A LOVE ORDAINED

Loveday's hands were clasped together in a tight ball beneath her breasts. She could feel the pulses in her throat at Adam's words. A few years, he had said . . . and he had meant nothing, of course. She knew that . . . they were strangers, and yet they were not. Something stronger than reality was tugging at her senses. As if they had met before, loved before, in some other life, whether past or future she could not guess, but the feeling in her was so forceful it would be like denying her very existence to be unaware of it.

Impulsively, she knelt on the damp ground as if to arrange the flowers more prettily. But instead, she leaned forward and smelt the freshness of the earth, touching her lips to it briefly, as Adam had touched his lips to hers. The sweet red earth beneath which her mother slumbered.

'He's the one, Ma', she murmured gently. 'No other will do.'

Also by Rowena Summers in Sphere Books:

THE SAVAGE MOON

The Sweet Red Earth

ROWENA SUMMERS

SPHERE BOOKS

First published in Great Britain by
Sphere Books Ltd 1983
Copyright © 1983 by Rowena Summers
Reprinted 1983
This edition first published by Sphere Books 1996

TRADE
MARK

Set in 10/11 Compugraphic English Times

Printed in England by Clays Ltd, St Ives plc

Sphere Books
A Division of
Macdonald & Co (Publishers)
Brettenham House
Lancaster Place
London WC2E 7EN

To my three, and theirs.

CHAPTER ONE

Loveday watched the canopy of the night sky, where a yellow moon slid in and out of grey clouds, dappling the spires and roofs of the town with mellow light. It was as balmy as midsummer, despite the fact that September was nearing its end, and she'd have preferred to keep her eyes heavenwards, instead of plodding along with the rest of the little company: to keep her mind on more poetic things, and not the stark reality of this particular night, and the request that had brought it about.

'I promise 'ee it will be a fine funeral!' Ralph Willard, General Store owner, had nodded and spoke stoutly. Mostly to cover his guilt at not seeing how ill his wife was until it was too late. And worse, not really caring.

'Bury me by torchlight, Ralph,' she had whispered hoarsely through the veil of gauze hiding the shameful disfigurements of the smallpox. 'I can't bear to think even the spirits will see what I've come to. Promise me you'll see to it! This one last request!'

He'd tried not to show his disgust as the claw-like hands had raked his own. He remembered her when she was buxom and rosy, and had gone into his arms with the ease of melting butter. That was before he'd strayed from the marriage bed and taken to scrumpy-supping at all hours; and long before the hideous illness had changed her beyond recognition.

Silently, he'd begged her to die quickly, and now that she had, he could act the bereaved husband by this show of grief, and make the local townspeople of Taunton nod their heads sagely, and think he wasn't such a bad fellow after all. He'd spent more than he could afford on the funeral Meg had wanted – the black hearse with its gleaming horses adorned

1

with their black crêpe trappings and high nodding plumes – the flaming torches to lead Meg to the churchyard and to light the faces of the mourners and those of the curious who'd lined the streets to witness Ralph Willard's burst of generosity.

He knew it could only benefit him as regarded their future custom at the store. Even in his bowed walk at the head of the mourners, he'd felt a ripple of sympathy in the crowd, and their satisfaction that at least poor Meg Willard had been given a good send-off, and pretty little Loveday would have a spectacle to remember.

Loveday fidgeted, one small foot rubbing against the other to try and bring some warmth back into them as she stood between her father and her Aunt Emily in the churchyard, but nothing could stop the shivering inside her. The solemn echoing of footsteps on the pitched flint stone of the streets still resounded in her head. The torchlights, held high to take her mother more flamboyantly to her grave than she'd ever lived her life, had made ghostly flickering shadows against the houses of the narrow streets through which they passed, and multiplied the faces of those who'd turned out to watch until it seemed as if an army surrounded them. They all crowded now around the long gaping hole in the ground that was to receive her mother's box, and Loveday stared instead at the toes of her boots, caked with the damp red earth, and tried to pretend that she wasn't there at all.

Or else to remember the churchyard in daylight, when it was very different from the gloomy depressing place it was now. Then, despite its crumbling air of decay, and the willow baskets of assorted bones and bits of skulls that were temporarily dumped near the church porch whenever a new grave was dug, the churchyard was a children's playground. Somewhere to race among the leaning headstones and shriek with pretended terror when a friendly hand suddenly gripped the shoulder from behind.

A place where the old men of the town liked to gather and sit awhile in warmer weather; where in summer swarms of white butterflies visited the flowers like dancing rose petals.

It was where Loveday had first seen the boy.

She felt a sharp dig in her ribs.

'Pay attention, Loveday. Reverend Cox is praying for your poor mother's soul.'

Aunt Emily, her normally florid farmer's wife face pasty with melancholy, admonished her. Loveday paid attention, not wanting to antagonise her aunt on this day of all days. She usually managed it without really trying. Aunt Emily was forever rebuking her for being too forward with her eyes in a way that was unseemly. As a child, it had been pretty, but now that Loveday was almost sixteen, it most certainly was not, Aunt Emily would say darkly to Loveday's father, and that he should keep a careful eye on his daughter. Loveday was too mature for her years, Aunt Emily chided her, too generous by nature, which was something her father, Ralph, was not. At least, not in his business dealings. His sister Emily closed her ears to rumours of his behaviour in other quarters. And now that Loveday's mother had gone to her rest, Emily was determined to see that her niece was brought up according to Christian values. She glanced at Loveday's wan face now, all the prettiness in it temporarily washed out by grief and the paleness of moonlight, and was satisfied.

Out of the corner of her eye, Loveday saw her cousin Matthew give her a sly wink. She made only the smallest grimace back, not wanting to be in league with him. She didn't really care for her cousin Matthew, though she felt it was probably wicked to feel so. The Willards were a family, and her mother had always told her to honour the family. It was a circle, unbreakable by those outside it as long as those within it kept it whole. It was one of Meg's own philosophical sayings that Loveday liked to ponder on in the darkness of her bedroom.

All the same, Loveday had her own opinions about Matthew, and no-one could stop her having her own thoughts. He was the second eldest of her four cousins, all brawny farmer's sons living up Quantock way, and as rough as the land they tilled. So different from the boy . . . she let her thoughts drift back to him. She'd seen him several times

3

now, and the first time had been in this very churchyard, some months ago. She'd wondered about him ever since. She'd guessed he was no farmer's son. Maybe he'd attended the College School, where the sons of gentlemen went. His voice had been educated, though still with a pleasing Somerset softness. He'd passed by with an older girl who was probably his sister from the way she grumbled at him to hurry, but Loveday hadn't really heeded the girl's fine clothes and leather boots. She'd been too taken with the boy.

His voice, though more educated than her own, wasn't overly so; he wasn't what her cousins would call, derisively, posh. His hair was dark and springy, but tamed into shape instead of being as woolly as hill sheep like the Willard boys'. He'd passed so close to Loveday she'd seen that the skin on his face was smooth, not wind-coarsened like Matthew's. When she and her companions had made some giggling noise in their games, the boy had turned and glanced at her for a moment. She'd seen that his eyes were brown, the colour of treacle toffee, like that in the jars at her father's store.

The girl had called him Adam, and Loveday had rolled the name around in her mind ever since, liking its sound and its strength. She hardly realised how often she compared him with her cousin Matthew, and found her cousin wanting.

Loveday heard a sudden hollow sound. Clods of heavy earth were striking wood from a distance, and she realised the Reverend Cox was nearing the end of his intoning, and soon they would go back to the house for the beanfeast. She'd shocked Aunt Emily by calling it that, but that was all it was, Loveday thought, with a sharp stab of grief for her mother, who'd never been so fêted in her life. She suspected she was the only one who had really cared about Meg Willard, the only one who had wept wildly at her dying. But since Loveday kept her weeping for her private moments, none had seen her grief, and the town had stamped her hard, just like the rest of the wild Willards.

It didn't matter a jot to Loveday. *She* knew she mourned, and so did her mother, wherever she was now. Anyway, she knew she needed to be stoical, because when they got back to

4

the house, Polly Reeves would be bright enough for all of them. Loveday felt the usual sickening little lurch in her stomach, remembering Polly Reeves and all the help, so-called, she'd given Loveday's father in the last six months since she came to live-in at the Willard house.

She forced her mind to the occasion, to see Ralph pumping the hand of the Reverend Cox, and to see that some of the mourners were beginning to disperse, while others tiptoed to peer down into the grave as if to catch a final glimpse of her mother's coffin before the red earth went tumbling all over it. The thought made Loveday shiver all over again.

'Are you feelin' cold, Loveday? I'll give 'ee a warmin' if 'ee's a mind to it.'

She jerked away from Matthew's heavy hand on her arm, only to find it sliding down to squeeze her rounded buttocks under cover of the darkness. For a long time now he had seemed obsessed by the feel of her body, Loveday thought, shrinking away from his touch; always trying to smooth and fondle under the guise of boisterous games. Once, he'd said scornfully that the budding breasts beneath her apron had been no bigger than beestings on a gnat, and he couldn't see what she was making all the fuss about. It hadn't stopped him pressing against them whenever he got the chance, and now that they had blossomed into a more womanly shape, the speculative gleam was in his eyes more often than not.

'I'm all right,' she told him sharply. 'And just remember Pa won't want you roughing about the house when you come back there tonight.'

'I know what your Pa's wantin'' he lowered his voice to whisper leeringly in her ear. 'That Polly Reeves is a fine 'un, and now your Ma's gone –'

Loveday's face burned with rage as she spun round.

'You shut up, talking like that, tonight of all nights, you great pig!' Her long fair hair swung out like a mare's-tail in her fury, and without thinking where she was, her arm came up, her small palm lashing out a crushing blow against Matthew's astonished face. At once, there was uproar and indignation.

'You vicious little tart!' Matthew bawled out, nursing his singing cheek. 'You'll pay for that.'

'The wildcat!' Aunt Emily screamed. 'Did you see that, Jack?' She implored her husband. 'Struck our Matt as if she was demented. She's a throwback, that one. And this is the child your brother thinks to send to us for a week or two.'

Ralph Willard strode across to his daughter, while the Reverend Cox stood scandalised for a moment at such a scene over a woman's grave not yet filled in. Irresolutely, he wondered if he should intervene, then decided wisely to walk away and leave the fighting Willards to find their own salvation. He'd thought that at least on this occasion they might manage to control their outbursts of temper. The sweet woman who'd just died was the only sane one among them, Reverend Cox thought sorrowfully, and God help the rest of them without her calming influence.

Loveday's teeth rattled in her head as her father shook her. The sky spun, a blue and yellow kaleidoscope in the flare of the torchlight.

'Show me up, will you, wench?' Ralph roared. 'You'd best come to your senses and remember your place, and you'll start by saying sorry to your cousin for striking him on such a sacred night!'

'I will not!' Loveday shouted back. 'And if you must know, it was on your account that I hit him, because of something he said about you and Polly Reeves.'

'Polly's an employee, as you and everybody else know,' Ralph snapped, but a little of the fire had gone out of his voice now, as he glanced out from under thick brows to see the effect this conversation was having on the onlookers. He let go of Loveday so quickly she would have fallen headlong in the grave after her mother if her oldest cousin Zeb hadn't grabbed her. She didn't mind Zeb touching her. He was only fourpence in the shilling, but blunderingly kind, and she shook herself free of him and rubbed at her sore arm where Ralph had gripped her, her flashing blue eyes daring anyone to come near her again.

Ralph turned on his brother Jack now.

'You'd best teach your spawn a thing or two on keeping his trap shut,' he burst out.

The crowd brightened. A good scrap between the Willard men was worth getting pins and needles in the legs for, and was enjoyed by all, including the participants. In terms of breaking the blood ties, it meant less than nothing, and in Ralph's own words, it spiced things up and gave 'em summat to think on when they were apart.

'There's nothin' wrong with my boys!' Jack Willard had whipped his snuff box from his weskit pocket, stuffed and squeezed and snorted violently till his eyes streamed. 'It's yon girl of yourn lookin' as if she knows what's what afore her time that's going to cause trouble, you mark my words. And no wonder, wi' your fancy piece livin' in the house.'

Ralph suddenly saw that the small crowd had pressed nearer, hoping to hear a juicy titbit of news to chew over at the market square. And he'd no intention of losing the small trading advantage Meg's smart funeral had given him. He put a pious look on his gross features.

'I won't rise to your bait tonight, Jack,' he said loudly, to the crowd's disappointment. 'My heart's still too full of grief to lower myself to arguing. And if you want to avail yourself of some hospitality tonight, I'd suggest you keep a civil tongue in your head, and tell your boys to do the same. Come along, Loveday. You may take your father's arm for the walk home.'

She would as soon have held a crawling creature, but Ralph gripped her close to his side, and to those away from the sudden skirmish, they gave the appearance of loving father and daughter, united in their grief. They were so unalike; he, with his bulbous nose and the look of his farming stock still denying him the courtesy he craved, now that he was a tradesman in the town. She, delicately-featured like her mother, with the corn-coloured hair and eyes of midnight blue, and a fire in her belly that was as earthy as her heritage, as yet unrealised.

They walked at the head of the small procession that led back to the living quarters above and behind the small general store, with its single bowed window frontage and the sign above that said Ralph Willard, Prop. His pride and joy, to become owner of a business since working for the old proprieter all his life, and finally to have the shop bequeathed to him when the old man died with no living relatives. Only to find that local townspeople still regarded him quaintly as the farmer's boy with no business head; only to himself did he admit that they were right, and that was one reason why he regarded Polly, with her quick brain and London ways, as such a treasure. He had other reasons too . . .

The lamps were on in the house, throwing a soft smoky glow over the worn furniture, when the mourners crowded into the tiny rooms. Polly, her face cheerful above her pert high-necked blue dress and white apron, flitted about with trays and plates and hunks of home-baked bread and wedges of cheese for the men, together with slices of hot-roasted ham and tart pickles. There were daintier sandwiches if required, but for the Willard family, a feast was a feast, whether its origin came from a birthing or a burying, and was meant to be enjoyed. There was tea or there was punch, and gallons of good Somerset cider to wash away the grief, on which there was no use in dwelling. It was the way of things.

The tiny rooms were packed with people and Loveday found herself pushed against the mantel in the parlour. Pushed and propped there by her cousin Matthew, so that it felt hard against her shoulder-blades as she raised herself on her toes to try and avoid him. The strong smell of scrumpy from his breath told her he'd already imbibed enough, and one hand was held firmly round a pint jug, the other caressing her slender waist.

'You're to come to the farm for a coupla weeks then, my girl,' he didn't bother hiding his satisfaction in the knowledge. 'We can have some fine old sport there.'

'I'm too old for games, Matthew.'

'Not the kind o' games I've got in mind, you ain't!' Matthew's laugh was coarse, his eyes roaming leisurely down over the high black bodice of her mourning dress, as if he could see right through the cheap stuff and the petticoats to the soft white flesh below. His look always made her feel undressed, and started a hotness of embarrassment running over her. Out of the corner of her eye Loveday could see her aunt looking her way disapprovingly, just as if it was she who was encouraging this tête-à-tête in one corner of the room, she thought indignantly.

She dodged out from under Matthew's enclosing arm.

'I must help with the food,' she said quickly. 'Polly can't be expected to do everything.'

'No, she'll want to keep her strength up for tonight,' he said meaningly, and Loveday thought she had never hated him so much. To suggest such evil things on the night of her mother's burial . . . she had her own suspicions about her father's attachment to Polly Reeves, but so far they had behaved decorously whenever she was about, and to her knowledge her mother had not been aware of the gossip surrounding Ralph and the trim young woman only half his age who'd come down to the country from London seeking a position, and descended on Ralph Willard's doorstep like a homing pigeon to act as assistant and occasional book-keeper.

Loveday grabbed a tray of food and began handing it round to the other black-clad figures. She hated black. The groups of relatives and friends reminded her of flocks of crows gathering to peck at titbits and scratch each other's eyes out if they got half a chance, which wasn't a bad way of describing it, she thought, as she heard her father and uncle in full swing again from the next room.

'Taken over the place, lock, stock and barrel,' her Uncle Jack was saying loudly. 'Family by the name of Goss, who know as much about cider making as yon Polly in there. The old man's kept on all the employees that worked for Lundy's all these years, and jaunts about the big house like a lord. Damned foreigners from Bristol, so they tell me, though I heard tell his wife came from these parts, and their son's been attending the College School here in Taunton, till he took on the life of a gentleman.'

Jack Willard gave another snort and drag on his snuff, and

Loveday heard the bellow of a sneeze a minute later. For some reason she couldn't explain, she found she was holding her breath. Her uncle went on speaking after a violent blow into his handkerchief.

' 'Course, our boys have ferreted out a bit about 'em, including the gentleman son,' his voice was derisory, then ended in a guffaw. 'Young Matt took a few shilling off 'un t'other week. Seems young Master Adam Goss ain't averse to gambling on the cocks any more 'n the rest o' the young 'uns!'

Adam Goss. Although it was the night of her mother's funeral, and she still bridled at the way the rest of the folks here were gabbing on as if it was just another social occasion, Loveday couldn't stop the spreading of a smile on her generous mouth. It had to be him, of course. The boy in the churchyard, whose dark brown eyes and fancy style and rich warm voice had occupied more of her day and night dreaming than she'd realised herself until this very minute. And her own cousin Matthew Willard, whom she despised and avoided as much as possible, actually knew the object of her dreaming. Had sported with him in Matthew's favourite spare-time occupation of cockfighting; shared in the close cloying intimacy of the hideous bloody fighting that always sickened her when her cousins dragged her out to Matthew's little arena to watch; Matthew had spoken to Adam. Matthew must be persuaded to tell her all he knew about him.

'Here, girl, what are you about?' Ralph roared at her retreating back, as Loveday dumped the tray of food in his arms and threaded her way through gesticulating arms and noisy farming talk in contest with the merits of town living. Past Polly, who told her smilingly not to worry and she'd placate her father for her, and whose words for once had no effect whatever on Loveday. Into the tiny parlour, where by now the four Willard brothers lounged against the mantel, big clumsy Zeb and the lusty Matthew, and the two younger ones, gawky compared with the other two, but still a match for any man in the room, Silas and Tom. Loveday marched up to them and told Matthew she wanted to talk to him. His pale blue eyes sparkled. It wasn't often his fiery girl cousin expressed a wish to talk to him. He felt a stirring in his loins as he always did when he felt the force of those deep-coloured eyes of hers looking directly into his. She could bewitch any man she chose with those devil-eyes, he thought lustily, and he'd have her afore too many more days were past. He'd made up his mind to that a long while back. He dumped his pint jug on the mantel with a thud.

'Right you are, my Lovey-dovey,' he told her, his nick-name for her making her squirm inside. 'Let's get away from these emmets and have a proper conversation, if we can find a quiet space.'

Loveday wasn't eager to be alone with him, but she had no wish for everybody to know of her curiosity about Adam Goss. She led the way to the passage between the rooms, where there was no lighting except the dim glow from the open doorways of the rooms leading off it. She was uneasy at her choice of place, but there was no other where she could put her questions and not be overheard. Before she got the chance to say a word, she was pulled roughly into Matthew's arms, and the smell of cider on his breath enveloped her as his fleshy mouth fastened on hers. She wrenched her face away from him, but he had her fast, pinned against the wall, his large body moving eagerly on hers, as if to simulate everything he dared not do here and now, but which he'd left her in no doubt he'd like to do.

'Matthew, for pity's sake,' she gasped out, 'this isn't what I asked you here for.'

'It should be then,' he growled. 'You've kept me panting long enough, my Lovey-dovey. Wouldn't you like to find out what you've been missin' so far? When you come up to the farm, we'll set the hay flyin' in the barn, you and me, girl. I've a fancy to see you spread on a bed o' hay. I'll be the crowin' cock then.'

Loveday glared into his grinning, lascivious face. Even in the gloom, she could see the desire in his pale eyes, and feel the hardening of him against her. Against her will, the tips of her breasts peaked and hardened in response, but it wasn't with an answering desire. She was afraid of him. Until now, she had hardly realised how much, but he had a strength in him that she had seen pitted against fox and rabbit and used to battle against the elements. If he was determined to break her, she would be as helpless as a kitten to his demands. Her only recourse was never to give him the opportunity he sought. Never another chance like this one.

'Remember my mother's newly buried, Matthew,' she said in a choked voice. 'If you've no respect for me, at least have some for her. She always showed you kindness.'

Matthew tipped up her chin with a rough hand.

'Kindness is what I'd show to you, my maid,' his voice suddenly thickened. 'All I ask is that you be nice to me, and let me be the first –'

Loveday jerked away from him as his meaning became clear. His idea of kindness was to make her his slave, she raged, to take her innocence and fornicate with her on every possible occasion. The idea of his body forging into hers made her shudder. Coming from farming stock, Loveday was fully aware of the nature of things, but Matthew Willard was not going to be the one to enter her. When that day came, it must be done with love and tenderness and mutual desire, and those were qualities she could never feel for this oaf.

'I wanted to ask you about someone,' she decided to ignore his words, and the little movements that were still grinding against her. She would pretend they weren't happening, like she'd blotted out the scene at the churchyard earlier that evening. They meant nothing to her, therefore they didn't exist. And her reaction was the worst form of insult ... except that to Matthew Willard, it had the effect of enraging him and exciting him even more. But he would indulge her for the moment. His time would come, and meanwhile she could feel what he was offering, for all her high and mighty ways. He had no doubt of that.

'About who?' he grunted. Loveday became wary.

'The old Lundy place,' she said carefully. 'Did I hear it's

been taken over by some out-of-town folk? Is there a young lady living there now? I think I've seen her walking in town.'

'There's two of 'em,' Matthew said at once. 'Two tight-lipped sisters who think they're both lady-muck and wouldn't give you the time o' day. The boy's all right though.'

'What boy?' Loveday said innocently, but not innocently enough for Matthew. He was pressed too close not to notice the sudden quickening of his cousin's breath, and the way her fine young breasts seemed to heave against him. But not for him, he sensed, in a rare moment of perception. He let a stray finger circle one deliciously taut button and then the other before he laughed.

'I'm thinking you already know what boy,' he taunted. 'These little beestings tell me so. Not such beestings now though, are they, my pretty Lovey-dovey? More like –'

'Stop it, or I'll scream out to my Pa,' she whipped out. 'All right, so I've seen Adam.'

Too late, she knew she'd said too much. Matthew leaned back from her, then his mouth came down on hers again, his tongue forcing her lips apart, and ranging round the inside of her mouth. She struggled to free herself, and suddenly he let her go. She could taste the cider he'd drunk. It was in her mouth, and it seemed ominously symbolic.

'You be nice to me when you come to the farm, and I'll see you get to meet Adam Goss,' Matthew whispered against her cheek, and then he swaggered away from her, as if he'd just lost tuppence and found a shilling. She could sense his triumph, as if, knowing himself and all the rest of the wild and lusty Willards, his cousin Loveday would be unable to resist the chance to get what she wanted, whatever the price. And Matthew was the price; but he'd reckoned without the sensitivity she'd inherited from her gentle mother, and if he'd known how she recoiled from his suggestion at that moment he'd have been honestly outraged.

CHAPTER TWO

It was late by the time they all left the Willard house to go home, and even though Jack Willard and his family would be up at dawn the following morning, they lingered on till nearly the last, being the closest family, apart from a distant relative of Meg's, who departed early on for her journey back to Hampshire.

But at last Loveday and Polly had done all the clearing up and washed the plates and jugs at the stone sink, while Ralph snored gently in the corner of the parlour. The sleep of the just, Polly whispered to Loveday with a giggle, just about able to be revived enough to be hauled off to his bed. And with just about enough sense left in his noddle to open the shop next morning without falling over his own feet.

Loveday listened to her good-natured prattle. She wasn't so bad, she supposed, if you could overlook her strong perfume with which she lavishly sprinkled her body, and the high-pitched giggle that grated on the ears, especially today . . . today was already yesterday, Loveday thought, with a tired, muddled sliver of philosophy, because it was past midnight, and already it was the start of a new day without Meg's presence in the house. Until yesterday, she had lain in waxen splendour, in the front parlour, and Loveday had felt obliged to tiptoe about the house as if Meg would awaken at any minute. But not so Polly. Loveday's brief moment of affinity with her vanished as the older girl wiped her hands dry on the stout drying cloth and stood with her hands on her hips, eyeing Loveday impatiently.

'Come on now, lovey, your Ma's dead and gone, and there's no use whimpering about, is there? Time the rest of us hit the pillows. You go on to your bed, and I'll shake up your Pa. If needs be, I'll mix him a powder for the head he's going to have tomorrow morning.'

She shooed Loveday out of the scullery as if she was an errant cat, and while normally Loveday would have resented such treatment and snapped back at her, tonight

14

she was too weary to object. She'd let Polly know her place once she'd had a good night's sleep, for if her poor mother had been too sickly to stop Polly infiltrating from the shop into the house and into far too intimate a relationship with Ralph, then Loveday certainly was not. As yet, she didn't know how far that relationship had developed, but she was determined it was going no farther.

Once in the darkness of her room, Loveday undressed in the light from the window, pulling on her cambric nightgown over her bare skin, and giving a small shiver at its roughness. Before she got into bed, she stood by the window, from where she could see the tall square tower of St. Mary's church, beyond which was the churchyard. Loveday said her own private goodbye to her mother in that moment, turned away from the moonlight scudding across the sky, and dived beneath the bedcovers.

But she was unable to sleep, despite her tiredness. The torchlight tableau was still too vivid in her mind; as too, were tales of body-snatchers who stole bodies from newly dug graves, to cart them away and convert the bodies into soap. Loveday shuddered in the darkness and the musky cocoon of her own breath, knowing now why not too many folk bought soap from the store ... why, they might be washing themselves in their own family, for all they knew. She switched her thoughts away from such horrors, wishing she dared have the courage to stand guard over Meg's grave in defence of such an abomination.

She would think of sweeter things. The old Lundy place, halfway between the town of Taunton and the mysterious folds and hollows of the Quantock Hills, in which was tucked the Willard farm, where Jack Willard and his family lived. The old Lundy place was situated in the lush vale of Taunton Deane, ripe and sweet-scented in spring and summer with the regimented apple orchards, pink-blossomed like confetti in spring, the whole area pungent with fermenting apples as the cider making season began. And now the Lundys had left, and the Goss family had taken over. Adam Goss lived there now, halfway between here and her uncle's farm, the centre link in a chain.

Loveday moved restlessly in the bed, suddenly too hot beneath the covers after all. She threw them back, feeling the tautness of her breasts beneath her nightgown as she did so. For a moment she let her hands rest lightly on herself, letting her palms curve over the swelling breasts, and wondered just why they affected a man so potently. Such as Matthew, who sweated and breathed more heavily whenever he could fasten his large hands upon her for a quick squeeze until she pushed him angrily aside. How would they affect Adam Goss, Loveday wondered? She was sure he would not squeeze or pinch or be rough; he would be gentle, and loving, and if seduction was his goal, then it would be an exquisite seduction, and she would love him all the more because of it.

Loveday's face flamed in the darkness. Such wanton thoughts to be filling her mind! Aunt Emily would wash her hands of her, and say it was no more than she expected, from the blatant come-hithering of her blue eyes. She forced her eyes to close and to will sleep to come. But when it did, it was peopled with ghosts, with cries and lamentations and the cracking of bones, and the leering black-hatted faces of grave robbers hacking open coffins that were still newly covered with earth. Loveday awoke in a drenching sweat, too terrified to remember anything at all except that she was very frightened ... no longer on the verge of sixteen summers, but a vulnerable child again, seeking comfort at the place where it was never refused. Without stopping to collect her senses, she slid out of bed and padded along the passage on bare feet until she reached the room where her father and mother slept, looking for the warmth of soft arms and soothing words.

'Come on, Ralphie!' Polly giggled as she tugged at the arms of the man sprawled out in the armchair. The snoring was still rhythmic, the buttons on his weskit popped open with the fullness of cider and food. She ran her hands lightly over his belly, laughing softly, feeling the excitement take hold of

16

her. When it was all over, Ralph had said; when his wife was dead and buried, and in a decent time for the good folk of Taunton to forget Meg Willard had ever lived, then he'd marry her.

But Polly was impatient, and always had been. She'd already had the best of him, but now she wanted his name too. She, who had lived the high old time of it in Soho until it became uncomfortably hot for her kind, wanted respectability! It was a laugh really. Not that she intended doing without her little comforts . . . there was many a man who could catch Polly Reeves' eye when she became Polly Willard and gave up the bookkeeping and the shop assisting, and did her little afternoon entertaining in the back parlour while her husband attended the shop. And only Polly knew just how she intended to do her entertaining!

'What's goin on?' Ralph slurred, feeling Polly's hands pulling at him. As she leaned forward over him, he breathed in her strong scent and the womanly odour of her that was far from displeasing to him. He seemed unable to rouse himself from the chair, but his masculine instincts were roused as always. There was some reason why he should refrain from sating his desires this night, but he was too befuddled by good company and a bellyfull of cider to ponder on it. Especially when Polly's luscious body was bearing down on him that way.

'Beddy-byes, Ralphie,' she went on laughingly. 'Come on, now, up the apples and pears.'

'Put your head on the weeping willow' he burbled on, 'and plough the angry deep.'

'Something like that,' Polly laughed. She gave one almighty tug that got him to his feet, and the two of them swayed together for a moment, then locked in each other's arms, they lurched towards the stairs and climbed them unsteadily. Polly's intention was to tip him gently on the bed, and retreat to her own room next door, to which Ralph had often stolen in the middle of the night when his wife had been sleeping soundly with the aid of the sleeping draughts she invariably took.

17

But somehow the two of them rocked onto the bed together, still shushing inanely, and Polly found herself beneath the belching weight of him. He was pulling at his breeches with fumbling hands, and cursing at the drink that was making him useless.

'I wouldn't call that useless,' Polly giggled, as he managed to free himself at last from the best black suit in which he'd walked to his wife's funeral six hours previously. For a second she hesitated, wondering if she should remind him that tonight was not the best of nights ... but then she reasoned cheerfully that everyone had his own way of dispelling grief, and if this was Ralphie's, then who was she to object or condemn? She wriggled out of her clothes while he was still kicking his breeches out of the way, and pulled him down to her; and it was while her father was plunging away merrily, his backside bared to the cool night air and the glimmer of candle-light in the corner of the room, that Loveday stumbled through the doorway.

Neither of the two people on the bed noticed her ... for the first startled moment, Loveday found it hard to define that there *were* two people there. It looked like a tangle of arms and legs and bobbing bedclothes, and her father grunting as if he was in danger of bursting a blood vessel. And then she grasped exactly what was happening, turned and fled from the room, sobs welling up in her chest that he could do such a thing on this night that was sacred to her mother's memory. It was a loathsome, vile act ... somehow she didn't altogether blame Polly ... she'd seen girls such as her strutting around the town, and knew what a sorry end they usually came to; it was her *father*, the so-called respectable tradesman, who drew all her disgust. Fresh tears for her soft, gentle mother ran down her cheeks when she reached the sanctuary of her own room, and for the first time, Loveday was thankful Meg Willard had gone to her grave before she knew what a seducer of young women her husband had become.

She never slept again at all that night. She went downstairs to the cold scullery soon after six o'clock, pale-faced and tight-jawed, feeling she'd grown up in a single night. No longer able to feel respect for her father, or even to look him or Polly in the face, so that in his usual early morning grouchiness, Ralph took her silence to be sullenness. He swilled down a cup of strong tea, laced with a powder to try and stop the racking in his head that came from too much good Somerset cider, too little sleep, and too much Polly.

'You'll have to put on a better countenance than that when you stay at your Uncle Jack's, girl,' he growled at his daughter as she dumped a plate of greasy bacon in front of him, home-cured from Jack's farm. The sight of it turned his innards nearly inside out.

'I don't want to go there,' Loveday sulked. 'Why should I go? And anyway, people will talk if there's just you and Polly left in the house.'

'There won't be,' Polly put in quickly from the doorway. Bright as a button even at six o'clock in the morning, the thought ran irritably through Loveday's mind. While she herself felt as if she'd been dragged through a hedge . . . it should be Polly who felt like that, instead of looking so perky.

'Polly's sister's comin' to stay awhile, miss, so you can just get that disapproving look off your face,' Ralph snapped.

'It's not me who disapproves,' Loveday lied. 'I'm thinking of your reputation, Pa. How would it look for you and – and her to be here on your own?'

She swallowed suddenly, seeing just how the pair of them would have high jinks if it happened. And if Polly's sister was anything like her, it probably wouldn't make a ha'pence of difference to the night-time activities. The thought was depressing. It was like discovering you had jumped on to a wheel that would never stop turning. Love, that she had thought to be such a romantic and ethereal emotion, was suddenly tainted in her mind, and her young sweet dreams that had somehow been woven around the noble head of Adam Goss felt like bile in her mouth. The image of her cousin Matthew's leering face and roaming hands made a mockery of it all, and now her father was thinking of sending her to stay at the farm. It happened every year, and Loveday had never thought anything of it. It had been a change of scene, even though she'd spent most of her time helping out her Aunt Emily in the preparations for Cattern's Eve and the feasting, after which Ralph and Meg had always taken her home.

This year, everything would be different, Loveday realised. Meg would not be coming to the farm to join in the celebrations on November 24th, the traditional country day to celebrate the beginning of winter. Polly would come with her father instead, and presumably the unknown sister, and nothing would be as it was before.

'Your Aunt Emily's expecting you as usual,' Ralph said shortly, as if following her thoughts. 'And you always tell me you enjoy the preparations. There's little enjoyment here, my girl, penned behind a shop counter all day and half the night, to wait on folks' pleasure.'

'There's other enjoyments,' Loveday muttered beneath her breath. 'At least, for some people.'

Polly stared at her thoughtfully, and then her voice became sly.

'You'll be finding out some of life's other enjoyments for yourself soon, Loveday. Wait till your Pa tells you what he's got in mind for you –'

'Hold your tongue, you ninny.'

Loveday stared at her father suspiciously.

'What have you got in mind for me, Pa? You're not thinking of sending me away to work as a skivvy, are you? I'll not do it!'

It didn't matter that she worked as a skivvy for the four of them . . . no, three now . . . that was different. She had no objection to blackleading and scrubbing and mending for her own family, but it was lowering for a tradesman's daughter to skivvy for other folks. They weren't too far up in the social scale, but they were better than some.

'Nor would I suggest it,' Ralph said testily, clearly annoyed with Polly for putting in her spoke. 'Well, since the

20

ninny here has started off, I'll have to put the rest of it to you. Finch Viney's been round, askin' to come courtin' –'

'No!' Loveday jumped to her feet, her fine-boned cheeks flooding with furious colour, her blue eyes flashing darker at her father's words. 'You can't expect me to go courtin' with Finch Viney, Pa!'

'Why not? He's a good man, wi' a business that'll never come to grief, and he's a fancy for you.'

'He's old and he smells, and I curl up inside whenever he looks at me,' Loveday burst out, feeling the smart of tears in her eyes. 'He's got the stench of blood on his hands.'

'Well, you stupid girl, what else would you expect a butcher to have?' Ralph was clearly put out at her vehement reaction. Especially since he'd had a kind of unspoken agreement with Finch Viney that there'd be unlimited supplies of good fresh meat on the Willard table once Finch and Loveday were officially affianced. Trading at Ralph's general store had been poor of late, and the coffers were low, and with Polly's extravagant taste in clothes, Ralph knew he was goin' to need every ha'penny he could lay his hands on when he and Polly were wed. The chance to be rid of Loveday as an extra encumbrance, and to fill his belly at the same time, was a temptation he couldn't refuse.

Besides, the girl would be all right wed to Finch. The man wasn't old, no more than thirty-three, though he supposed that to Loveday he'd be goin' on a bit. And he had a fine paunch on him that led the way into a room afore he came into it himself, but then again, what else would you expect from a butcher who had access to all the best cuts of meat? The girl should be glad to have the chance of making a good match. As to the bedtime capers, well, there'd been talk as to Finch's preferences, as there always was over an unmarried man of his age, but the man had made the request of Ralph, and he was satisfied Finch Viney would be as horny as the next man given the right woman to rouse him.

Ralph eyed his daughter now, her full breasts almost bursting out her bodice with the rage she was getting herself in. Time she was taken in hand and tamed, and if she was

21

anything like the rest of the lusty Willards, she'd soon find out there were other pleasures in life than children's games played in and out the headstones in the churchyard!

'You won't make me, will you, Pa?' she said suddenly, unexpected tears shimmering in her eyes like liquid sapphires. Giving her a look of Meg as she'd been when Ralph first took her to bed and delighted in her. A rare rush of affection overcame him for his daughter as he patted her hand.

'I'm only doin' what I think's best for you, girl,' he said gruffly. 'You give Finch a chance, that's all I'm askin'. Once you get to know each other better, you'll forget all about his work, and a man's hands don't make up all of him, remember.'

He gave a clumsy wink, but to Loveday it was the most insensitive action he could have done. It linked the future activities of herself and the odious Finch Viney with the eager bed-bouncings she had witnessed between her father and Polly Reeves last night. The night of her mother's burial. The idea of it almost choked her.

The sound of barrows clattering down the pitched flint stone street seemed to move her into action. She wouldn't stay here and listen to any more of this. Outside, the townsfolk of Taunton were going about their everyday business. Babies were being born and folks were dying, and the future of Loveday Willard meant less than nothing to any of them. She had a sudden urge to be in the midst of them, anonymous as a mouse in the fields, and to try and forget the outrageous suggestion her father had put to her. She twisted away from the two pairs of eyes still watching her, and flounced out of the room, saying she would be about her house duties, and disappeared to her bedroom.

Instead, she grabbed her dark shawl from her wall closet and flung it over her grey working dress. She could still hear the shrill quick tones of Polly's voice, interspersed with the gruffer ones of her father, as she slipped down the passageway and out into the fresh clean air of the late September morning, with no other purpose in mind than to get away from the pair of them. And wishing she could escape her own thoughts as easily.

Already, at that early hour, shop blinds were being hauled up and new displays of provisions and fresh vegetables straight from the farms displayed on wooden trays outside. Windows were being rubbed and washed into a sparkling freshness, and shopkeepers were gathering on the narrow pavements outside their own little patches to nod and blink and pass the time of day, and beam at it being such a fine old morning, as if they'd specially ordered it for the purpose of trading.

Loveday's footsteps took her into little meandering alleyways and wider, more splendid roads that were still little wider than two hands' span, and came to rest eventually at the end of the lane where Finch Viney's butcher's shop was situated. The low eaves overhung the pavement, from which the huge meathooks forked out, and even from a distance, Loveday could smell the fresh bloody aroma that emanated from Finch's shop early each morning. When she'd called there to buy meat, it was to stand chattering with the good wives of the town, while Finch kept up a bawdy and lively conversation with them, while hacking away at bone and gristle as if his worst enemy lay under his cleaver. And every few minutes wiping his bloody fingers on the coarse blue and white striped apron, that was varying shades of red and brown where the animals' blood had congealed. Sometimes too, Finch would run his fingers through his hair to push it back from his forehead, and by the end of the day his hair would be stiff and tacky. Loveday gave a great shudder at the thought of those same hands reaching out for her in the intimacy of the marriage bed.

It must never be, she vowed. Whatever plans her father had in mind for her, it must not include marriage to Finch Viney. Surely he must see how impossible it would be. Loveday felt the blind panic rising up, knowing of old how determined Ralph could be when he had a goal in mind. And it would be a very respectable marriage. As he'd so rightly said, a butcher was a respected tradesman, and never likely to go out of business. Loveday could do far worse ... and in her soul, she knew she could do far better! Not because of the man, but because of that sensitivity she'd inherited from Meg, that said a woman should know more at the hands of a man than merely his lust. There should be tenderness and mutual devotion, and that was what Loveday wanted for herself. Meg had spoken as if she herself had known it. Perhaps she was only deluding herself, or perhaps Ralph had been different in those early days of which Loveday was ignorant. Loveday only knew it was what she wanted too ... to love and be loved.

'Look out, girl!' A clatter of wheels thundered towards her, and Loveday jumped out of the way as a cart piled high with goods hurtled past. She'd do better than to wander about aimlessly, head in the clouds, dreaming of impossible things. Already the town was coming to life, the air filled with more smells than merely Finch Viney's butcher's shop. The East Street candle and soap manufactory was emitting its usual nauseating odours; the warm pungent scents of leather and glue came from the shoemaker's; fishwomen were already squabbling and fighting in the direction of the fishmarket, and ale ran freely along the gutters, glinting in the sunlight like liquid gold.

She had been foolish to rush out of the house, for there was nowhere she could go. She was likely to get a thrashing from her Pa when she returned for not attending to the household duties. An elderly woman pushed a flower barrow towards her, the blooms piled high and scenting the air more sweetly than any of Polly's perfumes would have done. Loveday searched in the pocket of her grey dress and found a penny. She walked resolutely up to the old flower seller. She had found some purpose at last.

'What can you give me for a penny, if you please? My mother was buried yesterday, and I want to put some flowers on her grave.'

The old woman peered at her through short-sighted eyes.

'Is it Meg Willard's daughter?' she wheezed, and Loveday nodded. The woman took the penny and thrust it somewhere deep in her clothing, then she took three roses from a box, and added a sprig of fern and some beech leaves, already turning to the colours of autumn, and pressed them in Loveday's hands.

'For your mother, my lamb, who brightened up many a dull day with her smile, and I'm thinkin' you'll be doin' the same. Take these and go quickly, afore I regret my good nature in partin' with more than a penn'orth.'

It was warm and pleasant in the churchyard. The old men were already wending their way to the benches to sit awhile and the morning dew on the flowers in jars and pots crowned them with diamonds, while the fragile network of spiders' webs shimmered in the sunlight. Loveday threaded her way to the scene of yesterday, already slightly removed in her mind and less traumatic. Now, instead of gloomy onlookers crowding round a black gaping hole in the ground, lit by the flaring, smoking torches, there was a neat mound of soft damp red earth, undisturbed by body-snatchers or ghosts or creatures of the night. Here, her mother slept peacefully . . . Loveday stared down at the earth, realising she had nothing in which to put the flowers she had just bought. She should have brought a jar with her. She looked round her, as if to find inspiration, and suddenly her heart gave a gigantic leap, as if it would soar right out of her chest.

Away to the right of her, standing in the church porch and talking earnestly to Reverend Cox, was Adam Goss. Loveday felt the quick colour stain her cheeks at the unexpected sight of him, and the fluttering in her throat was like a quivering of butterflies' wings she couldn't stop. She watched as his dark hair was ruffled by a small breeze, then settled tidily on his neck once more. She was suddenly overcome by the most tremendous wave of emotion she had ever known, even greater than the sense of loss after her mother's death. This was a more positive emotion, a sudden urgency not to let this young man leave the churchyard without speaking to him, just once. Wanting to be near enough to feel his breath when he spoke, and to know he looked at her

... really looked ... if it never happened again, the impulsiveness in her was too much to let her miss this golden opportunity.

Loveday picked up her skirts and hurried, without really seeming to, to the church porch, where the two figures there paused in their conversation.

'Excuse me, Reverend Cox,' her voice was breathless, unconsciously provocative. 'Have you some old jar I may use for my mother's flowers?' She held out the posy as proof of her words. She didn't look directly at Adam Goss now, but she didn't need to. He looked at her, and that was all she wanted.

'Ah yes – Loveday, isn't it?' Reverend Cox sounded a little irritated at being interrupted. 'If you go around the back of the church, you'll find something.'

He turned his back on her slightly, and she guessed he was still thinking about the uproar she and her family had caused last night. She felt dismissed, and then incredibly, she realised Adam Goss was addressing her.

'Was it your mother who was buried yesterday? I heard Matthew refer to his cousin as Loveday.'

'Yes. Yes, it was. Yes, I am.' Oh, how stupid she was sounding, Loveday raged, stammering and reddening as if she had never spoken to a young man in her life before. She took a deep breath. 'I believe I've heard my cousin Matthew speak of you, if you are one of the family now living at the old Lundy place.'

Adam laughed, and Loveday thought she had never seen such even teeth in a man's mouth, forgetting completely how few men's mouths she had looked in. Everything about him was enchanting her, and with the wild Willard blood racing inside her, she was already falling headlong and tempestuously in love.

'We prefer to call it Goss House now,' he informed her lightly, 'but it's the place to which you refer. I've become fairly well acquainted with your cousin Matthew in past months.'

And all this time she had avoided going to the Willard

26

farm up Quantock way, Loveday moaned silently, because of Matthew's growing attachment for her body. And if she had, she might have met Adam so much sooner . . .

'If you will excuse me, dear young Sir, I have church business to attend to,' Reverend Cox said sternly, as if to suggest that Adam Goss might have better things to do than chinwag with Loveday Willard. He turned and entered his domain, and the two of them barely saw him go.

'Shall we find the pot for your flowers?' Adam said in a scratchy kind of voice. He was taken aback at the sight of this girl, about whom Matthew Willard had referred so ribaldly. He'd expected a facsimile of the oafish farmboy, a red-cheeked country wench, who, according to Matt, was ripe for the taking . . . instead of which, Adam found himself almost meserised by the delicacy of Loveday's flower-soft skin, by the lustrous blue of her eyes, and the ladylike air that was the more tantalising because it was spiced with a sensuality she couldn't quite hide. The fact that he vaguely recalled seeing her before, dancing among the headstones with children, only enhanced his impression of her as something slightly fey, a glorious earthy creature who could wind herself into a man's heart without even trying.

Adam shook off the heady sensations, and offered her his arm as they trod over the uneven ground, and as for Loveday, pressed suddenly close to his side, she was transported into heaven.

They found an old pot easily enough and filled it with water from the spring, and Adam walked silently back with her while she placed the flowers inside it and forced the pot to stand firmly on the mound of earth. They both stood and stared at it, united briefly, and now finding nothing to say, strangers once more.

'Well,' Adam said at last. 'I had better be getting along. I'm leaving on the morning coach, and just called to pay my respects to Reverend Cox.'

Loveday's spirits plummeted.

'Leaving?' she stammered. 'Where are you going?'

She had no right to ask, but he seemed not to find it

27

strange that she did. She could almost imagine there was a faint regret in his voice when he told her.

'I'm to go back to Bristol for some months to stay with some relatives while Mr Brunel is in the city. I'm to go as an engineer with him,' he spoke with sudden pride, but all Loveday heard was that he was leaving the district.

'I've never heard of him,' she pouted, her eyes downcast, and Adam laughed.

'The day will come when all England will have heard of Mr Brunel,' he assured her. 'And farther afield than that. He's destined to be a great man, little Loveday.'

His words patronised her. 'I'm not little,' she said hotly. 'I shall be sixteen years old in a month's time. Old enough to be wed!'

He laughed again, his dark eyes dancing with amusement. To her astonishment, he leaned forward and touched his lips to her soft mouth for a fraction of a second.

'Don't be so impatient! If you can manage to wait a few years until I'm back in Taunton Deane, I might think of marrying you myself!' He was teasing her and she knew it, but it didn't stop her heart thudding or her head spinning. Before she could think of a smart reply, he had turned on his heels and was walking away from her, to turn with a wave at the gate before he was swallowed up in the morning crowds.

Loveday's hands were clasped together in a tight ball beneath her breasts. She could feel the pulses in her throat at his words. *A few years*, he had said . . . and he had meant nothing, of course. She *knew* that . . . they were strangers, and yet they were not. Something stronger than reality was tugging at her senses. As if they had met before, loved before, in some other life, whether past or future she could not guess, but the feeling in her was so forceful it would be like denying her very existence to be unaware of it.

And he knew it too. The knowledge whispered through her senses like a warm breeze kissing her face. Uplifting her and calming her, so that she could blot out all other consider-ations for the moment, such as the fact that it might be years before she would see him again. That was another thing too.

Something deep inside her told her it would not be that long. A conviction too psychic to put into words. All her mother's high-flown beliefs and ideals that Ralph had pooh-poohed as being so much bunkum and akin to witchcraft, flowed through Loveday with an exquisite energy of well-being.

Impulsively, she knelt on the damp ground as if to arrange the flowers more prettily. But instead, she leaned forward and smelt the freshness of the earth, touching her lips to it briefly, as Adam had touched his lips to hers. The sweet red earth beneath which her mother slumbered.

'He's the one, Ma,' she murmured gently. 'No other will do.'

CHAPTER THREE

Adam made his way to East Street, from where all the coaches departed, mail and passenger. His baggage was already safely deposited with an urchin who sat minding it for a penny, and he was thankful yet again that he'd per-suaded his father and sisters not to come to the town to see him off. For one thing, his father wasn't half as well as he looked, with the bronchitis that was plaguing him earlier this year; for another, he couldn't stand his sisters' fussing over him as if he was a babe in arms. The time for all that was long past. The third reason was that he'd wanted an affectionate word with Reverend Cox, with whom Adam had struck up an odd kind of friendship. Lastly, if he hadn't gone to the church that morning, which he surely wouldn't if his family had accompanied him, he wouldn't have seen Loveday Willard.

The horses came snorting round the corner, hooves rattling and manes flying, reminding him of the flaxen hair of the girl he'd just left. She had just the same proud air about her as these fine beasts. Adam flung the penny at the urchin, retrieved his baggage, and mounted his seat. He wouldn't admit to himself that his eyes searched the streets through which they passed out of Taunton for one last glimpse of her, nor that she remained on his mind for much of the long journey to Bristol, and that with every mile the lurching coach·covered, he felt a swift regret that it took him farther away.

That oaf Matt shouldn't have related so much about that cousin of his, Adam·thought ruefully. From the beginning, it had made him idly curious, no more. He had called at the Willard farm to ask for some milk, knowing that country folk were always free in their offer of refreshment, and since his horse had lost a shoe, Adam had had a hot and dusty walk back through the forest, and been glad to catch sight of the Willard farm tucked in the hills.

'You'll be from old Lundy's place then,' Loveday's Aunt Emily had commented, eyeing up the young man with approval, and comparing him favourably with her four sons, slurping companionably from huge jugs, while Adam Goss drank without spilling a single drop as befitted a gentleman.

'That's right. We've been here a few weeks now,' Adam informed her. He'd seen Matt's eyes suddenly glisten.

'Are you a gambling man?' he said.

'Hush up now, Matt,' his mother reprimanded him. 'Can't you see Mr Goss would have no truck with your cock-fighting? He'll be interested in finer things, the stags, I've no doubt.'

'Do you have a fighting cock?' Adam's interest was awoken as Matthew nodded. His brother Zeb gave a huge guffaw.

'Only the champion for miles,' he preened as if it was his own. 'Nobody can match Matt's bird.'

'Would you be interested in coming to our next little contest, Adam?' Matt said impatiently. Let his mother call him Mr Goss. He and Adam were of an age, and he'd be damned if he was giving him an inch. He quite liked the look of him, for all that he was a bit of a dandy. At least he'd talk more sensibly than Zeb about the things that mattered, like cockfighting and gambling, and girls, and a damn sight more intelligently than his two younger brothers, who were only interested in farm animals.

'I might be,' Adam grinned. 'Tell me where and when,'

It was arranged, and within three days Adam was back at the Willard farm, in the outhouse where Matt had set up his little arena, with coins jingling in his pocket for the sport. Matt's bird was a gleaming purplish-black, for whom he had a fond affection. He had named him Prince. The rival cock that day had been brought by a neighbouring farmer's son, a massive bird with a beak torn in a previous fight. Each man had his supporters and the wagers were put in a basket on the side.

The skirmish had been brutal and bloody, both game cocks urged on by their supporters, with voices that got more excited and coarse as the blood began to spill.

'Kill the bastard, my beauty,' was Matt's constant yell, 'peck his ass.'

Ned, the rival owner, bawled back insults at the cock and its owner.

'I've seen more fight in a corpse than in either of you dung-heaps! Come on, Whitie, gouge his eyes out. Pay 'im back for last time. Come on, fight, you bugger.'

By the end of contest, both heads had been bleeding and nearly bald of feathers, half their bodies pecked raw. On this occasion, Whitie, the rival cock, had dug one of its steel spurs into Prince's head, and the bleeding was profuse. Matt merely stuck the bird under his arm until the wagers were shared out, the onlookers dispersed, and only then did he bathe Prince's head with a mixture of milk and water and a rough tenderness.

'He's to be ready for next time,' Matt informed Adam, 'I can't leave him to recover in his own time. He's money to me, ain't you, my fancy?'

'I thought you'd gone soft for a minute,' Adam grinned. 'From the way you were stroking him, I thought you might have imagined you had a girl there for a minute.'

Matt grinned back. 'You ain't met my cousin Loveday yet, have you? 'Course you wouldn't, bein' new hereabouts. She don't come to the farm too often. A bit high and mighty, livin' in the town, see? And afraid of what's comin' to her, I reckon.'

'And what is coming to her, Matt?'

Matt gave a low rich laugh, and made an unmistakeable gesture with one hand. He sprawled out in the hay on the floor of the outhouse, his mouth fleshy, eyes lust-filled as he thought of his girl cousin. Adam threw himself down beside him, squinting up at the slivers of sunlight through the gaps in the planks of wood in the roof above.

'What's she like then, this Loveday? She must be pretty good. I can't see you going for somebody high and mighty somehow.'

'I've had my eye on our Loveday for some while now,' Matt went on. 'She was allus a good looker, even as a babby – well, far as I can mind. She's only two years younger than me, and she was a skinny little runt till just recent. These last months though, she's got a fine pair o'tits on 'er, and a cute little ass just ripe for squeezin'. Course, she don't let me get my 'ands on it too often. But I will, never you fear. I've got myself marked down for breakin' her in, come what may, and it's one job I mean to relish!'

Adam had felt a momentary envy for the lusty Willard girl who was evidently only holding her cousin off until she chose the right moment to be deflowered. And an even sharper envy for this country boy who was getting what he wanted so easily. He'd pictured Loveday as big and buxom and a bit simple-minded, even if she did come from the town. It was obvious she'd be stamped in the same mould as Matthew Willard.

The coach lurched over a heavily rutted piece of track, and Adam gripped on to the handrail to steady himself. He couldn't have been more wrong about Loveday Willard. It was almost impossible to see her connected in any way with

32

the uncouth Matt, who was as rough and ready as they came. Or to imagine Loveday hollering and shouting the way folks knew all the Willards did. It hadn't taken Adam and his family long to learn that their fighting was legendary, both the farming section and the townspeople. Once any two Willards got together, fighting inevitably broke out.

But surely not in Loveday's case! The image of her face came back to haunt him during all the long and tedious journey to Bristol. He'd half expected a trollop . . . instead he'd seen a vision. He mocked himself for getting so poetic about a girl to whom he'd spoken for such a brief time, but in the back of his mind was a new indignation now for the fate Matthew Willard had in store for her. To be ravished by that oaf who smelled of the farmyard . . . Loveday's clothes had been cheap, but they'd appeared clean, and Adam guessed that she'd be fastidious in her personal habits. There was a glow about her that told him so without actually knowing it.

He must be going daft in the head, he thought shortly. How could he imagine he knew so much about a girl he'd just met? The fact was, he'd thought he'd known her for so long now; it was six months since he'd started going to the farm on odd occasions, and sensing his interest, Matt had embellished his tales of his town cousin, until Adam had felt he knew her as well as he knew Matt. Now, to find her so different, and yet still in some uncanny way familiar to him, was disturbing, to say the least.

He realised he was angry with Matthew Willard for putting the idea in his head that his cousin was tarred with the same rustic brush as himself. Adam was no prude. His own temperament ran deep and passionate, but he prided himself he was not hell-bent on ravishing young girls the way Matt seemed to be, and neither had he expected to be spending so many hours thinking about this particular one!

Matt's description of her had been crude, using his own graphic words. Adam recalled a girl, well-rounded in the places where it mattered, with a dipping, slender waist just right for curving towards a man's body. In his sudden burst of imagination, he could feel the crushing of her breasts against him, and smell the musky odour of her; he could imagine his fingers entwining in that corn-coloured hair . . . good God, what had got into him today, he thought angrily? He gave the gentleman seated opposite him in the swaying coach such an aggressive look the man glanced hastily away, wondering if he was about to be assaulted. Adam heard him clear his throat uneasily, and forced a smile to his face.

'I beg your pardon if I startled you, Sir. My thoughts were elsewhere – on – on business matters.'

'Ah.' The gentleman looked relieved. 'And may I ask what business that might be, since we have a long distance to cover, and I prefer a pleasant conversation to black looks!'

Adam laughed out loud. It would be good to talk, and forget the nonsense about how it might feel to hold Loveday Willard in his arms . . .

'You may, Sir. I'm to be an engineer – though I confess, that's rather too grand a term for it just yet. But I'm to join the undertakings at Box, instigated by Mr Brunel. My father and I agree that it pays to begin on the bottom rung of the ladder to fully understand the job.'

'The railway tunnel! A very dangerous operation, I understand. They say it's to be almost two miles long. Can that be right?'

Adam nodded, feeling a swell of pride. Not that he had been involved in anything more than the navvying work so far, and was somewhat glad he hadn't had to work on the hazardous sinking of the shafts through the hill top, one of which had been sunk to a depth of 300 feet.

'It's a great feat of engineering,' Adam said. 'And think what it will do for the West. A great rail link from London, and all sprung from the imagination and foresight of one great man!'

'I see you are an admirer of Mr Brunel!'

Adam laughed, realising his enthusiasm had run away with him as always. 'Ever since I was twelve years old and watched the ceremony on Clifton Down to begin work officially on the bridge across the River Avon. I saw Mr Brunel that day, and ever since, I've wanted to follow in his footsteps.'

'I witnessed the same ceremony,' the other nodded. 'No-one could help but be impressed. But that was in 1831 – and you've never wavered in six years? It wasn't merely a boyish dream?'

As Adam shook his head he knew it wasn't quite the truth. There had been times when he'd wondered if it was merely as the stranger commented, and if the reality was to be a disappointment after all. Particularly now his father had been forced to retire to the country with the family. At first, Adam had been loud in his objections, but he'd become more interested in the cider business than ever he had expected to be. There was something very basic and rewarding in seeing the presses crush the apples into pulp, and watching the golden liquid trickle out; awaiting the exact moment of fermentation for the fruit to turn into a potent brew, allied with the heady musty smells of the crushing room and the huge silent kegs in which something almost magical was taking place.

'But a fine young man like you will be leaving a girl behind, I'm thinking?' his new friend said jocularly, seeing the sudden faraway look come into Adam's eyes.

'Oh, I've met a girl,' now why had he said such an idiotic thing?

'You'll be writing to her, I've no doubt,' said his friend comfortably. 'And she'll be waiting eagerly for your words of love, if I know anything about young girls!'

The gentleman settled back on the hard seat for a nap, and Adam gazed out into the unwinding countryside. Write to Loveday? How could he? It was something he'd never considered. He didn't know her, nor anything about her, except what Matt had told him, and what was instinctive inside him. He didn't even know if she could read. No, he didn't think so. But he could write to his sisters and suggest they make her acquaintance, since she was the cousin of Matthew Willard, whom they had met once.

Adam grinned ruefully. Neither Sarah nor Grace had

wanted to repeat the experience. The two of them enjoyed being ladies of the manor, if you could call Goss House by such a grand name, but neither of them would ever stoop to befriending such as Matt or Zeb or his two raucous younger brothers. Neither would he want Matt to get too friendly with his sisters, Adam suddenly thought keenly, knowing his nature only too well.

Still, maybe there was a way he could word the letter to his sisters so that they'd think it a kindness to call on Loveday, and in that way he'd get news of her. He leaned his own head back against the bouncing wood of the seat and closed his eyes, too intrigued by this new idea to consider how sweetly and smoothly he was becoming enmeshed with Loveday Willard.

Loveday's footsteps were jaunty as she made her way back home from the churchyard. Even though she now knew Adam had gone away, they had met; she had spoken to him; she had seen the way he looked at her, and all her feminine instincts told her there was a bond between them. Too subtle as yet to be recognised by any but themselves . . . no more than a reaching out of the senses, and a knowing. She hugged the secret of it to herself, and that other, more splendid secret too! Adam had asked her to wait for him, and he'd marry her! Oh, it was all a lot of teasing nonsense, of course, but words once said could never be unsaid, and one day, if God willed it so, it would happen.

She turned into the doorway of Willard's General Store, forgetting completely the way in which she'd flounced out of it earlier. The doorbell jangled as she closed it behind her, and the next minute she was almost knocked off her feet as her father's face seemed to leap in front of her, red and scowling, and she felt the ring of his huge hands as her ears were boxed soundly.

'And just where d'you think you've been, my fine wench?' Ralph shouted, all the more incensed at the first sight of her beaming face, as if butter wouldn't melt in her mouth, while he'd been combing the place for her. He caught sight of the caked earth on her boots. 'Have you been larkin' about with some boy? If you bring trouble home here, I'll wring your bloody neck, my girl. You've to wait a month afore I see you courtin' wi' Finch Viney, out of decency for your mother, but by God, when the month is up, the sooner you get safely knotted to Finch, the better. I'll have no trolloping from my own daughter.'

Loveday found her voice, and all the hurt screamed out.

'You're a fine one to call me a trollop! What about *you*? You disgust me! You couldn't even wait until the earth settled on my mother's grave before you were taking Polly into her bed. You make me sick with your hypocrisy! And if you think I'm going to let Finch Viney court me, you can think again.'

Ralph's swipe caught her on the side of her cheek, stunning her into silence. Through the pain of it, Loveday could feel the swelling begin, and knew she'd look a sorry sight before the end of the day.

'You'll do as I say, you bitch,' Ralph thundered, his face apoplectic. 'And what I do is my own affair. I'll have no criticism from my own daughter – and you'd do better than to listen to gossip.'

'I haven't been listening to gossip,' Loveday shouted, fighting back the tears that threatened from the pain in her cheek and the sides of her head. But she wouldn't let him see . . . she *wouldn't* . . . she gritted her teeth. 'I *saw* you both in my mother's bed last night, like a pair of animals.'

Ralph's breathing sounded suddenly laboured, her words knocking all the fight out of him for a moment. He hadn't known she was there. He'd been so careful until now. It was one of his unwritten rules that he and Polly should be discreet until such time as Meg died. She'd been frail for some months, and the smallpox had come along as a gift from heaven . . . he felt even more guilty as the unbidden thought swept into his mind. He was guilty enough with this fiery chit standing in front of him, accusing him of fornication, and the fact that she had every right to humiliate him didn't make it any easier to suffer.

'You keep your mind on your own business and I'll see to mine,' he snapped. 'When you're old enough to know what you're on about, then you can say your piece.'

'I thought the idea was to get me married off to Finch Viney!' Loveday stormed. 'If I'm old enough to be thinking of courtin', I'm old enough to know what goes on!'

Ralph ground his teeth. The girl had always had a quicker wit than he had. She had her mother's cutting turn of phrase when it was needed, though in Meg it had always been gentled by her breeding. This piece had too much of him in her to mind her words, and he'd be well rid of her. He'd start now.

'You can get yourself round to Finch's shop and purchase the mutton Polly's wantin' for the stew,' he ordered. 'An' make yourself pleasant to 'im. I don't want 'im scared off the idea of wedlock by thinkin' he's getting tied to a wildcat!'

'Why can't Polly go?' She ducked under his arm and whirled out of the store before his hand could clout her again. Enough was enough, and there was already a small group of spectators in the street outside, straining to hear what the Willard fight was all about. Fortunately they made so much noise among themselves speculating, they missed the half of it. But they didn't miss the way young Loveday came storming out, cheeks flushed with rage, and with an ugly dark mound on the side of one of them.

They scattered to let her through, one section thinking it a shame that such a pretty miss should be so knocked about by her brute of a father; the rest siding with Ralph in taming such a headstrong girl afore she came to too much harm and brought shame on his good name.

Loveday ignored them all, walking with her head held high until she had retraced her steps to stand outside Finch's shop. Only then did she begin to wilt a little. She'd achieved nothing in confronting her father with all she knew, and she'd only succeeded in being sent round here, where she least wanted to be. And knowing Ralph as well as she did, he'd be scheming in all sorts of ways to be rid of her as soon as possible. A wave of misery swept over her, because the one person to whom she could always run to with all her troubles would never hear them again.

Finch Viney caught a glimpse of the wan face outside his shop window. His simple heart leapt in his chest. Through the thick green glass, he was not yet aware of the marks of Ralph's attack. Finch only saw the girl for whom he had a fondness that astounded him. He'd cheerfully expected to remain unwed all his days, chirruping with the old dames who came into his shop daily, and allowing himself to be teased unmercifully by the smart young wenches. Finch didn't mind their teasing. It was the only bit of social life he got. After working hours, nobody ever bothered with him. If it hadn't been for his belly, that none could ignore, he'd merely have melted into the background like April snow.

And then, one night when he'd happened to see Ralph Willard staggering down the street after a gutful of cider, Finch had offered him assistance, and while the older man clung to his arm on the unsteady walk back to Willard's General Store, Finch had very daringly stammered out his admiration for the fine young lady Miss Loveday had become.

'Oh ah, fine enough,' Ralph had grunted. 'But needs a man, me boy. Fine an' burstin' out of her bodice, and needs a man to keep her satisfied of a night. You know what I'm meanin'!'

Finch had laughed in embarrassment and said he did, and Ralph had grown expansive to this fine young gent who'd bothered to come to his aid when he was temporarily unwell.

'A man such as yourself, Finch!' He'd dug the butcher in the belly. 'Respect – Respect – Res*pectable*!' He finally got the word out. 'How would you like to take 'er on then? Fancy her, do you? Fancy a bit o' the night sport with my Loveday, eh?'

'Well, only if we were wed, naturally,' Finch had said hastily, lest Ralph should think his intentions were dishonourable. To his amazement, and still not really knowing how it had all come about, he'd felt Ralph slap him on the

39

back and tell him he had his permission to come courtin', only he'd better wait until Loveday was sixteen, so as to stop folks talking.

And then the smallpox had taken off Loveday's mother, so there must be a delay for decency's sake, but it was only two weeks now before Loveday's birthday, and Finch found himself seized with an eagerness of which he hadn't known he was capable.

He strode outside now, as he saw Loveday peering in, his round face full of smiles, his side-whiskers making his cheeks look even wider. But his smiles faded as soon as he saw her properly.

'My sweet girl, what's happened to you?' Finch said, appalled. 'Have you been in an accident? Come inside, and let me bathe your face before any of my customers arrive.'

The concern in his kindly voice made Loveday swallow back the sudden lump in her throat. She'd come here sullenly, under protest, hating Finch, not because of who he was, but because she was being pushed towards him against her will. Not that he'd ever been less than kind to her, and she allowed him to take her through to the scullery at the rear of the shop.

It wasn't a normal scullery. There were bits of evidence of his trade everywhere; blood and skins tossed in a bin for burning later; piles of old newspapers for wrapping meat for customers; knives ready for sharpening.

Finch led her to the stone sink and ran the cold water, rinsing a mutton-cloth before squeezing it into a compress and pressing it lightly to her cheek. Loveday winced, her blue eyes blurring at the shock of the cold compress. It was too much for Finch. Closer to her than he'd ever been, with her mutely appealing eyes gazing up into his, he felt himself to be a man after all, with all a man's urges that he'd sometimes suspected were denied to him.

Daringly, he placed his free arm around Loveday's waist.

'I'd never hurt you, Loveday,' his voice was suddenly hoarse. 'You know that, don't you? And I think you know I've asked your Pa's permission to come courtin'. What do

40

you say, Loveday? It's what *you* want that's important.'

She still hadn't said a word. Sometimes she'd compared Finch Viney in her mind to a large pink pig, amiable and grunting, but suddenly she realised he was the first person ever to ask what *she* wanted. In those few seconds he'd made her feel important. Not that she could ever feel romantic about him. She could never love him, but it was something to know that he respected her enough to speak to her like this. And what if he did come courtin? Going courtin' didn't mean she had to have a hasty marriage. It didn't mean she ever had to marry him. Courtin' could go on for years . . . until the time Adam Goss came back into her life, as Loveday was certain in her soul he would.

'It's a big decision, Finch,' she murmured, more submissive than folks usually heard Loveday Willard talk.

'But you'll think it over?' Finch said eagerly, wishing desperately he'd had the foresight to put on a clean striped apron that morning, instead of the tacky one he was wearing so close to Loveday's trim young figure.

'There's no harm in thinking,' she smiled suddenly, not really thinking of him at all, her thoughts winging away to where a passenger coach might be right now on its road to Bristol. So immersed in her sudden yearning she didn't notice it was Finch Viney who put a tentative hand on the rounded swell of her breast, just to test her reaction to it, and was surprised and delighted to find its instant response. He let his hand remain there for an instant and then removed it, but the unexpected desire raging through him was a new and explosive sensation to Finch. It gave him sudden confidence in himself as a man, and he had every intention of making his engagement to Loveday as short as possible, now that she had given him her assent. He went around beaming for the rest of the day, ignoring the giggling young brats who carried on the usual sport of baiting 'fat old Finch with his belly in the ditch'.

CHAPTER FOUR

'You can't sling 'er out, Ralphie!' Polly stood with her hands on her hips, straightening up from making the bed in which she and Ralph Willard had spent the night until she'd stolen back to her own room just before dawn. 'She's your own kid, after all, and she'll be movin' on someday soon. She's not so bad really.'

'That's rich, comin' from you!' Ralph snorted. 'You know what she thinks of you, don't you, Pol?'

Polly laughed her throaty laugh and sidled round towards him, running her slim fingers inside his shirt in a way that made his chest hairs curl up of their own accord.

'Well, she's right, ain't she?' she said intimately. 'I don't pretend to be no saint, and you knew that the minute you laid eyes on me, didn't you, sweetheart? But I'll tell you what you can do. Fix a bloody great bolt on the bedroom door, so she can't come getting a cheap thrill at our expense!'

She giggled, suddenly imagining the sight that must have met Loveday's eyes the night before. Ralph was an energetic and noisy lover, and starved as he'd been for God knows how long in his wife's bed, he'd taken on a new lease of life since Polly had come on the scene. And no doe-eyed sprat was goin' to queer her pitch now, Polly thought suddenly, all the laughter leaving her. She'd angled long enough for this position, and it would only take a word in the wrong ear from that daughter of Ralphie's, for the prim and proper Taunton dames to outlaw the store if they thought there were any goin's-on there.

'Maybe we should tie the knot to make it all legal, Ralphie,' she began, and saw at once that she'd made a mistake.

'Talk sense, woman,' he snapped. 'Meg's just buried, and it's going to cause enough talk with you staying on here at all.'

'You ain't thinkin' of sendin' *me* away, are you?'

He pulled her into his arms and felt her arching towards

him in a cloud of the cheap scent she wore.

'No, I'm not,' he growled. 'But it'd be best if you get that sister of yours down here as soon as possible. Make it look as if it's you that's desirous of a chaperone for the sake of both our good names. Can't do no harm, and this sister of yours needn't make any difference to us, I take it?'

'Not a bit,' Polly's spirits were restored. 'I'll see to it today, Ralphie.'

He patted her rump as the doorbell sounded, and left her to the task of writing laboriously to Ellen to say she needed her in the country for a spell, and to put on her best prudish air for reasons she'd explain later. Polly grinned, knowing that last hint of mystery would do the trick. Ellen would be intrigued, and her one-time acting ability would come to the fore. Polly had no doubt she'd play the part of spinster sister to perfection.

Behind the counter of the store, Ralph Willard faced his first two customers since closing all day yesterday out of respect for last night's funeral. He put on a melancholy face, seeing the wives of the china dealer and the most eminent chemist in town, whose custom was to be valued.

'Good morning, ladies,' Ralph said solemnly, as befitted a newly bereaved man. 'Is there something I can get for you both?'

The women glanced at each other, then Mrs Oak, the chemist's wife, spoke forcefully.

'We heard that your daughter has been in some kind of trouble, Mr Willard. There's been some talk this morning, and since Mrs Phillips and myself are concerned about young people's welfare in this town, we thought to make it our business to enquire if the child was quite well.'

The interfering, fousty old rat-bags, Ralph raged inwardly, though his face gave nothing of his feelings away.

'I'm afraid poor Loveday's still grieving badly for her mother,' he said piously. 'Perhaps you're referring to a nasty fall she had early this morning when she was too beset with grief to mind what she was doing and fell into a doorpost.'

43

'Fell into a doorpost,' Mrs Oak repeated sceptically. 'It didn't look that way when an acquaintance of ours said she saw the child outside Viney's butcher's shop earlier on.'

Ralph's face broke into a smile.

'I can set your minds at rest there, dear ladies,' not by so much as a twitch did he reveal his fury at their nosiness and the tight-corseted self-righteousness with which they drew themselves up. 'Dear Loveday would be wantin' the reassurance from her intended that she was still the pretty young thing we know her to be. You know the way young girls are.'

'Loveday's intended!' Mrs Phillips, who prided herself she knew all the town's gossip before it was even fact, leaned forward. 'Loveday and Finch Viney, Mr Willard?'

'Oh, dear ladies, please forget I said the words. Of course, it's quite unofficial, since the dear girl's not yet sixteen until two week's time, and naturally, the month's mourning for her mother will take all her thinkin' –'

'Naturally, naturally,' as Ralph might have predicted, this new bit of gossip was fast taking precedence over the news of Loveday's bruised face. He surprised himself by being so devious, when everybody knew the Willards were more often than not at each others' throats, but he had the business to think of, and he didn't intend starting off married life with Polly by having people shun his store. And these two old dames were just the sort who could start that particular ball rolling. As they would have pressed for more details, to his relief Loveday herself came marching through the shop door, a newspaper parcel in her hands. The bruise was darkening on her cheek, but Ralph came swiftly round to the front of the shop and squeezed her to his side, willing her to back him up.

'Well now, my lamb, you're feelin' better, I trust, since payin' a visit to Finch's shop? He'll have set your mind at rest that you're none the less handsome because of a silly old fall against a doorpost!' he said jovially, his fingers digging unobtrusively into her arm. 'And he's sent some of his choice cuts for his future father-in-law, has he? A fine

44

upstanding young fellow-me-lad as I've been telling these two ladies, and unfortunately our little secret is out, Loveday, but I'm sure you won't have any objections to two of our most genteel customers a 'knowin' it.'

He saw them preen out of the corner of his eye, but he was more anxious at Loveday's reaction. If the contrary little madam let him down now, he'd add another bruise to match the first as soon as the old dames were out the shop door. To his astonishment he saw Loveday smile sweetly.

'It won't matter who knows it when another month is up, Pa,' she murmured demurely, 'and I know it would have set my mother's mind easy to know my future was settled with a God-fearin' man like Finch Viney.'

Ralph was well pleased with her, and the two ladies were smiling and telling themselves there was nothing wrong with a young girl who could speak so modestly, with due respect to her mother's memory and the teachings of the church. They overlooked the fact that the Willards were rarely to be seen in any church, and consoled themselves instead by remembering that Finch Viney regularly put in an appearance, his pink round face agleam with perspiration as he bawled out the hymns half a tone higher than anybody else. Never mind. In Finch Viney, Loveday Willard would find her salvation after all, and the two ladies purchased several more items from Ralph's store than they intended, just to show their goodwill and give their approval.

Upstairs in the coolness of her bedroom, Loveday flung off her shawl and threw herself flat on her bed, the springs squeaking beneath her, her mind filled with a hundred different things at once. Was it really only this morning that she'd gone storming out of the house in a red rage to come so unexpectedly and breathlessly upon Adam Goss? Only a few hours since she'd spoken to him and felt the touch of his kiss on her lips, and then felt the plunging sense of loss at his leaving? And then to have her father knock her about and discover herself almost trance-like walking into Finch Viney's arms, like a fly caught in a spider's web. Suddenly

Loveday wanted to laugh and laugh, and weep and laugh, and weep and weep . . . to find with such certainty all that she ever wanted out of life, and then to commit herself to someone else.

And those so-respectable dames in the store . . . the laughter overcame the weeping again, for what did it matter that they and everyone else would now think she was going to marry Finch Viney? Loveday herself had made her own vow, there in the quiet churchyard on the sweet red earth that was settling on her mother's grave, and if she gave her promise to a dozen men, she thought recklessly, it would mean nothing, for her heart would belong to only one.

But oh, her father was as cunning as herself, and she couldn't help but admire his quick thinking, knowing how the old dames would have borne down on him to make him repent of his bad ways if they'd known he'd been knocking her about.

He came in through her bedroom door a minute later, and she scowled at him. It was time he started knocking, Loveday thought frostily . . . not that he'd be finding what *she* had found in his bedroom last night, but she had a right to her privacy too. It was such a change to see him smiling, she bit back the words and sat up on the bed as he came near. He gave her a sudden enveloping hug, and smoothed down the tangles of her hair. By God, but she was goin' to complement Finch Viney's bed, Ralph thought swiftly, with that wanton look about her and the yielding body that was takin' on a womanly shape faster than blinkin'.

'You're not a bad girl, Loveday, and that was a clever bit o' thinkin' downstairs. Has Finch said summat to you?'

'We had a bit of a talk,' Loveday said carelessly. 'I said I'd think about it. You wouldn't want me to do more than that just now, with Ma hardly cold in her grave, would you?'

Her clear blue eyes dared him to pursue the subject, but Ralph was satisfied. She was a Willard, his girl, and once a Willard made up his mind to anything, he'd move heaven and earth to get what he wanted, and that went for the womenfolk too. Not that there were many true Willard women about ... in fact, his Loveday was the only one, Ralph realised. Emily, his brother Jack's wife, had produced four brawny sons but no girls, and it had been left to Meg to give him the baby girl whom everyone had said at her birth was going to turn out a beauty. And so she had. Ralph got up from his daughter's bed, suddenly feeling she was too old now to have him treating her like a little girl.

'We'll be havin' company to stay afore long,' he said, suddenly awkward, and forgetting Loveday had already heard this bit of news. 'Polly's sister Ellen's coming down for a spell, before you go off to Jack's place.'

Loveday looked him in the eye again, with that directness of hers he found so disconcerting.

'Are you goin' to marry Polly, Pa?'

'You shouldn't be askin' such a thing at this time,' Ralph blustered, his face deepening in colour as he remembered that Loveday had seen them together last night. The ring of the shop doorbell let him make his escape before the conversation got any more uncomfortable, and while he and Loveday were on reasonable speaking terms, he'd prefer to leave it at that.

Loveday lay back on her bed again, staring at the ceiling. She was sure her father would marry Polly. What she wasn't sure about was if she really cared. Whatever he did couldn't hurt her mother now, and that was an inescapable fact, and Loveday wasn't so green she didn't know her gentle mother had been far too fastidious to enjoy the drunken fumblings of a lusty man like Ralph Willard. It had been been all too obvious when Meg had explained certain things to her daughter in the springtime of that same year when Loveday began the change from a child to a woman.

'Men will desire your body, Loveday,' Meg had said delicately. 'And desire can be like a flame, all-consuming and blind to everything else. Don't mistake desire for love, my darling, and be very sure before you give yourself in marriage to a man that you love him, for without love, the bodily acts between you will be hateful. I hope I'm not frightening you.'

'No, no! It's right that you should tell me, Ma, rather than learn it from anyone else. Should I know more?'

Loveday had burned to know the details of these bodily acts that were at once so wonderful and so terrifying, but here Meg's courage and delicacy failed her, and she had ended by saying the time for that would come later, and meanwhile Loveday might observe the animals on her uncle's farm, for all procreation was begun in the same way.

For the first time, Loveday was eager to visit the Willard farm that spring, and to look curiously on things which previously she'd ignored. Only to find that her cousins were grinning behind their backs at her, and that Matt in particular was promising to give her a finer education in such matters than she'd ever find in pigsty and field. She'd tossed her head at him and told him not to be coarse; but it wasn't until last night, when she'd blundered upon her father and Polly so energetically employed, that her education had been really complete.

From the enjoyment both of them had emitted, Loveday was forced to conclude that Ralph and Polly loved one another. And Meg had said that as long as love was present, nothing that took place between a man and woman was wrong. Loveday passed a hand across her forehead, a small frown between her brows. It was very puzzling. She was on the verge of womanhood, and yet she was still as ignorant and as vulnerable as any street urchin in many ways. Probably more so, from the insistence of her mother to keep her sheltered from vulgar ways, and to accompany her on every excursion to the Willard farm. This year would be the first time Loveday had been packed off there on her own, while Ralph and Polly stayed behind to mind the store, with the chaperone of Polly's sister Ellen safely installed.

Matthew Willard was thinking much the same thoughts as he strode the morning-fresh fields at the Willard farm to chase the cows out to pasture after milking. Zeb was lumbering ahead, stooping every now and then to gather the dew-spangled mushrooms into a canvas bag slung round his milking smock. Zeb was very partial to mushrooms and when they got back for breakfast, their mother would fry up a great sizzling panful on the old farmhouse range, to go with slices of their own fat bacon and thick home baked bread. Zeb was happy in such thoughts, but Matt's were concerned with a different kind of hunger.

He'd watched his cousin Loveday change from a gawky maid, with big doe-eyes that looked too big for her face, to a wench who could make him rise just by letting his thoughts roam around the developing shape of her. There was a prize there that was goin' to be his for the takin', and the time was drawing near. When Loveday came to help his Ma with her preparations for the family feasting on St. Cattern's Eve, she'd be past her sixteenth birthday and as ripe and ready for spreading as she'd ever be. Sweet sixteen and never been stuffed, Matthew chortled gleefully to himself as he swung along after Zeb, kicking the tardiest cows along with an energy borne of anticipation. Sweet Loveday was going to have a stuffin' to remember, or his name wasn't Matt Willard! It was one to chalk up the next time he saw his new friend, Adam Goss. He and Adam had chewed over the girls they'd had . . . not that many in Adam's case, Matt had calculated, but he was going to delight in telling of how he'd got his leg across this snooty cousin of his . . . a pity Adam had had to go off right now and wouldn't be back till Christmas-time. They might have made it a threesome one dark night in the barn Matt had already set out in his mind as the place for the deflowering.

'Somethin' funny, is there, Matt?' Zeb's shadow blotted the horizon as he came back to join his brother on the way back to breakfast, with the black and white cows already scattering in the fields and munching contentedly. Matt grinned. His poor old Zeb would never be able to think of wenching, and it was a shame to excite the poor devil's mind with things he'd never manage. He slapped him good-naturedly on the back.

'Not a thing, Zeb. 'Cept that I'm going to enjoy your mushrooms extra well today. They're good for what I need, see?'

Zeb laughed with him, not understanding, but glad that

Matt was in a good mood and not one of the black scowling tempers, that was as like as not to end with Zeb getting a clout for no good reason except that he was handy. He stomped back to the farmhouse alongside Matt, his buffoon's face beaming as brightly as the September sunshine. In the flag-stoned kitchen, the air was already humid and dense with Emily's first bread baking of the day, with little droplets of moisture clinging to the low ceiling. The bacon was already curling nicely in one black pan, and Zeb tipped his bagful of mushrooms into the one waiting to receive them, the fat just beginning to buzz. No need for washin' 'em when God's good morning juice had cleansed 'em, was the saying, and Matt grinned as his two younger brothers let out great gaping yawns at the breakfast table, to be clipped around the head by their father. They'd been very late getting home last night, and there'd been barely time to lay heads on pillows afore it was time to be up and about the farm's business again, but there'd be no sympathy from Jack Willard, nor none from Emily neither. Farming was a job that took no heed of birthings and dyings, 'cept when it was stock that was involved. Pigs and chickens still had to be fed, cows to be milked, and 'twas no use telling any of *them* that Meg Willard was just buried. Tears must be wiped away and business carried on as usual. It was no use crying over things that couldn't be changed.

But Emily Willard had had a fondness for her sister-in-law, despite the fact that in background and temperament they had been poles apart, and couldn't dismiss her passing that easily, and while she passed round the heaped plates of food, she looked keenly at all her menfolk.

'You're to be 'specially thoughtful when Loveday comes to visit this time, boys,' she included her husband in the term. 'She'll be missing her Ma, and it's a bad time for a girl to lose her mother, just on sixteen. It's a special time in a girl's life.'

'Why is it, Ma?' Zeb asked, open-mouthed, with bacon fat dripping down his chin. Matt and his other brothers grinned, letting Zeb ask all the questions as always, while they reaped the answers.

'Because she's near to bein' a woman, that's why,' Emily snapped, 'an' I'll have no teasin' of her the way you allus do, you hear me?'

'Loveday's got bumps on 'er chest!' Silas burst out.

'Do they hurt, Ma?' Tom gurgled for good measure, while Zeb continued to look from one to the other as if they were the ones soft in the head.

' 'Course she's got bumps on 'er chest,' his slow voice informed them. 'She ain't no different from cows and sows and all female women, is she? Why shouldn't she have bumps on 'er chest?'

His brothers were convulsed with laughter at this piece of wisdom coming from Zeb, until their father shut them up with a sharp rebuke.

'Sometimes I think our Zeb's got more sense in his noddle than you three knot-heads put together. Now you mind and do as your mother says, an' leave the girl alone when she comes.'

'We won't have to go round wi' long faces on account of Aunt Meg dyin', will we, Pa?' Silas scowled. 'She'll be over it by then, won't she? An' we won't have to stop the celebratin' on Cattern's Eve, will we?'

'Of course we won't,' Emily said at once, before there were ructions so early on in her kitchen. 'Just remember Loveday's a girl, that's all, and girls are different from boys.'

Matt spluttered into his mug of black tea to force himself against making a crude comment that would get him a whack about the head, big as he was. His Ma didn't have to remind *him*, even if two of his brothers were too young to be bothering about such sport, and the other was too dumb to know what he was missing!

He took on the corn scattering to the chickens that morning, though it was usually Tom's job, since he needed to inspect his game-cock's leg, torn near across by the latest fight to which he'd put him this week. It was mending tolerably well with the rough splint and twine Matt had bound it with, and Prince came crowing towards him as soon as he recognised the odour of his boots, listing sideways, feathers fluttering.

'You'll do, my beauty,' Matt ruffled the cock beneath his

neck feathers. 'And come November, I'll be crowing as loud as you! I'd put the wager on it myself if I cared to trust another soul with the knowledge!'

There was only one he'd tell, and he'd already told Adam he was going to be the one to break in his cousin. A pity though, they couldn't have arranged a proper wager, with a spy-hole for Adam to see he did the job properly, and a triumphant cider supping at the end of it all. He'd even have persuaded Adam to provide the stuff from his Pa's cider farm. Not that Adam had much to do with the business end of it, from all he heard tell. Nor his Pa neither. Left it all instead to the old manager and workers who'd been there when it was the Lundy place, before Mr Goss had bought him out lock, stock and barrel.

Lording it over the countryside as if the rest of 'em were lower than themselves, and particularly Adam's sisters, riding round the hills and through the forest as if they had a bad smell under their noses whenever Matt or his brothers chanced their way. Proper snot-nosed town dwellers, they two, Matt snorted to himself, thin-chested and frigid, a pound to a penny. Nothing there to stir a man's loins, even if they might be considered handsome by some.

Matt snorted again, not wanting to waste time thinking of the Goss girls. He'd too much else of importance to do that day. He'd promised to set snares to catch some rabbits, and his Ma would get the kitchen steaming again with the aromas of pastry and meat and thick oozing gravy with Matt's favourite rabbit pies. He felt his mouth water just at the thought. There were two things of vital importance to a man's well-bein', and one of 'em was food.

Loveday went about her household chores with more energy than usual that day. She'd already upset her Pa, almost before the sun was up, and that was something of a record, even for a Willard. She'd come to her decision about Finch Viney and put the smile back on Ralph's face, even if nobody but herself knew that she had no intention of letting the engagement ever be anything more than that. At least her Pa wasn't ranting and raving at her for the moment, and it would be nice to stay in his

52

good graces for a while. Her jaw was still stiff and aching from this morning's knockabout, though Finch's gentle administrations had taken much of the sting out of the bruise.

He *was* a gentle man, Loveday acknowledged. He should have a red-cheeked countrywoman for a wife, middle-aged and comfortably fat to match his own bulk, not a restless, strong-minded girl like herself. Someone placid and jolly, not a girl with a hot passionate nature that was only just beginning to emerge . . . Loveday shivered. An engagement only, it would have to be, she vowed as she rubbed away with the blacklead until the hearth gleamed like ebony; for the thought of submitting herself to the damp perspiring clutches of Finch Viney in the way she had seen her father and Polly entwined, was too much even for her imagination to bear. He was too old, too fat, too gross, too pink, too . . . Loveday realised she was clenching her hands together, numerating all the faults of Finch Viney, that far out-weighed all the advantages of being the wife of a respected butcher.

He was still a tradesman; Loveday could almost hear her mother's withering comment at that moment, disregarding the fact that she herself had married a tradesman, and that in his youth Ralph Willard had been as dashing and virile a catch as any army officer. For her daughter, Meg had wanted so much more.

'I won't marry him, Ma,' Loveday whispered to the glittering dust particles caught in the sun's rays through the window-glass. 'It's just a way of marking time until the real thing comes along, like you always said it would.'

Into her mind's eye came the image of a tall young man with dark hair, and eyes the colour of treacle toffee, and her soft full mouth curved into a sudden smile. She was still on her knees, the polishing cloth momentarily idle in her hands, seemingly gazing at nothing at all, and muttering to herself, when Polly came bouncing into the room.

'Dreamin', are we?' she said in her shrill quick voice. 'Your Pa wants me to help in the shop, Loveday, and I wanted to catch the mail coach with my letter. If you've finished there, and you've nothing better to do, you can take it along for me if you like.'

It wasn't an order, but it seemed like it to Loveday. She was about to snap back with an angry retort, but suddenly it didn't matter all that much that Polly was acting as if she owned the place already. Taking her letter would be an excuse to be out in the fresh air instead of brooding indoors, and experiencing the cold little shivers down her spine from time to time when she turned her head to speak to Meg, before she remembered . . . Meg was dead, but there was still too much of her essence around for Loveday to feel entirely relaxed as yet. Maybe once she'd been to the farm and seen things from a distance, real as well as emotional, she'd start to feel better. As it was, her nerves were still too taut for her to be seeing things in their right perspective. She forced a smile to her lips as Polly waited impatiently, tapping the letter on the table.

'I'll pick up your new hat from the milliner's as well, shall I?' she offered. 'It was supposed to be ready today.'

'Thanks, ducks,' Polly sounded pleased. 'You look as if you could do with some air. You take your time and I'll see you right with your Pa.'

She winked, making them conspirators. It was the last thing Loveday wanted to be, but again, it didn't really matter. There was a strange new feeling stirring inside her. She didn't want to think of it as excitement, because it wasn't seemly to feel that way so soon after Meg's death. But Meg had always been the sensible kind, and told her daughter time spent brooding was time wasted, and she'd be the first one to say Loveday must be cheerful and look to the future.

And today, in one magical moment that again seemed significant because it happened right beside Meg's last resting-place, Loveday Willard had glimpsed her future. How or when she had no idea, but that it was bound up with Adam Goss, she had no doubt.

CHAPTER FIVE

The two figures on horseback trotted carefully through the quiet thickets of the forest, hardly noticing their surroundings, or the glorious red and gold foliage of a Quantock autumn. Sarah and Grace Goss were bored. Bored with the countryside after the hectic rounds of their lively Bristol life, and even more discontented as they contemplated that they'd had the choice of coming here to the West country or spending a year or two with their aunt in London, by which time both of them would have hoped to make good marriages. Each of them admitted freely that this had all been a ghastly mistake.

'We could have been in London when the princess became Queen,' Sarah moaned. 'We could be there for the Coronation next year, and all the excitement of seeing the officers in the parks. We could be riding in Rotten Row instead of being buried here in the back of beyond!'

'We could always change our minds,' Grace said dismally. 'Father won't like it, but we could say that now Adam's gone, it's even more tiresome.'

'Lucky Adam,' Sarah sighed. 'I sometimes wish I'd been born a boy, then I could do just as I wished! I suppose if we both pleaded with Father, he might agree, just so long as he doesn't think we're all deserting a sinking ship! How will it look if you and I insist on moving away as well? We can't possibly go right away. I think we must stay until Christmas is out, at least. And we should see if the doctor is right, Grace, and that this really is the best place for Father's chest. If we have a damp cold winter, we might as well have stayed in Bristol!'

They eyed each other gloomily. Their father was taking a new interest in the cider making business, that had sounded so intriguing when the idea of buying up the old Lundy place had first been suggested to Norman Goss by a mutual acquaintance of his and the family doctor in Bristol. The idea of living in a place made sweet and fragrant in spring by the blossoming of many orchards, and then the business end of it all, the process by which the hard little cider apples became the fiery golden liquid that was the countryman's nectar, was very appealing to Norman. That, and the fact that he need merely slip into the role of businessman and landowner if he desired, while the industry went on exactly as before, in the capable management of Jed Hiatt, who knew the cider making craft inside out.

Sarah, Grace and Adam had found the idea quaintly exciting, with expansive promises on their father's part that if it didn't suit them all, they were at liberty to return to Bristol or go where they would. The girls had confidently predicted that once Norman's health improved, he'd get bored with the life of a country squire, and long for the gentlemanly attractions of his club and theatre-going friends in the city.

It hadn't happened that way, to their dismay. Adam had been the one to decide to follow his own inclinations and his longing to emulate Mr Brunel in the engineering field, while Norman had suddenly discovered he wanted to be more than a figure-head at the helm of his cider works. He wanted to be in on every bit of his own business, now that October was here, and the production of the new brew was begun from the season's apples. Suddenly there was a new incentive in Norman's mind, even to the printing of new labels for the flagons and bottles and stone jugs that were now to be labelled 'Goss Cider', 'lately Lundy Cider, and still with the same high quality and prestige of former days.

To Sarah and Grace's astonishment, their father had paid out handsomely in a tussle with the former owner, to buy out the name as well as the property and stock. Whereas they had thought the move to Somerset had been little more than a whim and a means of recovering his health, it now seemed certain Norman Goss meant to stay, and his daughters didn't like the prospect one bit.

They picked their way carefully out of the woodland to one of the shady lanes that wound in and out of hedgerow and field, and could disappear mysteriously into the mist as soon as the sun faded in the evening sky. But this was early morning, with a crispness about it that still did nothing to improve their tempers.

'And now this latest idea of Adam's,' Grace burst out, her brown eyes that were so like her brother's, flashing in annoyance. 'Gone from here two weeks, and sending a letter home, asking us in that imperious way of his if we'd pay a call on some girl whose father runs a general store. How on earth does he manage to meet such people! We shan't go, of course.'

'I think we ought, Grace,' Sarah argued. 'He did ask us specially. And her cousins are apparently neighbours of ours.'

'Those awful Willards!' Grace cried. 'That's no recommendation for the girl, is it? And such a strange name – Loveday. It harks back to medieval witchcraft, I'm sure of it.'

Sarah started to laugh.

'And you say the country's not having an effect on you! You'll be hanging garlic on the doorpost next, to ward off the evil eye – *and* I saw you looking curiously at Jed's corn maidens the other day.'

'Oh, stop it, Sarah. I don't want to talk about it. And if anyone makes me think of the evil eye, it's that Willard boy. He's coming this way along the lane. Pretend you don't see him.'

Sarah looked at her sister in exasperation. It was impossible to ignore Matthew Willard, stomping along the lane towards them in his grubby farmer's smock. He was brash and uncouth, but Sarah was fully aware of the virility of him, if Grace was not. There was an earthiness about him that could be as attractive as any high-glossed military man, though she knew better than to say such a thing to her sister! She saw Grace's gaze exclude all but the distant hills now, and knew that Matt was perfectly aware of it from his grinning face as he neared them. And then all Grace's finer feelings were forgotten as she gripped the reins wildly as her horse flared high into the air, an insect buzzing loudly in his ear.

Grace flicked wildly at the insect herself as it swerved into her face, screaming that it was a wild bee, and nearly unseating herself in the process. Matt grabbed at the reins and steadied the horse in a few gruff words.

'Tain't no drumble drone, my pretty,' he grinned to Grace. 'Weather's got too cold for 'em now.'

'Well, whatever it is, it's bitten me,' Grace screamed out, sliding to the ground from the horse's back and clutching her neck just below the jawline. Sarah dismounted quickly and ran back to aid her sister, but by now, Matt was peering into the white flesh that was pierced by the insect bite and turning an angry red, and thinking it must be his lucky day.

'Hold still, my pretty,' his breath was close to her face, and Grace wished she could avert her nose from the farm odour of him, but Matt said cheerfully that it was nothing serious, and a rubbing with elder leaves would soon soothe the pain. He grovelled in the hedgerow for what he required, and began to caress the offending patch of skin with some of the leaves, discarding those to apply the coolness of fresh ones.

'The rough side for drawing out the poison, the smooth side for healin',' he informed her. 'How does that feel, missy?'

'Much better, thank you. I'm – obliged to you, Mr Willard.'

Matt chuckled. 'I'll want payment, o' course,' he said, and before Grace could blink, he'd put both arms round her and kissed her soundly on the mouth. Then, while she was still spluttering with outrage, he went whistling on his way, to disappear round a bend in the lane, the bag of snared rabbits slung over his back, well satisfied with his morning's work and the unexpected prize at the end of it.

'And you still consider them our neighbours?' Grace burst out to her sister, scrubbing away the touch of Matt's lips on her skin. 'He's a lout, and this is the family that Adam wishes us to cultivate!'

Sarah eyed her sister thoughtfully, unwilling to admit she half wished it was her who'd had the insect bite and therefore the attentions of Matt Willard!

58

'Well, I shall visit Loveday Willard this very afternoon,' she declared, irritated with Grace's sensitivity, and quite glad to be doing something by herself, since she knew of old Grace would never unbend now she'd made her position plain. 'Adam would be upset if he thought we just ignored his request.'

She remounted her horse, waiting for Grace to do the same. Her sister sat stiff-backed, digging her heels into the horse's flanks to make him move on towards the Goss property, spread out among the lush pastures of the vale of Taunton Deane.

'You do as you please,' she threw back haughtily. 'Just don't expect me to join in your rustic pleasures. And if you're so intent on staying in the country, I shall ask Father if I can go to London to stay with Aunt Lucy. I'm tired of talking to people who smell as if they've crawled out of a dung-heap!'

She urged the horse on along the lane, while Sarah trotted after her at a more leisurely pace. In some ways it would be a relief if Grace did move off to London, Sarah thought feelingly. She'd never settle here in a hundred years, and it would make life far more comfortable, and perhaps this Loveday Willard wasn't so bad after all. Perhaps she could make a friend of her . . . if Adam thought so highly of her, she couldn't be such a dragon as her cousins. Not that Sarah agreed with Grace's description of them either. At least, not Matt . . .

There should be something special about attaining the age of sixteen, Loveday thought. If her mother had still been alive, she was certain the day would have been made more important than Ralph made it. Meg had been a great believer in the mystic qualities attached to birthdays, and the fact of willing a thing to happen by the very power of thought and the strength of self. Loveday hoped very much she'd inherited her mother's strength of self, though she was having to exercise all of it today in trying to stop her lips from trembling, because Ralph had virtually ignored the importance of this day.

It had been Polly who'd reminded him, and that in itself had been a bitter moment for Loveday. Polly who said she was going to bake a cherry cake since it was Loveday's favourite, even though Polly's culinary achievements were usually dismal failures, and she'd always say cheerfully that her artistry lay in other directions. Only at Polly's announcement at breakfast did Ralph's eyes jerk towards his daughter.

'Oh ah, 'tis your birthday, girl,' he growled, annoyed with himself at having forgotten. 'Well, give your old Pa a kiss then, and you can have the choosin' of the meat for our dinner today, since Finch will be wantin' to see you. And you can go along to Mrs Forster's and have yourself measured for a dress, if you've a mind. Nothing too fancy, mind. I'm not made of money.'

'She's a lucky girl,' Polly piped up enviously, to which Ralph laughed, whacked her on the backside as she passed, and said she could order a dress for herself as well, which completely destroyed all the pleasure in Loveday's birthday gift and made her long for the days when she and Meg would have pored over bolts of fabrics and studied Mrs Forster's own designs, and spent a delightful afternoon closeted up in her workroom with tea and crumpets as an added attraction. She had no intention of going along there with Polly, and thanked Ralph woodenly.

Neither was she enchanted with the idea of calling at Finch's shop that day. He'd called several times to chat over things with Ralph, as he delicately called it, and Loveday began to think of herself as the pot of gold at the end of the rainbow, and today Finch was reaching the rainbow's end. She took her basket from its peg, deciding to get the interview over with quickly. And thinking this was no way to view her future affianced!

Outside the house, the air was decidedly cool, and Loveday drew her shawl round her more tightly. The lovely Indian summer had gone, and the sky was overcast and heavy with clouds. The seasons had moved on, and already

Meg Willard was forgotten except by those who remembered her in their hearts, and Loveday suspected she was the only one. Ralph was too busy enjoying the spurt of trade in the store, and the diversions he found with Polly Reeves, to spend his time mourning.

Finch Viney was in the act of hanging fresh carcasses on the hooks outside his shop to keep cool and to attract customers to his fine cuts, when Loveday glimpsed him from the end of the street. He was as round as he was high, she thought glumly, and she felt a sudden burst of anger that Ralph should think him a suitable husband for her. Small boys danced round him, chanting bawdy songs of their own invention, which Finch took in good part. It didn't endear him to Loveday, who was more used to seeing her own father give such urchins a scuff round the ear at their insults. She gave a deep sigh, seeing Finch Viney for the first time as an old woman, and wondering how she could even go through with the farce of an engagement she'd decided upon. He'd expect to hold her and kiss her, and she'd have a job not to shudder away from his embrace, and the smell of blood that always seemed to cling to him.

'Loveday, my dear!' He'd turned and seen her, and his pink face went a deeper shade of puce in his pleasure. Maybe it would go deep purple when he threshed about in love-making, Loveday thought, the image of it suddenly making her giggle, so that Finch thought she was eager to see him. He put one fat pink hand on her waist. Loveday flinched slightly, murmuring that she didn't fancy the street urchins mocking her as well!

'Of course, my dear,' Finch agreed at once, ushering her into the butcher's shop as if she were royalty. At least that was something new, Loveday thought, and better treatment than she got at home or on the farm! But once inside, there was no stopping his hesitant arm encircling her, and his watery eyes looking shyly into her face.

'My fondest good wishes for your birthday, Loveday, and I have a gift for you. I asked your father if it was all right,' he added hastily as he rummaged beneath the counter for a brown paper package.

Loveday unwrapped it, her natural love of gifts temporarily halting the impatience she felt at Finch's words. It wasn't *fondness* she wanted from a lover . . . it was passion and excitement from someone as young and vigorous as herself. It wasn't a stammering pink-faced duffer who asked her father's permission for every move he made, but a man who would sweep her off her feet and make her dizzy with joy of him.

'Oh. It's – it's very nice, Finch,' she murmured, turning the small book of poems over in her hands. It would be hardly Finch's own choice of reading, if he read at all, but presumably he thought it suitable for a young lady. She conceded that he was probably right.

Finch pointed out that he'd written his good wishes inside the flyleaf of the book. It was laboriously written, in a hand obviously not used to penning love messages, or anything more demanding than his weekly orders and accounts.

Loveday felt ashamed of herself for despising him in those moments. It wasn't Finch's fault that he hadn't been as educated as some, and she leaned forward to press her soft young lips lightly to his cheek, at which he visibly trembled with what she assumed was pleasure. Poor Finch. A small smile played around Loveday's mouth, and in that instant she felt infinitely older and wiser than he.

'Your Pa told me how well you read,' he said, with pride in her accomplishment and diffidence at his own lack. 'I hope the book's to your liking, Loveday – dear.'

'It's fine, Finch,' she said gently. 'Now I'd better choose the meat for our dinner, as I've other errands to do yet.'

He became businesslike, as if relieved that he was back in his own domain once more, talking of topics he understood, fine cuts and stewing meats, and birds hung by the feet and looking so undignified . . . Loveday prodded one of these. Anything she liked, Ralph had said . . .

'We'll have a turkey,' she announced. Finch gaped. Only the rich bought turkey, apart from the farming folk who reared them on their own land. He wasn't sure if Loveday should.

'And I'll tell Pa we're to have it cooked for tonight, and you can come and eat it with us, Finch!'

She'd swear he blushed all over at her words. She was as good as saying he needn't wait the proper month of mourning before he came courtin.' She was saying the courtin' could start tonight, on her sixteenth birthday, and he wasn't too sure after all if he was prepared for such a forthright young lady who took charge of everything. She stared at him with those bright blue eyes of hers that were so candid and so beautiful . . . he caught his breath between his teeth.

'Well, if you're sure your Pa won't mind' he began.

Loveday laughed, a feeling of recklessness overtaking her. If she was old enough to be courted, she was old enough to make decisions of her own. And tonight she was going to have proper dinner, like the rich folks who ate at the end of the day. Sixteen was something special. Ma had said so, and she'd be rejoicing somewhere up there in that heaven of hers, to know Loveday intended doing things right.

'Leave Pa to me,' she told Finch. 'I'll be back later for the turkey, Finch. I don't want it dripping blood all over Mrs Forster's dressmaking establishment!'

She swept out. Sixteen *was* different, she decided. She felt more grown-up, more confident. Tonight she'd sweep her hair up with pins the way Polly did, and pinch her cheeks to make them rosy. She'd wear her best brown dress that fitted her better than any of the others, and emphasised the fact that she was no longer a child. This was her night.

By the time she'd spent an hour and more with Mrs Forster and made her choice of new dress, Loveday swung cheerfully back along the narrow streets to Finch's shop to collect the turkey. He was too busy to chatter with her now, and she carried the heavy bird in both arms until she reached Willard's General Store.

'What the devil have you got there, girl?' Ralph growled at once. As soon as she explained, his birthday goodwill vanished. 'Do you think we're made of money? And that

63

thing will take hours to roast, you ninny. You'd best take it back and tell Finch you want some cheaper cut of meat –'

'I will not!' Loveday's temper blazed. 'Ma would want me to have a special meal today of all days, and anyway, I'll see to the cooking of it. We'll have it tonight, and I've invited Finch, which I thought was what you'd want. And he's let us have it at a special price, seeing as though we're almost family.'

Ralph was taken aback at her vehemence. A bloody good job when she was safely wed to Finch Viney, he thought savagely, and then he could have the taming of her. Polly came through from the back of the shop.

'Oh, let her do it her way, Ralphie. It's her birthday after all. There's some cheese and bread we can have at midday, and it'll be nice to have a bit of a party to cheer us all up, won't it?'

Loveday didn't want Polly pleading on her behalf, and she stormed through to the scullery, her eyes smarting because Ralph had taken more notice of Polly's sweet-talking than any desire to let her celebrate her birthday. She took out her vengeance on the turkey, pulling and plucking at its feathers until the scullery was filled with a fine dusty cloud of feathers and the bird lay pink and plump in the roasting pan ready for the oven. Her arms and her back ached when she'd finished it and scraped at carrots and potatoes to put round it, then stoked up the fire well before putting the pan in the oven to begin the long slow cooking. It was nearing midday already, and to appease Ralph she cut hunks of crusty bread and wedges of cheese and put them ready for when he'd finished in the shop.

Her nose was still full of feathery dust, and after the midday meal, Loveday spent some time in her bedroom, washing herself and brushing the bits out of her hair. It was a while later that she heard Polly calling her. By then, Loveday's good spirits had diminished a little, and the abortive efforts to twist her long straight hair into a more sophisticated style had come to nothing. She wrenched open her door, ready to snap at Polly.

64

'You've a visitor, ducks. I've put 'er in the parlour. A lady, by the looks. Name of Miss Sarah Goss – 'ere, where's the fire?'

Loveday brushed past her, her heart leaping in her chest. Miss Sarah Goss . . . it had to be one of Adam's sisters. Something had happened to him . . . she never paused to think it was highly unlikely anyone would be contacting Loveday Willard if such an eventuality occurred! She burst into the parlour, her bosom heaving, and a young girl little older than herself turned with a smile. Not the haughty one Loveday had seen with Adam in the churchyard that first time, she realised swiftly. This one was more approachable, at least. She didn't stop to measure her words.

'Is Adam all right?' she stammered. 'There's been no accident, has there?'

At the other girl's astonished look, Loveday realised what a fool she was being, behaving in such a way. The hot colour sprang to her cheeks. What must this young lady think of her, to talk so freely about her brother, establishing an intimacy between them that didn't even exist! Loveday was consumed with embarrassment.

'Please forgive me,' she rushed on. 'Do please sit down. I'll ask Polly to make some tea in a moment, Miss Goss.'

'My name's Sarah. And you must be Loveday. I hadn't realised you knew my brother so well, but I'll set your mind at rest at once by telling you there's been no accident. And some tea would be lovely.'

Her ease of manner made Loveday feel even more gauche. To cover her flustering, she jerked open the door and called to Polly to bring some tea at once, and closed it again before she could hear the snappy reply. She sat on the edge of the sofa, wishing she felt as comfortable as Sarah Goss appeared to be as she relaxed in Ralph's best chair. She watched as the other girl drew out a letter from her reticule, and as if some sixth sense told her it was from Adam, Loveday felt her heart begin to thud. She strained to see the square, masculine handwriting, as she sat tensely on the sofa.

65

'My brother wished me to make your acquaintance, Loveday,' Sarah went on. 'And to let you know that he is well and settled at our relative's home in Bristol, though he is to start in his employment at the Box tunnel this very week.'

There was a small silence. That he had thought of her enough to make mention of her in his sister's letter and to suggest Sarah make her acquaintance was enough to send the joy surging through her veins. Even the tart arrival of Polly with a tea tray couldn't spoil her pleasure.

'Since it's your birthday, I'll excuse your manner, miss,' Polly snapped. 'And I hope you an' your fine friend enjoy the refreshment.'

Her tone said she'd have preferred to be serving up poison, but Sarah smiled more warmly when she'd gone.

'Is it your birthday, Loveday? I hope I haven't come at an awkward time.'

'Oh no! You've brought me the best birthday gift of all!' Loveday blushed furiously again at her impetuous words, and attended to pouring the tea and handing a cup to Sarah. The china wouldn't be as fine as she was used to, but the tea would taste the same, Loveday thought swiftly.

'I hadn't realised you and Adam knew each other,' his sister said delicately.

'We don't. That is, not very well.' Loveday looked down into the swirling bubbles in her cup. 'Perhaps you wonder why he didn't write to me himself if he knew me.'

She looked up to catch a look of embarrassment on Sarah's face that she quickly hid. Loveday's colour deepened.

'You think I would be unable to read it!' She guessed correctly. 'Would you think it an imposition to show me the letter?'

Sarah handed it over, and Loveday's eyes caressed the neatly written words, scanning the length of the letter until she found her own name, again feeling that delicious leaping in her chest as she did so. Had he felt the same, she wondered, as he fashioned the letters that formed her name? She began to read aloud with a fluency that left Sarah in no doubt that this was no simple tradesman's daughter as empty-headed as that cousin Zeb of hers, with his vacant looks and lumbering ways. This was someone with a quick brain and a warm sensuality about her that Sarah guessed would have appealed instantly to Adam's passionate nature.

'. . . Her name is Loveday Willard,' Loveday read softly, her mouth curving into a smile at the thought of Adam penning this very letter. 'She'll be feeling the sadness of her mother's death right now, and it would be charitable of you to call on her, Sarah. She is the cousin of the Willard boys who farm just north of Goss House near to the Quantock forest. If you can spare the time, tell her I'm well and I think of her . . .'

Loveday's eyes sparkled as she glanced up at Sarah. *I think of her . . .* Sarah was startled at such a look on account of such a simple message from her brother, and she warmed to the girl still more. Simply adorned as she was, in her plain grey dress and flowing hair, Sarah guessed she could be stunning given more opportunity. Settling back in the chair, Sarah replaced her tea cup on the tray and unfastened the ribbons of her bonnet, patting her own well-coiffed hair into place. It unconsciously stamped them as friends, and Loveday would have loved anyone who brought her news of Adam, but she was specially pleased to like Sarah for her own sake.

Her quick brain had already memorised the address at the head of the letter, and she had every intention of writing to Adam herself. But she kept the little secret to herself, wanting to surprise him when he received a letter in her own neat hand. A swell of gratitude for Meg's insistent teaching, despite Ralph's scoffing, filled her mind now as she asked how Sarah was liking the country.

'Well enough,' Sarah nodded. 'I'd like it better if I had a friend to visit. Perhaps we could be friends, Loveday. I fear my sister will want to leave here soon, and it would be very nice to visit each other.'

'Oh yes! And I am to go to my uncle's farm for several weeks soon, as I do each year at this time, and then we shall be only several miles apart!'

They each smiled, having separate and secret thoughts at that moment. Loveday, because of the connection between this sweet girl and Adam; Sarah, because she couldn't deny the strange, almost repellant attraction she felt for Loveday's cousin, Matthew Willard. Perhaps seeing him more often as she might in this girl's company, she could rid herself once and for all of the impossibility of such an attraction!

'Can you stay awhile this afternoon, Sarah?' Loveday said impulsively. 'Please say you can. As it's my birthday I have a great desire to rearrange my hair, and yours looks so lovely. Will you help me to fasten it like yours?'

Sarah's was dark and glossy, wound around her head in two swathes, and by the end of half an hour, Loveday's too was swept up on top of her head, revealing the long slender neck and emphasising the delicacy of her features. As something a little different, Sarah had braided the ends of the swathes in the latest fashion, and they sat like a gleaming golden crown in the centre of her head. Already, she was a beauty, Sarah saw. No wonder Adam had sounded so besotted by her.

Loveday was looking at her new reflection in a little hand mirror Sarah had in her reticule when the door opened again.

'You've another visitor, Loveday, and I'm up an' down these stairs like a yo-yo.' Polly's voice trailed away as she stared at the image in front of her. 'My gawd, your Pa won't know you tonight. Proper little lady, and no mistake!'

As she backed out of the room, Matthew Willard breezed in. As the two faces turned towards him, he gaped in astonishment. He'd thought to have a bit o' teasin' with Loveday and to bring her the homely gifts from his family. The pot of honey from Zeb's bees; a bunch of bracken and wild flowers garlanded by the younger boys; a cushion his Ma had made out of scraps of fabric and stuffed with chicken feathers; and a kiss from himself, Matt had promised lustily.

Now, faced with these two visions, he was unusually

tongue-tied. Sarah, without her bonnet and looking flushed and animated and more vulnerable without her snooty sister around; and Loveday, his Lovey-dovey, looking so smart and elegant it all but took his breath away. But the hesitancy was only brief, and he strode across the room, glad he'd left his milking smock behind and looked fairly presentable, and clasped Loveday in his arms to plant a great kiss on her cheek.

'Happy birthday, Lovey-dovey,' he grinned at the usual sparkle of annoyance in her eyes. She might have the look of a fine lady on top, but she was still a Willard, and the girl who took his fancy more than any he'd ever seen. Though Sarah Goss was runnin' her a close second today, Matt realised, with her glowing brown eyes just like Adam's, and her rosy cheeks. A fine pair o' maids, the two of 'em! A pity he couldn't linger, but he'd to get back for the milking, and his horse had gone lame and he'd have to walk him all the way back to the Willard farm . . . unless Miss Goss would be so generous as to give him a ride in the pony and trap tethered outside, that he assumed to be hers, and allow him to tie the horse on behind?

Sarah said quickly that of course she would be only too glad to do a kindness for a neighbour, not giving herself time to consider how scathing her sister Grace would be at such a conniving request. But of course it was genuine, and she tied on her bonnet with unsteady fingers, surprising herself at the reaction she felt, that was a mixture of a strange wild excitement, and irritation at her own foolishness. But she bade Loveday goodbye, and said she would see her soon, and tripped down the narrow staircase behind Matt Willard, an unlikely couple to be riding off in the late afternoon sunlight.

No sooner had they disappeared than Loveday promptly forgot them, rushing up to her bedroom to put pen to paper and transfer Adam's Bristol address on to it before she forgot it. Not that there was much danger of that! Then, before she had to begin the preparations for the evening's meal, she began to write her letter, and in the writing of it she felt as close to Adam as if he sat beside her, and she was pouring out all her thoughts and feelings for him to share them with her. She didn't think anything odd in the fact that she was unofficially engaged to Finch Viney. She never thought of Finch Viney at all, for compared with Adam Goss, he was as brittle chaff to sweet strong young wheat. She never wrote of love, but love poured out of her, unmistakeable and heady to the receiver.

CHAPTER SIX

Mid November was cold and damp, and in the Willard milking shed the swish swish, hiss hiss of the milking vied with the steady dripping of rain from the roof. Matt's head was rammed against the cow's side as he worked, his brother Zeb cajoling his own beast to keep still and be drained. And up in the farmhouse, Loveday was installed, by now helping her Aunt Emily prepare the food for Cattern's Eve on the 24th of the month, the traditional day for ushering in winter, at which the Willards gathered for the feasting. This year Meg would be missing, but Ralph Willard would visit, bringing with him Polly Reeves and her sister Ellen, newly arrived from London. As befitted neighbours, Jack Willard had extended an invitation to the Goss family to join in their celebrations, and to Loveday's delight, Sarah and her father had accepted, Grace declining due to another engagement. Against her will, Loveday had been forced to ask Finch Viney to visit, since the two of them were now officially courting, but he excused himself, thinking he would be too busy cutting up meat for other folk to enjoy himself. Loveday didn't admit to anyone how relieved she felt that he wouldn't be there.

70

Her only regret was that Adam was so far away. Since her first letter, she'd waited in an agony of impatience for a reply, wondering if she'd been too daring in writing to a young man. She'd haunted the mail coach every day to see if there was a reply, and one glorious morning she'd been handed a letter with the same square handwriting she'd seen before, this time addressed to Miss Loveday Willard. She'd taken it to a quiet corner of the churchyard to read it undisturbed, almost tearing it out of the envelope.

'My dear Loveday,' she read, and her heart had leapt at such a beginning. 'What a delightful surprise to receive a letter from you. It brought a breath of home to me – and dare I say I hadn't realised I thought of Somerset as home until I left it! There's an admission for you, and one I wouldn't confide in anyone else, but I feel you and I share many things already, Loveday. I wonder if you feel the same way?'

Oh, but she did, she did . . . she read on.

'Now I'll confess something else. This great dream of mine to be an engineer seems a dismal failure. I work on the tunnel alongside hundreds of other navvies, which is the term by which they call us. I see nothing of Mr Brunel, and the work is heavy and claustrophobic. In a gust of wind the candles can be blown out, leaving us in pitch darkness until they are re-lit, and it's not the happiest of conditions with the bad weather making water seep in from above so that the pumps have a devil of a job to deal with it. The roaring of the explosions and the stench of gunpowder take their toll of the weaker among us, and accidents are commonplace. Sometimes I wonder what drove me to come here, when I could be breathing in good country air instead of toiling in mud and filth. But how I must be depressing you!

Forgive me for going on so, Loveday, and I beg you don't betray my most secret thoughts to anyone else. They're for your eyes alone, but it relieves me to speak of it in this way. If you wish to write to me again, I would welcome a letter from you, and look forward to seeing you at Christmas-time, when I intend to come home for a week or two'.

She wrote back straight away. In her second letter, Loveday had said jocularly that her father was pressing her to walk out with Finch Viney, but that though she did as she was told, she could never take the situation seriously. It was as far as she dared go, and though she was bursting to have a reply, there was no time to receive one before she was packed off to Aunt Emily's.

But Loveday enjoyed the preparations for Cattern's Eve. Last night the younger boys had goaded her into singing some of the old songs with them, their raucous voices mingling with her melodious one.

'Cattern's Eve, yew 'oodn' b'lieve,
'Tis but a month tew Kirsmas Eve', they'd bawled out, and then,
'Now welcome welcome Winter with a right good cheer.
Away dumps, away dumps, nor come you not here.'

She had seen Matt watching her as she sang, his pale eyes glittering, and a funny little shiver had run through her. He often watched her lately, Loveday thought uneasily. She plunged her arms into the big pastry mixing bowl, trying to shake off the feeling that something bad was just around the corner. It must be the oppressive weather, she told herself, and the thought that right now, Adam would be toiling underground in the murky cold and wet, with only the guttering candles to light the tunnel. It was so far from his dream . . .

'Come on, girl. Don't waste the daylight. There's little enough of it now, and tonight it's fading fast. These pies should be done and into the cold cupboard. Stop your window-gazing and mind your work. You can go off to your room later if you've a wish to, with your book reading,' Aunt Emily grumbled.

Loveday kneaded the dough more vigorously, knowing her aunt couldn't understand the fascination with books. None of the Willard boys could read, and her aunt and uncle had only a sketchy comprehension of the written word. Loveday felt sorry for them, but knew better than to say so, knowing they'd only snap at her for being a snooty miss at thinking she was better than they. She worked silently with her aunt, remembering how her mother had enjoyed this too. Making the Cattern pies, with their fillings of mincemeat, and the sweeter ones oozing with treacle and honey and breadcrumbs, always traditionally shaped like a waggon wheel. To eat a spoke of the wheel was to ensure a safe winter season on the farm.

On the feasting day there would be ashen faggots burning in the hearth with withies whose symbolism was lost in the past. Eleven withies burned, and each time a branch burned through, a jugful of cider was drunk with a roar of celebration. There would be mulled ale besides and apple rings and pork collops and bacon slices, and the farmhouse would be decorated with ivy and winter sweet. Ralph Willard would be obliged to stay at the farm until the early hours of the morning until he'd slept off the effects as usual . . . and then race home in a borrowed farm cart to open the store with a head that felt as if a dozen demons knocked and hammered inside it.

Finally all the pies were done, laying on the scrubbed scullery table like pale yellow catherine wheels. They would have to be cooked in rotation, and would take the rest of the evening, but Emily always saw to the cooking and testing herself. Loveday stretched her aching neck, lifting the weight of her hair away from it and wishing she'd fixed it up the way Sarah had done for her to keep her cool. By now the younger boys were in bed; Zeb was playing with bits of paper and her Uncle Jack was snoring noisily in a corner. Matt was off on business of his own somewhere. Outside the night was dark and dismal, and the steamy farmhouse seemed to be closing in on her.

'I think I'll take a breath of air, Aunt Emily. You won't be needing me again, will you? Then I'll go up to my room with my books.'

'You do as you fancy, girl, but don't waste the candle too long into the night, and remember I'll want you up early tomorrow morning to help with the cleaning of the place.'

73

'Yes Aunt,' Loveday sighed, wondering if her aunt ever unbent enough to say a loving word to anybody. Presumably she'd done so at some time, since there were four sons to prove it. Unless that was just seen as her duty, and conducted in silence, as Meg had told her sometimes happened. It hadn't been that way with Ralph and Polly though, Loveday remembered, and quickly steered her thoughts away from the memory. She slipped outside into the chill of the night air, knowing it would be foolish to stand about when she'd been so clammy indoors, and walking briskly through the familiar surroundings, breathing deeply to clear her lungs of the cloying atmosphere of the scullery.

It was dark, but it was a soft velvet darkness, and despite the occasional flurries of rain, there was a moon above, so that the outlines of barns and outhouses were clearly visible. Behind her the old stone farmhouse was etched against the rising Quantock hills, and away to the right the darker mysterious forest, where no traveller ventured at night unless it was absolutely necessary. There was no light to be seen, not even away down the vale of Taunton Deane, where Loveday knew the Goss place to be. There was only the glimmer of light from the farmhouse behind her, and in front . . . she realised there was a soft glow coming from one of the barns nearby. For a second Loveday hesitated, wondering if it might be some ragamuffin bedding down for the night, or a sneakthief . . . she felt the stirrings of fear as her footsteps crackled on the gritty ground. and then she heard a voice she knew.

'Is that you, Lovey-dovey?' Matt called softly from the barn. 'I thought 'twas a wraith flitting' about in the light of the moon, with that pale hair o' yours flying round your head. Fair scared me, you did.'

The thought of Matt being scared of anything was enough to make her smile, as did her relief in finding it wasn't an intruder bent on mischief after all. She started to say goodnight, when he suddenly appeared at the barn door, his game-cock clasped firmly beneath his arm.

'Don't go, Lovey-dovey. I'd be glad if you can give us a

hand with Prince here. He's struggling so bad while I'm tryin' to bathe his head here, he's peckin' me near to death as well as himself. If I hold him still, perhaps you can do the bathin' of his head, and you'll be a mite gentler than me with him.'

Loveday hesitated. She wasn't fond of poultry, except on a dinner plate, but if Prince was bleeding, it seemed only charitable to help Matt with him. She stepped into the barn as Matt moved back inside, and the next second he'd slid round behind her and kicked the door shut. At the same instant the candle flickered and went out, and Prince went squawking across the barn floor as Matt dropped him none too gently. Loveday felt her cousin's arms close round her like a band of iron, and all the fear was back with her again as she smelt the animal sweat of his body and heard the rasping breathing close to her face. Her mouth was dry as dust as she tried to speak.

'Matt, let me go. Don't be stupid. The bird –'

His laugh was triumphant and Loveday felt the dampness trickle down her back as his hands pulled her into him until she could feel every sinew of his hard muscular frame.

'There's nothin' wrong with Prince, my beauty. It's you and me who've got business to settle that's long overdue, and I'm fair to burstin' to give you a birthday gift you've been askin' for.'

Matt's hand came to the front of her body as he spoke, to grasp her own hand and push it down between them, to where she could feel the hardness of him straining against the roughness of his clothing. Loveday began to shake all over, knowing he was much too strong for her, and that she was powerless if he was really intent on ravishing her ... and of that, there was little doubt. As if the touch of her unwilling hand inflamed his senses, his breathing quickened even more, and as she began to struggle, he gave her a sudden almighty push that flung her to the ground on the pile of straw. The shock of it winded her for a moment, and in that time Matt was sprawling over her, his hands fumbling for himself and pushing up her skirts as if he was suddenly possessed by a dozen arms. It all happened so fast that by the time Loveday drew in her breath to scream for help she could already feel his fingers around the secret womanly part of her that Meg had told her in the soft dignified voice should be her greatest gift to her husband.

There was no dignity in this, Loveday's mind screamed out as Matt's other hand clamped over her mouth, reducing her outcries to a choked gurgle in her throat.

'There's no use fightin' it, my pretty little Lovey-dovey,' Matt panted thickly. 'I've had 'ee marked out for this for a long time now, and it's a sport you'll enjoy once you know the ways of it. Don't waste your time in yellin', for I'd soon tell 'em all you came out here specially to meet me, and who's to question it?'

One arm lay heavily across her chest and throat until she thought she would die from lack of air. She couldn't breathe, couldn't think . . . She was almost slipping into insensibility, with dancing flame-coloured dots in front of her eyes, when a piercing pain between her thighs overcame all other sensations. As he took her maidenhead, Matt loosed his hold on her mouth and pulled her into his arms, so that they locked together as one person. She felt the sobs welling in her throat, but Matt's mouth was fastening on hers, preventing them from becoming audible.

She felt him thrust into her, and the newness of it almost tore her apart. The sobs became gasps of pain, but Matt was too drugged by pleasure to heed them. His Lovey-dovey had wanted this as much as he, despite her protests, he was sure of it. She was a Willard, and as randy a one as himself. She'd be enjoyin' it now if only she'd relax and stop makin' those whimpering little noises in her throat. Unless they were noises of pleasure . . . Matt had heard 'em before, with other wenches; his mouth curved into a smile, and he soared on with new energy, already thinking ahead to more comfortable places for this bit o' sport, perhaps creeping into Loveday's attic room at the farm when his brother Zeb was snoring fast . . . when he could have her naked beneath him and bury his face in the softness of her breasts. The thought excited him so much he suddenly climaxed, writhing against Loveday as if in excruciating pain, and cursing himself for not prolonging it longer.

'Christ, but that was worth it,' he gasped out against her hair, spread like pale silk on the coarse straw. 'You could make a fine penny or two with what you've got down there, my little sweetheart, and there's no man alive who'd have given 'ee a better breakin'-in than you've just had!'

Loveday's senses returned as he slid away from her, and she felt the dampness seeping out of her. She burned with pain and humiliation, and a torrent of hate for her cousin swept over her. She suddenly raked his face with her finger-nails, hearing him let out a howl of rage as the flesh tore, and she found her voice.

'You bastard!' she screamed. 'I'll never forgive you for what you've done. I'll tell my father, and yours, and you'll get the thrashing of your life –'

Matt's hand struck the side of her head, almost knocking her senseless, making her reel back against the straw. Outside, a roaring wind through the forest trees carried her screams away as if they were never uttered, and she lay shiveringly as Matt's eyes seemed to bore into hers. He knelt above her, a black demon.

'You'll tell no-one,' his voice was soft now. 'We'll keep this little game to ourselves, and if you start blabbing on, I'll do the same. I'll let all the young bucks for miles around know what a juicy bit of night sport they'll enjoy with Loveday Willard. You keep your trap shut and so will I, or you'll find a trail of bucks sniffin' round your door, and I don't fancy that'll please my Uncle Ralph, with his "good name" to keep up!'

All the young bucks for miles around . . . Adam . . . Loveday felt the stabbing tears in her eyes, and Matt's face swam in front of her. He'd done more harm than he ever dreamed, she thought bitterly. He'd wrecked a sweet young dream she'd barely begun to know, but his words frightened her. She couldn't bear it if Adam knew her cousin had raped her, and her mind refused to consider her father's reaction if

Matt slyly let on to him that his daughter had encouraged him; he'd never believe the truth of it from *her* . . . and deep down inside, Loveday knew she couldn't bear to speak of this to anyone. Not even to have some sort of revenge on Matthew, no matter how slight. She would still be shamed and condemned, and nothing could ever take away the stigma of her own shame now. She had lost something very precious, something that she had only hazily imagined surrendering to someone very dear to her.

'Surrendered in love,' Meg had told her softly, 'there can be nothing more beautiful between a man and a woman . . .'

Love was what she felt for Adam Goss, Loveday thought, with an agonised catch in her breath. What had happened here was *lust* . . . it was hateful, hateful.

'Well, Loveday?' Matt's voice was aggressive now. 'Do we have a bargain?'

Her blue eyes flashed.

'I don't bargain with trash,' she whipped out, jerking her head to one side as he would have struck her again. 'But I'll keep silent if you will. I've no wish for folks to know you've touched me! 'She could barely suppress a shudder of revulsion. 'And providing you promise you'll never come near me again.'

Loveday could see his grinning face in the moonlight through the square of window, and a sickness washed over her. Even if he promised, she knew of old that such promises were meaningless. Matthew didn't know the meaning of integrity.

'Oh ah, I'll promise to leave 'ee alone except when the needs take me,' he laughed coarsely, and circled her nipple with his finger, feeling it sharpen. 'Though I'm thinkin' you'll be aware of certain needs from now on, my Lovey-dovey, an' when you do, be sure as cousin Matt will be only too ready to oblige!'

Loveday scrambled up from the bed of straw. She felt dirty and abused, the lower part of her body throbbing and tender. Only a beast would make her feel this way. A lover would have more consideration, awakening her with his gentleness until her passion matched his. That she was capable of passion Loveday was quite sure, but not with *him* . . . not with Matthew Willard; but his threats would keep her silent, and they both knew it.

'Let me out of here,' she muttered, knowing she was fighting back the tears, and not wanting this oaf to see her weep. He stood aside mockingly, springing to open the door for her, and she stepped through into a sudden gust of stinging rain. For a few minutes Loveday stood still, letting the rain wash the tears down her cheeks, and wishing it could wash away the memory of Matt Willard's assault on her so easily. Then, as she heard movements inside the barn, she sped across the gritty yard and slipped through the back door and up the stairs to her attic room without anyone seeing her.

She pulled a heavy chest across the door to stop anyone forcing their way in, and only then did she strip off all her clothes and wash herself all over with the cool water in her washing-jug, scrubbing at every bit of her that he had touched, no matter how it hurt. It hurt far less than what he had done to her. Finally Loveday fell into an exhausted sleep, knowing she must be up early and behaving as if nothing was untoward, for fear her sharp-eyed Aunt Emily started asking questions. She slept with her arms tight round her body, as if to protect it, but already it was too late.

He tried her door the next night, while she lay shivering inside until he went away. But there were other places where he lay in wait for her during the next long week that led up to Cattern's Eve. She was obliged to go on errands for her aunt, to take eggs to scattered cottages in the forest, and somehow Matt was always there, eager to repeat the ravishing, no matter how she ran and schemed to escape from him. He was as cunning as a fox, and although the pain of the first time was no longer there, the humiliation was always the same . . . and one night she forgot to bar her bedroom door, since she and her aunt had been so busy that night she'd crawled to bed utterly exhausted.

Matt came into the room stealthily, and the first Loveday

knew was the sudden coolness on her skin as her nightgown was raised, and then the sliding of him into her. She'd been dreaming, a golden dream in which Adam came smilingly towards her, his arms outstretched to hold her, and for one exquisite moment she abandoned herself to the fluid movements of love, arching to match them and glorying in the caress of his hands on her breasts.

'That's it, my peach,' Matt's voice said hoarsely. 'It took a bit o' time, but now you're gettin' into the swing o' things! You're a fine and randy wench, girlie.'

Loveday gave a strangled gasp in her throat as his mouth sought hers. She tightened every muscle in her body, but it only served to excite Matt anew. There was no stopping him, and she could only pray it would be over quickly, and she thanked God she would be going home soon. She vowed never to come to the farm again, no matter what rift it caused in the family, and all Meg's teachings about the family being a close-knit unit, a circle, was mere will-o'-the-wisp, Loveday thought bitterly.

'You bastard! You stinking bastard,' she grated out between her teeth. 'I'll find a way to make you pay for this.'

It was suddenly over, and he gripped her chin in his strong hand, forcing her to look up at him.

'You do, and I'll see you end up on Blackboy Lane with the rest of the tarts,' he said menacingly. 'How will your snotty father fare in trade, having a prostitute for a daughter?'

Loveday lunged out with her fist and caught him in the fleshy part of his belly. He grunted and clipped her a blow on the breast that made her cry out and hold herself tenderly. Matt hauled himself off her bed and straightened his nightshirt while she averted her eyes from his dark-haired body and the unwelcome object that had invaded hers.

Early the following evening she and her aunt were putting the spread of food all ready for the feasting. Uncle Jack and the boys had collected the withies and the huge ashen faggots, and the fire roared and danced up the chimney, filling the farmhouse with a blazing warmth. Smoke spiralled into the night sky, and it grew so hot all the doors and windows had to be opened, despite the fact that it was nearing the end of November. The pies were laid out with great ceremony, along with nuts and sweetmeats, and since Sarah Goss and her father were to be guests this year, Norman Goss had promised to bring a barrel of best Goss cider to add to the festivities. Loveday knew that by the end of the night, the men would be rolling drunk and the women obliged to heave them upstairs to their beds. She hoped Sarah knew the road back to Goss House tolerably well, or that at least their horses could lead the trap there unaided.

She kept her eyes away from Matt, and he was too busy with the fire and the pouring of the cider to spend any time pondering on her quiet mood. Her pallor and the dark shadows under her eyes that Sarah had been troubled to see on their arrival, soon vanished in the heat of the fire and the small amounts of cider she and the women drank. It was only when Ralph and the two Reeves sisters arrived, that Loveday felt a sudden overwhelming of her emotions. For one thing, because it should have been Meg who came to the farm with Ralph . . . for another, because Ralph greeted her with a jovial look in his eyes and said a certain person must be thinking partially towards her to be sending her two letters while she was away, and holding up the two envelopes with Adam's square handwriting on it to tease her until she grabbed them from his hands, thankful that Sarah and her father hadn't witnessed the little scene.

Loveday excused herself for a few minutes and tore upstairs to her room, to rip open the envelopes. Her heart was thudding as her eyes flicked down the pages in the candle-light.

'My dear Loveday,' Adam wrote once more, 'it's such a pleasure to read your letters, though I felt a pang to hear you speak even teasingly about becoming attached to Mr Finch Viney. Is he the pink-faced butcher, or am I thinking of the wrong man? If so, I think your father should think twice about suggesting you go courting with him. A much more suitable person would be about eighteen years of age, dark-haired and eager to know you better. Can you think of such a suitor?'

She could think of two . . . one hated and one loved.

'I've no right to speak so freely on such a short acquaintance Loveday, but I have such an uncanny feeling about you. As if I have always known you. I had best stop now, before you think I sound like a lovesick swain, and stop writing to me'!

It was signed, 'With affection, Adam'.

Loveday tore out the second letter. It was brief.

'My dear Loveday,' she read, 'I'm sick with disappointment, but I may not be able to be home in Somerset at Christmas-time after all. The work on the tunnel is very slow, since the rains are heavy and the seepage alarming. There have been many accidents and I myself have had a badly bruised arm which needed attention at the Bath United Hospital. But I don't complain – there are so many others worse off than me, with battered heads and broken limbs, and even some fatalities. What a gloomy letter this is. But I wanted you to know that even if I don't see you, I shall be thinking of you, and looking forward to your letters.

Yours with affection, Adam.'

Loveday wept over the letters until the ink ran and smudged the words. Adam was such an honourable young man. What would he think of her if he knew how her cousin had assaulted her? That it was no fault of hers made it none the less shameful to her. She stuffed the letters back in their envelopes as she heard her aunt calling for her help and asking if she was sulking or just workshy? She dried her eyes and ran downstairs to where the feasting was in full swing, and the boys were lustily singing the Cattern's Eve songs and trying to make everyone join in.

'. . . yew "oodn" b'lieve, 'tis but a month tew Kirsmas Eve . . .'

And she'd hoped that Adam would be back for Christmas.

'. . . away dumps, away dumps, nor come you not there . . .'

The words drifted in and out of her head as the night rolled on. She saw Sarah whispering to Matt as if the two of them were cosy, which was impossible. Her father and Adam's, arms on each other's shoulders, roared out the ancient verses. Polly Reeves and her sister Ellen, an older version of herself but less flashy, helped hand round wedges of pie and screamed with laughter every time a new withie flared up the chimney; it was a scene old and familiar and yet this year everything was different.

Meg wasn't here, and no-one seemed to notice it except Loveday. Her world had changed because of her own cousin, who seemed to be sweet-talking her friend, so that instead of the little shared intimacies with Sarah, Loveday felt as if she stood back, observing and yet not really part of it all. She was the outsider, in this place she knew as well as her own home, and she was suddenly aware of a sudden blinding panic she couldn't explain. If only Adam was here . . . if only he'd be here for Christmas . . . if only he'd been here all along, then maybe somehow the terrible wrong Matt had done to her would never have happened. She didn't know how or if he could have prevented it, she only knew she would stake her life on his honour.

And the thought of staying here for two or three more days as she usually did to help with the clearing up and setting the farm to rights again, was more than she could bear. While the singing roared on, Loveday felt her shoulders shake as she burst into uncontrollable tears, and to her fury it was Polly Reeves, with her cheap smelling scent, whose arms were wrapped round her as she blubbered out that she wanted to go home with her father that very night.

'There, there, ducks, of course you must come home,' Polly trilled. 'You'll be missin' your Ma, and it's only natural that you should. You'll come home with us, won't she, Ralphie?'

Ralph nodded as Loveday looked at him through a mist of tears. She'd got her way, and she'd be rid of the hated attacks on her body from her cousin, but listening to the soft murmurs of sympathy among the revelling, she knew sorrowfully that they were all wrong. It wasn't Meg for whom she yearned at that moment. It was Adam. Adam Goss, whom she hardly knew, but for whom she had the same uncanny feeling that he had – that she had always know him. And she loved him, and wanted him, and had to close her eyes tightly for a moment for fear that everybody here would see the sudden look of wantonness on her face.

CHAPTER SEVEN

Three days before Christmas, Sarah Goss visited her friend, Loveday Willard in Taunton, and the two of them sat whispering and giggling in Loveday's tiny bedroom. By now Loveday knew that Adam wouldn't be home until the New Year, and that he'd be staying with his relatives in Bristol for the festivities when he wasn't actually working. But her eyes glowed and her heart sang, because he'd written in confidence to his sister since Sarah had informed him of the Cattern's Eve visit to the Willard Farm, and he now knew the two of them were friends.

'Adam asked me to give you a special message, Loveday,' Sarah said. 'I think he was too anxious about writing it to you himself, but he said to tell you not to let yourself be persuaded by the butcher – and that he'd dance with you at the next Summer Fair on the Green! Does that make any sense to you?'

Loveday laughed, exhilarated despite the fact that he was so far away.

'Yes it does! He's referring to Pa's idea of marrying me off to Finch Viney, of course,' Loveday pulled a face, glad that Finch had been so busy of late with the Christmas trade, they'd seen very little of him. 'And somebody will have told

Adam about the tradition of the Summer Fairs on Castle Green. Everybody goes to them, even the broom squires come down from the Quantocks – that's what they call the gypsies – they have donkey racing and sack jumping; poles are greased for the young men to climb to gamble for legs of mutton; there are penny stalls and hot potatoes,' her face flushed, 'and the gentlemen come down off their high horses long enough to dance with any tradesman's daughter who catches their eye!'

'And you've obviously caught Adam's eye!' Sarah said.

'You don't mind, do you?'

Sarah squeezed her shoulder affectionately.

'Of course I don't mind. It would be a laugh though, if we ended up related, wouldn't it, Loveday? If you married Adam, and I –' she stopped at the look in Loveday's eyes.

'You aren't going to say you and Matthew Willard, Sarah! Oh, please say that's not what you mean. I'd rather you meant you'd taken a fancy for Zeb than Matt,' she realised she had annoyed her friend at the sudden coolness in Sarah's voice.

'Why shouldn't I mean Matt?' she said. 'You don't own him, do you? And you must think very little of me if you think I could take a fancy for that other buffoon! I know Matt's rough, and my sister would look right down her nose if she thought I'd been seeing him, but what I do is no concern of hers – nor anybody else's, for that matter. And you and Adam had best conduct your own correspondence in future. I shall tell him I don't wish to act as his messenger.'

Loveday jumped up as Sarah made for the door, holding her arm and feeling a lurch in her stomach at the thought of losing Sarah's friendship over Matt Willard, of all people.

'Please don't be angry with me, Sarah. I only meant that I didn't think Matt was good enough for you, that's all. I didn't know you'd seen him since Cattern's Eve. You hadn't told me!'

Sarah unbent a little. 'Well, I haven't actually been seeing him. It's just that our paths happened to cross from time to time, and I don't happen to find him as repulsive as you seem to.'

85

The image of Matt's glistening face as his body pounded above hers, swept into Loveday's mind, making her suddenly nauseous. What would her gentle friend think, if she knew? They had confided in many things in past weeks, but curiously, each had kept silent about their involvement with Matthew Willard.

'It's just that I've known him all my life, and he's always teased me unbearably,' Loveday said weakly, knowing there was no way she could say more, with Sarah's clear eyes looking at her in the smoky candlelight. She could never admit that she had been ravished by her own cousin, for whom Sarah seemed to have found a strange fascination. Hopefully, it would as quickly fade, Loveday told herself. She looked so distressed that Sarah couldn't remain angry with her.

'That's all right then. I suppose I feel the same about Adam. Families are funny things, aren't they? We never think about how outsiders see them. I mean, I can't really imagine anybody falling in love with my brother. To me, he's just – my brother!'

She gave Loveday a quick hug and told her she'd see her again in a week's time. She'd be expected to stay at home and make merry with the family, and her father was looking forward to playing host to his workers for the first time since taking over the cider business. It was a tradition that had gone on when it was Lundy's Cider, and now that it had changed hands, Norman Goss had every intention of making Goss Cider a happy and contented family business. The workers would be invited up to the big house and given a Boxing Day meal with their families, for no work would be done for the two days of Christmas. Up on Exmoor and the Quantocks there would be fox-hunting for the gentry. Down here in the vale and on the hill farms, there would be rough-shooting and snaring of wild fowl, hares and rabbits. Farms would hold rabbiting parties, and Matt Willard had told Sarah carelessly she could come over to the Willard Farm if she had a mind to.

As she picked her way along the uneven Taunton street to where she'd arranged to meet her sister Grace at a tea-room, Sarah felt the little thrill of excitement run through her. She didn't need Loveday telling her she and Matt were hopelessly mismatched; nor that while her father had been happy enough to roar his head off in the singsong at the Willard Farm on Cattern's Eve and sup away with the best of them, he'd be none too pleased if he thought his pretty daughter was being sniffed round by a clodhopper such as Matt Willard. She didn't need telling that Grace would probably box her ears for her and tell her she was lowering the family standards. She knew it all . . . but none of it could stop the way she felt when Matt's pale eyes looked directly into hers, with that wickedness in them that made her legs feel as if they'd turned to water.

Loveday was still troubled by the thought of Matt turning his attentions to her friend, and wondering how she could warn Sarah against him. It would need great delicacy, but she couldn't bear the thought of Sarah undergoing the same humiliations that she herself had done. The scars were still sharp in her mind, and sometimes lately she thought they were etched on her face for all to read. She caught sight of herself now in the scratched square of mirror in her room, her mobile face still and serious, and her deep blue eyes looked suddenly huge and dark in the pinched whiteness of her face. There was a pallor about her that in the past weeks she had attributed to grief over her mother; to the fact of Adam going away so soon after their meeting; to the memories of the attacks on her body by her cousin . . . a gripping fear took hold of her, and involuntarily Loveday clasped both hands over her abdomen, where the churning made her senses spin.

It was only three weeks since Cattern's Eve when she had stayed at the farm. And two weeks since her bodily rhythms should have commenced . . . it was nonsense to think the lack of bleeding was anything more than a natural misfunctioning, after the combination of such traumatic events in her life; but there was a dryness in Loveday's throat, remembering the reeling of her head these past few early mornings, and the sudden retchings that had never affected her before. She knew the signs of carrying . . . a feeling of blind terror held her rigid.

It couldn't be! It was too horrible to contemplate, knowing that no man had touched her but her cousin Matt! The thought that she could be carrying his child in her belly was enough to make her retch anew. Beads of perspiration broke out on her brow, knowing Ralph would kill her if he found out.

He mustn't know! And anyway, it couldn't happen, Loveday thought desperately. She was turning herself into a shivering idiot, imagining the very worst that could happen to her. She wouldn't think of it. She wouldn't let herself think of Adam either, for if this terrible thing really were true, it would be the end of a dream, and she might as well join the rest of the whores on the bad side of town, knowing she'd be treated as an outcast if she didn't confess the father of the child. She'd be branded as a tart, unable to point the finger at the father, because she couldn't tell whose brat it was . . . she'd seen it all happen before, but she'd be beaten to a pulp before she admitted that it was Matt who'd raped her. She shuddered, hating him.

'What are you doin' up there, Loveday?' Polly's shrill voice sounded outside her door, making her jump as if she'd been stung. 'Has that friend of yours gone, because there's still work t' be done, my girl.' She pushed open the door and stared. 'Good Gawd, what's happened to you? You ain't takin' sick, are you? I'm not doin' all the work myself now Ellen's gawn back t' the smoke. If I'd had any sense I'd have gawn with her, instead of stayin' in this dump . . . 'ere, what's goin' on?'

Loveday rushed past the whining voice and clattered down the narrow staircase. A fat lot Polly Reeves had to complain about, taking over the role of pseudo-mother and common-law wife, whatever the good dames of Taunton thought. Loveday thought savagely that she'd like to scream the truth of it from the roof-tops . . . her sudden blaze of temper subsided as she heard Ralph buttering up a couple of them in the store, and bit her lips as she remembered her mother's words. The family was a circle that nothing must be allowed to destroy, but Meg hadn't taken into account the fact that one of the circle was rotten; Loveday remembered something else. Meg had firmly believed that if you willed a thing to happen strongly enough, it would happen. The force of your own will would make it so . . . Loveday willed desperately. For a whole week she willed her body to revert to its monthly regularity, and for a whole week she tried to ignore the rising bile in her throat each morning when she awoke.

As if to make recompense for any wrong she herself might have done in God's eyes by her own passionate nature, and so unconsiously making men too aware of her, Loveday was extra pleasant to Finch Viney when he joined them for Christmas dinner, though she almost gagged on the fat goose that was oozing with glistening gravy. She saw the satisfaction in Ralph's eyes, and told herself she was acting like a good daughter. She even avoided reading the letter from Adam that came on Christmas Eve more than once, though it didn't make any difference, for his words were locked in her memory the moment she'd read them.

'I can't be with you in person, dearest Loveday,' he wrote, 'but I'll be with you in spirit, and wishing I could claim a Christmas kiss from your lovely lips. Am I too bold? I think not. Already there's a bond between us too strong to be denied, and I'm impatient to hold you in my arms. One look in those glorious eyes of yours, and I know I shall see all the love I feel for you reflected there. Hurry up and grow up, my sweet Loveday.'

She felt as if she'd grown up too cruelly already, despite the joy of his words. The Christmas days dragged, not only because she and Adam were apart, but because of the gnawing fear inside her. There was no-one in whom she could confide her worry; not Sarah, and certainly not Polly. Not Aunt Emily . . . on Christmas morning she'd taken a sprig of holly and ivy leaves to the churchyard to lay on Meg's grave. The earth was hard with frost now, no longer sweet and red, but bleak and unreceptive. Fancifully, Loveday felt as if it rejected her; as if it was Meg who was turning against her for being the wicked girl she was, and the visit brought her no comfort at all.

A week after Christmas Sarah should have come to visit her again. It would have been good to indulge in frivolous chatter about bonnets and ribbons, and to get family news of Adam, but Sarah didn't come. A few days later one of the Goss employee's wives came into Willard's General Store and handed in a note for Miss Loveday Willard that apologised for Sarah's absence, but she was confined to bed with a very heavy cold and the doctor had forbidden her to go outside the house in this cold damp weather for at least another week.

Loveday crushed the letter into a ball and flung it on the fire in the scullery, feeling that the world was closing in on her. No news of Adam since Christmas Eve, no Sarah, not even any contact with the Willards at the farm since a brief visit on Christmas Day. Not that she minded that, and she'd skilfully managed to avoid being alone with Matt. The days were short and already it grew dark at four in the afternoon. The scullery was clammy with the stew Polly had put in the oven for the evening meal, and the smell of the mutton was beginning to bother Loveday. Polly had begun to look at her oddly a few times. As if she had some sixth sense about Loveday's anxiety . . . she still wouldn't believe it. The nausea didn't always come in the mornings anyway, so she lulled herself into thinking she'd been mistaken. It was just a bad bilious attack that was taking days to go . . .

Polly came into the scullery and gave the stew a prod with a wooden spoon, sending the aroma wafting round the room. Suddenly the smell of it was too much for Loveday. With a strangled gulp, she pressed her hand to her mouth and fled out of the room to the back of the store, where she spewed and retched over the small square of back yard, passing a trembling hand across her mouth when she'd finished.

'So that's it, is it?' Polly's voice was right behind her. 'I 'ad my suspicions about you, my fine lady. Gawn and got yourself up the spout, 'ave you? And what's your father going to say about that!'

Loveday clutched at Polly's arms.

'You won't tell him, will you?' she gasped. 'Promise me you won't tell him, Polly. It might not be what you think.'

The other girl laughed knowingly. 'I've seen that look on a

girl's face before now, ducks. Fair pinched around the nose you are, and that's a sure sign, apart from the spewing, and the fact that there's been no cloths to wash for a while. Think I hadn't noticed, did you? I may be noddle-headed to some of your fine folks, but I can still put two and two together when it comes to a bit of the other. So, what you going to do about it?'

Loveday gaped at her, tears glimmering in her eyes. Polly's words seemed to make it all inevitable for the first time, and Loveday was suddenly shaking from head to foot. A spark of sympathy showed in Polly's eyes, and she pulled her roughly indoors out of the chill air. Ralph was still in the store, so for a while there was no danger of them being disturbed, and Polly tipped a drop of brandy into a glass and told Loveday to get it down her to bring some colour back to her cheeks. She did as she was told, feeling as incapable of thought as a new-born child, and veering her muddled thinking away from the simile at once.

'I never thought old Finch had it in 'im, to be honest,' Polly was going on now. 'I thought at least he'd wait till after the wedding, but men will be men, thank Gawd,' she tried to cheer Loveday up. 'Oh come on, ducks, it ain't the end of the world, and at least it proves he's got what it takes, don't it? You'll just have to have the weddin' a bit earlier, that's all. If you make it soon, you can pass it off as a babe come before time. There's plenty of them in the world, I'm tellin' you.'

On and on she trilled. Loveday was barely listening. Her thoughts were far away, deep in some dark tunnel where Adam Goss was acting out his dream of being another Mr Brunel . . . and expecting to come home to his other dream. It was going to be a very cruel awakening. Dreams were for children, Loveday thought bitterly, and Matt Willard had taken her childhood away along with her virginity. He had ruined her life . . . some of Polly's words seeped into her brain.

'Finch?' she said vaguely. She heard Polly give a little laugh as she shook Loveday's arm.

'Your intended, my ducks. Gawd, you've got a short memory, ain't you? You ain't got a string of blokes linin' up to claim the babby, 'ave you?'

She laughed again as if such an idea was hilarious. Loveday forced a smile to her cold lips.

'Of course not! What do you think I am?'

'Well, a bit of a sly one, if you must know!' Polly gave her a knowing wink. 'Anyone could see you was goin' to be a looker, and that men was goin' to fancy you, but you must have been keen to get old Finch to dip 'is wick.'

Loveday felt her face flame with colour at her crudity.

'Don't talk like that,' she snapped. 'It wasn't like that. Finch didn't – we haven't –'

'Oh no?' Polly leered. 'I'm willin' to go along with one virgin birth like the bible says, ducks, but when it comes to the likes of you and me, there's only one way of gettin' up the spout, and you might as well admit that you enjoyed it!'

'I didn't!' Loveday was almost shouting now. 'I hated it if you must know. It was horrible!'

Polly looked at her in surprise, genuinely amazed at such a reaction, and concluding that the poor chick must be frantic with worry to take on so. And of course, Ralph wasn't known for his sweetness of temper. She patted Loveday's arm.

'I'll tell you what to do, ducks. You fetch your shawl and take yourself round to Viney's shop and you stay there till you've persuaded him to marry you in the next couple of weeks. I'll make it right with your Pa without letting on anythin'. It'll be our secret. You take it from me it's the only way out of this little lot. Finch will do right by you, and if he starts blusterin', well, you can think of a way to get your own way, can't you? A nice fresh young thing like you.'

Loveday rushed out of the room and up the stairs to get her shawl. She had no intention of doing as Polly said; she just wanted to get away from the shaming words that classed her in the same mould as Polly Reeves. She wanted to breathe clean cold night air and to merge into the shadows of the streets, and pretend this thing wasn't happening to her.

She walked for what seemed like hours, aimlessly and dully. She thought of Matt with hate; of Adam with love and regret;

of her father with fear, and of Finch . . . it would be wrong to do as Polly suggested, to urge Finch to wed her, knowing she carried another man's child. Not that Polly knew the truth of it, but Finch was a good man, despite his pot-belly and the fact that he repelled her. He deserved more than the legacy of another man's lust. Loveday swallowed. What was the alternative, a small voice whispered in her brain? To tell Ralph the truth and have the whole Willard family breaking each other's heads? Meg's circle would splinter into fragments, and Loveday knew it, and although she was not the guilty one, she felt as if she was. She was the one who had to bear the child and see the good dames of the town shunning her and her father's store, as the evidence grew in her belly.

For a moment she toyed with the idea of running away. Running to Adam, who would love her and want her, only she doubted very much that his love would stand the test of discovering what she had done. And she couldn't bear to look in his eyes and see the love change to disgust . . . the thought of deceiving him, the way Polly's idea meant she would deceive Finch, never occurred to her. If she went to Adam, it would be with the truth, and that was impossible.

So it all came back to Finch Viney. It was dark now, with a biting wind stinging her face and hands. Her boots were thin, and every stone in the road made its mark on her feet. She had walked and walked, and almost without realising it, she had arrived at the end of the street where Viney's shop still had a glimmer of light in its window. Even as she watched, the light went out. To Loveday it was symbolic, as if a light had been put out in herself, and she walked slowly forward, drawn by an inevitable force to her unwanted destiny.

She pictured Finch now, going into the back room behind the shop to prepare his solitary supper. A man like that, good-natured and kindly, needed a wife. But not *her*, Loveday's mind shrieked out in protest. Her footsteps stopped outside the shop, and she rattled the door handle before she could change her mind. She knew Finch well enough to know he'd come out to serve another customer, no matter how late, and seconds later he was peering out into the gloom, a lamp in his

93

hand, the flame shielded from the wind.

'Loveday, my dear,' his face went pinker than usual with pleasure. 'I've closed, but please come in. You look frozen. Is it some meat your father is needing for supper?'

'No. I – just wanted to talk to you, Finch. Is it all right for me to come in? Folks won't think badly of me, will they? We are practically engaged, aren't we?' She made herself say the words.

'Of course it's all right, my love, and you know I have the greatest respect for you, Loveday. Come inside and shut out the cold. Will you join me in some cold tongue?'

Loveday tried not to breathe too deeply as the smells of the shop met her nostrils. But she'd begun, and she had to go on. She nodded, telling him she could only eat a little as her appetite was poor of late. He insisted that they ate first and they could talk later, and she watched as he bustled about filling a huge pot with tea and then pouring them each a cup of the weak brew. At least it warmed her, and she picked at the food on her plate while Finch cleared his plate noisily and then asked her into the parlour.

It was pleasanter there, and Loveday made herself look at it from the viewpoint of being its mistress. It was adequate enough, and with a little imagination, a woman's touch could make it look more of a home. She realised Finch was edging beside her on the lumpy sofa, his arm sliding round her back. For a second Loveday was rigid, then she reminded herself of her mission here. To carry it through she had to pretend this was what she wanted . . . she let her fair head rest on Finch's shoulder with a little sigh that he took to be contentment. The fire in the hearth glowed in her face, hiding the pallor of it, and she chose not to imagine how red his own cheeks were. She could hear the shortness of his breath as she let the back of her hand rest against his thick thigh as if by accident. She loathed herself for what she was doing, but it was almost as if someone else was doing it, and not Loveday Willard at all.

'What was it you wanted to say to me, Loveday?' His voice was huskier than usual, and she knew he was affected by her presence in the warm intimacy of the room with its rosy

94

lighting. It heartened her. It wouldn't be so wrong if he wanted her, and she would try to be a fair wife to him. She choked back the the tears that crowded her throat, thinking how badly she wanted to be someone else's wife. But that could never be now.

'Finch, you do want to marry me, don't you?' she forced herself to say.

'Of course.' He had begun to believe it himself now, especially with the scent of her so fresh and lovely and so warm in his arms now the chill night air had left her. 'Someday, when you're ready, Loveday.'

She twisted to look into his face. Oh God, he wasn't backing out, was he? It sounded so feeble. Where was the urgency of a lover, wanting her so desperately he'd take her here and now, any way he could, if he really loved her? She wound her arms round his neck and placed a light kiss on his lips, keeping her eyes tightly shut as she did so. That way she could pretend it was Adam she kissed . . . she murmured against his mouth.

'Don't you want me, Finch?' She pressed herself against him, knowing he must feel the fullness of her breasts, and that he could hardly mistake her meaning. He spoke thickly against her check.

'Of course I do, Loveday, but I respect you. I've already said so. I can't – we mustn't – not until we're wed.'

She took one of his hands and put it on her breast, pressing against it until she felt his finger and thumb squeeze her nipple. She wouldn't let herself think of anything but her purpose. She wanted him to be panting for her, ready to agree to anything.

'Do you like that?' she whispered as he continued to squeeze.

'Yes,' he said hoarsely. Sweat stood out on his forehead, and Loveday suddenly grasped his hand and slid it down her body until it rested between her thighs over her clothes.

'It's warm there, Finch. Warm and sweet. You could be there every night if we were wed. I want to be wed, Finch. I want it soon. I don't want to wait any longer.' Her voice was breathy, tempting him, and she saw him swallow convulsively. He snatched his hand away, but she fastened it on her breast again and ran her tongue around his lips erotically.

'Perhaps in the spring then,' he began, still hoarse, his breath coming very fast.

'That's too far away, and I'm tired of waiting. My Pa's rough with me, and I want to take care of my own man, Finch. We could be wed in a few weeks if you'd agree. Say you will, Finch. Before January is out. We could keep each other warm all winter long.'

By now, Loveday was near to hysteria, though no-one would have guessed it from her manner. Outwardly, she was the complete coquette, teasing and captivating. Inwardly, she cringed from the fleshy touch of Finch's mouth, no longer able to pretend it was Adam's, firm and young. And seeing how Finch was affected by her pretence, his face red and shiny, his breathing rapid, a deep shame spread through her. He was too good a man to be cheated, but even as she began to draw away from him and murmur that she had better go, thinking it might be better to throw herself in the River Tone than lose all self-respect in deceiving Finch so, he gripped her tightly in his arms.

'Then so we shall, my maid,' he gasped. 'We'll go and speak to your father this very night, and arrange the nuptials as soon as possible. Before the end of January it shall be!'

She had won. Loveday remained as still as death in his arms, wondering what she had done in committing herself to him for the rest of her life. Her eyes glazed as she was forced to bury her face in his shoulder, and she wouldn't let herself think of it. Instead, she told herself it was the only way. She could never have thrown herself on her father's mercy about the coming child, for he would have none. There was no question of wedding the true father of the child, for that would truly be hell on earth. As for Adam Goss . . . a small sob escaped from her dry throat. Adam had been her distant star, her dream lover; to have confessed to him all that happened would be another kind of hell. He must think she had wanted this marriage to Finch Viney. He must never know the true circumstances, and neither must Finch. Once they were wed and the marriage consummated . . . Loveday almost choked at the thought . . . he must believe, like the rest of the world, that the child was his.

She extricated herself from Finch's arms and said they had best see Ralph right away, or he'd be angry at thinking she was spending so much time in a gentleman's house. Finch agreed at once, and within half an hour they sat opposite Ralph Willard and Polly Reeves in the parlour of the Willard home, with glasses clinking and arrangements made. If Loveday had expected her father to be surprised or suspicious, she was mistaken. He seemed merely relieved that she was behaving like a good daughter and accepting the man of his choice for her. Loveday should have been the one to be suspicious, but it never occurred to her until she saw Ralph put his arm round Polly's waist and give her a quick squeeze.

'That sets us free to name the day then,' he beamed, his bulbous nose gleaming with the effects of fire and cider. 'Me and Polly have decided to get wed, now poor Meg's been gone a good few months, but we weren't too sure how two women might get on in the house when the legal positions changed. Now it'll all be plain sailing.'

'Besides, it wouldn't be right for me to be living here alone with Ralph once Loveday was wed,' Polly began piously, and ended on a giggle as Ralph pinched her bottom under cover of the table-cloth.

Loveday's eyes were almost black with rage as she realised how Polly had manoeuvred this so neatly, and Loveday had fallen unwittingly into the trap. She hadn't wanted to help Loveday out at all. She'd just wanted her out of the house, so that she could persuade Ralph to marry her in a disgracefully short time after Meg's death. Loveday mourned the fact in her soul, but even that wasn't uppermost in her mind at that moment.

Across the table, Polly smiled sweetly at her as if to give her blessing, but there was a look in the other girl's eyes that was all too evident to Loveday. Polly didn't dare to actually wink at her, but the meaning was clear between them all the same. A look of triumph, of congratulations that Loveday had managed to dupe the poor old fool so easily.

Yes, they were in the same mould now, Loveday thought bitterly. Both using their bodies to get what they wanted. She had never despised herself more.

CHAPTER EIGHT

It was nearing the end of January. Deep beneath the ground, Adam Goss sweated and cursed alongside his fellow labourers chipping away with pick and shovel in the construction of the Box Tunnel. The air was fetid, yellow and heavy with the effects of gunpowder, and lit only by candles that were totally ineffective. Two men working nearby had collapsed that day. Another had been killed by a rock-fall the day before. Adam asked himself yet again why he was doing this. It was far from the idea of being an engineer, but that idea had quickly palled. Working with his hands appealed to him far more . . . but not like this . . . not in conditions that were dark and wet and dangerous, with water seepage and bad air causing all kinds of lung complaints and rheumatic disorders. He must be mad.

'Here, hold on, young chap,' a voice near to him said hoarsely, as he attacked the Bath stone savagely with his pick, sending slivers of it scattering in all directions. 'It's bad enough missing death by inches from horses and explosions without you trying to kill us all as well.'

'Sorry,' Adam muttered. Another man laughed with little amusement in his voice.

'Young Adam here wants to break through the hillside all by himself, though God knows how he's got the energy this morning after last night's little orgy. Have a good time with the scruff, did you, Adam?'

'Shut it, Phillips,' Adam snarled, to be met with derisory laughter on all sides. He didn't want to think about last night. He didn't want to think about anything, least of all the letter he'd received from his sister Sarah yesterday morning at his lodgings near the tunnel workings. If it hadn't been for the letter he'd never have seethed and brooded all day long, until he was ready to lash out at anybody who came near him. He'd never have agreed to go along with the group of lusty young blokes who were inclined to call him snot-nosed – and worse – because he didn't show much interest in the girls who hung around the mens' lodgings for a night of drinking and bed-sport. He knew they thought he considered himself too good for them, but last night all he'd wanted was to bury himself in the nearest soft white flesh available, and to hear soothing words in his ears, regardless of the fact that they were hazy and that he was befuddled by drink. All he wanted was to forget a girl called Loveday Willard ever existed.

'I don't know how to put this to you, Adam,' Sarah's letter had begun. He could sense the irritation in it as if she'd been standing next to him. 'And I think it's grossly unfair of Love-day to ask me to tell you, but she's changed so much lately, I suppose I shouldn't be surprised at anything! She snaps at me for no reason, and instead of being warm-hearted and affec-tionate, it seems as if she's weighed down by all the worries of the world. When she speaks, it's as if she's frozen, and her lips have a job to say the words.'

Adam had frowned, wondering what was coming. Sarah must have upset Loveday in some way. The girl she described certainly wasn't the Loveday he knew; he read on, assuming it to be some female tiff that had affronted his sister, and totally unprepared for what was to come next.

'By the time you read this, Loveday will be married to the pink-faced butcher, Finch Viney. How she could think of tying herself to such a man I cannot think. Particularly when I quite believed that you and she had a special friendship that might have become more. I am very disappointed in Love-day, Adam. I know there was pressure on her from her father to become engaged to the butcher, but she and I joked about it. It was all for show, she said, nothing more. I wonder now if she was lying to me, and the dubious prestige of being a tradesman's wife was irresistable after all. I shall never feel quite the same towards her again, though she assures me she wishes to retain our friendship – all spoken in that strange frozen way I mentioned to you earlier. I really don't know what to make of it all, Adam . . .'

She went on in the same piqued way, but Adam heeded none of it. There was only one sentence that speared his senses.

'By the time you read this, Loveday will be married to the pink-faced butcher, Finch Viney.'

How could she do this, he raged? She knew his feelings for her, and he knew hers for him. She loved *him*, not the butcher. Every glance they'd ever exchanged had told him so, few though they had been. Every line of her letters, even the way she had formed the characters in his name so lovingly, had told him of her love. And he had made no secret of his feelings for her. Why then had she been unable to wait? Why rush into this marriage that was doomed to failure from the start? Loveday and Finch Viney? It was as ludicrous as himself thinking he could be an engineer of Mr Brunel's stature with no experience and no qualifications. *And*, Adam admitted now, with no real aptitude for the intricate planning detail such work required. In the mood of depression Sarah's letter had plunged him in, he was ready to call himself the biggest failure that had ever lived.

All day in the tunnel he'd sworn and raged and in some adverse way proved himself more one of the men than they'd ever admitted before. By the end of the shift they were urging him on to join them in their evening's entertainments, and in a spirit of anger and bravado, he'd gone, indulging the night away in strong ale and petticoats that had left him with an explosive headache fit to burst his skull. And a temper to match. His fellow workers found a new respect for a man who could put such words together and find expletives new even to them.

But by the end of that day's shift Adam's anger was spent,

and he felt only a cold contempt for Loveday, assuming his sister to be right, and that she had wanted the security of marriage. She had been unable to wait until he came home, and had taken the first offer made to her. He told himself he despised her for letting it be Finch Viney, and as long as he continued to despise her he could smother all his other feelings. She was a cheap little drone after all, thinking she'd got herself a good catch with the butcher. Well, good riddance to her, Adam told himself, and when the companions of last night egged him on to join them again, he went unresistingly, finding a kind of comfort in the stone jugs of ale and the warmth of the scented female caresses that followed.

He'd intended going home soon after Christmas, with extra money in his pockets from the double shifts he'd worked to help compensate for the bad weather in which work had been almost impossible. Now he decided to stay on for a while, having no taste for going back to Somerset and seeing Loveday Willard flaunting herself as Mrs Finch Viney. Only to himself, in the cold reasoning hours of the night when sanity returned to him, did Adam admit that the panacea of drink and women was only a temporary thing. That one day he would have to go back and face her to find out the truth. It was contrary to his nature to blot out his troubles in a haze of ale. He'd always believed in meeting them head on, no matter how unpleasant, and it was only a matter of time before he'd have to face Loveday Willard. Only when he heard from her own lips that she'd married Finch Viney out of love would he believe it, and he would dare her to admit it when she looked directly into his eyes.

What stopped him storming right back was the doubt that Sarah had put in his mind. Generous he'd have sworn Loveday to be, in passion and temperament, but mercenary, never. By now she was wed to Finch, and the knot was tied. If it was less than love she felt for the butcher it would surely tell in a very short time, and Adam could no more imagine Loveday submitting to Finch's caresses than flying. Neither did he want to, he thought grimly, and put them both out of his mind.

*　　*　　*

It was Loveday's wedding-day. The day she both dreaded and welcomed, with a feverishness that astounded her father and was perfectly understandable to Polly. Ralph and Polly themselves had been married quietly the previous week, so there would be no impropriety in the two of them sharing the Willard establishment once Loveday was gone. How unwittingly she had helped Polly Reeves in getting what she wanted was still a bitter pill for Loveday to swallow, but she told herself that Polly would have managed it sooner or later anyway.

Out of deference to the late Meg Willard, Ralph's wedding had been unannounced, except by a brief dignified notice on the shop window informing folks that Willard's General Store would be closed for one afternoon this week and again the following week, and the reasons. He and Polly had foregone any family celebrations, but once Loveday and Finch were wed, there was to be a combined wedding party that night, with the farming Willards invited, and one or two friends. Polly's sister Ellen had declined from coming all this way from London again, and Loveday's friend, Sarah Goss, had dithered on whether to accept or not, but in the end had agreed to be called for by the Willards and taken home by them the same night. Crushed beside Matt in the crowded conveyance, Sarah told herself this was not the reason she had come, and guiltily knew that it was. His arm had crept round her waist to hold her safely as the vehicle lurched round corners, and his stubbly cheek had brushed hers more than once, and she couldn't deny that each contact gave her a quivering thrill. She was both glad and sorry when they reached the town house, where the ceremony was long over and the party had begun.

Loveday had been so stiff with her lately, Sarah had wondered if their friendship was worth anything after all. But on this day, when Loveday had become Mrs Viney, the new bride's cheeks had been flushed, and her blue eyes were bright as if with a fever, and she'd clasped Sarah to her with all the old warmth.

'I'm so glad to see you, Sarah,' she said tremulously. 'It's all been like a dream today, and I'm not sure how I'll feel when I wake up!'

'It's a bit late to think of that now, isn't it?' Sarah was half teasing, half tart, until she saw the shine of tears in her friend's eyes.

'Don't hate me, Sarah,' Loveday went on, so softly that no-one else could hear. 'One day I'll try to explain – if I can.'

How could she, when it involved her cousin Matt, for whom Sarah seemed to have formed such an infatuation! Loveday bit her lips together. How could she admit to this innocent girl beside her that she had been wicked beyond anything? Lain with her own cousin, again and again, albeit against her wishes – but in doing so she had started on the pathway leading to this day. Leading her into Finch's arms, and out of Adam's for ever.

Swallowing hard, Loveday turned to greet her family, as Aunt Emily pecked her cheek and peered at the solid gold band on her marriage finger, a look of satisfaction in her eyes.

'You mind and keep your vows now, my girl. Said before God, I'll remind you! Your mother's not here to tell you how to be a good wife and do your duty, in the marriage-bed and out of it –'

'You don't need to tell me,' Loveday said rudely. 'I'm as much wed as you now, Aunt, and I'll do things my own way.'

'You're not properly wed yet, Miss, but if you think you're too clever to have things told to you, then I wash my hands of you, and wish you a good night's bedding! I could tell you a few things to make it easier on you, but there's no talking to you, is there? Let's hope Finch will find a way to tame you!'

She turned away as Matt sidled up, a leer in his eyes, pulling Loveday towards him and planting a cousinly smack on her mouth. She resisted the urge to scrub the taste of him away, knowing the family would be thinking nothing of such an embrace, and then she heard his voice in her ear.

'Congratulations, Lovey-dovey, but it needn't stop us havin' a bit o' fun when I come to town, need it? I daresay it'll make things easier, with your man busy in his shop and me callin' on my cousin for a bit of a chat – and other things.'

Loveday wrenched out of his arms.

'Don't you come near me, Matt Willard, you hear me?' she raised her voice, but it was hardly noticeable in the din going on all around them. 'You've done all you're goin' to do to me, and if you try calling on me, I'll kill you!'

Matt began to laugh at her blazing eyes, then realised she meant every word she said. He pulled her close again and gave her another kiss, forcing her mouth open with his tongue. It was done briefly, but it was enough to sicken Loveday with the memory of other times, and she turned almost gratefully as Finch came bumbling up behind her to claim her in a dance as the music began on the old fiddle one of his cronies had brought along.

'Come on, wife, you can't let your cousin monopolise you any longer,' he chaffed jovially. 'You and me have got to start the jigging!'

She let herself be pulled away and into Finch's arms. The room spun as he swung her around, his pink perspiring face moving backwards and forwards and up and down, his hands clammy and tight on hers. Maybe if she spun fast enough, the baby would be dislodged from her womb, Loveday thought dizzily, letting herself become a puppet in his arms as the walls seemed to close in on her . . .

' 'Ere, give her air,' she heard Polly's voice saying in her ear. She felt the fan of a handkerchief as somebody flapped it against her face to create a breeze, and the room, that had merged into a water-colour haze, came sharply into focus again. Finch was leaning towards her anxiously, his great belly still heaving with exertion, and Polly was waving the handkerchief, while others stood about uncertainly. Polly was whispering to her.

'Come on, ducks, don't give the game away until he's got you bedded. I'll get you a drink of water if you sit still a minute.' She pushed through the curious watchers. 'All right, the excitement's over, and poor Loveday's goin' to take more water with it next time. She ain't used to the drink, and old Finch'll want her sober tonight, won't 'e?'

The curiosity subsided as she told the fiddler to start up again, and Finch sat holding Loveday's hand by the open window. The dancing began again, and only Matt Willard followed Polly out to the scullery while she fetched some water for Loveday.

'What's up with her? he asked. 'It's not like our Lovey-dovey to go all faint for no reason. She's not ill, is she? I ain't seen 'er like this afore.'

Polly had had plenty to drink herself, and all she heard was concern in the rough country voice. She forgot about discretion, and swore him to secrecy if she let on to him, so as to stop his unmerciful teasing of Loveday.

'You'll all know in time, and there's nothin' that's goin' to stop that! You can't hide this kind of job, and she'll be showin' all too soon now. But you be gentle to her, Matt, you hear? And if old Finch couldn't stop his eagerness in gettin' her to bed before the weddin', well, he's not the first, and it's all turned out for the best. She's wed to the father now.'

Matt couldn't speak for a minute as he felt the breath knocked out of him. Then he snatched the mug out of Polly's hands to take it to Loveday. Stupid bitch, he railed inwardly at Polly. Stupid, stupid slut, if she couldn't put two and two together. Who in their right minds would think it was Finch Viney's sprog Loveday carried! It was his, *his* ... for a second he preened himself, though the thought of the fat old fairy takin' the credit for his couplin' with Loveday made him puke.

He caught sight of his father roaring at some ribald joke his Uncle Ralph had made and sobered up at once. What in hell's name was he thinking of, feeling cocky at being the father of Loveday's sprog? There'd be nothin' short of bloody civil war among the Willard clan if it was ever breathed ... but Loveday must have known! And she was the clever one, saddling old Finch Viney with the fathering of it, and Matt would bet a thousand to one the old fool didn't know the truth of it. The water slopped as he reached Loveday's side with it. Finch straightened as Matt knelt beside her with false concern.

'There, my precious,' he oozed, 'can't have you faintin' away on your bridal night, can we? Wouldn't want to deprive ol' Finch o' the pleasures awaitin' him, would 'ee?'

His whispered tone reminded her that he knew only too well of her intimate pleasures. Loveday recoiled from him as she took the mug, her mouth trembling. She hated him all over again at the leering look in his eyes. Thank God he didn't know the whole truth of it. It was her one sliver of relief, that Matt couldn't possibly have guessed about the baby, and that she was marrying Finch Viney to give it a name and avoid a scandal. Under cover of the noise they seemed able to hold a private conversation that would have shocked everyone there if they'd overheard it.

'I hate you, Matt,' she ground out the words. 'Get away from me and don't come near me again. I won't forgive you for what you've done to me.'

'You won't forget neither,' he chortled, enjoying the fact that he knew the cause for her flashing eyes now. He wouldn't let on that he knew though. 'Have a good beddin' tonight, Lovey-dovey, though I doubt it'll come up to what you're used to!'

His laugh was low and coarse as he got to his feet, swinging away from her to seek out her friend, Sarah Goss, for a jig about. Even if he had to keep it to himself, the news about the bab was oddly stimulating. Matt felt drunk on it. He wanted to celebrate, even though Loveday's eyes were spitting fire at him, and there was a comedy in the thought of dancin' wi' pretty Sarah Goss, knowing she'd be glowin' at the contact.

Loveday watched him, feeling sick and drained, and Finch hovered near once more, anxious and attentive. The night had grown dark long ago. She swallowed back her distaste and forced a smile to her cold lips as Finch asked after her welfare.

'I'm better, thank you, but I'd prefer not to dance again if you don't mind,' she murmured.

Relief brightened his face. He wasn't built for jigging, and he was glad his little Loveday didn't seem overkeen on the sport. He was getting nervous as the evening progressed. The remarks from the older Willards and young ones alike had got more raucous, with gestures and winks lacking in taste. He avoided looking at the clock on the mantel, knowing he and Loveday couldn't remain here much longer. And that being alone together, the thought of which was sending cold sweats running through him, might yet be better than these wild innuendoes surrounding them. He cleared his throat.

'I think it might be a good idea for us to leave soon, Loveday,' he spoke apologetically, hoping he wasn't offending her in appearing too eager, though God knew that wasn't really the case. Finch already acknowledged that his bride was a stronger character than himself, and that he wouldn't want to see those magnificent blue eyes blazing at him in anger. To his surprise, she agreed immediately.

'Whatever you say, Finch,' she spoke demurely, the dutiful wife, and rose at once to link her hand in his arm. He was pleased, not knowing how dizzy she felt at any sudden movement, and that the thought of fresh air was like nectar. They made their farewells as quickly as possible, though it was necessarily some time before the family and few friends would let them go. When they finally stepped out into the street, it was to the resounding singing behind them to help them on their way to the nuptial bed.

'On with 'is armour, down with 'er drawers,
I'll show 'ee mine if you'll show me yours.'

Ralph and Jack roared a drinking song lustily from the upstairs window, the sounds following Finch and Loveday down the street, to the accompaniment of shrieks of laughter from others all wanting to shout their good wishes from the window, and Aunt Emily's voice severely telling them all they should be ashamed of themselves.

The bride and groom walked through the echoing streets to Viney's butcher's shop in silence, arms linked, but each trying to avoid thinking of the time when they'd be in the closest contact with each other. Finch was desperately trying to summon up all his courage and reminding himself that he was a man, and that once he and Loveday became

107

used to one another, it would be perfectly natural to behave as married couples did. And forcing himself to ignore the fact that connection with a woman had always seemed the most *un*natural thing to him.

Loveday held on tight to his arm, her small fingers curling round it like some encroaching vine. Every step she took was like a betrayal to the sweet young love that had grown so effortlessly in her heart for Adam Goss. She had firmly believed that some special empathy existed between them. That when he'd said lightly in the churchyard that day that he'd come back and marry her when she was old enough, he had meant exactly that. Almost without words, he had offered her a future with him, and she had accepted it. Since then, through their letters, love had grown as surely as his father's apples ripened on the trees, and something beautiful that God had bestowed on them, she, Loveday, had allowed to become tainted. She had destroyed it . . . a small sob was smothered in her throat as she realised Finch's footsteps had stopped, and that they were at the door of her new home. As she was ushered inside and the door closed behind her, Loveday felt as if she was being entombed.

The moment couldn't be put off any longer. Loveday was already curled up in the big bed Finch had had installed in his old room, so that it took up nearly all the available space. Outside on the narrow landing, an oil lamp burned very low to give a little light as Finch disrobed himself, and Loveday peeped through her lashes as he hauled the nightshirt over his portly shape. She saw his huge belly, liberally sprinkled with light hair, and quivering with the coldness of the fabric as it touched him. She saw the coarser mound of hair below, and the object that was supposed to stir her with desire. She shuddered, closing her eyes tightly, though at that moment it looked as harmless as a rag doll. Her resolve returned. Hateful though the thought of it was, Finch had to consummate this marriage to their mutual satisfaction for her plan to succeed. He had to believe the child she carried was his, for her status in the town to be assured. She pushed down the swift shame of it, and awaited him as the bed creaked beneath him.

He had left the oil lamp burning low, and through the half-open door it threw a soft dim light over the bed. Loveday uncurled herself slowly and lay submissively as he placed a tentative hand on her breast. It responded mechanically.

'Loveday – dear –' she heard him mumble. 'I'm afraid you don't have a very experienced husband.'

A completely ignorant one, his mind screamed at him. Ignorant and repelled by the very thought of the act he was now expected to perform.

Remembering Matt's confident impregnation, the diffidence of his voice made Loveday suddenly tender towards Finch. She laid one hand against his belly as if to assure him of their closeness, but that she didn't demand instant romping.

'It's all right, Finch,' she murmured. 'We have all night. We have the rest of our lives, don't we?'

If the thought hadn't suddenly made her sick, she might have noticed his little gurgling sound at the thought of threshing about with her all night long. Better to get it over with quickly, perhaps, he thought desperately, though nothing was happening down below. He knew it wouldn't. He *knew* it. His masculine pride asserted itself. Tonight it *had* to. Just this once it musn't let him down. Once he got the hang of it, perhaps . . .

And his little bride was so lovely, lying there; so wide-eyed and innocent, her silky fair hair spread on the pillow like ripe corn. He had a duty to do by her, and he must go gently, not to frighten her.

'We don't have to – to do it this night if you don't want to, dear,' he heard himself say. Her hand clutched at his wrist, pressing his hand more firmly on the fleshy contours of her breast, and he heard her breath quicken.

'Yes we do! Don't you want me, Finch? You do – you do love me, don't you?'

'Of course I do, Loveday. I don't want to – to disappoint you, that's all.'

Under cover of the bedclothes he was trying to find himself with his other hand, and cursing himself for the lack of reaction he found between his legs. How could any man fail to respond to the lovely vision alongside him? Perhaps if he raised himself so that she was looking up at him, so that he felt the master and in command. Finch grunted as he knelt astride her, pushing her nightgown gently upwards. She made no sound as he ran his tentative hands over her body, seeking the unexplored areas that were totally new to him, and willing his own manhood to exert itself. When it didn't, he gave a low curse, began sweating profusely, and muttered hoarsely that he was sorry, and that though it shamed him to suggest it, did Loveday think she could help him a little?

She looked up at him, not understanding, until he took her hand and guided it to the small limp penis. Waves of hysteria began to rise in Loveday's throat. It was the only thing that *was* rising, the appalling thought struck her. She could hear Finch panting heavily as he tried to move against her hand, and concluding this was what she was supposed to do, she gritted her teeth and did it. Nothing happened. Not by one twitch did the object beneath her fingers give any reaction. Furiously she pulled and pushed, until suddenly she realised that the man crouching in such an ungainly fashion above her was actually sobbing.

Loveday let go of him at once, horrified and ashamed. *Had she hurt him? She'd thought this was what he wanted. What was wrong? Why didn't he tell her?*

Finch was blubbering like a baby, his great belly shivering against hers and filling her with a disgust she couldn't hide, even while she pitied him. He was saying something, apologising like the great ninny he was, instead of getting on with it; suddenly, the import of what he was stammering became clearer, and Loveday gasped with shock and gripped hold of his shaking shoulders. She pushed him down on the bed with a violent effort, feeling it rock and creak beneath them, and then she was kneeling over him, but not erotically, only with disbelieving fury in her eyes as her hair swung like a gleaming curtain over his face.

'What are you saying, Finch?' she heard herself

screaming. 'It's not true. Tell me it's not true!'

She pummelled her hands against his clammy chest while his sobs went on. He wanted to die. He had never expected anything like this from her. He'd expected some understanding at least, some indication that as his wife she would stand by him; be a buffer between him and all the jeering he'd known through all the years; his helpmate and companion . . . he hadn't expected this fireball to come storming at him with fingernails like knives.

'I'm sorry, Loveday,' he wept. 'I couldn't tell you before we were wed. It was something I couldn't tell anybody. I didn't know for sure, you see, not even when the doctor said he thought I was impotent. I didn't believe it. I didn't want to believe it.'

Oh, but secretly he *had* wanted to, Finch knew, to his shame. Because then it meant he'd never have to do the thing that other men leered about that had always seemed so degrading to him. He'd never have to lie with a woman and act out the horror that other men spoke of so lasciviously. Never possess and be possessed . . . he felt a stinging slap across his face, then another and another as Loveday struck out at him.

'Impotent!' She screamed out as panic took hold of her again. 'You bastard! Do you know what you've done? Tying me for life to a man who can't even be called by that name? Making me go through this farce of a marriage, and all for nothing! You useless bastard!'

'Loveday, sweetheart,' he said weakly, terrified at such an unleashing of passion, and still unaware of its cause. Was the act of union so all-important to others? Finch felt a momentary pang for something he could never feel. He caught hold of her flailing arms. 'We can still have a good life together, can't we?' he pleaded. 'No-one need ever know. I'll be good to you and you'll want for nothing. I'm not rich, but we'll eat well, and surely this isn't everything? And in time, things might change. In a few months –'

'In a few months I'll be big with child and everybody will think what a clever chap Finch Viney was to perform so well

111

on his wedding-night!' Loveday was still screaming, too furious with the blow fate had dealt her to think what she was saying until Finch sat up in the bed, pushing her backwards so that she was doubled up on her heels and gasping out at the weight of him over her. His face was puce in the lamp light.

'Are you telling me you married me because you're carrying someone else's child?' he said hoarsely. 'That you've already been with someone else, you disgusting little bitch?'

He let his eyes roam over her naked lower half, and the sight of it and the thoughts that were filling his head now at her deception and all that had gone before, suddenly filled him with revulsion. To Loveday's horror, he let go of her with a sudden jerk, leaned over the side of the bed to reach for the chamber-pot, and was violently sick.

Outside in the night, some late-night revellers heard the sounds of shouting and screaming coming from Finch Viney's bedroom, and caught sight of the jumping silhouettes against the window. They smiled broadly to one another, telling themselves that old Finch was a dark horse after all, and all the tales about him must be untrue, if he could give that sweet little wife of his such a good bedding as to make her scream out for so long. He was a horny one all right.

CHAPTER NINE

They were late with the wassailing at Goss Cider that year. Usually it was celebrated on January 17, Old Twelfth Night, but what with the new owner being taken ill a few days before and not wanting to miss the custom, it was held back a week or so, till he could be wrapped up in scarves and woollies and enjoy the spectacle. And Sarah Goss could invite her friend Loveday Willard, to come to the Goss house for the evening. Only now she was Loveday Viney, of course. Sarah had to keep reminding herself.

Old Jed Hiatt, the cider manager, had presented himself up at the house, cap twisting in his gnarled hands, to make sure Norman Goss fully realised the importance of the occasion, and that it wasn't going to be missed out.

'Tis very important as to the fruitfulness of the apples, Master,' Jed said in his broad West Country burr that was almost unintelligible until heard a few times. 'Tis never missed out, and I 'oodn't like to vouch for the success o' next year's crop wi'out it!'

Norman Goss smiled broadly, already having heard tales of the wildness of the night of the wassailing, and guessing that Jed and his workers wouldn't be wanting to miss out on a night of free cider and lusty singing to which all for miles around were invited.

'You spread the word then, Jed,' Norman told him. 'And we'll set the date for the 28th. We won't be offending any good folk or bringing down bad magic on our heads by the delay, will we?'

He was laughing as he spoke, but there was no answering smile on old Jed's weathered face.

'You can scoff at old country customs, Master, but I'd remind 'ee to 'ave your shotgun at the ready to fire into the branches of the tree to scare away the evil spirits.'

'What, and shoot all the apples off.'

Jed's look was as withering as it could be, considering he spoke to his Master, who paid his wages and kept a roof over

113

his head for his wife and sons.

'Bain't no apples on the branches in January, Master, nor won't be unless you mind the wassailing. I'll be gettin' about my business, then, and spread the news for the 28th. 'Twill be as usual, I take it, with plenty of mulled cider to pass round, and no lack of victuals for the well-wishers?'

'Oh yes, yes,' Norman said hastily, and the man backed out of the room, a satisfied look on his face. When he'd gone, Sarah burst out laughing, her eyes dancing with amusement.

'I have the feeling Jed got the better of you in some way, Father! He was so determined to let things carry on the way they always have, I think he'd have got the shotgun to *you* if you hadn't agreed to it all!'

Norman gave a chesty cough that alarmed her for a moment, but he waved her to sit down again when she would have rung for some medication. It was only a chill, he told her testily, and the damp weather wouldn't let it pass off. Once the spring was here and the orchards began to blossom, he'd feel better. Already he was liking the country life, but he admitted it played the very devil with his chest in wet weather. And he was supposed to be benefitting from the air, he reminded himself! Remembering the pressures of his life in the city, he knew that he was, despite the weather that nobody could foresee.

'We'd best find out all that goes on,' Norman said now. 'We don't want to appear as ignoramuses at our own wassailing. I'll tell you what, my dear – you might take a ride over to the Willard farm this morning and bring back some eggs. I'm sure you can engage Mrs Willard in conversation about the wassailing, or one of the young boys if they're about. And be sure and let them know they're invited, of course.'

Sarah brightened at the thought. Her father sometimes thought it was a lonely life for Sarah now her sister was firmly settled in London, and Adam's plans seemed so vague of late. It was good that the Willards were handy neighbours and always ready to welcome the pretty Miss Goss. So well-mannered and refined, compared to her tempestuous niece, Emily Willard would reflect . . . so responsive to a bit of frolicking, Matt would grin to himself. Not too much . . . but he was just bidin' his time. There was no other young feller on Miss Sarah's horizon, that he was sure of, since none came visiting at this time of year, and there weren't another farmer's son who'd dare to poach on his preserves.

Matt was in the barn when he heard the sound of horse's hooves that morning. He lifted his head to see the bright red bonnet and matching cape that added to the glow on Sarah's cheeks, and called out to her as she tethered the horse in the stables nearby. For a second Sarah hesitated, not seeing the owner of the voice immediately, then walking uncertainly towards the barn with her heartbeat quickening. There was no sign of life from the big farmhouse save for a curl of grey smoke rising straight into the overcast sky. The only sounds were a scuffling in the barn and a male voice. Whose it was, Sarah wasn't quite sure, but the moment she stepped inside the gloom of the barn and felt the clasp of a strong arm round her waist, she knew.

'Matt, you're wicked,' she gasped, laughing as his unshaven face nuzzled into her soft one. She knew very well she should be outraged, that she should object strongly to the smell of him and the fact that she was the daughter of a gentleman, while he was . . . but she didn't object, and the wild exhilaration was singing in her blood as always when he embraced her so masterfully.

'You just tell me you don't like me bein' wicked,' Matt whispered in her ear. 'An' I'll tell you you're a liar, my fine lady!'

She felt his hand roam over her bodice and went weak because of it.

'I could give 'ee a fine present one o' these mornin's, young Sarah,' he went on thickly. 'When the rest on 'em's busy and away from the farm, you come callin' on me, and we'll have a fine old time together in the hay.'

Sarah pushed him away. He excited her and she admitted

it, but there were times when he frightened her too. When she knew very well his intentions towards her went much farther than she would ever permit. For that reason, she knew she must avoid being alone with him too often. There was a ruthlessness about Matthew Willard, and to her relief she heard the chatter of the younger Willard boys and the slow gruff tones of Zeb approaching the barn. She shook herself free of Matt's arms as they joined them there.

'I've been sent for eggs,' she said loudly, just in case anyone should think otherwise. 'And to ask you all to come to the wassailing on January 28th.'

'We thought there weren't goin' to be a wassailin' this year,' young Silas piped out. 'Pa was gettin' the glooms about it, an' sayin' the crops 'ood fail, what with a new owner an' all.'

Sarah felt a little leap of her heart.

'What nonsense! It's just an old country custom, that's all. You don't mean you take it that seriously, do you? Old Jed made it sound something of an evening's entertainment.'

'Ah, so 'tis, sweetheart,' Matt drawled. 'But don't you go scoffin' at country ways, or puttin' 'em to the test, or you'll soon find out whether 'tis all a game or not.'

For a moment she wondered whether his words had a double meaning for her, and gave a shiver. She had no intention of putting Matt Willard to the test and risking being alone with him when no-one else was around! A little bit of harmless flirting was one thing, but she'd seen a dark gleam in those pale eyes of his that was too animalistic to be ignored. She tossed her head.

'I'm going to visit your mother and collect the eggs. I can't waste time talking nonsense with you boys.'

Zeb barred her way for an instant, his large lumbering frame seeming to fill the doorway. His slow voice was kindly and solemn.

'Tain't nonsense, Miss Sarah, but 'tis nothin' to be afeared of neither. You'll like the singin' and dancin' and the ringin' o' bells, and the good spirits'll smile on 'ee all year round. 'Specially a body as pretty as you.'

116

He reddened furiously as his brothers hooted with laughter; old Zeb making a pass at a pretty girl! Sarah softened towards him, and thanked him quietly as she passed him, walking towards the farmhouse with her head high. The rough charms of Matthew Willard were beginning to grate already. Probably if she'd had a young suitor of her own since coming to Somerset, he'd never have affected her at all, Sarah admitted, in a moment of honesty.

The farmhouse door opened as she approached and Emily beckoned her inside, inviting her to a hot brew of tea and a home-baked scone, still steaming from the oven, and spread with melting butter and Emily's own quince jam. It was a little feast in itself, and it was no trouble to get the farmer's wife talking about the wassailing.

'Bless you, my dear, it's good that your Pa ain't ignored it altogether, though I daresay old Jed 'ood 'ave been gettin' anxious about it. Still, as long as it's done afore January's past, you'll be protected.'

Sarah felt her skin prickle. Such simple talk to bless the apple trees! But she was wiser now, and let Emily ramble on, her eyes wide and interested as she listened.

'You'll enjoy it all, Sarah. The singers will gather in the orchard and circle round the largest tree, while the dancers do their jigs. They'll sing to the tree, then cheer it, and fire shotguns to scare off bad spirits. Old Jed has the lightin' o' the bonfire by tradition, your Pa will pass round mulled cider if he's to carry on the old Lundy ways, and a bit o' toast soaked in his best cider will be put up the tree for the robins. They'm the good spirits, see?'

It all sounded like a lot of heathen rubbish to Sarah, especially when Emily added that once the tree was soaked with cider the handbells would be rung out and there'd be plenty of wild singing and dancing by all, because the next year's crop would be assured. Sarah kept a straight face, not wanting the keen-eyed woman to know how idiotic she thought the whole thing sounded. Not the festivities, though. They filled Sarah with excitement. Something else to brighten up this dull month, and coming a week after

Loveday's wedding, it would be good to see her friend again and discover how married life was suiting her. Sarah felt guiltily that she'd been very starchy with Loveday of late, and she missed the old easy companionship they'd shared.

By the time she left the Willard farm with the eggs wrapped securely in cloths and then carefully packed in a basket tied to the horse's flank, Sarah felt she knew all she needed to know about the apple wassail, and rode eagerly home to relate it all to her father. The only thing missing would be Adam, she thought sorrowfully. How he'd have loved it all. She'd write to tell him just how it was. Her last letter had been an awkward one, imparting the news of Loveday's coming marriage. The next would be bright and gay, and cheer him up, she promised herself. And she'd be sure that word got to Loveday and Finch – and to her father and Polly too – that they were welcome to attend the wassailing at Goss Cider on the 28th of the month.

The messenger from Goss Cider handed in the note for Mrs Viney at the butcher's shop the next morning. Finch put it to one side to give to Loveday later in the day, soiling the paper with his fingers and hardly noticing. He wasn't noticing anything much these days. His life had suddenly turned into a nightmare, and he couldn't think how to make the best of it. Such a short while ago he'd been leading a placid life with no worries save for the ribbing of the local boys, and he'd put up with that long enough for it all to pass over his head. He'd been happy in his way, enjoying the simple pleasure of knowing the old matrons looked on him fondly enough for his good services, and not needing or wanting the attentions of the younger ones.

The speed with which his fortunes had changed still bewildered him. He had allowed himself to be swayed towards this alliance with Loveday by her father, though he knew he'd never raised serious objections. He'd let the girl herself persuade him with her soft lips and beautiful eyes into thinking this was what he wanted. Now he knew to his horror, that he did not.

118

The abomination of his wedding-night still curdled inside him whenever he thought of it. Since that night, when he had discovered Loveday's wickedness, he had blundered out of the bedroom and spent the rest of the night between the scullery and his shop. Loveday herself, too revolted by his reactions, and feeling herself to have been as deceived as she was the deceiver, had snatched the bedclothes from the bed, wrapped herself in them and spent the night shivering in a chair in the parlour. Since then she had told Finch coldly that she would never enter his bedroom again. He slept there alone, while she made her own sleeping quarters in the tiny attic above. She wouldn't let her thoughts move ahead to when she would be too ungainly to climb up and down the narrow wooden steps.

Outwardly, folks assumed them to be the happily married couple, hardly seen in public, but that was only to be expected so early on in their new life together. In private they rarely spoke, and all pretence at a normal relationship was gone. Loveday bitterly regretted her marriage, and only refrained from rushing back to her father's house with her tale of outrage on Finch's own deception, because of the child. It was because of the child that she had married him, and because of the child that she must remain silent. Poor baby, Loveday thought mournfully, the innocent cause of so much hatred.

'There's a note for you,' Finch said gruffly at the door of the parlour, making her jump. She took it with distaste, seeing the blood-stains from his butcher's fingers on it. But as soon as she read it, it was as if the sun came into her life again, and a semblance of normality with Sarah's exuberant words.

'We're invited to the Goss's wassailing,' she exclaimed. 'It's to be on the 28th. We can go, can't we, Finch?'

'You're sure you want my company?' he spoke mildly enough, but with resentment still simmering in him. She looked no more than a child herself, yet she was as strong as steel. Finch knew he would never be a match for her, and it demoralised him still further to know how he had failed in the very essence of manhood. The thought of his failure gnawed away at him like some horrible disease, eating away at his vitals, destroying him.

'If you don't want to go, I can go with my father and Polly,' she spoke sharply. 'If you want folk to think my new husband's content to let me go off alone so soon after we're wed. There'll be plenty of young fellers to dance with round the apple orchards.'

'We'll go together,' he snapped, though it wearied him to do so. He wasn't made for arguments and fighting, and the appalling thing was that he was now part of the Willard family who gloried in such activities. He turned and stumped out of the room, not wanting those knowing eyes on him, seeing him for the half a man he was. He'd puff around the apple trees and warble with the rest of them, and no-one would know that Finch Viney wasn't satisfying his bride, he vowed. Downstairs in his shop, he hacked savagely at a side of beef, while none of the twittering matrons on the other side of the counter knew what torment he suffered.

He made no comment when Loveday put on her bonnet that afternoon and went to call on her father and Polly, after suggesting they travel to the Goss orchards together on the 28th of the month. It mattered little to Finch. He had no more desire to be alone with his new wife than did Loveday herself. In company at least, they did not have to meet each other's accusing eyes.

'It'll be a lark!' Polly was all enthusiastic when Loveday announced her reason for visiting. The two of them would never be friends, but they shared a bond that neither could deny. More than one, Polly thought keenly, eyeing her step-daughter's pinched face and huge eyes. Hardly the picture of the happy bride, Polly thought sagely, but perhaps the babby was making her feel sickly, and Polly didn't pursue the idea. 'I've heard tell about the old country custom, but never been in on it. There's dancin' as well, is there, ducks?'

Her eyes sparkled in her plump face. Ralph was a good 'un, but a bit of flirting under cover of the dancing never came amiss, and with the mulled cider to warm them, and

the novelty of dancing outdoors under a January sky ...
Polly prayed for a fine night, but if not, Norman Goss would
no doubt make other arrangements ... She beamed at Loveday, fiddling with the ribbons of her bonnet.

'Cheer up, me ducks. You look as if you've found a
ha'penny and lost a shilling. Everything all right in the bed
department, is it?' She winked at Loveday, her thoughts not
really on the young girl, but more on the high old jinks she
and Ralph enjoyed now they were 'respectable'. Polly
smothered a giggle as Loveday glowered at her, her face the
colour of fire. She would never let on to anyone what a farce
her marriage to Finch had turned out to be, least of all, Polly
Reeves Willard. She stood up to go.

'I'll have a word with Pa about the wassailing,' Loveday
said coldly. 'I daresay he'll arrange with Finch about hiring a
horse-trap to take us all. It'll be good to breathe clean country air again.'

She flounced out, and Polly was in no doubt that Loveday
referred to the clouds of scent with which Polly bathed
herself. Cheap little tart, to criticise *her*, Polly thought
scathingly, when she'd gawn and got herself up the spout by
the time she was sixteen! She turned to the copy of the
London magazine her sister Ellen had sent her, sighing
briefly for the nostalgia it brought, and promptly forgot
Loveday's troubles.

Loveday's spirits improved as the 28th drew near, though
she and Finch still hardly exchanged a word. There was a
feverishness about her that outsiders mistook for buoyancy
over her new status, and those less charitable called immod-
esty. For Loveday it was none of those things. It was the
feeling of a night's freedom, away from the claustrophobic
rooms she shared with Finch, where the smells of meat in
varying stages of freshness and decay, were ever present. It
was a chance to make her peace with Sarah again, and to be
in the place where Adam's family lived, and to be a part of
his life, however obliquely. He wouldn't be there, of course,
but she might get news of him from Sarah.

Finally, the night out would renew her youthful feelings for a while, instead of the overpowering weight of depression that marriage and her circumstances had brought her. She was still young, Loveday reminded herself, even though she sometimes felt a hundred years old. She was sixteen, and needed to laugh and sing and dance. On the night of the wassailing, she would forget all the bad things and enjoy the heady excitement of the occasion.

By the time the Willards and the Vineys arrived from Taunton, Norman Goss had thrown himself into the spirit of things, expansive in the idea of being the squire hereabouts and inviting all and sundry to share in the spectacle of the evening. Cider was drawn from the huge barrels and mulled to a warming heart; there was cheese and bread and nuts and pies; the night was crisp, but the revellers never noticed it. They were fired with excitement and well-being, the bonfire already flaring high into the night sky and lighting the faces of the watchers into glowing suns. The singers shrieked out the words of the old wassail song, while the dancers linked arms and circled them and the oldest tree in the Goss orchards; they were liberally doused in cider, both tree and participants.

'Hatsful, capsful, three bushels bagsful and a little heap under the stairs.' They bellowed to the tree, at the end of which the cheers rang out and then came the deafening sound of shotguns fired into the branches to scare the devils away. The January night exploded into a cacophony of sound as handbells jangled furiously, feet were stamped and roars of approval echoed skywards. Drunk with cider and excitement, men young and old, grabbed the waist of the girl nearest them and swung her round and round in a dizzying spiral. It was all part and parcel of the jollifications, new to Sarah, old and familiar to Loveday, but the effect on each of them was the same. Even more enjoyable now, since they had renewed their old friendship.

'Not so fast, Matt,' Sarah gasped laughingly, as he held her more firmly. Another young feller whom she recognised as the blacksmith's son, relieved Matt of her, as the girls were passed from arm to arm. She caught sight of Loveday's father panting and perspiring as he neared her; of Polly, as red-cheeked as any farmer's wife as she bounced up and down to the approving eyes of the male population; of Loveday, whirling faster than a cyclone, with skirts flying; of Finch Viney, standing glowering on the edge of a group of small boys baiting him. As Sarah passed by him, with the flare of the bonfire and the darkened trees moving alarmingly around her between earth and sky, she caught some of the words the boys were chanting at Finch.

'Fat old Finchey's got himself a wife,
Won't bring 'im nothin' but trouble an' strife!'
And,
'Bun's in the oven, she'll soon be showin',
Who put it there, there's nobody knowin'.'

The small boys yelped and scattered as Finch's arm came out to lash at their heads. They sang lustily, not really knowing the meaning of the skits, but to Finch every word turned a knife in his heart. It was as if everyone here knew of the wrong Loveday Willard had done him; even down to the infants of the county. He felt degraded and wild with a fury he couldn't express as he watched Loveday's bright blue eyes smiling up into the faces of the men and boys who swung her round in the dance. Her soft red mouth parted and shining, provocative and inviting, reminding him of that awful moment when he'd pushed her backwards on the bed and seen the secret part of her exposed to him for the first time. Finch shuddered, the scene still vividly horrific in his mind. He wanted to blot it out forever; to be rid of the scent of feminine odours in his house; to feel clean and chaste and untouched by lust. But that bitch had spoiled any hope of that, he thought, with a savagery unlike him. With every week that passed, he'd see evidence of another man's lust as her belly swelled, and finally there'd be the indignity of a squalling infant to whom she'd give birth upstairs above his shop. She'd give it her breast and he'd smell its milk.

Finch convulsed. Butchery was an honest, necessary

occupation, and all the sights and smells of his work couldn't compare to this. His eyes were wild with the vision of the future. Other men might delight in all the procedures that accompanied procreation, but he wasn't like other men. He blundered away from the chanting boys to reel among the apple trees and try to stop his spinning head from crashing into them as he spewed violently. The nightmare still went on, and there was no stopping it. Only one way. One way . . .

'Where *is* Finch?' Loveday said crossly, when the revelling gradually came to an end, and folks started to wend their ways back to farm and cottage and town house, heads rocking as if a hundred hammers beat there, but replete with food and awash with drink. 'Has anybody seen him lately?'

She clutched the arm of her friend Sarah for a moment, her own head seeming not to belong to her body, and a dull heavy ache inside her from too much of everything that night. It was too mean of Finch to be missing right now, when her father was staggering about making noisy good-byes to his relatives from the farm and showing them up in front of Sarah's well-mannered father.

Not that Mr Goss seemed to mind. He went round beaming at everybody, assured by his hospitality and the rituals that had been faithfully followed that there'd be an abundance of fruit on his apple trees in the year to come. Norman never doubted it, nor heeded the thought that six months ago he'd have looked askance at any man who suggested he'd honour such pagan rubbish. He was a country-man now, by God, and if he'd never quite been accepted as Squire Goss before, then he was now! It gave him a feeling of well-being such as he'd rarely felt.

'You haven't lost your new husband already, little lady!' he said jovially to Loveday as he joined the two pretty girls. The man must be a fool to wander off from little Loveday!

'He might have gone on home,' Loveday muttered, highly resentful of the fact, but knowing Finch often spent the early morning hours chopping and carving and arranging

124

with all the finesse of an artiste, despite the fact that his hands and clothes would be bloodied by the nature of his work. He could have *told* her, she thought angrily, if indeed he had gone on back to Taunton by some means. As his wife she deserved some consideration, though she knew full well he hadn't wanted to stay this long, when the night was long past and thin fingers of a pale daylight streaked the blackness of the sky.

Polly hovered nearby, dishevelled from the romping, but still elated by the occasion. She put her arm round Loveday's shoulder in a friendly way, ignoring the rigid response from her step-daughter.

'Come on, ducks, you an' me'll find your Pa an' take ourselves off home. We'll see you get indoors safely, and tell that man o' yours a thing or two!' she said cheerfully. 'He's not used to havin' a wife yet, that's certain.'

'Will you come and visit me in a day or two, Sarah?' Loveday turned her back on Polly. Sarah hugged her and said she'd be happy to come and see Loveday's new home, at which Loveday moved abruptly away with Polly, not wanting Adam's sister to see the smarting of tears in her eyes.

With Finch's disappearance the excitement of the wassailing was fading fast. All Loveday wanted was to get home and climb wearily into her attic bed. She ached from head to foot, and the jolting of the horse-trap all the way back to the town made her stomach feel as if a thousand knives jabbed at her. It seemed an eternity before the trap rattled to a halt outside Viney's butcher's shop and she let Ralph help her down.

There was a glimmer of light from the premises, so she concluded that Finch had got home before her. Loveday suddenly remembered the scowling looks he'd given her all evening as she whirled in the dance, and felt a strange unease. Finch had never been a man to draw fear from anyone, but there was fear gripping her now. She caught hold of Ralph's arm as he made to get back in the trap.

'Come inside with me a moment,' she stuttered. 'You and Polly. Just to make sure it's Finch in there.'

'Course it's Finch,' Ralph said soundly. 'Who'd want to break in and steal a few cuts o' meat.'

'Oh come on, Ralphie,' Polly was clambering down after him. ''Twon't take a minute, and she's only a young 'un after all. Lead the way, ducks, and we'll be right behind you.'

Loveday pushed open the shop door. Something heavy and inert stopped it moving more than a few inches, and she felt her father give it a great heave to get the object out of the way. There was an awful smell coming from the shop, the fresh blood smell that so nauseated Loveday on occasions; but the second the three people stepped inside the place they realised it wasn't coming from the cuts of meat hanging on hooks or lying on slabs.

It belched and frothed from the newly-severed artery on Finch Viney's wrist, where he'd hacked away in a fury with his butcher's saw, finding the only way out of a life that had become too much for him to bear. He'd come back here, beside himself with rage and frustrated torment, meaning to vent his wrath on the sides of beef and legs of lamb awaiting his attention. And suddenly the way out had been all too easy . . . and he lay, a ghastly yellow-grey colour instead of his usual pink, sprawled out among cutlets and joints in a pool of his own blood.

Loveday heard herself screaming, and felt herself being bundled back out of the shop into the morning air. She felt as if she was drowning, unable to gulp enough clean air into her lungs, yet all the time the terrible noises were wrenched out of her. Polly was shaking her, and Ralph was shouting at the folk who came running out of houses to see what the din was all about that there'd been a terrible accident and Finch Viney was dead. She heard it but she couldn't believe it, except that the sight of Finch lying there was terrifyingly real in her mind . . . the screams rose higher, and then someone was slapping her hard, and the screams dissolved into whimpering cries.

'The poor maid, to have such a terrible thing happen so soon after she was wed,' she heard hushed voices say.

'And to see it like that! 'Tis something she'll never forget.'

126

'Such a kind man, poor Finch Viney. Not such a catch as some, but never one to do harm to a livin' soul. To come to such an end.'

'Come away, ducks,' Polly's voice was muted in her ear, as if she was hearing it under water. There was such a rushing sound in her head, and a great sawing pain in her belly. Was she going to die too, Loveday thought dully? 'Your Pa will send for the constables and do whatever needs to be done 'ere. You and me'll take the trap on home, and you'll stay with us for now. Pale as death yourself you are, and the quicker you gets a drink o' brandy down you and I tucks you up in bed, the better.'

Loveday let herself be propelled. If Polly had led her straight to the river and tipped her in, she couldn't have protested. But she didn't. She steered Loveday towards the trap and got her to the Willard house, pouring brandy down her throat till Loveday thought it was on fire. And helping her up the apples and pears to her old room, where everything was so exactly as she had left it such a little while before that Loveday felt the stinging salty tears fill her eyes again.

If only Ma was here, she wept silently. Polly did her rough best, but she needed her Ma. Her teeth were chattering and she knew that Finch's death was no accident, no matter what folks thought. She knew she was responsible because of her wickedness. A searing pain shot through her and she felt a sticky dampness between her legs. Oh God ... oh God ...

'Polly,' she gasped, clutching at her belly. 'What's happening to me? It hurts – it hurts.'

Polly gave her a quick looking over and made her swallow a drop more brandy.

'Now then, ducks, it seems as if the babby don't want to stay around without his father,' she said sympathetically. 'We'll see to it, never fear, and nobody need know anything at all about it 'cept you an' me. When your Pa comes back, I'll keep him out of here if this little lot ain't over by then, an' you can sleep the day away in your old bed tomorrow. After that, we'll sort things out between us. I'm not altogether surprised after all your cavorting at the Goss place earlier on, but maybe it's better so. You're no more than a babby yourself in some ways, an' it's only justice that you ain't landed with Finch Viney's young'un after he's gone.'

Loveday's anguished gasp stopped her prattle for a moment, and Loveday gurgled as Polly tried to push more brandy past her lips. It trickled down her neck and Polly tutted at such a waste, but the pains were coming fast now and the expulsion was swift, and exhausted though she was, Loveday could still feel a burning, shaming relief that she was no longer carrying Matt Willard's child. It was all over, and the only victim was poor Finch Viney, poor impotent, pink-faced Finch. She could even feel pity for him now, as Polly moved quickly about the room, clearing away the soiled sheets and making her comfortable. She could be the same as she'd been before . . .

CHAPTER TEN

Within weeks all the excitement over Finch Viney's death had subsided. Suicide was never suspected, and it was just concluded that poor Finch had had a bellyful at the Goss's wassailing and so caused the accident to himself in a drunken state. Sympathy was all for the little bride, so ashen-faced in her black at the burial, propped up by her father and his new wife; and only the two of them, Loveday and Polly, knew that she was still weak from the miscarriage.

She still remained at the Willard house, and Polly had told Ralph sharply that he must leave his daughter to her care now, since it needed a woman's touch to comfort her at such time. And Ralph, hardly recognising his spirited Loveday in such a subdued manner, was only too glad to do as Polly said. The girl must have been genuinely fond of the butcher, he thought generously, and agreed without hesitation to her one hysterical outburst.

'I can't go back there until all the meat's cleared out, Pa! I can't bear to see it or smell it, and I want it all taken away. Arrange for what's still good to be sold to Randall's on Elmore Street, and see that the rest of it's burned or buried, and the shop cleaned and scrubbed and every bit of butchering equipment sold. I want it to look like a new place when I see it again.'

'You don't ever have to see it again if you don't want to, Loveday,' Ralph said gruffly. 'There's still a home for 'ee here, and room for the three of us.'

'No, Pa. I've got my own home now, and when I feel more settled, I'll decide what to do with it. Just see to it all for me, please. There'll be money from the meat and fittings, so you won't be out of pocket with the payin' for it. Finch told me awhile ago that if anything ever happened to him, the shop and rooms would belong to me, so I suppose I'm a woman of means now!' She tried to smile, but her mouth trembled, knowing that whatever his faults, she'd never have wanted Finch to end up so horribly. She forced her thoughts away from the scene that could still wake her in the night in a nightmarish sweat.

'It'll all be done exactly as you say, Loveday, and don't go frettin' about the payin' of it,' Ralph grunted, but Loveday knew him well enough to know he'd be relieved there'd be money on her account, and that he wasn't going to be footing any bills. He had enough to do with Polly's fripperies. But he went along to Randall's butcher's shop on Elmore Street and arranged for the deal to be done. Randall's, a bigger concern than Viney's, promised to clear out the premises that very day and to give a fair price for good meat and fittings. Ralph would be obliged to get the slaughtermen to dispose of the rotten carcases before they started carrying disease. A good thing Finch's demise happened in a cold spell, Ralph thought cynically, or the whole neighbourhood might be suffering with belly-aches by now.

Loveday sat by the window of her old room above Willard's General Store and watched the rain trail down the glass in slow snails' tracks. She found it hard to lift herself out of her depression. She had thought for one magical moment that everything would be as it was before, but with each day that passed she knew everything had changed. It was as if the earth had shifted beneath her feet, leaving her unstable, unsure of herself, alone and afraid. There was no place for her here, for nothing would persuade her to live permanently with Ralph and Polly, kind though Polly had been to her lately. She was in no hurry to go back to the home she still thought of as Viney's butcher's shop, even though her orders had all been carried out, and Polly was trying to get her to make a short visit there, to prove to herself that there was no vestige of the place as it had been. It was just an empty shop-front and back room, Polly assured her, newly painted and smelling of nothing but turpentine and paint. Polly had been there with Ralph, and told Loveday that the longer she put it off the harder it would be.

'I want all the upstairs furniture sold,' Loveday had said suddenly. 'Everything that was in it when Finch was alive. I want it to be completely empty, and the rooms upstairs painted too. Ask Pa to see to it for me, Polly.'

Polly began to wonder if her brain had turned. She had tried cajoling and harping, and now she tried a bit of funning.

'I'm startin' to wonder what plans you've got for the place, ducks. Not goin' to turn it into one o' those fancy bawdy-houses, are you, all silks and soft lights?'

Loveday's eyes snapped at her. 'Don't you dare suggest such a thing to me! It's what I might have expected, coming from you, but don't class me as one of your sort.'

Polly bristled. 'That's a laugh, Miss! I know all about what sent you scurrying to wed Finch Viney, and don't you forget it. A word dropped in your father's ear would have

130

you out of here in no time at all.'

Loveday clutched at her arm, her fingers biting into Polly's soft skin.

'You wouldn't tell him? He'd kill me, and he'd know you were in league with me. He wouldn't want to know you'd been deceiving him all this time, and helping me on the night Finch died. He'd think he married a lying bitch, and he'd be right!'

Her voice rose shrilly as Polly shook her off, rubbing at her reddened arm.

'All right, all right, I was only teasin' you. I've no wish to tell your Pa, but I'm thinkin' it's time you and me parted company, Loveday. I'll ask your Pa to get your place stripped and painted like you want, then you'd best see about gettin' some new stuff and movin' back in there.'

It was an order and Loveday knew it. And she knew that Polly could persuade Ralph without any trouble at all that it was time for Loveday to leave. She stared at the dismal rain-swept afternoon, feeling the damp tears on her cheeks, and wishing she could summon up the nerve to write to Adam.

Despite Polly's jocular remark about starting a bawdy-house, if the truth were told, the very last thing Loveday wanted was any contact with men. Since losing the baby and the trauma of Finch's death, it was as if all her feelings and emotions were frozen inside her, locked away in an ice-box that was her heart. She wanted to write to Adam . . . yet she couldn't. What could she say to him? How could she begin? And she had heard nothing from him for weeks. He must know of her marriage, and probably about her widowhood too, yet there had been no word. She was still in a state of shock, but not realising how deeply it went, Loveday feared that all her capacity for loving had gone. And what she intended to do with the little house and shop that now belonged to her she had not the faintest idea.

Sarah had thought long and hard about penning her next letter to her brother. She remembered how she had intended it to be cheerful and bright, after her recent news about

Loveday's marriage and uncertain temper. Now, she felt hardly inclined to cheer him with details of the wassailing, since it had ended so tragically. In the end, she wrote a brief little note, and enclosed an account from the weekly newspaper that embellished the tragedy of poor Finch Viney and the poignancy of his bride being married and widowed within a week.

Adam could not have been more shocked. The image of Loveday's face as he had seen it, smooth petal-soft skin and those huge, lustrously tempting blue eyes, danced in his senses. But she would not look so vibrantly beautiful now, after such a cruel blow, he thought. She would have loved the fellow, and to write to her now would be an insensitive action. He must wait. The bitterness of knowing Loveday herself hadn't waited for him was temporarily forgotten. And if he couldn't in all conscience write to Loveday, he would write to Sarah and ask her to convey his sympathy. It warmed him a little to know they were friends, and to think of Sarah consoling Loveday, when he'd have given much to sweep her into his arms himself.

But this was hardly the time, Adam checked his passionate feelings. Loveday would need time to recover, mentally if not physically, and time was on their side. He wrote back to Sarah immediately.

Loveday's sad eyes brightened as she saw a familiar figure approaching Willard's General Store along the rain-glistened street, and threw another stick on the tiny fire in her room, and was ready to welcome her friend inside as soon as she heard Sarah's footsteps outside the door.

'It's so good to see you,' Loveday clung to her hands and Sarah was shocked to see the change in Loveday. She had waited awhile before visiting, thinking it best, and that Loveday would want to be surrounded by her family, but the girl who greeted her was almost wraith-like, with none of her old vitality. Any reserve Sarah might have had was shed in an instant, and she clasped Loveday in her arms.

'I've thought about you so much,' she spoke thickly, tears

studding her lashes. 'I wanted to come so much, and then when I heard from Adam, I knew I must. Forgive me, Loveday, for being so tardy.'

'You've heard from Adam?' Sarah suddenly realised Loveday had come to life. She no longer stood limply in Sarah's arms, but seemed to sparkle, as if charged with sudden energy. 'What does he say? Is there a message for me? Does he – does he forgive me?'

To Sarah's consternation, she suddenly burst into tears, and her voice was muffled as she leaned against her friend's shoulder.

'Oh Sarah, I've been such a fool. Such a stupid, wicked fool.'

A noise behind them stopped her short as Polly appeared in the room with a tray of tea and two slices of seed cake.

''Ere you are, don't say I don't do nothin' for you, ducks. An' don't you go worryin' about that snivellin', Miss,' she addressed Sarah now. 'It's the first proper cry she's 'ad in days, an' a body needs to cry to wash all the misery out of 'er. You stay an' cheer 'er up, for Gawd's sake, or we'll all end up in the madhouse.'

She clattered down the stairs again, and it was Sarah who poured the tea and pressed a cup into Loveday's shaking hands as they sat in front of the paltry fire.

'Yes, I've heard from Adam, and he sends you his sympathy, Loveday,' Sarah said gently, knowing she must tread carefully. The reference to the madhouse frightened her, but Loveday certainly looked strange and wild-eyed now, with fierce spots of colour in her pale cheeks. 'He'll write to you himself in due course, but it didn't seem the right time.'

Loveday bit her lip to stop it trembling.

'I did a wicked thing, Sarah,' she whispered. 'I married a man I didn't love, but it was worse than that. I married him when I loved somebody else.'

'Adam! I thought so!' Sarah said softly. 'And I know my brother well enough to guess that his feelings towards you are the same. So why on earth did you marry Finch, Loveday? It doesn't make any sense to me.'

Loveday looked at her friend, sweet, innocent Sarah, looking so bewildered and wanting to understand. And felt a burning shame at her own wickedness. How could she tell Sarah she had been seduced by her own cousin, for whom Sarah seemed to have a fond regard? How could she confess that she had sought the security of Finch Viney's good name for her bastard child rather than face the scorn of the town? That she had hurled abuse on poor Finch's head on their wedding-night on discovering he was impotent, when she had tried to seduce her husband in such wanton ways? And all the time professing to love Adam, Sarah's brother, with a love that was young and pure.

There was nothing pure about her, Loveday thought bitterly. She was bad, and deserved to suffer . . . but she had never meant to make Finch suffer too!

'Pa wanted me to marry Finch,' she knew she was hiding behind her father, but anything was better than letting Sarah learn the truth and seeing her turn away in disgust from such a wicked tale. 'I just let it happen, Sarah. Once we were engaged and then the plans were being made for the wedding, it seemed too late to do anything about it. Pa kept on about the security, and I just let myself be persuaded.'

She kept her eyes averted, not wanting to see any doubts in Sarah's face. Knowing it was unlikely that Loveday Willard could be persuaded to do anything she didn't want to. Sarah saw the muscles working in her friend's throat and changed the subject.

'What will you do now? Stay here?'

'Oh no! At least, only for a while. Then I'll go back to Finch's – my – house, though what I'll do with it I don't know. It won't be a butcher's shop again. Perhaps I'll take in lodgers – I don't know yet.'

'Come and stay with us for a few weeks, Loveday,' Sarah said impulsively. 'You like the country, and I'd be so glad of your company now it's such dull weather. Please say you will. I know Father would be pleased to have you, and I don't even need to ask him. We could go back this very day if you like. Pack a few things in a box and come home with me to Goss House. The trap is calling back for me in an hour, so you've plenty of time. What do you say?'

Home to Goss House . . . never had anything sounded sweeter to Loveday's ears. She hugged Sarah and wept a little, and said it was the best place on earth she could think of right now. Away from the town and its painful memories; away from Polly and Ralph; and sharing Sarah's smooth and comfortable life, in the home that was also Adam's. She didn't say any of that to Sarah, but her gratitude said it all.

It was no problem informing Polly and Ralph of her invitation. It was almost painfully obvious that Polly was glad to be rid of her mournful step-daughter, and Ralph promised heartily that by the time she came back to town the Viney house would be just as she wanted, and he'd get some suitable furniture installed if she wished him to.

'Yes please,' Loveday said distantly. 'The kind of things my mother would have chosen, no cheap rubbish. There's money enough for that, so make it nice, please, Pa. And I'll go back to being called Loveday Willard, since I was hardly wed to Finch long enough to be entitled to his name. I'll be Loveday Willard again for Ma's sake.'

He agreed blusteringly, as if she embarrassed him somewhat, but Polly flushed darkly. Polly knew, as Loveday meant her to, that as far as she was concerned, Meg Willard still reigned here, and if there were any trollops in the family, it was one with a cockney accent who didn't belong and never would.

But inside the hour Loveday forgot them as she and Sarah rode in the Goss trap away from Taunton and towards the winter greyness of Taunton Deane. It didn't matter to Loveday that the bare trees dripped moisture and the red earth squelched beneath the narrow wheels and made tracks that filled almost immediately into red rivers. Spring was coming back to her heart, and by the time it laced the apple trees with a latticework of green again, she prayed that the wounds of the past six months would be healed. Loveday was resilient, and she couldn't deny a wild sweet thrill that soon she would be living in rooms where Adam had spent so much time; her eyes seeing vistas that were familiar to him; touching the same chairs, eating from the same plates, sleeping in the same sheets . . . her breath caught in her throat, knowing the ice around her heart was melting rapidly, with a sharp exquisite excitement that made her suddenly long to see him again, and to see his clear brown eyes looking into hers.

The day came sooner than she had expected. There was a limit to the number of shifts a man could work in the tunnel at Box before the need for daylight and clean air became an explosive need inside him. Hours of back-breaking work shifting the lumps of rock and passing them back in heavy buckets made the hands raw and tempers short. Treading the uneven ground, made dank by water seepage and horse-dung, and the incessant fears that what happened to one man could happen to another, took their toll. No man could go on without a break, and almost as soon as Adam had sent his letter home to Sarah, he knew he must get out for a while or go mad. He would be back, he told his disgruntled foreman, but he was taking one week off, and no man was stopping him. And it was more than a rest at his uncle's house in Bristol he sought. He boarded the earliest coach leaving for Somerset and arrived at Taunton feeling dirty and unshaven, but never more thankful to see the endless countryside stretching away in the distance as he hired a trap to take him on to Goss House. When he was rested and refreshed and looked more presentable, he would ride back to town and seek out Loveday Willard, whether it was proper or not.

The house looked welcoming and inviting as Adam neared it; solid and enduring in its foil of greenery, the blue-misted mounds of the Quantocks behind it, the sweet red earth that produced the bountiful crops of apples beneath. Adam felt a sudden swell of pride in the thought of being part of all this. Like his sisters, he hadn't altogether welcomed the move from town to country, but after sweating in the mud and clay of the Box tunnel for several months on

136

end, the sight of it was never sweeter.

And surely he must be having hallucinations, he thought now, as the door of the house burst open on hearing the approach of the trap, and a flurry of blue skirts appeared as his sister screamed out his name in excitement. Followed by his father, pleasure written over his gaunt features, and another figure, dressed in demure grey, but with a disbelieving smile on her lips that made his heart leap . . .

'Why didn't you let us know you were coming, Adam?' Sarah hugged and kissed him.

'It's good to see you, boy,' Norman pumped his hand up and down. 'Back for good, I hope.'

'Only for a week, Father,' Adam said, his eyes still on Loveday and seeing the brief disappointment in her eyes. God, but he'd almost forgotten how beautiful her eyes were, deep blue and the most expressive eyes on earth. He forced himself to look at his father, registering with a little shock that he looked even thinner than before Adam had left.

'We have a visitor, my boy, as you see,' Norman kept his arm round Adam's shoulder as they went into the house out of the cool air. 'You won't have heard about Loveday's troubles –'

'Yes I have,' Adam put in quickly, colouring a little as he saw his father's surprise. 'Sarah told me in her recent letter, and I can't tell you how sorry I was, Loveday. I meant to write to you myself, but it was difficult.'

He realised Norman was looking even more astonished now as Loveday murmured something inaudible in reply. She and Adam recognised the falseness in his words. How could he be sorry that the man Loveday had married was dead? Adam was no hypocrite, and they both knew it. And his father was biting his tongue with difficulty, and wondering at the apparent intimacy between his son and the Willard girl, of which he had known nothing. He hadn't been aware they knew each other, let alone be on familiar enough terms to carry on a correspondence; young people went their own ways these days, he contemplated . . . he would speak to Adam later, but for now nothing must spoil his homecoming.

137

'How lovely to have you home to escort us about the country, Adam,' Sarah broke into the little silence. 'It's a little unnerving for two young ladies to ride too far afield on their own, but we shall feel much safer with your protection.'

Her words were innocent and half said for her father's peace of mind, but the little raise of her eyebrow conveyed the message to Adam that the three of them could be riding well away from Goss House, and that Sarah would be quite willing to disappear discreetly, to give Loveday and Adam time alone together. He knew her well enough to read the hidden message in her words, and agreed readily.

'I shall want to visit all the places round about,' he nodded. 'And to renew a few old acquaintances, like Loveday's cousins.'

This too was said on his father's behalf, lest he should suspect too great an interest in a girl newly widowed, but Adam didn't miss the sudden little frozen look on Loveday's face. For a second Adam remembered vividly the coarseness of Matt Willard's assurance that he'd be the one to break in his luscious little cousin . . . he'd been thwarted there, because of the mismatched wedding between Loveday and Finch Viney, but the thought wasn't one to give him any satisfaction. He forced himself to think of other things, and agreed that he was parched and hungry and that a meal would be very welcome, since it was late afternoon and a while since he'd eaten anything.

But he had a hunger greater than the need for food. He and Loveday had to talk. He needed to hear from her own lips that her father had forced her into the preposterous marriage with Finch; that she had never loved him nor wanted the marriage. He needed to hear her say there was only one love in her life, and to see proof of it glowing in her eyes. He saw it now as she sat across the great oak table from him, and wondered that no-one else seemed aware of the magnetism between them. He saw it and felt it, but he wanted more. He wanted to hear her say it, whether it was too soon or not . . . that didn't matter any more. Too many pent-up emotions in the past months were bursting to emerge. He had seen, touched and smelled

138

death too often in the darkness of the tunnel for it to demand his respect any longer. He had learned the urgency of living life to its utmost while it lasted, and he wanted his life to include Loveday Willard.

The four of them talked long into the evening, but for two of them the others hardly existed. Loveday smiled dutifully when Norman passed a comment in her direction, and Adam told them something of the dangers of his work, though far from all of them. He was aware of every change of expression on her face; while she listened, hearing nothing but the timbre of his voice, and watching the strong mobility of his mouth and imagining its touch on hers. All the bitterness he'd felt at her marriage had somehow evaporated, because she was here and so was he, and that was all that mattered. Eventually he pushed his chair back from the table.

'I must walk off that meal,' he smiled at his father. 'And take a look around, since it'a a fine night. Who's coming with me for an inspection of the estate!'

'Not me,' Norman smiled. 'I've too much respect for my doctor these days, and the night air does my chest no good. You young ones go if you've a mind, and I'll take a nap by the fire until you come back.'

Loveday and Sarah fetched their shawls, and Loveday's hands trembled as she wrapped it around her slender body. She could still hardly believe the miracle that had brought Adam home when she was a guest in the house. Meg had told her always to believe in fate, and it was fate that was throwing them together . . . and who in their right minds would dare to deny such a force? Who would want to, the sweet thought raged through Loveday's mind, when she had loved Adam Goss for so long?

'Loveday,' Sarah joined her in her room, noting the luminous brightness of her friend's eyes, and the rosiness of cheeks that suddenly seemed to bloom as if touched by an artist's brush. 'If you and Adam want to talk privately, I can easily slip back to the house by the back door for an hour, and then rejoin you by the cidersheds. It would look best if we returned to the house together, since Father will be refreshed by then and looking out for us.'

139

Loveday gave her a quick hug. The world was suddenly more beautiful. Outside her window the thatched and timbered cider sheds that stood some distance from the house and grounds loomed invitingly white in the mild February night, softened by moonlight and the whisper of gentle breezes through the apple orchards beyond. They were destined to be her trysting place with Adam, and her heart beat unevenly at all they had to say to one another.

He was waiting for them near the front door of the house, and Sarah told him quickly what she intended to do. Her plan was met with eager approval, and Loveday's hopes soared. He did love her, and her heart sang because of it. The three of them strode out together in the direction of the cider sheds, but once in the shadow of the trees, Sarah slipped quietly back to the house and left them alone. Adam pushed open the door of the cider shed nearest them, and immediately they were enveloped in the piquant sweet-sour aroma of apples and fermentation, musty and heady. It was dark in the low raftered building, but the moon cast light and shadow on the giant cider press with its great wooden screw and slab, from which the crushed apples would discharge their golden potent liquid.

Piled up at one side of the shed were bales of straw which was used in alternate layers with the crushed apple pulp to form the *cheese* from which the juice flowed, a cloudy amber hue until it was fermented to throw off all impurities and emerge as the pure ambrosia given its rich colour by the red earth . . . but neither of the two intruders into the cider shed gave it a second thought. Through the moonlit windows the straw formed a thick matted bed, and Adam drew Loveday down on to its yielding weathered softness. There was no need for words as she moved into his arms. They held her in sweet imprisonment as his lips descended slowly on hers, in a kiss that went on and on . . .

'If a hundred churchmen condemned me for wanting you so soon after your harrowing experiences, it would make no difference, Loveday,' he said, his voice husky against her mouth, his hands in her hair and moulding her to him as if he couldn't get his fill of her. 'I would still want you as I've always wanted you.'

'And I you,' she was breathless, stars bursting in her head at the wonder of it all. Adam and she . . . God was good, giving her this second chance; she felt the pressure of his lips again and gave herself up to the dizzy rapture of it. Pressed in his arms, the crude straw became a scented silken bed, worthy of a king's lady, because she was here with him. Nothing else mattered. No-one else existed, nor time nor place . . .

Adam's palm gently covered the softness of her breast, and there was no feeling of revulsion inside her as there had been with Matt, no self-disgust that she'd known at Finch's touch, only the longing to love and be loved, and for something so right to happen between them that it would exorcise all the badness that had gone before.

Adam knew she was his for the taking, but he held himself firmly in control. What kind of man seduced a woman still haunted by the memory of her husband's death, no matter how much he wanted her, and how deliciously spontaneous her response? Loveday was made for loving, but he would despise himself if he gave in to his desires so urgently at such a time. And there were still things needing to be said between them.

'Why did you marry him, Loveday? Didn't you take me seriously that day in the churchyard when I said I'd come back for you? It was said in jest, I'll admit, but I thought our letters since proved my feelings for you were deep. And yours for me, I thought.'

'You thought right! Don't ever doubt it, Adam.' she said passionately.

'Then why this marriage? I can't believe you felt an undying love for the butcher if you already loved me! And nor do I believe you'd submit meekly to your father's wishes. I believe I know you too well for that!'

She felt her teeth digging into the soft inner flesh of her mouth as the tone of his voice changed. She could sense the smouldering anger in him despite his avowed love for her. She was in the circle of his arms, but suddenly she felt as remote from him as the moon above. He didn't know her at all. He didn't know the wickedness in her. If she had been the victim of Matt Willard's seduction, then she had been ten times more wicked in her own seduction of Finch Viney, cajoling him into marrying her to give a name to her unwanted child.

And the final wickedness, driving Finch to his death by screaming at him and flaunting her shame as if to underline his own inadequacy as a man. Finch had been as much a victim of his own nature as she had been of hers, and had paid the price, together with her own innocent child . . . was there no end to wickedness? Loveday took a deep shuddering breath as she felt the grip of Adam's fingers on her shoulders.

'Pa wanted to marry Polly,' she stuttered. 'he wanted me out. If I hadn't agreed to marrying Finch, I'd have had to go skivvying or worse, and found my own way in the world. You'd gone away, and how was I to know you weren't just dallying with me? I wasn't in your class.'

To her relief he seemed to accept her fumbling words, and folded her in his arms again.

'Don't talk of class,' he said roughly. 'It's nothing to me or my father, but if there was no chance of you staying at home when your father wed Polly, couldn't you have gone to your uncle's farm? I'm sure they'd have taken you in.'

He felt her shudder in his arms.

'I wouldn't have gone there,' she said tightly. 'It would have caused endless trouble between Pa and Uncle Jack. There seemed no alternative but to marry Finch. He was kind, and undemanding –'

'The thought of him lying with you at night drove me insane,' Adam was suddenly fierce, and she jerked up her head to look at him. His face was dark above her, but she could see the shape of his features; the well-defined head with its soft curling dark hair; the contours of his cheeks and firm-jutting chin; the set of his nose and the flash of his eyes as the disturbing image of Loveday in Finch Viney's embrace forged into his mind.

Loveday's soft mouth trembled, remembering it the way it was.

142

'If that's what troubles you, Adam then you can put it out of your mind, because nothing ever happened,' she murmured delicately. 'When Finch died, I was as pure as on the day he married me.'

It was the truth, and yet it was the biggest lie of all, for she had been sinful long before the farce of her wedding-night . . . Adam stared at her.

'Was the man a fool then?'

'No, don't say that. Spare him a little pity, Adam. He spent his life being baited by the wags of the town, and I suspect he married me in a sense of desperation to prove himself as much a man as anyone. Only – he wasn't. Do you understand? I – I can't explain more –'

'Good God, you mean he was impotent!' Adam seized her meaning at once, and then the full import of her words sank into him. She felt the brush of his lips against her cheek, her closed lids, her mouth.

'I can't be a hypocrite and pretend I'm sorry, my darling,' his mouth moved against hers, sensuously, arousingly. 'Oh, I'm sorry for him, naturally, that he couldn't know a wife's ultimate sweetness, but I'm elated that yours was denied to him! You belong to me and we both know it, don't we, my Loveday?'

'Oh yes, Adam!'

He pulled her into a sitting position and she swayed against him as his kisses became more ardent, melting in his embrace as if she craved nothing more than to be locked in his arms forever. Her loosened hair tumbled like silver gilt around her shoulders, lit by shafts of moonlight, and to Adam the sight was both ethereal and beautiful. And she had not been defiled by the fat-bellied butcher after all . . . and nor would she be by him, he vowed. Loveday was too innately good for her reputation to be ruined by a moment of passion. He shifted slightly away from her clinging arms.

'It's unthinkable that we should make our intentions known yet, my lovely,' he said softly. 'But this time we'll have no misunderstandings. When the good folk of Taunton allow you to stop mourning officially, you and I will be wed. When

143

the leaves of autumn begin to fall – do you agree?'

Her kisses were all the answer he needed, even though autumn seemed centuries away to Loveday. But she knew he spoke sensibly, and it would be their secret. The sweetest secret of all.

"I must return to Box after this week, my darling,' he began.

'But I'll never see you then,' she cried out. 'Do you want to leave me so soon?'

'I never want to leave you again,' Adam said roughly. 'But I can't stay here and not want to make love to you either, and I won't risk your good name by compromising you. I'll go back as I said I would, and the time will pass all the quicker. Perhaps when I come home in the autumn for good I'll learn to be an apple grower and make Goss Cider the best in the country! Will that please you?'

'Yes,' she whispered, her face hot against his chest where she could hear his heart's erratic beating. His words stilled her protests. He thought her pure and she was not. He ached for her, but he respected her good name too much to risk a scandal. She didn't deserve him, Loveday thought, with a little rush of emotion, but she would do as he asked of her and be patient, and try to prove herself worthy of him.

CHAPTER ELEVEN

It seemed as if everyone was infected by the sudden mood of gaiety brought to Goss Cider by the arrival of young Master Adam. From old Mr Goss himself and pretty Sarah, to the poor young maid so recently widowed, and putting such a brave face on it. To the housekeeper, Mrs Hiatt, and the housemaids, cheered by the sight of the handsome young gent. To Jed Hiatt, long-time cider manager, surprised and gratified at the new interest young Master Adam was taking in his domain, and about which old Jed was only too pleased to chinwag.

He liked to see how the young master always found time to escort the two ladies about, whether the three of them went riding together, or visited the cider sheds for a look round, as now. It warmed Jed's simple heart to see them listening attentively as if his words were of prime importance to all three, to learn how the rich fruit of which he was so proud, could be turned into liquid gold.

The tall dark gent was flanked on either side by the two pretty girls, one fair, one dark. A sight to brighten a muggy February morning with the mist veiling the hills and a golden vapour rising from the dew-fresh grasses as the sun struggled to appear in the slaty sky.

The year was still new, but Jed had a countryman's instinct for sensing that spring would come early, for the earth was barely frost-touched, and already there were patches of white snowdrops sparkling among the ropy roots of gnarled trees. Soon there would be violets and celandines and the sun-splashed gold of primroses to lighten the dull days.

It did old Jed's heart good to watch nature's bounties unfold as inevitably as the seasons followed one another, and to know he was a part of it, as was his good woman. It did him even more good to realise Master Adam's growing interest in the land of which he was now a part, and to sense that it weren't merely to impress the ladies.

'Will you tell my sister and Miss Loveday the procedures, Jed? The way you told it to me,' Adam requested, and it was no hardship for Jed to ease his limbs awhile and explain to the pretty young ladies what Adam had enjoyed hearing already.

'Well then, young sir, I'll need to tell it from the beginning, and that's the point when we collect the apples from the trees. We don't use 'em right away for the cider making, 'cos they need to mature. To do that we heap 'em outside the

145

sheds on the grass, in great pyramids of red and green. A fine sight they look too. Then they go in the mill where we grind 'em down to what we call pommy, a thick soggy substance.' Jed nodded his head to the far corner of the shed. 'You'll see yon bales o' straw?'

The smile that passed between Adam and Loveday went unnoticed. Both paid attention, but both were seeing the sweet image of themselves here in this very shed last night, when the straw bales had been a love-nest, softened and shadowed by moonlight, and the humble surroundings had been turned into a place of enchantment by their discovery of each other.

'. . . then a layer of clean straw goes on the flat bed of the mill,' Jed was droning on. 'Followed by a layer of pommy, then one of straw, and onwards in like fashion till it's all built up into what's called a cheese.'

'I thought cheese was for eating.' It was Sarah who spoke quickly, seeing that she was the only one who seemed to be listening properly now, and fearing that Jed might be offended. Her brother and Loveday seemed to be in some other world for the moment, and Sarah felt a swift envy. Not that she begrudged them their precious moments, even though some might say Loveday had no business to be looking fondly at a young man when her husband was so recently buried. But Loveday would do exactly as she wished, and if some divine providence had sent Adam home at just this time when Loveday was here, why should anyone question it?

Jed's ruddy face broke into a broad smile.

'Bless 'ee, Miss Sarah, there's cheese for eatin' and cheese that's a term in cider makin', and there bain't nothin' similar in 'em at all!' His accent broadened with his smile.

Out of the corner of her eye, Sarah could see that Adam was far more interested in Loveday at this moment than the story of cider making. It was as if the smell of the apples was intoxicating him . . . or else it was Loveday's presence alone that was doing that. Even when he didn't look directly at her, he kept her in his periphery vision. He knew every

146

curve and contour of her face. He knew the exact proportions of her tip-tilted nose and the variety of expressions in her beautiful eyes that could darken with passion and inflame his senses so stunningly.

' . . . then the cheese is squeezed by the old wooden press that's done more years of service than I can count, young misses, and 'tis still in fine fettle and will outlast the likes o' you or me! It takes three men to stand in the gallery up above and turn the screw on it. Another man shears the edges of the cheese clean before the final pressing. A right old mess it looks when the juice is all pressed out of it, but we don't waste nothing. The old dry pommy and straw mixture is passed on to the farmers for cattle-feed . . . '

His three listeners had seated themselves on an old bench along one wall. Loveday's hands lay motionless on her lap. Why had he never noticed them before, Adam wondered? They were smooth and soft, the fingers long and neatly-tipped, curling round each other on the folds of her dress and cloak. He imagined her hands holding him, and felt a sudden fire shoot through him at the thought of their untutored caresses. Now that he knew the butcher had known nothing of her sweetness, she was as pure and unsullied in his eyes as an angel; he felt Sarah's foot digging into his ankle, and dragged his thoughts away from their delightful meanderings.

' . . . some cider makers add beetroot or other aids to improve the colour of their brew, but we need no such artificial aids,' Jed was saying proudly. 'The copper in the soil hereabouts sees to that, and we've got the best crop of apples too, the "blacks", to produce the best cider for miles. You'll have seen the kegs for fermenting?'

'They can hardly miss them,' Adam grinned, and chewed on his lip as Jed gave him a stern look. He felt Loveday fighting to suppress a giggle at his side, and his spirits soared. He was in love for the first time in his life, and no intoxicating drink could ever compare with the way his blood flowed when he thought of her, or the heady sensations her touch evoked in him. He held out his hand to her as Jed led

147

the way to the fermenting shed, and her fingers remained in his for a moment longer than necessary. Adam could still feel their warmth even when they were removed, as he followed dutifully behind Loveday's trim straight back, unable to resist noting the womanly flare of her hips and the neat little waist. The urge to possess her was tempered by a flood of tenderness. She had been through so much in past weeks, and the knowledge that she loved him was making all the hurt he'd felt at her marriage recede into oblivion. He wanted her, but this was not the time . . .

Inside the fermenting shed it was pungent, the smell of the fermenting cider almost overpowering. Jed pointed out the huge cider kegs, all filled now with the fermenting liquor that was his pride and joy.

'These kegs are made of seasoned oak and very thick,' he informed them. 'There's hundreds of gallons of cider in each one, and come the summer, there'll be many a farm worker who'll be thankin' Goss Cider for makin' his day less parched as he toils in the fields! Now, was there anythin' more you wanted to see, or can I get on with my work now?'

His smile was deferential, his voice mild, but leaving them in no doubt that if they had little to do but idle their time, then he was made of different stock. Adam thanked him for his time and he and the girls made their way out of the sheds.

The air was mild, and it seemed destined to be a fair weather day. Both Adam and Loveday were filled with an energy that sprang from their new awareness of life and living and each other. It was obvious to Sarah that the best thing she could do would be to leave them alone, but the proprieties made her hesitate. Even here, in the comparative wildness of country life after the more correct ways the family had followed in Bristol, decorum was still to be prized. Besides, what would her father think if these two went off on their own too many times?

As the three of them strolled back to the big house together, Sarah wasn't the only one to be thinking similar thoughts. Adam yearned to be alone with the love of his life, and as for Loveday, she bubbled as if drunk on champagne, and the fact of her recent widowhood was as easily shed as an unwanted shoe. She hadn't wanted marriage with Finch Viney. In her own mind it had been forced on her by the circumstances Matthew Willard had induced. At a distance now from the horror of finding Finch with his wrist cut, Loveday could view the whole episode calmly. It was not her fault. If Finch was weak enough to end his own life, then it was his choice. He hadn't thought enough of her feelings to care whether she laughed or cried at his death. And though she wasn't so heartless as to laugh, she had done with crying. She was young and strong, and Adam was beside her.

She turned towards him at that moment with a smile of such brilliance that he caught his breath. God, but she was so beautiful, he found himself thinking. Beautiful and tempestuous, and far too alive to waste her life in mourning for that mild pink butcher husband of hers. Adam was still intent on finding out the true reasons for her marrying him, and if that swine of a father of hers had forced her with threats of violence or ejection, then he could hardly blame sweet Loveday for taking the only way out at the time.

If only he had been here . . . the attractions of returning to Box and the dank muddy tunnel workings were fading fast. Ever since coming home he had toyed with the idea of staying, but the fever of desire with which he was filled every time he looked at the girl beside him made him afraid of his own feelings. He wasn't made in the same style as his sometime friend, Matt Willard, who had gloated at the thought of deflowering this lovely girl. Adam's mouth tightened, and surreptitiously, he squeezed Loveday's small hand for a second, feeling its instant response before he let it go.

'We could always pay a visit on your aunt if you wished, Loveday,' he said casually. 'I'm sure she wouldn't object to my accompanying you.'

'No!' The word exploded violently from her lips, to the astonishment of the other two. 'I've no wish to go to the farm! I only want to stay here. I don't want to see anybody else but you and Sarah and the people here at Goss House.'

Sarah interposed quickly as Loveday's face reddened with

anger and tension and a rising panic at the thought of seeing Matt again. 'It's all right, Loveday. You don't have to do anything you don't want to. Adam was only thinking it might be a pleasant diversion for you. He doesn't fully realise the terrible strain you've suffered. You've looked so well these last few days, I think we've both forgotten a little.'

She stopped in embarrassment, remembering too how volatile Loveday could be, and how their friendship had itself been strained on more than one occasion. But Adam caught hold of Loveday's hand openly now, his face troubled.

'I'm sorry if I upset you, Loveday,' he said. 'You must know it's the very last thing I wish to do. And perhaps I was being too devious. I thought a long walk alone might have sounded too presumptuous, so a visit to the farm was a good excuse. We needn't have called there – '

'It's a good idea,' Sarah put in, seeing the way his mind was working, and speaking for Loveday, since she seemed to be temporarily silenced by the thought of visiting anybody. 'In any case, I promised to sit and read to Father this afternoon as he likes me to do, so I'll be quite happy to stay indoors. And I want to be here when the doctor comes to call on him.'

Adam looked at her sharply. 'Is he ill today? Why has nobody told me the doctor has been sent for?'

Sarah put a restraining hand on his arm as he would have rushed towards the house.

'He has the recurring cough and the weak chest he has always had, Adam, but no-one has sent for the doctor especially. He makes routine visits every few days, and today is one of those times. Please stop making such a fuss, and if you and Loveday want to take that walk, I shall tell Father you went off to visit Loveday's aunt at the farm. Whether you arrive or not is up to you, isn't it?'

Loveday's nerves were settling down again. Until Adam's casual reference to the farm, she had had no idea of how abhorrent the idea of seeing Matt again would be. Not that he had any idea about the miscarriage, of course. She

150

thanked God for it, even though she thought that God would probably disown her if she were to die right now, and she thanked Him for the miscarriage too, wicked or not, because if the baby had been born, Matt Willard would have been adding up the months on his fingers and knowing the truth of it, if no-one else did . . .

'I'd like to go for a walk, Adam,' she said hurriedly, steering her thoughts away from unpleasant directions. 'I feel the need to be out in the air these days, rather than the cloying confines of four walls around me, however pleasant they may be.'

She added the last, in case they should consider her ungrateful for their hospitality, but all she wanted to do at this moment was walk through the spring-like vale with Adam, as if there was no yesterday and no tomorrow, only the magic of the here and now, and being with him. As they neared the house a horse and trap clattered through the gateway and a young man alighted, carrying a brown leather bag. Loveday didn't miss the way Sarah's cheeks were suddenly tinged with pink.

'It's the doctor,' she said quickly to the other two. 'He's recently moved to the area to replace old Doctor Dodds, and is a distant relative of his. Come and be introduced.'

The young man approached smilingly. He couldn't have been more than his mid-twenties, Loveday thought rapidly, appraising the smart yet tasteful appearance, the shock of sandy-coloured hair and engaging smile that would be reassuring to patients young and old. And which was more than appealing to Miss Sarah Goss, by the look of things! And Sarah had said nothing to Loveday of this new arrival in their midst! It was the doctor's first call since Loveday had arrived at Goss House, and now she burned with curiosity to ask her friend about him, since it was obvious the rustic charms of Matt Willard were fading fast with this new arrival. Loveday's spirits rose, relieved beyond measure that her friend wasn't still obstinate about the attachment to Matt Willard that had so bothered Loveday.

'Good afternoon, Doctor Chard,' Sarah's fingers were

already being held in a firm clasp by the young doctor, and it was obvious to anyone with eyes to see that it was a lingering hand shake. Sarah forced herself to make the introductions. 'May I introduce you to my brother, Adam, and to Miss – Mrs Loveday Viney?'

Loveday opened her mouth to speak, then closed it again. It was hardly the moment to insist that she preferred to be known as Loveday Willard again, but privately she avowed to herself that everyone must be informed as soon as possible. She had no wish to be reminded of the farce of her marriage, nor of Finch . . .

'I'm pleased to make your acquaintance, Mr Goss,' Doctor Chard said warmly. He had a country burr that was pleasing to the ear, and his smile embraced them both as he looked at Loveday. 'And yours too, Mrs Viney.'

'I trust these frequent visits of yours shouldn't cause me any alarm?' Adam said at once. If Loveday hadn't thought it so unlikely, she would have sworn that the doctor's face became as tinged with colour as Sarah's!

'Not at all, sir, but your father is not in the best of health, and never will be, which I'm sure you know already. Since I am new here, I want to reassure my patients as much as possible by my presence. It can be disturbing to older patients to see a fresh new face.'

It was not only elderly patients who were disturbed by Geoffrey Chard, though not in the same way, Loveday thought. Sarah seemed to hang on his every word, watching his mouth as he spoke, as if she were imagining its touch on her own. And oh, didn't she know exactly the way such overwhelming sensations could affect the pulse, making the skin glow and the blood sing? Loveday thought, with a sudden rush of empathy. Wasn't it happening to her every moment she was with Adam?

'My father will be waiting to see you,' Sarah was murmuring now, as if these pleasantries had gone on long enough, and she wanted young Doctor Chard to be sitting opposite her in the comfortable drawing-room, where he would take port with her father and exchange the gossip of the day, once the brief examination was over, and the stability of Norman Goss's immediate condition reassured. Sarah would want to sit prettily, her cloak removed, the fine contours of her figure displayed in the deep blue gown she wore ... suddenly, Loveday knew just why she'd dressed so alluringly that day. Sarah would want the firelight to enhance the colour in her cheeks and lips, and to deepen the glow in her eyes. Loveday felt as if she could read every skittering thought that would be filling her friend's head right now. She leaned forward and gave her a light kiss on the cheek.

'We'll see your father later,' she said softly. 'We'll take that walk to my uncle's farm now, and be back in a couple of hours, Sarah. It was very nice to meet you, Doctor Chard.'

Adam echoed her words, and as he and Loveday made their way out of the gateway to strike towards the slopes of the hills, Loveday glanced back to see the doctor offering Sarah his arm as they entered the house. Out of sight of them all, Adam tucked her hand inside the crook of his arm, pressing her close to his side as they walked briskly in the cool fresh breeze.

'Are you thinking the same as I am, Adam?' she spoke with a hint of laughter in her voice. 'That it isn't only your father the handsome young doctor comes to see?'

'My thoughts exactly,' he smiled back. 'And not an unpleasant idea at all. I can think of worse suitors for my sister!'

He spoke lightly, yet they both thought of the same man at that moment, and Loveday gave a small shiver against him.

'You're cold,' he said immediately. 'Perhaps this wasn't such a good idea after all. We should have taken the trap and taken a ride instead of walking.'

'Oh no, I prefer this, Adam! I like to be walking the narrow lanes with the hedgerows almost touching on either side. Sometimes it's as quiet as a church, and then you emerge into the daylight with the hills all around you. I love it, though I hadn't realised how much. I always thought I was a town girl, but there's something about this place that touches my soul.'

She blushed deeply, not usually given to speaking so freely about her inner emotions. Meg had instilled this aesthetic quality in her, and combined with the passionate earthiness of her Willard heritage, Adam found the combination totally fascinating. She could have the look of a wanton and the finesse of an angel at one and the same time, he thought, with a heady rush of love for her.

'Anywhere with you is the most perfect place on earth for me,' he burst out, his voice thickened. Still in the seclusion of the quiet lane, he pulled her roughly into his arms, his mouth taking possession of hers in a long sweet kiss.

It started out as a pledge of his feelings, but the way she melted into his embrace turned it into the most passionate of intimacies. He could feel her firm young breasts pressing tightly against his chest, their peaks sending new shafts of desire racing through his veins. He could feel the roundness of her buttocks as his hands wandered over her shape as if of their own accord, and the way their thighs seemed to lock together as they stood as close as one person. In everything but fact, he made love to her as sensually as if she lay naked in his arms. His imagination soared ahead of him, until he ached with the need of her. And she, his sweet darling Loveday, looking up at him with those expressive eyes that had darkened with an answering need . . . as he moved slightly away from her lips, Adam felt his limbs tremble at the swiftness with which love had enslaved him.

'Do you see now why I have to go back to Box for the time being?' he said roughly. 'Do you think I can stand to see you every day of my life and not want you? And even when you go back home again, I'd still have to seek you out. I couldn't help myself, and I won't ruin your reputation, Loveday. You mean too much to me.'

His hands were in her hair, rippling through the corn-soft silkiness of it, and the words almost tumbled from her lips . . . *What did it matter? What did anything matter but the love and need that flowed like a tidal wave between them?*

154

What did other folk matter . . . ? Even as she thought it, Loveday knew that to Adam, such things did matter, and so they should to her.

As far as the good people of Taunton knew, she was the poor young widow of a respected tradesman, and the daughter of another. She owed each of them something, and even more, she owed it to Adam to be all that he wanted of her.

'We have the rest of our lives, Adam,' she said in a softly husky voice, and knew she had said the right thing when his arms held her more tenderly, and his kiss was gentle. Right now she didn't need the excesses of passion to know how badly he wanted her. She knew it with a certainty that set her senses aflame, and dissolved the final remnants of anxiety at whether she would ever be able to respond to a man's loving again after Matt Willard's assaults on her.

She knew it by the fierce tide of longing exploding inside herself that she stemmed as insistently as Adam. All Meg's gentle teachings had been right . . . the love of a man and a woman could be as mystical as anything in heaven and earth, and Loveday felt her eyes prick with tears to know she had been given it.

'Let's walk on,' she whispered. 'We could gather some wild flowers to take back to prove we've kept our hands busy.'

The way he smiled at her made her blush, and she knew he would wish his hands to be busy at other things. But together they strode on, united more with every step, and Loveday thought she had never spent a more enjoyable day roaming the tangled oak coppices of the dark forests, or coming out into the glinting sunlight in a pastel-coloured sky. Everything she saw seemed more brightly lit, her senses heightened because she shared every experience with Adam.

They walked through sylvan glens, gathering curling wiry fronds of bracken and the first pale primroses, and a handful of wild daffodils. They walked through deep red lanes where the banks were tilted and coppery, and alongside silvery streams where water bubbled and gushed, and tinted red by the soil that seeped into it, and gleaming over its pebbled bed.

155

In sheltered places the short springy turf was already starred with daisies and primroses. It was an enchanted place, because they were together.

'Did you know the river Tone that runs through Taunton was named Tan or Tawny – it's not certain which – by the Saxons, Loveday?' Adam couldn't resist airing a bit of knowledge learned at his college. 'They named it so because the waters are often dyed brownish-red from the Quantock soil.'

'All those centuries ago!' Loveday marvelled, thinking how clever he was to retain such information in his head for such times as it was needed. She leaned forward and knelt by the little streamlet where they were gathering primroses, letting the clear water trickle through her fingers. With the sunlight playing through it, it was pink-tinged too. She almost expected it to leave a stain on her skin.

'I bet there's something else you don't know, my pretty Loveday, since your head is too beautiful to be bothered with too much learning!' His voice teased her.

Loveday tossed her fine gold hair, the strands blowing out behind her head. Did he think her incapable of learning? She could read and write, as he knew very well . . . the love and teasing in his eyes made her swallow her indignation, because of course he was more educated than she!

'Tell me then, and I'll be as wise as you,' she commanded imperiously. Adam laughed at her unconscious little show of pique, pulling her to her feet. He glanced down at their boots, caked in mud.

'Did you know that my name – Adam – has a Hebrew meaning?'

Loveday felt her skin prickle. Hebrew . . . biblical . . . ancient and the name of the first man . . . she shook her head breathlessly.

'Adam means "red earth"', he told her, and just for a second Loveday felt that strange spinning sensation again, as if heaven and earth were converging together. For an instant she seemed to see nothing, then it was as if a mist cleared, and Adam was laughing down at her, and asking if

156

she didn't think it was significant in this particular part of England, considering the state of their footwear?

It was even more significant than he supposed, Loveday thought tremulously. It meant his place was truly here. He belonged, at one with the earth, given the right at birth and baptism, and even more symbolic in Loveday's mind – hadn't she herself knelt at her mother's grave a few short months ago and kissed the sweet red earth as she whispered to Meg that she had found her own true love?

Loveday ran her tongue around her dry lips. How Meg would have loved this! How steadfastly she would have affirmed that Loveday's action and the knowledge that Adam had just given her established a bond that was too strong ever to be broken by mere mortal acts. There was a force that intended Loveday and Adam to be together. No matter what threatened them, their destiny was ordained . . .

'Well?' He demanded. 'Are you going to tell me you dismiss it as nonsense that a name could have a meaning?'

Her silence seemed to mean he thought she was sceptical. To his pleasure, Loveday suddenly hugged him close to her. He could feel her heartbeats through her clothes, as rapid as a wild bird. She spoke softly, yet it seemed to Loveday that her voice soared and carried above the blue-misted hills as if to some other plane.

'It's not nonsense. It's beautiful, and I love it, Adam. I love you, too. I *love* you, Adam!'

It was the first time she had said the words in her life. They tasted as sweet as honey on her tongue.

CHAPTER TWELVE

Polly Reeves Willard looked at her hands with distaste. No matter how many times she washed them, she couldn't rid her nails of the blacklead, and the cold water in which she scrubbed and stoned them was making the once soft skin reddened and chapped. It was one more item to make her resentful and bitter at the life Ralph Willard had led her into.

She couldn't deny that she'd gone into it willingly enough! Even before Meg had died of the disfiguring smallpox, Ralph had sought refuge and delight in Polly's bed, sneaking along the passageway in the dead of night and sliding in beside her almost before she knew what was happening.

And she wasn't one to raise any objections. It was an extra bonus to find a gent so willing and amorous under the very roof in which she'd come to work. It saved looking elsewhere, and added a spice to their relationship. Pretending to be the pert but still modest little shop-girl, newly come down from London, by day . . . while at night . . . a flicker of remembrance stirred in Polly now as she paused in her ablutions, her eyes misty for a moment.

'Ooh, Ralphie, you mustn't, ' she'd giggle, as his hands searched for every delicious rounded part of her beneath the bedcovers. His hands were everywhere, as if he was starved of everything womanly, despite his Meg. But she had never been up to much in that department, Ralph had told Polly hoarsely, while he'd made up for lost time with his new fancy. Meg had been passive and dutiful, while Polly and he performed athletic feats of which even Ralph hadn't known he was capable with his bulk.

'No such thing as mustn't, my little Polly Perkins,' he'd chuckle and wheeze as he throbbed beneath Polly's willing attentions. And for all that she made token protest, they both knew there was an earthy attraction between them that made the long nights worth living through. She was his little jam tart, he'd tell her coarsely, and if he didn't pound the ass off her afore he was done, then his name wasn't Ralph Willard.

Such talk in the musky atmosphere of the bedroom excited and stimulated Polly, and she'd firmly believed that when Meg died and she and Ralph made it all legal-like, they'd continue in the lusty way they'd begun. Especially now that haughty little madam, Loveday, was safely out of the way.

Polly spared her a moment of pity. But no more. The silly little ninny had brought it all on herself by gettin' herself knocked up by the fat butcher, and now she'd gone off to that fine friend of hers, Sarah Goss, with a face like putty. Got out of it all very well, in Polly's opinion.

Her brief feelings about Loveday ended abruptly. What was more important was the effect the whole episode had had on Ralphie. Turned respectable, he had, cashing in on the sympathy of the Taunton dames because of what had happened to Loveday. And his respectability included less of the bedroom capers that Polly knew now were the only thing keeping them together. Apart from that, Ralph bored her. He had none of the perky backchat of the London barrow-boys she and her sister Ellen had enjoyed. He never wanted to stir of an evening, just to snore the time away by the old range, his weskit buttons popping, a jug of cider at his side, and the snorings interspersed by the roar of a fart.

Polly was bored out of her mind. Ralph wasn't hard-up for a bob or two, but the way he hoarded his money in an old tin box in the attic, climbing up the rickety step-ladder every night with the day's takings, large or small, and counting it in his laborious way, was nothing short of miserly. He seemed to have forgotten that Polly was young and pretty, and wanted pretty things. She'd expected to have them. She'd dismissed her sister Ellen's dire warnings when she'd come to visit a few short months ago.

'You're a bloody head-case, burying yerself down 'ere, Pol,' Ellen had said bluntly. 'Quaint it might be, but there's all those bright lights waitin' for yer in London, and many a fine gent who'd be glad of yer company. Remember those fine old times we 'ad when we was doin' our turn at the old King's theatre? No lack of gents to choose from at the stage door, was there? Don't you miss it?'

She hadn't, not then. All this had been the new adventure, and besides, at the time she left London, there'd been a bit of bother with the law, and it had been best to lie low for a while. All that was past now, Ellen had told her, but the lure of being Mrs Ralph Willard and the thought of entertaining in her own home had attracted Polly more than London's bright lights.

Now . . . she frowned at her reflection in the mirror as she found a new line alongside her eyes. She was stagnating here, and Ralphie had clamped down firmly on any ideas she'd had about 'entertaining' in his parlour. Just as if he guessed the form such entertaining might be. Polly gnashed her teeth. Something had to be done, and soon, before she went mad.

On the same day that Polly was trying to decide what she could do to rouse Ralph to his former ardour, Norman Goss was realising that his son Adam and the little fair-haired widow, were becoming closer by the hour. Not in any scandalous manner, he was glad to see, for Adam had been brought up in a gentlemanly fashion, and acted accordingly towards Loveday. But anyone with eyes to see could tell that there was a blossoming attachment between them. Modest and yet unconsciously sensual on Loveday's part, protective and endearing on Adam's. Despite the newness of the girl's widowhood, it cheered Norman's heart to see the way she had changed during her visit to his house. Arriving so wan and pale and still stunned with shock, and now, with Adam's obvious devotion and Sarah's caring friendship, Loveday looked a different girl. Glowing and alive, where before she had seemed set to be following in the footsteps of her husband.

Norman Goss was too well aware of his own uncertain state of health to waste valuable time in mourning what couldn't be changed. If Loveday had been married years instead of days ... and if he, like everyone else, hadn't thought the couple so mismatched, and if Sarah hadn't confided to him privately that it hadn't been a love-match, and therefore he'd concluded Ralph Willard had put pressure on his daughter to be wed ... then Norman might have thought differently about the way the girl went about with stars in her eyes, and Adam looked as if the day only began when he was near to her. As it was, Norman was charmed by the total innocence of a relationship that seemed to him to have begun with startling swiftness, but which nevertheless seemed entirely inevitable.

He liked Loveday's spirit. She managed to combine dignity with femininity, yet he sensed that she was as strong as steel. She had the Willard guts, of which old Jed had yarned to him on more than one occasion. In the men it came out as wild and raucous fighting. In Loveday it was a trait Norman could only admire, seeing the way she conducted herself in his house.

The four of them, he and his two children, and Loveday, had just eaten a splendid dinner that Mrs Hiatt had cooked. There was roast duck and green peas, and mincemeat pie to be eaten with hot punch. It was long past Christmas, but with Adam home, Norman wanted to keep the Christmas spirit going. And he had an extra little gift of his own to offer Loveday. He smiled at her as the four of them sat in front of the roaring fire in the drawing-room now.

'What are your plans when you go back to Taunton, my dear?'

Loveday started, his question taking her by surprise, and jolting her into remembering things she would rather forget. But she couldn't entirely forget. Through all the euphoria of being here with Adam and the enchantment of loving and being loved, she couldn't quite forget that there was another world to which she had to return soon. She couldn't forget Finch, and sometimes she awoke in the night with her palms clenched and sweating, praying that Ralph and Polly had done all that she'd requested with the house and premises that had once been Viney's butcher's shop.

161

She shrugged her pretty shoulders in a gesture of vagueness, her hands spread out as if seeking help. Norman sensed that if he dared, Adam would have seized both Loveday's hands at that moment and pressed them to his lips, insisting that she remained here with him. However, there were proprieties to be observed, and Norman cleared his throat as he looked at Loveday enquiringly.

'I'm afraid I've barely thought beyond the present, Sir,' she murmured. 'While I am here, my father and – and Polly are clearing out all the old furniture and arranging for the place to be painted and cleaned, and installed with all new items. It was the only way I felt able to return there, but neither did I feel able to return to my father's house.'

She stopped speaking abruptly, before the resentment she felt towards Polly bubbled over. And Loveday had no wish to be ranting like a fishwife in front of these gentlefolk, even though thoughts of Polly could always evoke such a reaction.

Norman nodded sympathetically, clearly thinking it was her father's marriage and his apparent insistence on the wedding to Finch Viney that made Loveday appear so distressed.

'Father, do you need to ask Loveday questions at such a time?' Adam spoke up in defence of his love. 'After all the trauma of past weeks, can you not see how much better she looks since she's been here? Why stir up all the memories before it's necessary?'

He was transparent to the other three, but he didn't care. He felt indignant that his father should have spoiled this evening, and knew he had his own selfish reasons for not wanting to be reminded that Loveday's home was the butcher's premises.

'It's all right, Adam,' Loveday said swiftly. 'I have to go back, and it's only putting off the day by pretending it's not going to happen.'

'You know you can stay here as long as you like, Loveday,' Sarah said generously. 'Father and I will love to have you as our guest until you're completely well again.'

162

But she wasn't ill! And though Sarah had meant well, she had unconsciously reminded Loveday that she was only a guest here. Whether the future held anything different, for the present she didn't belong here. And once Adam had gone back to Box, even Goss House, that she had come to love, would be empty without him.

'Your father's being sensible, Sarah,' she acknowledged. 'I have to do something with my life.'

'The stock will all be disposed of?' Norman went on.

'Oh yes!'

The place would be empty and sterile, with no trace of Finch's presence or trade. It would be as if he'd never been, but Loveday hadn't considered what she would do with her time all day. Alone, the future suddenly appeared as a frightening void. But one thing was certain. She'd never go back to skivvying for her father again. That was Polly's job now, and one that Polly wouldn't be taking to very kindly, Loveday thought, with a glimmer of satisfaction.

'I have a proposition to make to you, Loveday.'

The three young people in the drawing-room all looked at Norman in surprise as he made his statement. Loveday felt her cheeks tinge with colour, wondering what Mr Goss could possibly have to offer her.

'As you know, the business here is thriving as it's always done,' he went on.' When the place was owned by Lundy Cider, there was a good reputation for quality to uphold, and I'm just as anxious for that reputation to be maintained now that it's Goss Cider. We supply farmers all the year round, and also the local taverns and send a quantity of stock to ale-shops, but there's never been a shop that's exclusive to Goss Cider.'

Loveday felt her pulse quicken, but as she would have spoken, Norman held up his hand gently to show he hadn't finished.

'Hear me out, my dear. I'm not suggesting you turn your establishment into some kind of ale-house. It wouldn't be proper, and nor would I want you pestered by louts and drunkards at all hours. But what I'm thinking of is a respect-

163

able shop, for which I'd be happy to pay you rent for its use. The premises would still belong to you. Since I understand from Sarah that you have a nimble brain and can read and write, it would be advantageous if you would see to the accounts and bookkeeping, for which naturally, I would pay you. Apart from that, unless you wished to work in the shop yourself, I suggest we install some older person to actually sell Goss Cider, or even a young lad, though I am in favour of an older person myself. Now, tell me what you think, Loveday. Is the idea completely repugnant to you?'

Her eyes were shining. 'Not at all! It appeals to me very much, Mr Goss.'

Impulsively she rose from the settee and ran to his chair, putting her arms round him for a moment and pressing a grateful kiss on his cheek. The gesture touched him unexpectedly, and from that moment he was her champion.

'How can I thank you for thinking of it?' Loveday went on huskily. 'It puts some purpose into my life, and I shall be proud and honoured to play a small part in the success of Goss cider.'

Her heart sang at the thought. The generous offer his father had made knitted the fabric of the relationship between her and Adam even more firmly together. In a small way, she was already part of his life through his father's suggestion. Suddenly embarrassed at the way she was kneeling by Norman's chair, she returned to her seat, looking for approval from the other two. Surely they would not object, or think it strange, the anxious thought flitted into her mind? But one look at the delight on their faces, and it was obvious they did not.

'How clever of you to have thought of it, Father,' Sarah cried. If there was the slightest hint of condescension in her voice it wasn't meant or heeded.

Loveday's mind worked like quicksilver.

'I could ask Mrs Mundy, the old seamstress who used to do a little work for my mother. Her eyes are too bad to do the sewing now, but she'd be glad of the work behind a shop counter all day, especially if her crippled husband could be

164

sitting there beside her. Poor old dabs have been sorely in need of work lately, and there's none more respectable and sober as those two!'

'How good you are to think of them, Loveday,' Sarah exclaimed. 'You have a generous heart.'

Adam's warm smile said far more than Sarah's words. Loveday was his dear sweet girl, spirited and rising above all obstacles. She was a survivor, his Loveday, and in the midst of it all, sparing a thought to be charitable to those less fortunate than herself. Norman Goss nodded his approval as Loveday lowered her eyes, her cheeks pink with excitement and joy at the way things were going.

And oh, just a tinge of guilt at the way these fine people thought she was being so kind as to think of the Mundys, when in reality it had been a flash of inspiration on her part to mention them. Knowing they'd be servile and grateful, and Loveday Willard would be goin' up a step in the world because folks would be sure and call at an establishment where the respectable Mundys worked, bein' such God-fearin' church-goers. And the Mundys had had a finger in everyone's pie over the years, with Mrs Mundy doin' the sewing for half the dames in Taunton, and old Chipper Mundy, who'd fashioned many a crib with loving hands for a new-born bab before the rheumatism screwed up his joints.

There'd be no shortage of fine folk willing to patronise Goss Cider at the little shop in Taunton . . . and not least of Loveday's inspired suggestion had been the desire to see the admiration in Adam's eyes, and the nod of satisfaction on his father's face. She needed their approval like the desert needed rain, and knowing that she had it sent her spirits soaring.

'So be it,' Norman declared, as solemn as if intoning a legal oath. 'Once you're settled back home again, Loveday, I'll call and see you and we'll see about installing the stock and altering the name-sign. I won't rush you, my dear – '

'Oh, I don't mind!' She was bubbling inside at the very idea. It would be a new life, a new beginning, and Adam's name would be above her shop door. It was a sign . . . an omen . . . Meg Willard would be in no doubt of it, and Loveday was her mother's daughter. Norman stood up and patted the top of her shining head.

'Well, we'll give it a few days for you to think it over, in case you think of changing your mind, eh? This is only a verbal agreement so far. I'll come to see you, and if you're still of the same mind, I'll get things started and have a legal document drawn up to say you're leasing the premises to me for a term to our mutual satisfaction.'

The eloquence of him passed over Loveday's head. There'd be no changing of her mind! Not when his father's suggestion was drawing her life and Adam's that much closer together!

'I'll leave you three young ones to talk together,' Norman went on, his cough reminding them all that he wasn't a well man and needed his sleep. Sarah jumped up at once and offered her father her arm, throwing a smiling glance back towards the two left in the firelit room. And once the door closed behind them, Adam seized Loveday's hands in his own. There was no doubting his delight at the turn of events.

Loveday looked into his brown eyes that always reminded her of the richness of treacle toffee, feeling that she must surely burst with love for him. And he found it hard to keep his own desires in check at the radiance that glowed on her face. As if she'd been given the moon and stars because of a modest little suggestion on his father's part . . . but it was more than that, of course. Adam was as charmed by the idea of their two lives becoming entwined as Loveday.

'Oh Adam,' she breathed. 'Isn't it marvellous? How kind it was of your father to do this for me.'

'And for himself, don't forget,' if he didn't bring the prosaic into his voice, he knew it would be hoarse with passion, and already his feelings were in danger of running away with him. And he'd vowed to himself that he wouldn't be the one to defile his innocent Loveday. No-one would touch her until she came to him unsullied on their wedding-night. Adam felt the warm quick little breath of her on his cheek and swallowed back the urge to crush her in his arms here on the soft carpet in front of the flickering fire in his father's house. The urge was in danger of becoming a raging need, but somehow he controlled it.

'Father will have thought long and hard about this before he made the suggestion, Loveday, and he'll be certain it will be a profitable venture. But I'm none the less pleased for all that!'

'Pleased!' Loveday pouted, her cheeks still flushed, her eyes shining like deep sapphires. Around her face, the corn-coloured hair was like a golden halo, wisps of it slipping away from the swathe into which it was pinned. She looked like an angel, Adam thought, his breath catching in his throat, a beautiful golden angel, but his carefully measured words had the effect of making her withdraw from him a little, which was all to the good at that moment, from the uncomfortably pulsating feelings in his groin.

'What an inadequate word to use for something so exciting!' Loveday cried. She shook off Adam's hands, rose to her feet and skipped round the room, her skirts billowing out around her, 'How can you talk of merely being pleased, when it feels as if all my nerves are tingling with pleasure at having some purpose in my life again, when I thought I had nothing but dreary years ahead of me? Nothing but the gloom of being Finch's widow, when I wasn't even his wife in the real sense of the word . . . '

The elation vanished as if a cloud had blotted out the sun. Because if it hadn't been for Finch dying, she wouldn't have been in the position she was now, to accept Norman Goss's offer, and to know he was in fact setting the seal of approval on her relationship with Adam. And it was because of her that Finch had done the terrible thing to himself . . . the laughter changed to tears so quickly, Adam could hardly believe it.

At once, he had leapt to her side, to gather her shaking body into his arms, to feel the softness of her breasts pressed against his chest, and the curving shape of her moulding into him. But now there was only tenderness filling his mind as he held her sobbing frame close, his hands gentle on her hair, feeling the damp heat of her cheeks next to his own and her trembling mouth as she tried to fight back the tears.

'Hush my little love, hush. You've had so much to contend with, and you've been so brave. But it had to come out this way, or you'd have burst with the tension inside you. God knows I wanted to kill you and the butcher both when I heard you'd married him, but having heard from various sources what your father is like when he gets his rag up, I can understand how you were driven to it. And finding him the way you did must have been a dreadful shock. But it's over, Loveday. It's a chapter of your life that's past, and you're very young still.'

As he stroked the softness of her hair and felt its silkiness slip out even more from its confining pins, Adam felt a slight misgiving. Her eyes swam with tears as they looked up so trustingly into his face, and at that moment it was a child's face. He had almost forgotten how young she was, no more than sixteen, but with that child-woman air she had, it was easy to forget. But for a child of sixteen to cope with all she'd been through, it was only to be expected that this sudden new security was shaking her as emotionally as anything else. He must take care not to go too fast himself. If there was one thing they had on their side, it was time. He ignored the fact that he'd thought as much before, and then she'd upped and married the butcher . . . this time, there was no man alive who could keep them apart.

'Loveday, look at me,' he said gently, as her lids closed momentarily over the brimming eyes. Her long lashes were darkened and spiked with tears, her petal-soft face streaked with them. The blue eyes opened obediently, and Adam kissed the salty cheeks one by one, with no trace of passion.

Neither of them noticed when Sarah opened the door to come and sit with them, then decided against it, and closed it as quietly behind her. They noticed nothing but the flickering firelight illuminating the other's features, and the emotion charged atmosphere between them.

'We will be married, I promise you,' Adam went on, his

voice low and tense, because suppressing his natural desire to pull her more savagely into his arms was taking its toll. 'But you need time to recover mentally and emotionally from the last few months, and my presence here is partly hindering that recovery.'

Loveday's voice was fierce now. 'How can you say that? If you cannot see that I'm more alive now than I've been in my whole life, and if you don't know that it's all because of you, then you're a fool, Adam Goss!'

'And you're a fiery little creature that can twist me round her little finger by one flash from those sparkling eyes,' he agreed, laughing. 'But this time I know I'm right, Loveday. I'll have no arguments – and if our love is worth anything, then it's worth waiting for, isn't it? Worth a little time apart – or don't you think you're capable of waiting patiently for me? You won't be looking at any other young men while I'm gone, will you? No brawny farmer's sons who'll call in at the new Goss Cider shop for their measures?'

He was merely teasing. Confident in the love they shared, Adam never seriously considered that he could lose her a second time . . . and as she swayed into his arms in answer to this tender embrace, he missed the sudden look of shock that crossed Loveday's face, and the blanching of her skin as mention of brawny farmer's sons brought her hated cousin Matt Willard vividly to mind. He need never doubt her, she said hoarsely in his ear, and made her jangling nerves relax as he protested that he never would, and surely she must know he was only jesting.?

Matt and his brother Zeb trudged out across the fields early next morning, their thick boots squelching in the sea of red mud that oozed up through the sparse covering of grass. It was a dripping, melting day, and it did nothing for Matt's temper to have Zeb breathing noisily alongside him. There were fences to be mended, and the life of a farmer didn't stop for the vagaries of the weather, but a less docile companion might have made the task ahead of them more bearable. It was bad enough to be working in dank conditions where the

169

cold and wet penetrated one's very bones, without this stupid oaf beside him.

Matt had been in ill humour for days now. If he'd ever admitted such a thing to himself, he was sorely troubled about his cousin Loveday; oh, not with any thought of doin' the right thing by 'er, since the startling news that Polly Reeves had confided to him. But what was to happen now? He asked himself the question a dozen times a day. That old Finch Viney had sliced his wrist and freed his new wife was one thing, but presumably only he and Polly and Loveday herself knew the truth o' her situation – and Loveday didn't even know that Matt was aware of it!

No, what troubled him was the thought that she might go blabbin' to her father on the truth of it now. Or even come a-runnin' to his mother, her Aunt Emily . . . not that there was much love lost atween they two . . . but they was fam'ly all the same, and it was fam'ly a body ran to in trouble. Matt knew well enough that there was no fam'ly like his own for closin' in when danger threatened from outside, and none like his for findin' a fittin' punishment when one of their own had hurt another. The thought of his father's wrath coupled with his Uncle Ralph's if they ever got to know he'd been the one to put Loveday up the spout was enough to make his skin crawl. And the only one he could take out his temper on was the half-baked brother plodding alongside him.

What made it even made galling was that there was no-one he could tell about how good it had all been at the time, Matt thought with a surge of resentment. Nor that secretly he thought himself a fine ol' boy for havin' made a bab in Loveday's belly. When he wasn't worried sick at bein' found out, with his guts sawin' inside him, he felt as crowy as a bantam cock on a shit-heap . . . and there wasn't a bloody soul he could tell it to.

'Come on, you bugger,' he shouted to Zeb, sprinting into a run. 'I'll race you to the fences.'

And it didn't help when, after winning for most of the distance, Zeb's lumbering frame suddenly lurched past him,

170

to crash into the rotten fence post and send it splintering to the ground with Zeb sprawling on top of it.

'You're supposed to be mendin' em, not breakin' 'em down, you silly bugger,' Matt hauled his brother to his feet and cuffed him one round the side of the head.

'It was your fault. You started the race. You were so close behind me I couldn't help fallin' – '

'Oh, shut up. You're about as much use to anybody as a fart in a colander. I suppose you'll be tellin' me next you forgot to bring the hammer and twine,' Matt said sarcastically.

'No I didn't,' Zeb pulled them out of his pocket, rubbing at the side of his head where his skin throbbed. He couldn't fathom out what he'd done now to irritate Matt, but it never took much, and his slow-witted brain couldn't be bothered to try to work it out. He dragged up the broken fence post and looked at it doubtfully. With all his weight on it, it had snapped right off at the base.

'Well, don't stand there all day, blockhead. Find a stake somewhere so we can bind what's left of the post to it and drive it back in the ground. Christ's boots, do I have to do your thinkin' for you as well? If I don't get me somebody sensible to talk to pretty soon, I swear I'll be as dippy as you!'

Zeb cast his eyes around for a likely piece of wood to act as a stake. His face brightened. Over his shoulder he threw out a piece of information Matt might be interested to hear.

'I saw a friend o' yourn yestermorn, Matt. That dandy gent who come up 'ere for the cockfightin' a few times. Do 'ee mind who I mean?'

Matt's pale blue eyes lost a little of their belligerence.

'Adam Goss, you mean? Where'd you see 'im then? He's away up near Bristol somewheres. You tellin' me you got spirited away in the night and seen 'im in one o' your funny turns?'

'No, I ain't,' Zeb never lost his mild-mannered tone, though his ruddy cheeks were even ruddier at Matt's sceptical look.

'It were when I took the cart over to the Lundy place – I

171

mean the Goss place yestermorn to get the pommy for the cattle, and I seen 'im there. Large as life and twice as pretty, he were, walkin' round the place wi' 'is father, so there!'

Matt spun him round. Lord dammit, he thought he'd done Matt a favour by tellin' 'im, but it seemed his brother wasn't angry with 'im, just eager to know more.

'Why the four an' 'alf didn't you tell me this before, you loon? Me an' Adam could 'ave been jawin' together a couple o' days since, if he's been home awhile.'

'I couldn't tell you afore I seen 'im, could I? An' that were only yestermorn – '

'If you say that once more I'll throttle you,' Matt snapped, but his thoughts were streaking ahead. Adam Goss ... it was like the answer to a prayer. Here was the very person in whom to confide. Hadn't he boasted to Adam that he'd be the one to lift Loveday's skirts? And wasn't this news of the bab the very proof that he'd done as he'd said he would? Never mind the hasty weddin' to the butcher ... Adam was a learnin' man. He'd be able to tot up the months on his fingers and know the truth o' Matt's words when the time came for Loveday's birthin'. Never mind what other folks thought about it bein' a hasty hatchin' after a honeymoon dip; Matt knew, and Adam would know, that the bab was a Willard bab as no other, sired and mothered by good Willard stock!

There was an endin' to gloomy days after all, Matt thought, as the notion of it sped through his mind. The two of 'em could watch Loveday grow ... at least he could, and Adam could when he came down to these parts again ... and hide their sniggers together. A secret had no relish unless it was shared, an' knowin' that never in this world would he dare to acknowledge the bab as his own to the fightin' Willard family, at last he'd found the perfect crony with whom to share his bit o' news.

'Is this piece o' wood all right?' He heard Zeb's docile voice in the midst of his milling thoughts, and grunted his approval. But Zeb sighed with relief. He could never follow the quick-thinking of his brother, and he was often too slow

172

to miss out on a clipped shoulder or a fist in the face when Matt got his dander up with 'im. But just now he could see by the lift to Matt's chin, and the way he went striding about the sticky red earth and hammered in the stakes Zeb handed him as if he had somebody's throat beneath his big hands, that Matt was in a fine and cocky mood again.

To Zeb, it didn't matter why. Nor did he ever dream, as his mind wandered off in search of the music of the morning that came from the flutter of butterflies wings and the chatter of crickets and the sighing of the breeze through bracken and gorse, that his striving to please his brother had already begun a chain of events from which there was no turning back. As destructive as it was inevitable.

CHAPTER THIRTEEN

The fencin' took all mornin', and then there was work to do at the farm, turnin' the cattle back into the fields again from where they'd not wander off now. There was milkin' to be done and the feedin' of the pigs and cleanin' out of the pens, and the endless feedin' and beddin' of the beasts, and the humpin' o' the cartload o' pommy, the waste dry straw and apple pulp from the cider makin' that always went to any farm willin' to collect it. And Matt took it as a sign of good fortune that his father had sent Zeb down to the Goss place to bring the cartload back here and deliver the news that Adam Goss was back in Taunton Deane.

Late, o' course, Matt thought scathingly, thinking that his brother might have managed to tell him the previous night, and that he needn't have wasted another day afore gettin' some decent company, instead of his halfwit brother. Still, mebbe Adam was stayin' a spell, and they could

173

arrange another cockfightin' match if he'd a taste for it, an' have a few wagers on the side.

By the time his day was ended, Matt was perking up by the minute. He'd have ridden over to the Goss place earlier in the day if he could have been spared, but his father was in a tetchy mood and it didn't do to get him riled at such times. The two younger Willard boys had already had a switch taken to their backsides for cheekin' their father that day, and Matt had no wish to be the next. Big as he was, Jack was bigger, and a son was a son to the end of his days. If he needed a thrashing, he'd get it, as all the Willard boys knew to their cost.

So it was early evening when Matt finally set out to make the re-acquaintance of his one-time friend, Adam Goss. Astride one of the stocky Quantock ponies that was sure-footed on the treacherous ground, icy with frost now after the rain-sodden day, Matt picked his way along the dark narrow tracks. Lit by a pale moon, he saw the outline of Goss House ahead of him, with the long low outbuildings of the cider sheds, and the symmetrical rows of apple trees beyond.

His blood quickened. He'd already partaken generously of a jug of Goss cider at supper, and he felt in an expansive mood. He was goin' to enjoy tellin' Adam about his pretty little cousin and her fruity little snuffy. By the cowcake, but it seemed a lifetime ago! Not too long for Matt to recall how sweet it was, though, nor to savour it in his memory, as the glitter in his eyes and the throb in his loins reminded him.

He'd be wary of approachin' her for the present though. What with the way his Ma had told him she'd turned a bit queer in the head since Finch's death, according to Polly Reeves, an' didn't want no visitin' from folks, not even kin. An' specially since she must be showin' round with the bab a little by now. The thought of it excited him, nonetheless.

He pictured her the last way he'd pinned her beneath him, in the tiny room at the farm, her silky pale hair all spread across the pillow, lookin' up at him mutely, afraid to yell because of what he'd said he'd do to her if she did. Afraid of

174

rousin' the rest o' the Willards, and hearin' Matt tell how she'd begged him for it.

How he'd forged into her then, and how he ached suddenly to do it again, he thought savagely. Feelin' the roundness of her soft belly firmed up because of the bab that was inside it. The bab that belonged to both on 'em, and nobody else! It was enough to make the seed spill out of him again just at the recollection of her head twistin' beneath him, and he had to make a great effort to control it. He had no wish to spend the next couple of hours in sticky breeches.

But he'd done summat no fancy town gent had done, he crowed to himself. Sired a bab . . . unless Adam had done it somewhere up in Bristol or wherever it was he was workin'. Matt doubted it. His sort would do things proper, the weddin' afore the couplin', and anyway, it took a fine and lusty fellow like himself to make a bab! By the time he arrived at Goss House, Matt was cock o' the roost in his head. He slithered off the back of the pony, and slapped its flank, feeling his head spin a midgin and his knees buckle ever so slightly, but by the time this night was out, he fully expected that he and Adam Goss would be drunker than lords, and he'd merely got a head start, that was all.

Inside Goss House, Loveday and Sarah were dressing for the evening meal. Loveday loved the elegance of the way they lived. It had never been this way at her father's house, though she dimly remembered a time when Meg had tried to bring a more genteel way of living to the Willard household. It had been a losing battle from the start.

'Why should we pretend to do as mincey rich folks do, when the old ways have allus been good enough for we?' Ralph would roar at his cowering wife. Not that she cowered too often, but there were times when he raised his hand to her and reminded her that in a Willard marriage, it was the man who set the style of the house. And at such times he would always revert to his farming dialect, as if to remind Meg still more that there'd be no changing him.

Loveday guessed that Polly Reeves was probably finding

out the same thing for herself. The only one to change Ralph Willard was Ralph Willard himself. There was no woman alive who could do it.

Maybe if Finch had lived and they'd settled into some kind of life together, Loveday could have brought a little of her mother's breeding into the Viney household. She was sure she could have done so, for there was no-one so easily pliable as Finch, and it would have been child's play to make him do the things she wanted.

Loveday shuddered, wishing thoughts of Finch hadn't entered her mind. She tried not to think of him at all, but at times she just couldn't seem to help it. She seemed to see his fat pink face looking at her reproachfully, or glistening with sweat as he tried to do his husbandly duty by her on the night they were wed. Or else the sheer horror of the moment she'd screamed out the truth of her pregnancy at him, and his bolting for the chamber-pot at the realisation.

Sometimes she couldn't rid her mind of him, and at such times Loveday knew Adam was right. She needed time for the mental and emotional scars to fade. Maybe she wouldn't ever be able to go to Adam in the way a loving wife should, after all she'd suffered at the hands of Matt and then Finch's dismal failure ... maybe it had unknowingly soured her responses towards all men ... how could she tell? She loved Adam desperately, but until they lay in the same bed together and he possessed her body and soul, how could she tell what her own reactions would be?

Loveday shuddered again, wishing she didn't get these terrifying thoughts, but knowing she had too questing a mind to ignore them. They chilled her through and through, and the only way she could blot them out was to think instead of these lovely days she and Adam were sharing. Days she hadn't even dared to imagine before the joy of his unexpected arrival. She accepted that he would leave soon, and it was the only cloud on her horizon, but the promise of their future together was like the coming of spring after a dull and dismal winter, and just as certain.

She turned to her closet and took out the dress she would

wear that evening at dinner. A rich deep rust colour that accentuated the contrast of her flaxen hair and deep blue eyes. She splashed cold water on to her face and shoulders until they glowed, knowing she wanted to look beautiful for Adam. A small humming sound escaped Loveday's lips, and she wondered briefly when she had been so truly happy.

In the drawing-room, Adam stretched his long legs before the fire and thought of her. His love, his darling... and wondered whether to tell his father just how far their relationship had gone, or whether to leave it for the time being and let things take their course. Adam and his father had become very close in this past week, and he knew Norman was loath to see his son leave for the tunnel workings again.

Adam too, knew that his heart wasn't really in the move. But he'd made a promise to himself and to his foreman, that he'd return and see the present work through at least. He must go back to Box, even though the heart of him would be left behind here. The ambition he'd nurtured for years to work as Mr Brunel worked seemed to be a very feeble one now. He felt guilty at his own lack of interest in what had once been the only thing he'd burned to do. But that was before Loveday.

The fire crackled companionably in the hearth, throwing its usual warmth around the room, and lighting up the comfortable home. Adam looked round thoughtfully. Yes, it was madness to try to compare the hazards of crawling underground in grey mud and filth with tons of rock above, and sweating, blaspheming men for company, with the life he'd once known, here and in Bristol. The kind of life he and Loveday would share once they were man and wife.

A discreet tap on the door and the entrance of Mrs Hiatt made him turn his head. The housekeeper's face was dark and tight-lipped with disapproval as she folded her arms over her bolstered bosom.

'Yes, what is it, Mrs Hiatt?' Adam enquired. Some problem in the kitchen, no doubt, and until his father came stiffly downstairs to join him, Adam supposed he'd have to try to sort it out.

'There's a – a *person* to see you, Sir,' Mrs Hiatt's voice said that whoever the person was, it had no business being here. Adam felt his mouth twitch in amusement until he saw the glare in the woman's eyes and hastily stifled his laughter lest she thought he was laughing at her.

'What kind of person, Mrs Hiatt? Has he stated his business – assuming it *is* a gentleman?'

The housekeeper snorted. 'He's no gennulman, Sir, and that's for certin knowledge! I'd get rid of 'un as soon as 'tis proper, if I was you, Sir, beggin' pardon for puttin' my spoke in to what's no business o' mine!'

'Good Lord, somebody's been upsetting you, Mrs Hiatt.' Adam got to his feet, unable to stop the smile spreading across his mouth now. 'If it's some tinker, I'll soon send him on his way.'

She sniffed, not too sure whether the young gent was funning with her or not. ' 'Tis worse than a tinker I'd call that 'un!'

She swished out of the room with her black skirts rustling in indignation. As Adam followed her out, she paused with her hand on the door leading to the kitchen quarters.

'You just get rid of 'un afore your father sees the state he's in, young Sir,' she said tartly. 'And remember that decent folk come sober to their dinner table, and that yourn'll be ready in half an hour!'

The door banged behind her, as she was prompted to react more strongly than usual to the likes of one of they rough Willards darin' to call here of an evening, when decent folks were gettin' ready to act civil to one another! The cheek o' the varmint! He hadn't asked for Miss Loveday, so mebbe he didn't know she was staying' here, and a good thing too. Otherwise it was like as not that all the rest on 'em would come a'callin'. Mrs Hiatt's face went white at the thought. The girl was only to be pitied, and they did say as how her mother had been summat of a lady . . . but as for the rest on 'em . . .

Adam opened the front door of the house and peered out into the darkness. At first he could make out nothing but a swaying bundle of branches on the moonlit steps in front of the house, and then the branches steadied themselves for a moment and he realised it was a set of arms and legs attached to an unsteady trunk.

'What do you want?' Adam asked sharply, as the reek of cider met his nostrils. 'If it's charity you're after, you'd best come back sober, for we've no truck with drunkards here.'

His voice trailed away as the woolly-headed figure chuckled. There was something familiar about him . . . if the entrance-hall hadn't been so dimly lit, and the fellow half hidden in the shadows, Adam might have recognised him instantly. As it was, it took a few more seconds before it suddenly dawned on him who his visitor was.

'Ain't you pleased to see me, Adam?' Matt drawled. 'We've 'ad some fine ol' sport together, you an' me, ain't we? With the fightin' cocks an' all! I ain't here for your charity! Just to chinwag over a new kind o' sport I've been enjoying till recent. One you'd like to hear about, my fine friend!'

'Matt Willard!' Adam thought there was no-one he'd less like to see at that moment. The oaf was already three sheets to the wind, and likely to start hollering about the place if he wasn't humoured. And his father's health wouldn't stand too much raucous excitement . . . besides, upstairs Loveday was getting ready for dinner. If she came down and saw her cousin behaving so disgracefully, she'd be shamed and humiliated.

Adam grabbed Matt by the arm and hauled him away from the house, the two of them stumbling down the flight of steps and into the darkness of the gardens.

'Hey, hey, hey, wait a minute,' Matt spluttered. 'I got summat to tell you. Summat that'll make your toes curl, me boy!'

'All right, but you can tell me somewhere else,' Adam said quickly. All he wanted was to get him as far from the house as possible. Somewhere where they wouldn't be overheard. With any luck, Matt would get his tale over and done with and he could send him packing before dinner. Adam steered him past the cider sheds where the huge wooden presses stood, and the racks of jars and jugs proudly bearing the name of Goss

Cider on them. Past them all until they reached the fermenting shed, farthest away from the house. Adam bundled Matt inside, where the sweet-sour smell of the fermenting juice in the huge kegs filled the air. He closed the door behind the two of them, and got him up the wooden steps to the platform that ran round the top of the shed, where Adam knew the lanterns stood ready. Quickly, he lit one of the wicks, and the lantern threw a soft warm light that bobbed about as he hung the lantern into position on its nail and turned to look at Matt Willard.

'Good God, what have you been doing to yourself?' Adam exclaimed. 'You look terrible!'

Matt breathed in deeply, a stupid smile on his coarse features. 'Terrible and like to be more so, with this lovely smell to fill me lungs still more, boy!' He turned his head to take in the sight of the cider kegs filled nearly to the brim with the golden liquid, still brown-frothed as it worked to throw off its impurities.

'Christ's boots, it's a drunkard's delight to be in a place like this,' he grunted.

Adam was suddenly impatient. Had the fool come all this way on some whim just to talk nonsense with him? He shook Matt's arms.

'Tell me what you want and get out of here,' he snapped. 'My family will be downstairs for dinner soon, and they'll wonder where I am – '

'Oh ah, your posh fam'ly,' Matt's moods were mercurial tonight. He was suddenly resentful of these fine city folks who'd invaded his territory with their long noses that looked down at folks who'd lived here for generations. He was sick of girls like Grace Goss, who'd flounced off to London and wouldn't have given him her snot-wipings. And girls like Sarah, whom he'd known very well had had a fancy for him, and who hadn't looked at him twice since he'd almost forgot himself and got over-amorous with 'er. Not that it bothered Matt that much, for he'd as quickly tired of the whey-faced city girl; it was the principle of the thing that mattered.

And now Adam, whom he'd really thought of as his crony,

was standin' here lookin' disapprovingly at him, every inch the master . . . Matt's temper boiled over.

'Mebbe you'd like to hear a bit o' news about *my* fam'ly,' Matt's harsh voice seemed to echo round the wooden building, and Adam thanked his stars they weren't likely to be overheard as long as he managed to keep the other appeased.

'All right, if I must,' he said indulgently. 'What bit of news could you possibly have that would be of interest to me, Matt? Get it over with and then leave, if you please.'

'Then leave, if you please,' Matt mimicked insultingly, and then, as Adam grabbed him by the scruff of his coat in a burst of anger, he started yelling.

'All right, let go of me and I'll tell you! It's about your precious little Loveday, if you want to know. Only she ain't yourn and never will be, I shouldn't think. Not now she's gone and got herself up the spout – '

The lash of Adam's hand across his throat winded him for a second.

'What are you saying, you toe-rag?' Adam shouted into his face. A red mist seemed to rise up in front of him, and for a moment he thought he could kill this leering oaf swaying in front of him.

'That stopped you, didn't it?' Matt went on hoarsely. 'Got herself up the spout, she has, an' who put the bab there?'

Adam lunged towards him again, this time pinning him against the wooden wall of the shed. The lantern swung with the vibration, the dancing light illuminating the frothy dark liquid in the kegs nearby.

For a moment Matt was taken by surprise at the strength of the other young man. Adam might have all the advantages of breeding and wealth, but Matt had never considered himself anybody's minion, certainly when it came to brute strength; but he had forgotten the effect that the months working in the Box tunnel had had on Adam, both physically and mentally, and he was beginning to discover that Adam Goss was afraid of no-one.

'You're not fit to lick Loveday's boots,' Adam grated. 'And you must be sick in the head to degrade her name with your foul suggestions.'

181

Matt found his voice again. 'They ain't so foul, my fine gent! They was very sweet if you want to know. Lyin' in the straw an' spreadin' her legs was every bit as sweet as I expected.'

He dodged the swing of Adam's fist. 'Told you I'd be the one to break 'er in, didn't I? Want to know the details, do you?' he crowed. 'First in the barn an' then in her bed – '

'Shut up, you bastard,' Adam's breeding deserted him as he almost screamed the words. 'You keep your filthy shit-talk to yourself. What girl would want to lie with a stinking ape like you, anyway?'

Matt's eyes glittered. He kicked out at Adam with a vicious thrust at his groin that sent Adam staggering backwards, his face contorted in agony.

'Your sister seemed to take a fancy to me once,' he heard Matt's smug voice. 'But she don't have the tits on her that Loveday's got. Know what I mean, boy? A man needs a good handful to nuzzle against on a cold night.'

'You're lying,' Adam shouted, nearly beside himself with rage and pain. 'She'd never give in to you – '

'Didn't have no choice, did she? And didn't take long gettin' to like it neither. An' ended up with a bab in her belly, like I told you.'

Adam suddenly felt sick. He was talking almost to himself now, his eyes flashing hate at the rough lout shadowed against the lantern-light and seeming to tower over him in triumph and aggression.

'She told me she was as pure at Finch's death as when she married him. The poor devil was impotent . . . and I believed her . . . I still believe her.'

Matt gave a coarse laugh. 'I daresay he was. Either that or a pansy-boy! Real clever of my little Lovey-dovey, weren't it? Gettin' hitched to the butcher to give my bab a name! The Willards were never slow when it come to craftiness.'

Adam had been leaning back against the wooden wall of the shed, arms outstretched as if needing support to keep erect. But it was just as if something suddenly exploded inside his head at Matt Willard's sickening revelations. Whether he really believed them or not didn't matter any more. All he wanted to do was to stop the grating voice and the flicker of recollection in the farmer's eyes. It degraded Loveday even more to know the oaf was still savouring every moment he'd spent with her . . .

As if he was a coiled spring suddenly unleashed, Adam felt himself hurl forward to push against Matt with all his strength. He was already drunk with fury, and semi-intoxicated in the fruity enveloping smell from the fermenting cider. He barely noticed the scream of terror from Matt's lips before he too lost his balance and followed him into the deep frothy brown liquid.

For what seemed like endless seconds Adam felt himself plunging deeper into the blackness before he kicked out automatically and struggled gasping to the surface.

His ears sang. His eyes stung. He gulped for air like a grounded fish. His lungs felt full to bursting. Stars were exploding inside his head. There was cider outside and inside his body. The sticky brown froth clung to his hair and got in his eyes. He was a thousand times more disorientated than any sociable jug of cider had ever made him. His eyes wouldn't focus. They streamed cider. He threshed about trying to find the curved oaken side of the keg, and it seemed an ocean away from him. A sickening sweet ocean that was going to drown him if he didn't find a way out of it soon. A desperate feeling of panic gripped him as he tried to remember the rudiments of swimming.

'Adam, help me!' He heard the scream close by, and it was as if a tidal wave suddenly closed over his head as clawing hands pushed and pulled at his body. His head went under again, and when he managed to surface, it was to hear Matt still screaming and blubbering, all the bravado gone. 'I can't swim! I'll drown! Help me, you bastard. Don't let me drown.'

Why not? Savagely, with a desire more basic than lust, Adam knew that was exactly what he wanted to do. It would be so easy, just to push the struggling woolly-headed pig beneath the cider, and to let him struggle until there was no more life left in him. To let him drown in the stuff, his lungs clogged with froth, his body bloated and distorted . . . it was a temptation that was almost irresistible.

Whether Adam would have carried it out or not, he was too stupefied with the raw cider inside him to consider. But some instinct greater than his fury somehow gave him the strength to haul Matt's head above the surface, to hear him gasping and retching and threshing, the normally gutteral voice falsetto with terror as he continued to beg for help.

Adam's legs felt too heavy to move the few feet to the rim of the keg that was becoming vaguely visible through his stinging eyes. He thought he would never move them. There seemed to be no co-ordination between his head and his limbs. He couldn't even remember clearly any more just how he and Matt Willard had got themselves into this situation. The effort of trying to remember made his head spin like a top, and there was an enormous throbbing pain gathering above his temples.

His arm was beneath Matt's jaw now as he thrashed about trying to feel the edge of the oaken keg. It was taking so long he began to think he'd never find it, and they would circle round in the fermenting liquid until eternity claimed them both, locked together in a kind of embrace.

Adam felt a sudden wild urge to laugh, knowing that for some reason the sight of them would be totally ironic. To embrace someone meant you loved them, and though his senses were too befuddled to recall the reasons, he knew that for Matt Willard he felt only hate. But such an evil, all-consuming hate that it shocked Adam to the core to know he was capable of such a feeling. Even in the exploding muddle of his mind, the hate was there. Only the reason for it was blotted out by the intoxicating liquor that felt as if it was consuming him up, rather than the other way round. Gobbling him up with greedy, seductive, moist lips that were sweeter than any wine, red as the earth.

They gobbled at him, wanting his very soul, and he had to blink the froth out of his eyes to escape the illusion of so many glittering shiny lips, as the waves of cider rippled around him in the circle of light from the swaying lantern above. The light

184

began to dance more quickly and became brighter. Adam heard voices, fogged by the muzzy sensations in his ears. His arm was still beneath Matt's chin as if fastened there. He could hear his mumblings, so he hadn't throttled him yet, but maybe this was the moment they were both to perish. Now, with the bright lights stabbing his hurting eyes, and the voices surrounding him . . . he was hallucinating . . .

There was a sudden splash beside him, and then another, and strong arms were prising him and Matt Willard apart. Perversely, he heard himself scream as they were parted, as if he wanted to remain clinging to this devil-friend. If he was going to die, then so was Matt Willard, the bastard.

'Hold still now, Master Adam, we've got you,' the voice made sudden sense. He recognised it as belonging to one of the cider workers who worked for his father.

His father! Through the weird unreal sensations that gripped him, Adam had a moment of lucidity. Norman Goss would probably see this night's escapade as a frolicking by himself and Matt that had got out of hand. Assuming that they'd come into the cider shed for a free tasting and ended up with a dip that had almost had a tragic finale.

But such fleeting thoughts couldn't sober Adam up so easily. As he was hauled ignominiously out of the keg, he swayed on his feet, still hideously near the churning cider, and felt himself clutched by nausea. He retched against the wall of the shed, barely noticing his companion being dragged out beside him.

Matt had fared better than Adam. He was more used to the roughness of the cider, more used to consuming it in great quantities, and when there was some mention of a doctor, he shouted that he wanted no doctor, just to get on home and away from this madman who'd almost drowned him. For the first time Adam heard his father's voice speaking coldly and finally.

'I doubt that it was my son who began this affair,' Norman Goss dared anyone here to disagree with him. 'If you think you can find your own way home I suggest you leave this minute before I thrash your hide for ruining a good batch of

185

cider. If it wasn't for the fact that I'm thankful to find my son still alive, I'd have the law on you for this. As it is, if I ever catch you near here again, I shall personally leather you within an inch of your life. Do I make myself clear?'

'Ah, so 'ee do,' Matt slurred, his voice gravelly. He looked a grotesque sight, with scum tangled in his hair and terror silvering his pale eyes. Adam turned away from him, knowing that he must look as bad, and hating himself for it. And for letting his father down like this. He would have stumbled out an apology, if only he could have made his lips and tongue do what he wanted them to do.

He vaguely heard Matt lurching down the wooden steps and lumbering across the ground outside. He would have been left to find his own way home, since that was what he appeared to want, but for one of the cider workers, who hove him across the back of the sturdy little waiting pony and whacked its backside to send him on his way.

'We'd better see about getting a doctor for my son,' Norman said rapidly to another of his workers as Adam gave a low groan. There was a shooting pain low in his groin that fought with the hammering in his head. He wasn't sure which was worse, or if the worst thing was the agony in his arms where he'd tried to keep Matt above the cider, or the heaviness in his legs. He was enveloped in pain, but he shook his head violently, gasping as it almost took him off-balance and shot him headlong into the keg again.

'I don't need a doctor either, Father,' his voice sounded distant and woolly to his own ears. 'Just a bed and a cold cloth for my head, and no *fussing*!'

Norman's lips compressed. Tomorrow he'd find out the truth in all this, but then old Jed nudged him. He had Jed to thank for noticing the flickering light in the cider shed, and he felt obliged to listen to him now.

'I'd say he'll be all right after a night's sleep, Sir, 'cept for a head like a bucket, o' course. He'll be too pained to remember much on all o' this, I'll wager, but I'd say he's brought up most on it by now. The doctor ain't really needed. If you'll take my advice you'll put the young sir to bed with a tot o' brandy to keep up his strength and leave 'un there till morning!'

Adam retched again at the mention of brandy. Tonight's experience was enough to put a man off drinking for life, the thought staggered through his brain, but he saw his father nod and then willing hands helped him more carefully down the steps and out of the shed than they'd escorted Matt.

Outside the air was stunningly clean and pure after the musty atmosphere of the fermenting shed. It felt good for a moment, and then Adam felt his head reel anew at its effect. He felt so ill . . . no-one guessed how ill he felt . . . he tried to mumble an apology to his father, but he was hushed up and told that explanations could wait until morning. His feet dragged as the helpers almost lifted him along, and he wondered what a tale they'd have to tell tomorrow. It humiliated him afresh.

At the open door of the house he saw two figures standing anxiously, his sister and Loveday. There was something he had to scream at Loveday; it eluded him as Norman waved the two young women away and told them this was not women's work. He roared for a man – servant to follow the men up to Master Adam's room, to strip him and clean him and put him in fresh night-clothes before his head touched his pillow, for he saw no reason for his house to resemble a bawdy-house or a tavern.

He took charge, knowing it was the only way he could control his seething anger against his son for disgracing them all while they had a guest in the house, and showing himself for a drunkard in front of their workers. Norman's pride was sorely affronted, but he would die before he showed it. It was a mark of his breeding that a gentleman behaved as if no situation was beyond him, and none but himself knew how Adam's appearance had shocked him, nor how he fought to suppress the racking cough made worse by his sortie into the cold damp night air.

When he had seen the workers out of the house with a jug of cider for each of them for their trouble, Norman took a deep breath and strode into the drawing-room, where the two young women awaited him. Each turned anxious eyes towards him, and he forced a thin smile to his lips and forestalled their questions.

'If we are to have any dinner this evening, I suggest we go into the dining-room straight away before the food is all ruined. And since we are only three tonight, you will both have to make do with my company. I think a little singing and pianoforte playing would be agreeable afterwards, don't you? And let me say just once that Adam's name is forbidden at the dinner-table this evening and for the rest of this night. Now – an arm each, I think. A gentleman can consider himself fortunate to have such lovely companions!'

Loveday could only admire him. Everything he said was spoken in the same even tone, but there was never any question of going against his wishes. She smiled into his eyes, and might have wondered if she'd imagined the horror of seeing Adam brought in as if he'd been in some drunken brawl, save for the tension she felt in Norman Goss's arm as she rested her hand upon it.

If she had known it was her cousin, Matt Willard, who was blundering through the night slung across the back of his pony, who had been her beloved's companion earlier that evening, Loveday's small feeling of anxiety would have flared up into a raging fear.

CHAPTER FOURTEEN

Matt was beyond giving any instructions to the pony as it plodded steadily over the crunching ground towards the Willard farm. He ached all over, and those bastards who'd thrown him unceremoniously on the pony's back had been anything but gentle.

188

Still, he felt his mouth curve into a fleshy, beatific smile. It had all been worth it to see the look on Sir Poncey Goddammed's face when he'd told him about his Lovey-dovey, worth the soaking in the cider keg an' all. He sobered up rapidly as he thought of how near he'd come to drowning, and he'd been aware enough that Adam was near to keeping his face under the brew in his fury.

He heard himself muttering and shouting and blaspheming all the way across the darkened tracks, not really knowing where he was heading, and not really caring. It was nothing short of a bloody miracle, he marvelled later, when he felt the pony stop short so fast he nearly shot over its flanks, and squinting through red-rimmed eyes, Matt realised he was beside one of the outhouses at the Willard farm.

'Well, I'll be buggered,' he tried to whistle through lips like sausages. 'They do say the devil takes care on its own, so I reckon as how they must be right, me beauty.'

He slid off the animal's back and gave it a slap to send it on its way, chuckling into the darkness and swaying on his feet. Then the miracle of why the pony had stopped resolved itself, as a shadowy figure appeared in front of him, a wraith until he realised it was Zeb in his nightshirt, with a blanket draped round his shoulders.

'Is that you, Matt?' Zeb whispered hoarsely.

'God's teeth, who the bloody hell d'you think it is?' Matt snarled, his heart thumping erratically. 'What d'you think you're doin' outside like this?'

Was it the middle of the night or summat? He couldn't think sensibly. It had been mid-evening when he'd left the Goss place, but since then he'd jogged for hours and hours on the pony's back, going round in circles probably, and every bone in his body felt stretched like elastic and just as ready to snap.

'I been lookin' for you, Matt,' Zeb went on placidly. 'I made your excuses to Pa and pretended you was asleep in bed. He was about ready to tan your hide when you didn't show your face.'

The fact that this loon had covered up for him irritated

189

Matt even more. He took a few steps, and it felt as if his legs were about to crumble. He'd never make it quietly up the twisting staircase indoors. He'd have to bed down in the barn. It wouldn't be the first time, and mebbe his sodden clothes would dry off a bit if he wrapped himself in a bundle of straw. He shrugged away from his brother.

'Piss off,' he hissed. Why in God's name did it feel as if the whole world was against him this night? Hadn't he done what he set out to do? Hadn't he and Adam chortled over the fact that he'd won his bet and got his leg across his little Lovey-dovey?

The frown on his forehead deepened. No, by God, it hadn't turned out the way he'd intended it to, and now he remembered it all very clearly. That poncey Adam had nearly drowned him and he'd never forgive him for that. But he'd needed to crow over his little secret, God damn it, and Adam had spoiled everything by turning all churchified on him, as if he'd gone and done summat criminal, when all the world knew a maid was meant for beddin'.

His pale eyes gleamed. He turned and looked back towards Zeb, standing uncertainly in his blanket shroud.

'Come in the barn and chinwag a spell,' Matt said with deceptive friendship. 'First off you can find me a horse-blanket while I strip off this wet clobber.'

Zeb followed trustingly. 'Where you been, Matt? Been takin' a swim? I thought you couldn't swim. You been a-drinkin' too, Matt?'

On and on he went like a wheel. Well, he'd soon shut up when Matt got started, he thought gloatingly. It was about time this half-wit got his education completed. He'd learn a thing or two tonight . . . and if his tale hadn't got the reception he'd expected from Adam, then at least he wouldn't get half-killed by his loon of a brother! It was about time Zeb learned there was more to matin' than the frantic couplin' of a cock an' a hen, or the awkward clambering of one beast aboard another. He was about to find out about the softness of a woman, and the sweet smell of her that could set a man's senses tinglin', and the excitement of ridin' her.

190

'Sit you down. Zeb,' Matt said, and grinned as his brother complied. Like a lamb to the bloody slaughter, he thought gleefully.

When Adam awoke, it seemed as if he'd hardly been asleep for more than a few minutes. Yet he knew it must have been more like hours, because the sky had that unearthly silvery light in it that came as dawn was approaching. He'd woken because his head thought it was somewhere near his feet, and he wasn't sure where one ache ended and the next began. But one thing of which he was quite sure was that he was now stone cold sober, with all that had transpired in the fermenting shed crystal clear in his mind.

And the pain of Matt's revelations overshadowed all the humiliation he'd felt on seeing his father appear. The shock of hearing that uncouth lout gloating about winning his bet and laying with Loveday . . . and all the rest of it . . . the worst of all, that Adam tried in vain to push away from his mind.

It couldn't be true. He wouldn't let it be true. He couldn't and wouldn't believe that his sweet Loveday could be so wicked and devious as Matt Willard had suggested. Already with child from their unlikely coupling, and then to marry the butcher merely in order to give her bastard child a name?

Adam felt the dryness in his throat, and ran his swollen tongue around his lips. An insistent voice inside his head told him to face things squarely, and not to be so besotted with love that he wouldn't admit that it was possible.

Hadn't Loveday given him every encouragement in her letters? Hadn't he fully expected her to be waiting for him to marry her, when she was a little older and recovered from the death of her mother? And hadn't he been stunned and perplexed as to her reasons for the sudden rush to the altar with Finch Viney, when he'd have sworn on a stack of bibles that Loveday was a match for her father any day, no matter how loudly he ranted at her to marry someone of his choice?

It just wasn't Loveday to submit meekly and willingly, unless there was a very special reason. The blood pounded

191

sickeningly in Adam's head as the tormented thoughts ran round his mind. There was no escaping them. And the deception still went on, he thought . . . she was hiding the fact of her pregnancy very well, for no-one would ever guess . . . Adam's thoughts became very bitter.

How long would it be before she announced to the world that the poor little widow had been left with a child to bring up? A child that would be born prematurely because of her grief, naturally. His thoughts veered away to another tack.

Hadn't Loveday told him tremblingly that Finch was impotent? That she was as pure now as when they were wed? Which was the lie? Adam sat up in bed, gritting his teeth as the room swam at his sudden movement. Suddenly he didn't want to face her. He couldn't ask her. Not yet. He couldn't trust himself. There was a violent side in him he hadn't even realised himself until last night. If Loveday's deep blue eyes brimmed with tears at his accusation he was as likely to shake her by the throat as to beg her forgiveness. He couldn't trust his own reactions. And the thought that she might shrink away from him in despair and admit that it was all true, was even worse to contemplate.

He strained his eyes to focus on the clock on his mantel. It was barely four o'clock. But already the decision was being made in Adam's mind. He moved carefully out of bed, wincing as the stab of pain in his groin reminded him of Matt's vicious kick, and dressed himself for travelling.

Within an hour he was ready to leave. In that time he'd written a letter to his father, begging his forgiveness for the shameful exhibition he'd shown him last night, and since he was due to leave here in a day or two anyway, he considered it best that he should leave right away. He would take the pony and trap into Taunton to await the coach for Bristol, and pay a boy a copper or two to bring it back to Goss House. Perhaps the next time they met, they would each be able to forget the unfortunate incident.

Adam had chewed the pencil before adding the final words to his letter. It would be very odd if he didn't mention the two young ladies.

'Please convey my regret to Sarah and her friend for not saying goodbye, but I feel it's best to go quickly. And give my good wishes to Mrs Viney in her new venture with Goss Cider.'

He signed it 'Your affectionate and contrite son, Adam.'

He stared at it when it was finished, knowing he was putting Loveday at a distance from himself by his formal wording. But for the present it was the only way he could bear to think of her. And since the rest of his letter was just as formal, he hoped his father would not think it strange.

Guiltily, Adam knew very well he would be saddened that Adam had chosen to go this way, sneaking off like a thief in the night; but for his own peace of mind he had to get away. He couldn't breathe here. He suddenly felt he was being stifled. He didn't stop to think of Loveday's reaction.

One day there would be a reckoning between them and he knew it. But to stay here right now and watch her lovely mobile face, with the suspicions festering inside him and yet totally unable to demand the truth from her, was more than he could do. There had been too much conviction in Matt Willard's voice.

Adam swung his travelling bag under his arm and opened his door cautiously. Everyone still slept, and he moved quietly down the wide staircase and out of the house.

It was Sarah who brought the news to Loveday, bursting into her room without even knocking on the door. As soon as she saw Sarah's tear-stained face, Loveday whirled round from her dressing-table, knowing instantly it had something to do with Adam.

'Adam's gone,' Sarah gasped out. 'He left a letter for Father and he's gone back to my uncle's in Bristol and then he's going back to that dreadful tunnel again. I know he said he'd go back, but somehow I always hoped he'd stay. Especially now, since you and he – ' she saw Loveday's stricken face and ran to her, taking her cold hands between her own.

'Oh Loveday, what can have happened? You and he were so happy yesterday, and now Father's downstairs with a face as grey as a December sky and racked with coughing. I've insisted on him sending for Geoffrey today – Doctor Chard, I mean.'

Her cheeks coloured, and Loveday thought fleetingly that at least her father's cough was an excuse for the good-looking doctor to make an extra call. But the thought was merely dancing in and out of her senses. There was only one all-consuming thought that she couldn't understand. *Adam had gone!* She couldn't believe it. *Why?* What could have happened? She licked her dry lips.

'Was there – any message in the letter – for – for either of us?' she said huskily. She felt her mouth tremble, and knew that if he hadn't given a thought to her she was about to burst into tears.

Sarah nodded. 'The briefest of mentions. In the two sentences that he referred to you, he called you my friend, and Mrs Viney. Loveday, what's happened?'

Tears blurred Loveday's eyes. She was completely stunned, unable to conjecture. Unless it had something to do with last night. The two girls had been told strictly to stay indoors when there had been talk of trouble at the cider sheds, with rumours of robbers and horse-thieves among the kitchen staff, quickly suppressed. And then Norman Goss had been so extraordinarily calm later, insisting that Sarah should play the pianoforte and the two girls should sing for their supper ... and they'd seen that Adam was all right, even if he'd looked as if he'd fallen in a ditch when he'd been helped indoors.

When she didn't answer, Sarah spoke a shade more positively.

'Anyway, we're to go into the study after breakfast and Father's to explain certain things to us about last night. I suppose it must have some bearing on Adam's leaving,' she echoed Loveday's thoughts, her voice wavering a little. 'When we were little, Father always used to call us into his study when he wanted to tell us something serious. I hope this isn't going to be too awful.'

She turned and fled from the room, leaving Loveday

staring dully at the door. Whatever it was, nothing was as awful as Adam going off like that without even a special note for her. And referring to her so coldly in his father's letter as Sarah's friend and *Mrs Viney* . . . the slow trickle of tears ran down her chiselled features unheeded. Her brief happiness was over.

The two girls sat opposite Norman Goss in his study, over-looking the cider orchards at the rear of the house. The trees were bare now, but already a fine network of grey-green cob-webbed the branches with the promise of spring and a fine new crop of apples. Loveday knew she should be interested in it all now, since she was to be a small part of Goss Cider, but all she wanted was to hear about Adam.

Norman's face was set as if it had been put in a mould. He'd thought long and hard as to how much the girls need be told, and had decided there was no need to embarrass and pain the young widow further by revealing that it had been her ruffian of a cousin who had caused all the furore last evening. And he had instructed his staff that on no account must there be gossip about the incident that would upset their guest. The child had been through enough already . . . and glancing at her pale face now, he knew she was as bewildered as himself over Adam's sudden departure. It was up to him to smooth the path as much as possible.

'Now then, my dears,' he breathed heavily to disguise the fact that a bout of coughing was almost on him again. 'You'll be as saddened as I am that Adam has gone back to his work so suddenly, but he's gone and there's no use in crying over spilt milk or even spilt cider, is there?' He lightened his voice to a teasing tone, but he might as well not have bothered. There was no glimmer of a smile from either sweet face, merely a mask of politeness and confusion.

'But what happened, Father?' Sarah burst out. 'Yesterday we were all so happy, and Adam didn't even have any dinner with us! You must tell us what you know!'

Norman looked at his daughter thoughtfully. For a short time he'd suspected she had had her head turned by the rustic

195

fellow, but thank God it all seemed over, and the pleasant Doctor Chard was the main attraction now. And there'd be plenty of opportunities for Sarah to see him in the future, Norman thought grimly. He raked his throat as his breathing rasped.

'We had an intruder last evening, my dears,' he informed them. 'A sneak-thief. Adam was taking the air when he heard something and went to the cider sheds to investigate. The ruffian took fright and hid in the fermenting shed, where Adam followed him. They fought, and fell into one of the cider kegs. It could have ended in tragedy, but thank God they were discovered in time and hauled out. Unfortunately the brute ran off before we could do anything more.'

'Was Adam hurt?' Loveday's heart thudded. 'He looked so distraught when we got a glimpse of him last night.'

She had given Norman the thread of explanation he needed.

'Not really hurt, Loveday, save for his pride, and of that Adam has plenty. He had a few bruises, naturally, but after such happy days here, he would not want you to see him in such a state. You know the way an animal seeks the darkness in which to crawl away and lick his wounds? Adam's pride is very much the same, I'm afraid. Rather than show himself as less of a man, he decided to leave here a day early. It *is* only one day, after all!'

But one day more with Adam was worth a lifetime with anyone else . . .

It didn't explain everything. It didn't explain why he'd gone without a word to her. Without even a note pushed beneath her door, or a few words of love. It was as if these past idyllic days had never been. Loveday swallowed the lump that suddenly blocked her throat. She was alone again. Was she destined to be always alone? It was a fearful thought, and one she couldn't dismiss. Was she destined to be some kind of Jonah on all the men with whom she came in contact? First Finch, now Adam . . . ?

Stop it, she told herself. It was nothing to do with her that Adam had been involved in a fight with an intruder last night. Nothing at all. She hung on to her dignity, reminding herself that it was hardly seemly to show too much despair in front of Norman Goss. She was still the young widow, come here to regain her strength after her husband's death, not his son's affianced.

'Oh well, he's gone and there's nothing we can do about it,' she heard Sarah say resignedly. 'But it's flattened the day for us, hasn't it, Loveday? And it's raining, so there's nothing we can do out of doors. We shall have to amuse ourselves by sketching or sewing.' She looked at Norman. 'You'll be sure and let me know when Doctor Chard comes, won't you, Father? I want to have a word with him.'

'Of course, darling,' Norman's face relaxed into a smile that remained until the two girls had left him alone, and then he let the raging cough have its way with him in a violent paroxysm.

Sketching or sewing . . . could anything sound so dull when all Loveday wanted to be doing was held in Adam's arms? He couldn't have wanted her enough, she thought bitterly, or he'd never have gone off like this. And that last little exchange between Sarah and her father, it underlined the fact that for other folk life still went on. Sarah was even humming beneath her breath now as they went back upstairs together, because her Geoffrey Chard was coming to call, albeit on her father's account. Adam's departure wasn't the end of the world as far as Sarah was concerned.

The enormity of it didn't overwhelm Loveday until she closed the door of Sarah's room behind her, and the two girls sat disconsolately on the bed for a few disorientated minutes, thinking what to do with their time. And then Loveday's shoulders began to shake and her limbs felt as if they'd turned to blubber as the grief of this new parting assaulted her senses.

Sarah folded her in her arms without a word, rocking her back and forth as if she was a little child. Loveday rarely cried in public. Never at her mother's funeral, and not for Finch . . . but this was a raw unexpected grief, and only Sarah knew how much she cared.

'Oh Sarah, I loved him so,' she gasped out the words. 'How could he do this? I don't understand . . . I don't understand . . . I know he thought of these days as precious, the same as I did. How could he go off with no word for me at all? The little mention he gave me in your father's letter is more of an insult – a slap in the face! And what have I *done*? I can think of nothing!'

She wept uncontrollably. Was it merely because she was a Willard after all, and whispers of their family wildness had made Adam pause and think before commiting himself totally to her? Was he having second thoughts now about marrying her and hoped she would flounce off and turn to someone else? Nothing made sense.

There was only one thing Loveday could think of that would cause Adam to turn against her, and that was a secret that was known only to herself and Polly Reeves and to no other living soul. And for all Polly's faults, she was certain she would never have told Adam . . . how could she, when they had never come in contact with each other?

Besides, thank God, that little matter had been resolved by nature. Loveday bit her lips hard. Was that something bad in her too, that she had caused her own child to die before it had had a chance to live? New sobbing racked her at the thought.

'Hush, darling,' Sarah's voice was thick with emotion at such a display of anguish. 'You've got nothing to blame yourself for, and I'm sure it was as Father says. Adam has a lot of pride, and he wouldn't want you to see him looking bruised and hurt.'

'But that doesn't explain why he went off without a word!' Loveday cried.

'No, it doesn't,' Sarah had to admit it. 'And I shall write to him and demand to know how he could be so heartless.'

Loveday could write too. But somehow she knew she wouldn't – at least, not immediately. She had her pride too.

She swallowed back the tears and squared her shoulders, wiping away the tears with an inadequate wisp of handkerchief.

'I'll try to restrain myself from flooding you again,' she

gave a crooked smile. 'And I won't let your father see how upset I am. He'll be grieved enough on his own account without worrying over me.'

You're a survivor, Adam had said . . .

The sound of a rider approaching the house caught Sarah's attention. She moved quickly to the window and turned back to Loveday with flushed cheeks.

'It's the doctor. Will you be all right if I go and talk with him, Loveday? I want to be sure that Father's as well as he thinks he is.'

Loveday gave a watery smile. 'Of course I'll be all right, and you don't think I'd deprive you of the chance to talk with your Geoffrey, do you? I'll compose myself in my own room, Sarah – and – bless you for lending me such a sympathetic ear.'

They hugged each other, and then Sarah went tripping down the stairs, with an eagerness in her step that told its own story. Loveday walked slowly back to her own room. Suddenly there was no place for her here. Without Adam it was just another house. Norman Goss was kind but he had enough problems of his own with his ailing health; as for Sarah, her dear friend was already head over heels in love, even if she herself didn't realise it. Loveday felt so much older than Sarah at that moment, the older, wiser one . . . which was an ironic thought, since she had been so foolish in all her doings with men!

Sarah was gone a long time. When she came back upstairs her eyes were sparkling. She was relieved to find Loveday looking calmer, even if the colour was high in her cheeks. She ran to clasp her friend's hands, and the book Loveday had been aimlessly staring at slid to the floor.

'Geoffrey has asked Father formally if he may call on me, Loveday, and of course he has said yes! I'm sure it has made Father feel a hundred times better to hear a bit of happy news today, after all the upset this morning and last night!'

'I'm so pleased for you, Sarah,' Loveday hoped her voice didn't sound too wooden, for she was genuinely pleased, and yet now that her bout of crying was over, it felt as if all her emotions were locked away inside her heart. It didn't pay to release them. It hurt too much when all your hopes and dreams came tumbling down, but she smiled with her lips and listened to her friend prattling on, and thought how lucky young Geoffrey Chard was going to be to have this vivacious girl for his wife.

She took a deep breath. She had been wondering how to say what was in her mind, but now it was made a little easier.

'Then, since you'll be so taken up with entertaining very soon, I hope you won't mind if I decide to return home tomorrow, Sarah. It's been a wonderful time here for me, until . . . ' her voice trembled a little, but she went on firmly. 'Oh well, I just feel that I must start living my own life again and not rely on other people to prop me up, that's all. I'd like to discuss the business arrangements with your father about the shop. You – you aren't put out at the thought of my leaving so soon, are you, Sarah?' she added anxiously.

She needn't have worried. There was only admiration in her friend's eyes, perhaps tinged with a little relief now that her courtship was formally to begin. The same admiration that was in Norman's eyes later in the day, when the dignified young woman in the soft grey woollen dress sat opposite him in his study and discussed the business arrangements he proposed with all the aplomb of a craftsman.

She was a game little maid, Norman thought. Though not a maid, of course . . . he let his eyes rest briefly on the womanly shape of her. A fine young woman to have so much tragedy in her life in so short a time, and one he'd be proud to have as his daughter-in-law, providing Adam hadn't let the foolishness of last night spoil his chances for good and all!

'We'd better shake on it, my dear,' Norman smiled at her, and at once her arm shot out as straight as an arrow, and he clasped the slim young fingers in his own for a moment. 'To our mutual business venture, and may it be a great success. And I think we should celebrate the arrangement with something finer than cider, even though it's the stuff of life around here!'

200

He went to a side table and poured them each a glass of port, handing Loveday's to her with a smile.

'Here's to us both, Loveday, and to your survival after all your troubles!'

He tipped his glass towards her before draining the drink. So he didn't notice how her hand shook as she sipped hers more delicately. So strange that he should use almost the same words Adam had used. *You're a survivor*, Adam had said . . . well, never had she needed to prove it more.

'I shall escort you back to Taunton myself tomorrow,' he went on. 'I daresay Sarah will want to come as well, and it will be good for you to have company the first time you enter your home once more. Though I've no doubt it will seem a different place if your instructions have all been carried out as you wished.'

'I've almost forgotten just what I asked my father and his – wife to do,' she murmured. Though she could never forget the sight of Finch's body humped behind the door, and the spreading stain of blood surrounding him. She shivered.

As if he could read her thoughts, Norman patted her hand.

'All memories fade in time, my dear pretty Loveday,' he said softly. 'Even the good ones we would keep with us for-ever. You may take an old man's word on it.'

He leaned forward and kissed her forehead, telling her lightly it was also an old man's privilege to claim a kiss from a pretty girl, but all the same he was deeply moved to see how well she conducted herself. He had heard about the wild Willards, and had cause to curse the one who'd come here last night and started the rumpus with his son, and he had heard about the gentleness of Meg Willard, the mother of this girl. He hadn't known Meg, but if Loveday was half the girl her mother was, then he found himself wishing he had. Such women didn't appear too often in one man's lifetime.

CHAPTER FIFTEEN

If ever she'd made a mistake in her life, Polly thought furiously, she had made it when she tied up her lot to Ralph Willard's. She'd thought she was bein' so clever, preening herself in front of her sister Ellen on her visit down from London, and parading round the town expecting the Taunton dames to accept her now she was respectable and none could doubt it.

None had to show it neither, she thought grimly. Old Ralphie and his like might think she was a bit o' good sport when a bit o' female company was desired, but Polly was learning fast that in country places, even one no bigger than a pocket handkerchief compared with London, a pert young second wife with a well-turned ankle, who'd hitched herself to a bulbous-nosed widower almost before the ground was cold on his first wife's grave, was given the cold shoulder. And it riled her somethin' wicked.

Even young Loveday got better notices from the Taunton dames than Polly did . . . and there was a tale or two Polly could tell about *her* if she chose to . . . not that she would. Even if she wanted to spread a bit o' gossip about her irritating step-daughter, what would be the point? Loveday weren't 'spreadin' in the belly no more, and it'd only be Polly's word, an nobody was going' to believe that!

Gawd, but Loveday had squirmed out of her situation all right and no mistake. Nippin' off to those fancy friends o' hers, and leaving her and Ralphie to do the donkey work at the butcher's shop, not that Polly had minded that much. It was a lark really, turning the dreary place into a smart little establishment like it was now, with light-coloured paint and fresh new wallpaper, and all the trappings of the butchery business gone. Filled it with the kind of furniture Loveday had wanted they had, an' never a thought of envy until it was all finished, and Polly had looked round the Willard premises she shared with Ralph and felt the boredom wash over her again.

'Why don't we change a few things, Ralphie?' she'd

whined in her piping voice that sometimes grated on him so much, he wondered how he could ever have found it coy and sensual.

'I don't want nothin' changed,' he'd growl. ' 'Twas good enough for Meg with her breedin', so it's good enough for we.'

As always, Polly would feel her temper rise.

'I 'ope you ain't saying' I ain't got breedin' then,' she'd snap. 'I knew finer gents than you when I lived in the smoke, that's for sure, Ralph Willard.'

Whenever he could, he'd answer with a fart, watching her fan the room in an exaggerated manner with one o' the wispy little bundles of feathers she kept for such occasions.

'*And* they had better manners!' She'd add furiously. 'Still, brought up with pigs, I s'pose you're bound to end up acting like one in the end.'

A belch usually followed and Polly's tone would become icily sarcastic.

'I wish some o' your townsfolk you toady up to could see you now, you rat-bag! They'd have second thoughts about includin' Mr fancy-tradesman Willard in their club walks.'

She knew that would get to him. It always did. Ralph's greatest desire was to be elected into the local tradesman's Friendly Society and he hoped that this year would be the one his nomination was successful. On Oak Apple Day he dearly wanted to march through the streets of the town with the rest of them behind the town band, holding his flower-decorated banner aloft, since he'd be a new member, hopefully, and not credited with the official brass sign on his pole until he'd been attached to the club a whole year. He wanted to march from church to inn and back again, joining in the feasting and holding his head high, and proving once and for all that Ralph Willard, Prop, was as good a tradesman as any in Taunton.

Polly dodged the swipe from his hand as she mocked him. Bloody silly tuppeny-ha'penny clodhoppin' club, and he thought the world was goin' to open up to him if he belonged to it!

'Anyway,' she sulked, 'what are folks going to think if you can't even buy your wife a new bonnet for the spring?'

She'd never known a man so mean with his money. And

now that they'd had the shock of discovering how Loveday had fallen on her feet, it had made Polly even more resentful of her lot.

Gawd, what a shock that had been. Hadn't known nothing about it, till some gossipy old crone had said casually in the store that little Loveday was looking well, and wasn't it a mercy the kind gent had seen to it all so tasteful-like? Polly and Ralph had looked at each other and muttered a reply, and as soon as the crone had gone they'd shut up shop and gone marching round to Viney's. To stop short with shock as they read the new sign tacked over the door.

'*Goss Cider!*' Ralph said incredulously. 'What's going on here that I don't know about then?'

'Now hold on, Ralphie, before you burst a blood vessel,' Polly put her hand on his arm. 'Loveday's a grown-up married woman now, even if she is a widow and only sixteen, but she don't have to be beholden to you no more. Calm down, Ralphie, an' let's find out without telling the rest of the street that it's all a mystery to us, eh?'

He saw the sense of it. There'd been enough gossip about his family already, though it was hard to stop his temper exploding, when he discovered the new shop had been in operation for weeks now and he'd known nothing of it!

Inside, new shelves had been installed, and the gleaming brown cider jugs stood waiting for sale. An old woman he vaguely recognised asked him his business, while a pipe-smoking hunched-up old man rocked away in one corner on a creaking chair. Real cosy, it looked, but where was his girl?

'My daughter,' Ralph demanded. '*That's* my business.'

'I know who you are, Ralph Willard,' the woman said tartly, 'and there's no need to shout at me. I sewed many a garment for your sweet wife – your *late* wife, I should say,' she added, with a disapproving glance at Polly. 'I'll ring for Miss Loveday.'

She pulled on a cord and they heard a bell jangling somewhere above, and seconds later Loveday's light footsteps came down the stairs. She looked well, Polly saw. Much better than when she'd gone fleeing to her friend's house, but she was strung-up still. It was obvious to Polly, if not to her father.

'What took you both so long?' Loveday said lightly. 'I expected the news to get round long before this that I was back. Will you come through and take some tea with me?'

They followed dumbly at this new confident Loveday, who appeared to be mistress of her own business now, and prospering at that. But once in the parlour, which was more homely, if far more elegant than his own, with the little touches Loveday had added to the bare furnishings, Ralph let out his voice in a customary bellow.

'And what kind of daughter lets a father find out her movements from a town gossip, I'd like to know?'

Loveday's eyes flashed. 'And what kind of father marries his daughter off to a man like Finch Viney for his own gain?' she snapped back. 'I don't consider I owe you anything!'

'You were quick enough to agree as I remember it, but that ain't the point. Didn't Polly and me do all you asked for us while you were away? Weren't it all to your liking when you got back, with no trace of you-know-what left behind?' He was getting more aggrieved every minute.

'Your father's right, Loveday,' Polly said quickly. 'You might have let us know. We'd have asked you round for supper one evenin', and o' course Ralphie wanted to know how you was farin'. It's only natural.'

There was nothing natural in the way he was glowering at his daughter now. It was everything back to normal, Loveday thought, as she poured the boiling water into the tea-pot and left it to brew.

'If you must know, I was afraid you'd find some objection to what I'm doing,' she said flatly. 'And nobody was going to make me change my mind this time. Mr Goss has been very kind to me. It's his business now, but the premises still belong to me, and he just rents the use of the shop and pays the wages. Mrs Mundy and her husband are respectable folk and I'm seeing to the accounting books. It's all legal and proper, and there's nobody who can say any different. And I wanted to get it all done by myself. I leaned on folks too heavily before I went away, and now I can stand on my own two feet.'

'That you can, my pretty,' Polly breathed as Loveday glared defiantly at the two of them. Ralph seemed to have lost the power of speech for the moment. He was used to Loveday's ranting and screaming at him, but he wasn't used to the sight of this new dignified Loveday in the soft wool dress and crisp lawn collar, her golden hair swept to the top of her head and pinned there with some kind of jet ornament he dimly remembered Meg owning. She confused him, this confident daughter of his, and he took refuge in scowling and poking about the place with a suspicious air.

'You'll find nothing wrong, Pa,' it enraged him to hear her voice tinged with amusement. 'I don't have any secret lovers hidden in cupboards, and I'm not running any kind of bawdy-house, if that's what you're thinking. Did you really think it so strange that I didn't come running to you the minute I got back to Taunton? You pushed me here, and here I'll stay.'

'You've still got your acid tongue on you, despite your fancy friends, I see,' he snapped. 'Well, where's that tea then? Let's have some if you've made it, for I can't shut up shop all day. I can't afford to miss out on trade, even if some folks seem to have struck it lucky.'

Loveday hid a smile. Oh, but the moment was sweet. She'd been determined not to go near her father's place, knowing it would only be a matter of time before he found out about Goss Cider and came storming round here. And from the look of envy on Polly's face he was in for a tongue-lashing from her tonight as well. Polly envied everything she didn't have, and her new home was a credit to her, Loveday thought with satisfaction. She was happier here than she'd have believed possible, in spite of hearing nothing from Adam in the three weeks she had been back.

But that was something she wouldn't let herself dwell on too much. What good did it do? She kept busy with other things, and left the crying to the long silent hours of the night.

'We'll be goin' then,' Ralph drained his cup noisily, not waiting to see if Polly had finished or not. 'I daresay we'll see summat of you occasionally then, miss?'

'I daresay,' Loveday spoke drily, feeling superior to him for

206

the first time in all her life. Yet the feeling only made her oddly tender towards him, seeing how totally discomfited he was by her manner. Ruefully, she knew instantly the sense of the saying that blood was thicker than water, because when he offered her a rough cheek to peck, she did so dutifully. Though she drew back at once when Polly obviously expected the same.

After all she'd done for her too, Polly raged, as they made their way back to Willard's store. She nearly had to run to keep up with Ralph's striding walk, and knew he was still sorely put out about the whole situation. If only Loveday had told them first. Polly was none too pleased with that little madam. Looking so prosperous and a catch for any man, and in a bloody good place to find one too, a shop selling good cider. The bitch had it all, Polly thought resentfully.

She banged the cooking pots about that evening, thinking up ways to get Ralph into a sweeter temper, since she was fed up with the rough edge of his tongue. She dressed up in one of her low-cut dresses that had her dumplings boiling over, and splashed herself with the cheap scent he used to like. To her fury, he let out a great bellow of rage the minute he saw her, when he'd shut up shop for the night.

'You silly little tart, what have you got yourself up like a whore for, tonight of all nights? I told you a parcel o' folks from the club committee will be round to give me the once-over, and what are they goin' to think when they lay eyes on you? They'll think I've taken on another fancy-piece instead of a wife! Get into some sober clobber before they arrive and sprinkle some vinegar round the place, as if you've been cleanin' summat, to get rid of that stink. They'll think they've come to a bawdy-house otherwise. And fling the windows open a spell to let the smell out!'

Polly glared at him as he put his words into action without waiting for her. Truth to tell, she'd forgotten all about his rotten stupid club with all the excitement over Loveday, and for two pins she'd appear even more scantily dressed later, just to spite him. Only it just wasn't worth it, and she flounced out of the room, banging the door so hard it rattled everything in sight.

207

But she was seething all the same. The place stank of vinegar now, and she scrubbed her skin to get rid of her scent. She put on the pious act Ralphie wanted for his precious committee, and when they finally left, he told her gleefully that it was all right. He'd been accepted at last, and she could have a new spring bonnet as long as it didn't cost too dear, but that she'd have to make it last till next year, because he wasn't made of money.

She seethed as he belched now that his company had gone, and seethed when he took her in his great thick arms that night, and told her she'd been a good girl and mebbe it was time they celebrated in the best way he knew how. She let him get on with it, completely immune to his gaspings and poundings above her.

A couple of weeks later she had a letter from Ellen again, asking when she was going to get tired of the country life, since it would be nice if Ralph could spare her to come back to London for a visit. It would be fun, and they could have a high old time, just the way they used to.

Polly thought wistfully of those times. The excitement of the coffee-houses and the stage doors, and the fine and dandy gents who treated a girl as if she was china. The horses in Rotten Row and the snugglings in the park . . .

'Why can't I go, Ralphie?' she said petulantly, as he gave her a flat refusal. 'I'd only be gone a couple of weeks.'

'Because wives of honest traders don't go off to London for a couple of weeks, that's why! I'd trust you about as far as I could throw you, my girl, and besides, where do you think I've got money to chuck about on holidays for you? Next thing, you'd be telling me you needed fripperies as well, and there'd be no end to it.'

He settled down in the chair, closing his eyes as if to close out any more mention of such a thing. His chin was layered over his throat, and it was only seconds before the snorting and snoring began. His hands were locked across his great belly, his legs sprawled halfway across the room, leaving no room for Polly to sit near the fire if she'd wanted to. She looked at him with disgust. To think she'd been fool enough to marry him, and even more fool enough to like his groping hands on her. She gave a shudder at the thought. She felt as trapped by him as if he'd locked her up in chains. And there was pretty little Loveday, with everything she wanted, and no pig of a husband to answer to . . . and there was her sister Ellen in London, still enjoying the good life, while Polly was the lackey to this red-faced monster.

He'd be out for hours now, having drunk his way through a jug a cider. Polly's lips twisted. Ralph had been off to Loveday's place several times since they'd discovered her new situation, and come back smiling with a jug or two or cider, since Norman allowed her a discount on it. Which meant he thought he could quaff a greater quantity than usual.

Polly's resentment bubbled over. Before Ralph settled down for his drunken evening, she'd been left to twiddle her thumbs as usual while he did his nightly addition in the old tin box in the attic. Ralph didn't believe in banks, and there must be hundreds of pounds up there now, away from any chance of robbers finding it.

She felt her heartbeats quicken so fast it almost sickened her for a minute. And then the excitement took over. Why not? Why bloody not? Didn't he owe it her for all the good times and hard work he'd had out of her? He'd never miss a few notes.

Her eyes suddenly glazed. Why stop at only a few? Why not take the whole bleedin' lot while she was at it? Shoot off back to London and set herself and Ellen up for good an' all . . . change their names maybe . . . he'd never find her even if he did come chasing after her, which she doubted. He didn't have the guts for travelling, for all his bluster. An' even if he set the law after her . . . well, with all that loot in the attic, she and Ellen could be across the sea to France if they wanted. Start up a whole new career in French Paree with all them moustache-twirling hot-eyed continentals.

Polly's face flushed. What a bleedin' fool she was to stay here one minute longer than need be. But she was going to be crafty about this. No tearing about and waking Ralphie out of his stupor before she got clean away. She had to think first.

Put on her bleedin' thinking cap and not get carried away at the thought of the future suddenly dazzling brightly in front of her.

It was twenty-four hours later that Loveday heard a hammering on the door of her shop fit to wake the dead. For a moment she panicked. She'd closed the shop and the Mundys had gone home, and if this was some drunken reveller outside intent on clearing the shelves of jugs of Goss Cider, she'd be helpless to protect herself. She hesitated, heart pounding, praying that there might be a constable about to apprehend the caller before she had to do anything about it. And then she recognised her father's voice.

She rushed to unbolt the door with shaking hands, furious now the danger was unrealised, that he could make such a spectacle of himself. But her fury stopped abruptly at the sight of him; hair awry as if he'd been clutching and tearing at it; weskit buttons popping as if he hadn't bothered to dress himself tidily or put on a top coat in the keen night air; his face purpled with rage that was near to apoplexy, and tears streaking down his face.

'Pa, what in heaven's name's happened?' Loveday gasped, dragging him inside the shop, where he swayed on his feet. Not from drink, she realised rapidly, but from sheer unbridled shock.

For a second it seemed as if he would choke on his spittle, unable to get the words out, and then a torrent of abuse was unleashed in a roaring voice.

'She's done it this time, the bitch! The stinking, raddled, poxy bitch! If I ever get my hands on her, I'll kill her! How I could have let myself be sweet-talked into marryin' her, God only knows. He must have summat agin me to let me fall for a whore like that one! *Cheap bitch.*'

'Pa, stop it!' Loveday caught at his arms as he waved them about like windmills. He was demented, she thought fearfully, and he was going to do her an injury in a minute if he didn't stop threshing about with the sharp-edged tin box he was clutching.

'Look, calm down, will you, and tell me what's happened?

It's obviously something to do with Polly – '

It was just as if the mention of her name set all his nerve-ends jumping. He let out a howl of rage and stamped his feet as if there was an army of emmets beneath them. In desperation, Loveday lashed out her hand against his face, though it was something she'd never done in her life before and she feared his violence would turn on her, but it had the effect of sobering him up a fraction, and the eyes glaring at her now were a little less wild at last. She managed to steer him into the back room somehow, and pushed him into a chair. It seemed he hardly knew where he was. In his mind he was still wherever it was that had caused his temper to erupt. Suddenly he banged his fist on the table, rocking the cup and plate there.

'Ah, I'll tell 'ee, so I will, girl,' he bellowed. 'I'd tell your mother if I thought she still 'ad ears to 'ear and weren't moulderin' beneath the ground, God rest the soul of a good woman!'

Loveday felt the anger rise like bile in her mouth. How *dare* he go all pious over her mother after the way he'd carried on with that Polly Reeves? She couldn't bear to hear her mother's name on his lips.

'Leave my mother out of it, Pa,' she snapped. 'It's a pity you didn't think more of her when she was alive, but it's too late now, and you've got what you wanted, so say your piece and go home. I'm tired.'

He scowled at her with dislike in his eyes. Why couldn't he have spawned a child who'd speak to him with respect and cringe from his wrath like any normal one would? Not a Willard though.

'You're no daughter to me, are you?' Ralph suddenly shouted. 'Where's the respect I'm due then, eh? Where the help when it's needed? Didn't I help you out after Finch killed himself? Why'd he do that, I wonder? Couldn't stand your sharp tongue, mebbe. Was that it, you ungrateful baggage?'

Loveday leaned against the edge of the table, her knuckles white as her face.

'I don't have to listen to this, Pa. This is my house. Now if you've got something to say, say it, or get out. If you don't, I'll send for a constable and have you thrown out!'

211

For a second he'd forgotten why he'd come, but now it all came back to him, and Loveday stared in horror as his shoulders began to shake uncontrollably. Oh God, she couldn't stand this . . . he thrust the tin box across the table at her.

'Open it! Go on, open it!'

She did as she was told, but since she'd never seen it before, it meant nothing to her. Until she saw the note inside, that and nothing else, written in scrawly, untidy writing.

'Bye bye Ralphie. I won't say it was nice knowin' you, because it wasn't. Not lately anyway, you great fartass. Give your next ladylove my deepest sympathy.'

'You know what was in there, girl?' Ralph's voice was choked now. 'All my money. *All* of it! And the bitch has taken every penny and gone.'

'*What*? Stolen it, you mean?'

Ralph glowered at her. 'Of course *stolen* it. Can't you understand plain English no more? She's gone, and I ain't got a clue where to find 'er.'

'Well, you must go after her and get it back. Get the constables on to her, Pa. You mustn't let her get away with it!'

He shook his head violently. ' 'Twont be no use. I know 'er too well. You wouldn't believe the tales she's told me of how her and that sister of hers skipped the law afore now. She'll have planned all this too well.'

'She can't have got far. How long has she been gone? An hour?'

'Last night as far as I can tell.'

Loveday stared at him, aghast. 'Last night? But how is it you haven't discovered it until now? Didn't you wonder where she was, Pa? I don't see how you didn't miss her.'

Not with the cheap scent she always wore that filled a room so that decent folk could barely breathe . . .

'I keep tellin' you, she's clever,' Ralph couldn't talk without shouting yet, and Loveday whisked the crockery away quickly as the table thumping started again.' She's got me to bed afore now, when I've had a belly-full o'drink,' he avoided Loveday's eyes as they both remembered the night of her mother's funeral. 'She must o' got me there last night and left

212

me to sleep it off. Mebbe that's when she went up to the attic and got the tin box.'

He choked again, and Loveday tipped a splash of brandy into a glass and handed it to him. In the circumstances it seemed a medicinal necessity.

'When I woke this morning with a head like thunder, there was a note on 'er pillow.' He dragged it from his weskit pocket and pushed it towards Loveday.

'Dear Ralph, I was called on in the night to go and sit with my friend Marcia, who's suffering with the consumption. I'm sorry to leave you to yourself, but if I'm not back by evening, there's cold pie and potatoes and pickles you can eat till I get back. It's feared that Marcia might be dying, so I may be gone awhile. Your loving Polly.'

Ralph snorted as Loveday pushed the letter back.

'Loving Polly indeed. I'd as soon love a scorpion as love 'er again. And this Marcia friend of 'ers – some trollop she's taken up with – turned up as primped as ever a while ago askin' to see 'er. That's when I knew summat was up all right. And I was right, weren't I? An' what's goin' to happen now, I'd like to know? I don't want to see that bitch again, that's for certain sure, but I want me money back! All me savings that was goin' to see me right in me old age. Money for the bills and new stock, and a new weskit for the club walk at the end o' May.' He suddenly began to blubber hysterically. 'All this time I've schemed and whined to get elected into the club, and promising 'em a fine fat contribution to funds, more'n anybody else, I wouldn't wonder, and that poxy bitch has gone and ruined it all.'

He reached across the table and clawed at Loveday's hands. She was repulsed at his blubbering, but his grip was too strong for her to break away from it.

'You've got to help me, Loveday,' he said shrilly. 'You're the only one who can. You owe it to me and for your dear mother's sake. You've got to give me some o' that money Finch left you to set me right. I'll pay 'ee back when I can.'

'Are you *mad*?' She managed to snatch her hands away from him. 'I've got no money. What I had from Finch's stock

213

all went on the re-furnishing of this place. There's nothing at all! I own this property and that's it. I've nothing to give you, Pa!'

He stared at her as if not comprehending, and then he slumped back on his chair. She had never seen him so crushed.

'That's me done for then. She's done it for me. I might as well go an' end it all in the river. Ralph Willard 'll never hold his head up again, an' all because o' the sins o' the flesh. 'Tis a wicked wicked world, Loveday, and I must be a real wicked sinner for God to punish me like this after 'twas He who gave me the urges o' man.' He was doleful to the point of being ludicrous.

She had heard this last resorting to God's ways before, and knew it wouldn't last forever. Soon, Ralph would be his old rip-roaring self again . . . though this time was different, she admitted anxiously. Always before, he'd soaked himself in drink and come up fighting. If there was no more money for drink, he was just as likely to put his words into effect and drown himself in the Tone. She had to be sure just how bad it was.

'Have you got bills outstanding, Pa?' she asked. He nodded mournfully.

'So many creditors you'd think they was beatin' a new path through the town leadin' straight to me door,' he moaned. 'Polly was always grousin' that I gave her nothin', but it weren't true. She had plenty, and she was extravagant with the cookin' too, not like your Ma, who could stretch a slice o' bacon to do the work o' three.'

Loveday didn't want to hear this. 'Then it's really that serious, Pa? Can't you hold them off a while longer?'

'I've already held 'em off so long the bills are growing whiskers,' he said eloquently. He looked at her, defeat in his face. 'You sure you ain't got nothin' put away somewhere, Loveday, me dear? Just summat to tide your ol' Pa over till things brighten up?'

She squirmed. She couldn't bear to hear him begging.

'I've told you, there's nothing. Why don't you try Uncle Jack at the farm? He can always find a bob or two when he needs one.'

'No good. He'd dig deep for his brother if he could, but all the money in farmin's tied up in the animals and the land. He couldn't spare what I need. No, I'm finished and that's the end on it,' he allowed his voice to waver, knowing her too well. Knowing she wouldn't fail him, no matter what. He didn't look at her now, but he heard her deep sighing breath as she looked at the slouched figure opposite her. He was her father and she felt nothing for him, because he'd been bad to her, and he'd brought all this on himself. She should tell him to go and stew in his own juice, and yet . . .

A sudden gust of wind whipped up the back street behind the shop, flapping the tree branches against the window like the rap of fingers. Like a little reminder . . . Loveday seemed to hear the soft echo of her mother's voice in the sighing of the wind, telling her that the family was like a circle, strong and whole and complete within itself. Telling her that it was her loving duty to go to her father's aid, because nothing could change the ties of blood. To Ralph she owed her very existence.

'Pa, I'd like you to go now, and leave me to think about this,' she said evenly. 'I'm not promising anything, because I'm no miracle worker, but there might be a way. I'll have to consider a lot of things, but you must promise me you'll not do anything rash until I get in touch with you again.'

'And when will that be, Loveday dear?' his voice was suitably humble. 'You can guess I'll be near to spittin' pins till I know what my fate is to be.'

'I don't think you need to be quite so dramatic about it,' Loveday said shortly. 'And if you want my honest opinion, I think you're well rid of Polly Reeves.'

'Oh ah, you're right, me dear girl. She was never worthy of followin' in your mother's footsteps, that she weren't. She were allus too painted and scented and – '

'All right then. Promise me now. You'll go home and stay calm and sober until you hear from me again,' Loveday's voice was jerky now. If he didn't go soon she'd lose her control and shriek and spit and hurl abuse on him to rival any fish-wife, and she'd no intention of getting down to his level.

215

'I'll hope to visit you tomorrow evening.'

He lumbered to his feet, still clutching his tin box, a pathetic sight with the unaccustomed gratitude in his eyes. She preferred the old Ralph after all, Loveday thought in surprise, the one she was used to. She avoided his awkward kiss and let him out of the shop door, and only when he'd gone clattering down the street on the pitched flint stones did she let go of the iron control and crumpled to the floor exactly where she was, beating her fists against the flagstones in anguish until the knuckles bled.

As soon as the Mundys were settled in the shop the following morning, Loveday appeared in her best navy-blue wool dress and shawl, her hat speared by a pin, her boots polished until they gleamed. She might not be back till late afternoon, she told them, and was assured that they'd manage fine and it was time she took a day off to go for a spin. Loveday smiled grimly as she climbed into the trap she'd hired for the day, extravagant or not, and swished the reins to get the pony started, thinking this was anything but a spring outing.

All night she'd tossed and turned, wondering what she could do to get her father out of this mess. Knowing there was only one way and not even that was certain. Supposing she was humiliated when she made her proposal? She had no way of telling what her reception was going to be.

But she sat straight and proud in the bouncing trap as she rode through the streets of the town, and more than one lounging fellow took a shine to the fine sight she made, and the dames thought what a brave young woman she was turning out to be after all, considering everything.

Sarah greeted her with cries of delight as she rode into the grounds of Goss House, and Loveday ignored the painful pangs of memory of all the halcyon days she and Adam had shared, and the shock of his leaving, since when she'd heard nothing from him. But it wasn't Sarah she'd come to see, even though she was obliged to admire the shiny pearl ring Sarah now wore on her finger, and hide the twist of envy she felt.

By the time her business was done and she urged the pony

216

back towards Taunton before dusk settled around her, Loveday felt almost numb and totally exhausted. A sleepless night after so many sleepless nights before, when she'd wept over Adam's abrupt departure, had taken the colour from her cheeks and left dark shadows beneath her beautiful eyes. Norman Goss had thought she looked more like a beautiful and tragic heroine from a novelette than a flesh and blood woman. But what she'd come to say was said passionately and sincerely and from the heart. And she'd done what she set out to do.

She delivered the pony and trap back to the hiring yard, and walked to Willard's Store. As soon as he saw her, Ralph pulled down the shop blind and closed up for the night, ushering her into the parlour with excruciating servility. Facing him, Loveday slapped a piece of paper down on the table and told him he'd better read it.

'What's this?' He frowned at it. If he'd expected pound notes to be put in front of him immediately, he was disappointed, Loveday thought.

'It's a note from Mr Norman Goss, agreeing to buy my premises, lock, stock and barrel, though the barrels are already his by rights, instead of merely renting them from me. It promises me a handsome payment because of the prime position the shop holds, and because of the goodwill he says I've already brought him in the sale of Goss Cider since we opened. As soon as he's seen his solicitor and had the thing made legal, the bank will honour this note and the money will be paid to me. And as soon as it is, you can have what's needed, which will be most of it, I suppose, and my debt to you will be paid in full, Pa. I think I'll have done all a daughter can be expected to do then.'

There was a small silence while Ralph digested all she said, and Loveday's stomach curdled as she watched the changing expressions on his face. Incredulity, relief, gloating delight . . . she watched them all, and wondered if it had really been worth it. She'd felt as bad as if she was prostituting herself, going begging from Adam's father, too proud and dignified to give a proper explanation, save that she wanted to be free of

217

the responsibility of owning the place, and would prefer to be a living-in tenant, working exactly as before, but with the property belonging to Goss Cider as well as just the contents.

If Norman thought there was more to the request than Loveday let on, he didn't comment on it. He had an interest in the girl, and he didn't like the wan pale look about her, but if he could help her, it made little difference to his capital, and he agreed more generously than she could ever have hoped. As she left, she couldn't resist asking after Adam.

'He's well,' Norman said cautiously. 'But I fear he has little time for letter writing.'

She nodded, for didn't she know it. And told herself it was high time she put him out of her life and her heart, since he'd shown so plainly that his professed words of love were meaningless. But it was as impossible to do that as it was to escape the effusive hugging of her father at his good fortune, and his avowal that he'd pay her back one of these fine days, as God was his witness.

'Leave God out of it, Pa,' she said wearily, rising to leave. 'He's had enough of your promises, same as I have. I'll see you get the money as soon as I can.'

She stepped out of the store, momentarily clean and refreshed, as if she'd rid herself of Ralph for ever. But she hadn't, nor ever could, and in some ways he was like a great millstone round her neck, which was a wicked way to think of her father, she thought shamedly. But what had he done for her now? Made her shame herself by going to Adam's father, as the only way out of the mess Ralph had got himself into by taking up with Polly Reeves, and any good she might have gained by selling the property was lost to her because she'd be handing it all over to Ralph.

It had been a piquant situation to know that she had a property good enough for Norman Goss to want to rent. It gave her a special kind of status . . . no, she didn't feel clean and refreshed at all in what she'd had to do, she thought dismally. She felt dragged down and humiliated, not least because Goss Cider now *owned* her.

218

CHAPTER SIXTEEN

As the month of May blossomed forth, there was little to show that any change of fortunes had occurred in either Willard household, save that Ralph Willard had attracted the sympathy of the townsfolk when it was known that his flighty wife had upped and left him. A reaction on which he seized eagerly, and played it to the full with a flair which would have tickled Polly, had she been there to see it.

He was the respected tradesman at long last, a member of the Alltrades Club, and eligible to march through the town on Oak Apple Day with his flower-strewn banner, holding his head high, and knowing it was a mark of acceptance to all classes. His florid face was more often piously solemn than anything else, at least in public, and none but those who also frequented such places knew that for solace he sought the darker streets on the wrong side of town, where he could buy all the cheap scented skirt he wanted for the price of a pork pie. Ralph had found his place in life at last.

Loveday rarely came to visit him, but it didn't matter. In fact, the farther apart they were, the better it was. He felt a little uneasy at the way he'd had to go to her, and preferred not to see the look in her eyes that reminded him of it only too well. So he never sought her out, and it seemed to suit them both. But not so his sister-in-law, Emily Willard, who marched into the Goss Cider shop that had lately been Viney's butcher's shop, and banged her hand on the counter, startling a dozing pair of old biddies into wakefulness.

'Now then, Pru Mundy, I've come to see my niece, since she can't find time to visit with her relations no more. Just you tell her I'm here while I chinwag with ol' Chipper, though from the looks on 'im he's nearer to the grave than the cradle.'

'I'll have to see if Miss Loveday's available,' Mrs Mundy said crossly, annoyed at being found sluggish when this sharp-eyed and sharper-tongued farmer's wife bustled in. She was a Willard all right, Mrs Mundy reflected. Years of living among 'em had marked her down all right. She stabbed a finger towards the back room. 'She may be in there doin' the books,' she said haughtily, as if this countrywoman would have no notion of the exacting work Loveday had to do in the thriving business.

'Then I'll go and see,' Emily said, before the other woman could make a great to-do about pulling the bell-cord. She pushed open the door to the back room and was shocked as Loveday looked up from the accounting she was poring over.

'Well now, me girl,' she said, miffed to cover her concern. 'I suppose you know it's more'n three months since we've seen 'ee? An' a right sorry sight 'ee looks, all thin and pinched around the face. If this is what your fancy new business does for 'ee, it's time 'ee came to the farm for a bit o' fattenin' up!'

Next minute she was taken by surprise as Loveday sprang to her feet with a cry of pleasure at seeing her, hardly realising how she'd missed her, until the sight of her had taken her breath away. She hugged her aunt, the tears spurting to her eyes, and Emily cleared her throat, never guessing how easily such emotions came to the surface these days. It was most unlike Loveday to be so effusive towards her, and it touched her rough soul.

'It's good to see you, Aunt Em,' Loveday dabbed her damp eyes. 'You'll take a cup of tea and some seed cake, won't you? I baked it yesterday, so it's just right for eating now.'

'O' course I will, me dear, and I must say you look nicely set up here now. A bit different from when ol' Finch was in charge, ain't it? It was an unhappy ending for 'un, but it's made a woman of 'ee, Loveday, even if 'ee do look so pinched. It's a fair doing for a woman to be a property owner at your age.'

Loveday kept her eyes averted. No-one in the family but herself and her father knew the truth about that. She felt obliged to ask about her uncle and cousins.

'Same as ever,' Aunt Emily snorted. 'Large as life and twice as ugly, as they say. An' wantin' to know if you'm comin' to the farm for the sheep-shearin' as usual this year, since I'll be glad o' your help.'

'Oh. I don't think I can this year, Auntie. What with the shop and all.'

'Rubbish. There's nothing to selling a few jars o' scrumpy that they two out there can't see to! What else have they got to do with their time, 'cepting sit around waitin' to peg it? What else have *you* got to do on Oak Apple Day, come to that? Not courtin' again, are you?'

'Of course not.'

'There ain't no "of course not" about it, me girl. Fine young wench like you ought to have fellers round her like bees to a honey-pot.' She conveniently forgot the times she'd warned Ralph about his daughter's knowing eyes and curving womanly shape. 'Well, far as I can see, there's nothin' to stop you comin' out of the farm the evening afore, an' if you insist on it, goin' back afore dark on the Day. But I could do with your help for feedin' all they hungry men, Loveday. Unless o' course, you feel obliged to stay in town an' watch your Pa parading round like a duck's dinner now he's come up in the world?'

'No, I don't,' Loveday said sharply. 'You heard about him belonging to the club now then, did you? And about Polly leaving him, I suppose?'

'Ah, we heard. News took its time in reachin' us though, so I s'pose nobody wanted our thoughts on't.' She sniffed expressively. 'I daresay they weren't much different from yourn.'

'I daresay they weren't,' Loveday muttered. She'd forgotten the Alltrades Club parade. If she wasn't at the farm, her father and a lot of other folks would think she was slighting him if she didn't watch it. And she couldn't *bear* to see him strutting about.

'All right, I'll come as usual,' she said reluctantly. 'As long as Mrs Mundy doesn't mind.'

Walls were thin in the property, and when Loveday showed her aunt out, it was to have Mrs Mundy say stiffly that she'd be only too pleased to continue serving Miss Loveday, leaving no doubt that it was on her account and not the rough countrywoman's that she offered her and Chipper's time.

221

Anyway, it would be all right, Loveday told herself. She'd make sure she was never alone with Matthew, and it was only for one night and one day. She'd survive ... she turned abruptly and went into her back room. Such a phrase always reminded her of Adam, and she was trying very hard to forget him, since it seemed he'd forgotten all about her. She'd swallowed her pride just once and written to him, begging him to say what she had done to displease him, but in the end she hadn't sent it. Instead she'd ripped it to pieces and waited in vain for a letter from him that never came.

Loveday knew the rituals of the sheep-shearing by heart. The day before Oak Apple Day, which was May 29th, several of the surrounding hill farmers as well as her Uncle Jack himself, would round up the sheep and bring them down from the hills ready for the washing. It was a Quantock custom to share in the preparation and the shearing, in the assumption that many hands spread the load. Since the day's operation was accompanied by much scrumpy drinking and merry making, at least on the Willard farm, the benefits were doubtful. But the work had always gone on at the Willard farm for them and their neighbours, simply because it was the only one with a good shallow pond in which to dip the sheep.

'Dippin' 'em cleans the wool,' Uncle Jack had told Loveday when she'd been small enough to bounce on his knee and join in the singing, and then help Aunt Emily hand round the hot meat pasties she'd helped to bake.

To Loveday it had seemed magical that the piles of fluffy grey-white clippings from the sheeps' backs could ever be turned into cloth fit for wearing. And though in those childhood days she'd wept over the poor pink shorn sheep, so thin and miserable without their shaggy covering, she'd long ago become used to it.

Sometimes, if the weather had been particularly warm, she might stay on at the farm a week or two then, to spend whole days with Aunt Emily going a-hilling to pick the whortleberries that grew in such a purple profusion on the tiny bushes among the Quantock heather. They had been

222

days of enchantment then, seeking out the little jewel-dark currant-sized fruit with the earthy flavour, with the hot sun on their backs and the hum of insects to accompany them through the maze of bracken. Sometimes bringing home a sheaf of the miniature, red leaves of the fruit to press between the pages of a heavy ancient book that was never read, since reading at the farm was considered time wasted.

She and Aunt Emily would make whortleberry pies, and jam, until the whole kitchen steamed with the cooking, and the luscious fruity aroma made all their mouths water. And Loveday would be taken home to Willard's Store, carefully carrying a pie she'd baked specially for her mother . . . and proud of her pie-markings.

She wouldn't be staying on at the farm after Oak Apple Day this year, Loveday thought keenly. The sooner she could get away once the feasting was over, the better. And it hadn't got warm enough yet for the berries to be ripe for going a-hilling, so there was no use in Aunt Emily trying to persuade her.

In the late afternoon on the day before the sheep-shearing, Loveday heard the shop bell tinkle, and then a voice she hadn't heard for a long while sent the blood sickeningly to her cheeks.

'Where be 'ee, Lovey-dovey?' Matt hollered out, standing with hands on hips and gaping all round the new fine shop his cousin now owned. Mrs Mundy gave him one of her best frowns, but Matt never even noticed. Instead, he was thinking that little Loveday had done all right for 'erself, and wonderin' just how she was still gettin' away with the fact that she was hidin' a bab beneath her skirts!

His Ma had said never a word on't when she'd come home from visiting Loveday, though Matt had quizzed her as intently as possible without raising too much suspicion that his interest was a mite more than natural.

'She's middlin', 'was all his Ma would say. 'What more 'ould 'ee expect after such doings as she's 'ad to live through? Mebbe a spell away from the town'll do 'er some good, mebbe not. She's a strange little body at times an' no mistake.'

Matt's eyes roamed over Loveday's strange little body when she appeared swiftly in the shop on hearing his voice. Still as comely a wench as ever, he noted, if not as sparkling as she once was. Truth to tell, he'd been more apprehensive at comin' to fetch her at his mother's request than he'd have thought possible, since he had no way o' knowin' whether Loveday would start screamin' and carryin' on at him for what he'd done to 'er . . . but standin' so proud, an' with the pleats an' folds of her dress hidin' her shape, a body 'ould never guess.

'I thought you'd be too busy at the farm to spare anyone to come for me,' Loveday said tartly. 'I expected to come in a hired trap. It wouldn't have been any trouble.'

'Now you didn't really think I'd leave 'ee to come all that way on your own, did 'ee, me darlin'?' Matt grinned, his coarse face darkening a little as she made it so plain she weren't pleased to see him. An' in front of they old 'uns sat there like stone statues too. Matt was none too pleased with Loveday's reaction. Stuck up as ever, his pretty little Lovey-dovey . . . but he could forgive 'er a lot, he thought, as she swished away from him into some back room and said she'd collect her things right away then.

She still had a gleam in they deep blue eyes of hers that reminded him of other times when she hadn't been so distant from him. Even though she hadn't wanted it, he'd made good and sure she knew what a man's body was all about. She'd had a right horny breakin'-in.

'You been keepin' well then, Loveday?' he asked innocently, as she climbed into the farm trap beside him and they clattered off down the roads leading out of the town.

'I'm all right,' her voice was scratchy. Never again could she feel easy with this uncouth lout to whom she was allied by ties of blood. Never could she forget the humiliation suffered at his hands. She heard him give a throaty chuckle as he whipped the horse into faster action.

'That you be, my pretty, and like to be bloomin' like the spring blossom afore long, I'll be bound.'

Loveday stared straight ahead as they covered the lanes

leading towards Taunton Deane with its apple orchards and lush pastures, averting her head a little as they passed the property belonging to Adam's father. Matt was talking in riddles, she thought crossly, and she couldn't be bothered to try and decipher them. She wished they didn't have to pass Goss House. It reminded her too painfully of the way Adam had rejected her in leaving without a word.

Neither Sarah nor her father had had any satisfactory explanation to give her on the few occasions she'd seen them since then. And to Loveday it seemed obvious that the son of the house was regretting his sudden passion for a young widow with far lower status than his own. And having second thoughts about tying himself to a girl who'd given in to her father's wishes and married another. Maybe this was his way of paying her back, Loveday thought bitterly, when the long dark nights had been spent in tossing and turning, her pillow damp with tears. Maybe he had already forgotten her . . . but she didn't find it so easy to forget.

All the way to the Willard farm, Matt kept up a coarse and ambiguous line of talk that she ignored as far as possible, closing her ears to the sly references to times past. Only when he stopped the horse and cart at the farm did Loveday turn to him with a freezing look.

'Don't you dare to come near me while I'm staying here tonight, Matt Willard. If you do, I swear I'll kill you, and that's a promise.'

She swept away from him, leaving him gaping, but well aware that it was a threat he'd best not ignore. There was too much ragin' Willard tension in his Lovey-dovey just now that he recognised all too well. A pity . . . but Matt could still bait 'er, he thought cheerfully. He could still find out how she was farin' with the bab in her belly, and it would be a lark to let on to her that he knew all about it, since his hintin' hadn't provoked her into saying a word about it!

She could forget Matt as she was welcomed into the warm and steamy kitchen, everything the same as ever, with her aunt bustling about and getting food ready for the morrow. And instructing Loveday not to waste time in chit-chat, but to

225

tie on an apron and start mixing the pastry dough.

'The men are out bringin' down the sheep,' Aunt Emily told her. 'We'll give 'em supper tonight and a bite to eat after the shearin' in the mornin'. Will you be staying on afterwards?'

'No, I must get back,' Loveday spoke quickly, her hands already at work in the big mixing bowl, not looking at her aunt. 'I can't leave the shop in the hands of the Mundys for too long.'

Her aunt bit back the remark that family business was more important than selling cider to drunkards, and that Loveday had nothing else to rush back for . . . in the circumstances it would have been tactless. Though appraising her niece, Emily Willard could see none of the grieving widow about her. Of course, it was four months now, and she'd hardly been a bride afore she was a widow, but there was still summat not right about Loveday. Emily, not usually a greatly perceptive woman, could feel it as surely as she pummelled the bread plait beneath her hands. The girl was as strung-up as any of Finch's Christmas geese had ever been.

'A couple o' the Bagley boys have asked to stay overnight to be up an' ready for the shearing in the mornin',' Aunt Emily went on. 'They'm starting at five o'clock as usual, so we'll be up early to feed 'em all. An' you'll be sleepin' wi' me, Loveday, since we'll have to be shiftin' beds about to accomodate 'em all.'

She was astonished to see the look of relief that spread over Loveday's face, as if the sun had suddenly shone out of her eyes. Why, mebbe the poor lamb was missin' that lump of a husband of hers after all, Emily thought wonderingly, and was a'feared to sleep alone.

She'd have been even more astonished and enraged to know Loveday's thoughts at that moment. If she was sleeping with her aunt, there was no way Matt could force his odious attentions on her! She began to cheer up. In twenty-four hours she'd be back in her own home, and her renewed contact with her farming cousins would be over.

Her eyes softened a little. There'd been genuine boisterous greetings from the young ones, and Zeb had shown her his usual good-natured warmth in his simple way. She hadn't seen her Uncle Jack yet, since he was out in the hills, and the boys were now going off to join him.

But there was too much work to do to waste time in worrying about anything. She was here and she'd best help, or she'd be getting a ticking from her aunt. And at supper that night it was easy to avoid being anywhere near Matt, with so many large male bodies to feed and clear up after. She was little more than a skivvy on such occasions, but for once it didn't matter. All she wanted was to get through the time at the farm, and be on her way back home.

Next morning when the ritual of cooking and clearing up began again, and the men set off to wash the sheep in the pond before the shearing began in rotation, Loveday's thoughts went fleetingly to her father. He probably wouldn't be up just yet, she thought, but soon he'd be shutting up shop like the rest of the tradesmen that day, and preening himself in his best bib and tucker, and parading round the town, a club member at last. She couldn't begrudge him his moment of triumph, she thought reluctantly.

It was late afternoon before the men began trickling back to the farm in twos and threes. Loveday was out feeding the hens when she saw Matt's large aggressive shape approaching her. She glanced around. Zeb was some distance behind, dawdling in the spring sunshine, glad to be free of the dusty sheep's wool that tickled his nose and throat.

'Well, my pretty, so here we are at last,' Matt said throatily. The barn was between them and the farmhouse, and Loveday began edging towards it and then stopped. She had no wish to be cornered inside with him. She threw down the corn-basket from over her arm, and the hens leapt squawkingly towards this unexpected food bonus, rivalling any of Matt's cock-fighting sorties in their efforts to satisfy their greed.

'You keep away from me, Matt Willard,' she spoke rapidly, the words tumbling out of her. Her face flushed as he laughed, his arms stuck out, hands on hips as he looked her over in an insulting fashion. She felt as if his eyes foraged beneath the spring dress and covering apron she wore, right through to her soft flesh. The hatred she felt for him made her skin crawl.

'Now why should I do that, Lovey-dovey?' he laughed coarsely. 'You ain't allus been so partic'lar, 'ave 'ee?'

'I never gave you any encouragement to touch me,' she spat the words at him, her deep blue eyes flashing with fury at his intimation.

'Liked it though, didn't 'ee?' Matt's voice said slyly. 'There ain't no bab sired in this world wi'out a spark of lust atween a pair.'

He couldn't have shocked her more if he'd stripped naked there and then. Whatever she might have said was lost to her as the horror of it hit her. He knew about the baby. Somehow, God knew how, Matt knew . . .

'When's it to be then, me pretty? You'll be sure an' bring it to see its Pa, won't 'ee? Even if no other folk but we two knows the truth on it.'

Loveday's breath escaped her in a sharp gasp. He didn't know all of it then. He believed she was still pregnant! But *how* could he possibly have known? There wasn't another living soul who knew, except . . .

'Polly Reeves!' she shouted furiously. Matt glanced uneasily towards the farmhouse, but they were well away from it as Loveday's voice rose hysterically. Zeb came nearer, stopping abruptly at the sight of his pretty cousin Loveday looking so angry at summat. His pale blue Willard eyes looked uncertainly from one to the other of them. But Loveday hardly noticed him.

'You don't mean to tell me you took any notice of her lies?' Her only recourse was to deny it totally. He could never prove it, and Polly was gone and good riddance. She glared at him scathingly. 'That's just the kind of dirt I might have expected from *her*,' she said witheringly. 'As if a baby would hatch from such a disgusting act with you!'

Matt lunged forward to grab her arm and dig his fingers into it. He was sorely put out at this reaction.

'Are you tellin' me there's no bab in your belly?' he forgot about discretion since there was only his loon of a brother standing by, and he was too much of a dunderhead to take it

228

all in. 'Can you tell me that to me face, Loveday Willard?'

For the first time in her life, Loveday felt she had the upper hand. She thrust her face close to his, grabbed his free hand and pressed it against the front of the rough apron. Pressed it hard to the taut flatness of her belly.

'Nothing there, is there, my clever cousin? No hideous little brat to carry your name on, thanks be to God! And if one had ever been born, I think I'd have strangled it at birth, so there!'

His hand struck her on the side of the face, causing her to cry out and almost lose her balance. She went crashing into the side of the barn, rubbing her bruised cheek. But she didn't care. It was worth it to see the fury in Matt Willard's face. She guessed now how he'd been saving up this titbit of information to taunt her with, and now she'd thrown it all back in his face.

'Do you think I'd have wanted anything belonging to you, you stinking pig?' she lashed at him. 'I've enough to remember of you to last me a lifetime.'

He rushed at her, pressing his body flat against hers, so that she couldn't escape him. She squirmed as she tried to free herself, but there was no escaping his fleshy mouth as it fastened itself on hers, forcing open her mouth, and feeling his tongue perform a pseudo act of love inside hers. She wanted to retch, but she was pinned and couldn't move. She felt Matt's body writhe against hers, his arms flattening her own to the wall. His knee pushed her legs apart, grinding against her thighs. Fully clothed as they were, he jerked against her as insultingly as if she was a farm animal ready for mating.

Suddenly she felt him being dragged away from her, and she almost fell, gasping and sobbing as she rubbed savagely at her mouth and spat out the taste of his saliva.

'You're not to hurt Loveday no more!' She heard Zeb's normally placid voice raised and agitated. She looked on in horror as his big hands went around Matt's throat and began to shake him as if he was a puppet. 'You said you pleased Loveday afore. You didn't say nothin' about no bab! Nor that she was hurt because of 'ee. You didn't tell me all on't, did 'ee?'

'Stop it, Zeb!' Loveday suddenly gasped out as she saw

229

Matt's eyes begin to bulge. Strong as he was, he was no match for the lumbering Zeb on the rare occasions he was roused. He took no notice, and in desperation she tugged at his arm. 'Please, Zeb, this is a bad thing you're doing. I'm not hurt any more. I'm all right, and I want you to stop hurting Matt. *Please*!'

Slowly the rage in her cousin subsided, and he let go of his brother so quickly, Matt staggered to the ground, choking and clutching at his throat. But he was going to be all right, and it was more important now that Zeb shouldn't repeat any of the things he'd heard. Loveday spoke to him quickly as the sounds of her uncle and some of the men returning from the shearing drifted towards them.

'Promise me all that's happened here will be our secret, Zeb. I don't want anybody else knowing about it. Do you promise me?'

Zeb looked from her to his brother, still muttering and hawking on the ground.

'But Matt hurt 'ee – '

'Yes, he did, but it's something I don't want to talk about or to think about ever again.'

He nodded slowly, his pale eyes still troubled, as if not understanding how such a wrong could be disregarded. But the next minute he heard Loveday answering his father's hollering, that the boys had had a bit of a scuffing match and the hens had got the best of it when the basket had been knocked out of her hand. He and Matt were both in for an ear-cuffing then for wasting good corn, but neither brother denied their cousin's story.

Loveday could hardly bear to look at Matt again. She counted the hours now until she could be ready to leave the farm, asking that Zeb should take her back and hearing Uncle Jack guffaw that the wench must be taking a fancy to 'un, but agreeing amiably enough. She'd have walked every step of the way back to Taunton rather than sit beside Matthew in the cart again.

But there was plenty to do before the time came when she was to leave. The sheep were all shorn and ready to go back to

230

the hills, and Jack Willard was given his dues for the washing and the housing of 'em for the day. Emily Willard provided her usual Oak Apple Day feast, helped out by the comely little niece with the hair like sunlight on a June morning, and the delicacy of features that contrasted so sensuously with her Willard temperament. There was talk of her trouble, poor wench, but it took awhile to filter to outlying farms, and she seemed to have overcome it well enough by the looks on 'er, they remarked sagely among themselves.

And today was a day for feastin' and singin' and cider suppin' before they made their unsteady ways back to their various farms. 'Tweren't a day for looking back and ruminatin'.

At last Loveday felt she could leave without causing too much eyebrow raising. She gave her aunt and uncle a dutiful peck on the cheek and promised them she wouldn't stay away so long next time. What she promised herself was somewhat different. She made little fuss of saying goodbye to her cousins, and breathed a long sigh of relief when at last she was jogging along beside Zeb in the farm cart and heading back towards Taunton. It was already turning dusk by the time they arrived, and Zeb wouldn't want to be hanging about. She watched as he lit the lanterns each side of the cart and impulsively pressed a swift kiss on his cheek for his gentle championing of her.

'He ought to be made to pay, Loveday,' Zeb muttered clumsily, and without waiting for an answer he clacked the horse into action and started the return journey.

Loveday went inside her shop and closed the door thoughtfully. No, she didn't want any sort of revenge taken against Matt. It was over, and she'd emerged miraculously whole if not entirely untainted. But no-one else knew of that, and the fact that Polly had been so foolish as to confide in Matt left her burning with rage. But as long as he'd told no-one else . . . Loveday shuddered, imagining it! She doubted that he would, knowing the effect such news would have on the entire Willard family, but outside the family, perhaps . . . Thank

God Matt had few friends or cronies, and she couldn't think of one person in whom he'd be able to confide and know that his appalling secret was safe.

She had hardly been back half an hour and recovered slightly from the tension of the last two days, when the shop door bell began to ring insistently. She'd sent the Mundys home with many thanks, and thought irritably that it was probably her father, come to gloat over his triumphant day with the Alltrades Club. Loveday was tempted not to answer it, knowing he'd be awash with drink and flushed with success, and fit to talk the tail off a donkey. And she was so desperately tired.

The bell continued to ring, and in the end she threw the door open crossly, peering out into the gloom of the night.

'Miss – Mrs – uh, Miss Willard, miss,' a hoarse voice stuttered out. A voice she vaguely recognised as being one of the workers at Goss Cider. She felt her heart miss a beat and then begin to thump uncomfortably. 'I've been sent to tell you, Miss, that Mr Norman Goss passed over an hour or so back. Miss Sarah said I was to be sure and call in on 'ee, Miss, afore I ride on to Bristol an' Box to inform the relatives and Master Adam, it bein' quicker than waitin' for the mornin' coach. Then I'm to send a fresh rider on to London to inform Miss Grace, expense bein' no object, as you might say.'

The man drivelled on, clearly agitated at his untimely task, while Loveday stood as if carved out of candle-wax. Outwardly calm as she thanked him and said she'd go to Miss Sarah as soon as it was daylight. Inwardly, ready to crumple and melt at such sad news, her spirit weeping at the death of that fine and gentle man, who'd been so much more a father to her than her own had ever been, in the short time she had known him.

CHAPTER SEVENTEEN

Adam knew he was going to be late for his shift that morning, and he didn't care. If the foreman decided to give him his marching orders when he arrived at the tunnel, then it would save him the trouble of deciding for himself. He was sick of the cold and damp. Even on the brightest day, it was a foul and gloomy place in which to work. He remembered grimly how he'd been fool enough to believe a man had to start at the bottom rung of the ladder to understand a job fully, learning as he went along for the best apprenticeship of all.

He'd learned plenty by now. He'd learned that he hated the smell and the seemingly endless task confronting engineers and navvies alike. He hated the raw necessity of sometimes having to crawl in mud and filth to drag away the bits of a man, with whom he'd been having a ribald conversation minutes before a rockfall splattered him against the rough jagged wall of the tunnel. He'd also learned that there was a dogged streak in him that wouldn't let him admit defeat and go home.

Maybe things would have been different if it hadn't been for Loveday's betrayal. Each day Adam hacked savagely at the rockface in the guttering candle-light, feeling that each splintering blow was a punishment to himself for believing in her. Loveday, with the soft golden ethereal looks of an angel; he might have been able to forgive one betrayal. In fact, he'd already done so, after her stumbling explanation about the butcher's impotence.

But two betrayals were too much for any man to forgive. Especially when it was that crowing bastard, Matt Willard, who'd gloried in her sweetness and lived to tell the tale. If he'd had any sense on that last night at Goss House, he'd have kept the bastard's head beneath the cider and drowned him. Only it wouldn't have made any difference. Matt had already told him and nothing could take away the memory of his gloating face. By now, probably everyone could see it for themselves, Adam's thoughts ran on, and she'd be getting their sympathy all over again, assuming it was Finch's child she carried.

No, he was better keeping well away from women, even though some of his work-mates thought him a rum 'un for refusing to go with them any longer when they frequented the local bawdy-houses. He didn't care. If any man dared to suggest he was anything other than a man, he soon discovered that Adam Goss had fists of steel and wasn't afraid to use them.

'Mr Goss, Sir!' He heard the raucous voice of the landlady at his lodgings as he still lingered beneath the bedcovers, loath to begin another day in the tunnel, and yet unwilling to find an alternative way of living.

'All right, I'm coming,' he shouted back irritably. Then he heard the rapping on his door. God damn the woman, he fumed, she was worse than a mother hen at times. He threw on a dressing-robe and went to the door. The woman stood there, pop-eyed in her serviceable morning attire. 'What is it? Has the tunnel fallen in or something?'

It had to be something dire to make her climb the steep stairs more than once a week to clean the rooms housing her lodgers. She puffed a moment while she caught her breath.

'If you please, Mr Goss,' she always spoke with more deference to this particular lodger, recognising him for a gentleman, for all that he worked the tunnel. 'There's a person come from Somerset 'specially to see you. Ridden all night, 'e has, so I reckon it must be summat mighty important.'

Adam was already pushing past her and taking the stairs two at a time. Some awful premonition took hold of him. It had to be his father, of course. Taken very ill, perhaps, or – one look at the face of the cider worker, his face drawn with fatigue and embarrassment at being the bearer of bad news, and Adam knew.

The man twisted his cap in his hands as he said his piece, touching his finger to his forelock as he realised he was now speaking to his master.

234

' 'Tis sorry indeed I am, Master Adam, to bring you such news, but I'm feared that your father passed over last evening. Miss Sarah wrote you a note, an' since I've called in on your uncle's family in Bristol, there's a note from 'un too.'

Adam had to fight back the lump in his throat as he ripped open the two notes, Sarah's written in obvious distress.

'Dear, dear Adam, please come home as quickly as possible. I cannot cope alone, and I need your presence. Geoffrey has been wonderful, and suggests the funeral be one week from tonight. I have written to Uncle Miles in Bristol informing him of the news, and a rider will take over from Bob Duffy to take the news to Grace and Aunt Lucy in London. I pray that we will be all together soon. Your loving sister, Sarah.'

He scanned the other note quickly.

'My dear nephew, I need not say how grieved I am to hear of your father's demise,' Uncle Miles was ever pompous in grief to hide his emotions, Adam recalled. 'If you will come here as soon as you are ready, we will leave for Somerset immediately. I will be remaining until after the funeral if you and your sister request it. I am presently preparing for departure, and await your arrival with doleful heart in the circumstances. Your affect. uncle, Miles.'

Adam cleared his throat as the two other people in the room watched him unblinkingly, looking to him to give them a lead. He asserted himself as quickly as his spinning thoughts would allow.

'Mrs Ellis, as you've heard, my father has died, and I must return to Somerset immediately. I shall not be coming back to Box, so you may let my room as from today. It's all paid up until the end of the week, so you may keep any sum due to me for your inconvenience.' He knew full well that his bed would be slept in that night by a replacement tunnel worker, and the woman wouldn't lose by his departure.

'But your job, Mr Goss, and your wages due – '

'I've more important things on hand at this moment,' he said sharply. 'If you would send word by one of the others that any wages due to me shall go to the hospital in Bath, for a few comforts for accident victims from the tunnel, I would be glad. It will be pitifully little, but it may ease someone's lot. And now, Bob Duffy, I'm sure Mrs Ellis will give you some breakfast and a warm drink while I dress and pack my things. Will you rest awhile? You look done in, man.'

'I'll be gettin' back as soon as this good lady'll do as you ask, Master Adam,' there was forelock touching again. 'Don't you worry none about me. But you'll be wanting a trap to take you to Bristol to your uncle's.'

'I'll send someone for it,' Mrs Ellis said quickly, clearly realising now that 'Master Adam' must be even more important than she'd thought, and that there would probably be a shillin' or two in it for her too, if he could afford to pass on all his wages due to a hospital. She'd see to it an' all. She might be poor, but any lodger could expect honesty from Flo Ellis.

Adam left the two of them together and went back to his room. Once there, he leaned heavily against the door and let the choking sobs well up in his throat. His beloved father was dead, and he hadn't been there to make his peace with him. They had exchanged letters since Adam had left so suddenly, but letters weren't the same. Norman Goss and his son had always had a close and loving relationship. Nothing had caused any rift between them, nor even any misunderstandings, until that last night at Goss House, when Adam knew his father was sorely distressed at his son's uncouth behaviour with a farm boy.

And why had such a thing happened? Because of Loveday Willard, that was why! Adam felt a twist of anger so sharp it was like a knife in his gut. Loveday's betrayal had more far-reaching effects than she could ever have dreamed, causing relations to be strained between his father and himself, and denying Adam the right to hear his father's forgiveness face to face. If it hadn't been for Loveday he'd have made several journeys home in the last few months, but every time he'd hesitated, knowing that everywhere he looked in that soft green country, there would be a reminder of her seductive sweetness. A sweetness that was as deadly as belladonna.

236

As he packed up his belongings and dressed himself for travelling, Adam knew he was shifting the blame for his not being there at his father's end, on to Loveday's slender shoulders. He knew it and couldn't stop it, because if he didn't blame someone, he would go mad with grief and self-condemnation.

But now he was going home, and he wouldn't be coming back. His future had been decided for him after all, and it would be up to him to take up the reins of the cider business in which Norman Goss had been so intrigued. It had begun to fascinate Adam himself, and it was one small way in which he could recompense his father, by keeping Goss Cider alive and thriving. He made a silent vow to himself. So be it!

Shortly afterwards, everything was settled at his lodgings, Bob Duffy insisting on being on his way like the loyal employee he was, and Adam was being transported in a hired trap to Bristol. His uncle welcomed him with one brief hug and covered his feelings on the loss of a brother by briskly taking charge, paying off the driver of the trap, and hustling Adam into his own waiting carriage. Miles Goss travelled in style, and he saw no reason to do otherwise now, even though he'd hastily draped black cloth at the windows and tied black plumes on to the horses as a mark of respect, and to show the world that the occupants were in mourning.

'A sad business, Adam,' Miles Goss cleared his throat noisily when they were on their way south-west. 'You'll hardly have had time to think what to do yet. As the son of the house, it will naturally fall on your shoulders to make the decisions. Which will it be, I wonder? It will keep your mind from dwelling too gloomily to give some thought to the future, my boy. Whether to continue with your engineering dreams or not, though I should think you've given the tunnelling a fair whack, and could start thinking about buying up your own company by now! Or to come back to Bristol with the girls. Back to where your roots are, boy. I'll wager your sister Grace wouldn't say no to that, if she's not too hoity-toity now after staying with your Aunt Lucy and her

237

fine London ways. I daresay Sarah might have different ideas, since I hear she's got herself affianced to a young doctor.'

Adam let him prattle on until he had to stop to draw breath. It was his way to sound so busy and businesslike, one could be forgiven for thinking he didn't care. Adam knew that he did care all the same.

'I've already made up my mind, Uncle Miles,' he said steadily. 'I shall become Goss Cider, just as my father did. I know it's what he would have wanted, and I must admit I feel a great affinity with that part of the world.'

With the red earth . . . the sweet red earth that was synonymous with his name. Loveday's soft voice marvelling at the fact swam through his senses . . . with an effort he blotted it out.

He felt his uncle's hand pat his knee, and knew it was a gesture of approval. It didn't matter that his uncle probably thought Adam was giving up a dream to fulfil his father's dream. He didn't believe in dreams any more. They were as intangible as the wind. Just when you thought you had one in your grasp, it scattered and vanished. He pulled his thoughts together.

The carriage was passing swiftly through towns and hamlets, and once they stopped at an inn for refreshment and to rest the horses. But each was eager to get on, and in the late afternoon the buildings of Goss Cider came into sight. As the carriage passed cottage and workers, they felt the same deference accorded them. In so short a while, Norman had been liked and respected, Adam realised. They drew up at the house, and Sarah's running feet and streaming eyes greeted them as she threw herself into Adam's arms first, and then her uncle's.

'Oh, I'm so thankful to see you both,' she gasped out. 'It's been a nightmare, Adam, and if it hadn't been for Loveday – '

'Loveday?' He said sharply. 'She isn't here, is she?'

Sarah flushed, puzzled at his tone, as if Loveday was the last person he'd want to see. She knew there had been some-

238

thing wrong between them, but that Adam could recoil so swiftly at the mention of her friend's name was more than disturbing. It was unbelievable after their previous closeness.

'She came at once when she knew Father had died,' Sarah said defensively, as the three of them went inside the house. 'Loveday *is* involved, remember, since Father installed Goss cider in her shop.'

'I'd forgotten,' Adam muttered. 'It's just that I think it only right that just the family should be here at this time.'

Sarah stared. 'You won't object if she comes to the funeral, I suppose?' She couldn't help the sarcasm creeping in. Adam was being so – so unlike Adam! And at such time . . .

'I can't stop the curious standing round a burial gathering,' he said, and then his face reddened darkly as Loveday appeared in front of him, bright spots of colour on the whiteness of her face at the insult she'd overheard.

He barely looked at her. In any case he was too agitated to register that there was no sign of pregnancy in her slender figure. To cover Adam's bad manners, Sarah quickly introduced her to her uncle, but the meeting was becoming acutely awkward, and Loveday ended it by saying it would be best if she went home now Sarah was no longer alone, since the Mundys had been in charge of the shop all day and it was hardly fair to them.

She looked at Adam. God in heaven, but he didn't know, the thought almost shrieked in her mind. He didn't know he owned the shop that had once been Finch Viney's. He didn't know he owned *her* . . . it had been a private matter between herself and his father, but the solicitor had drawn up all the legalities, of course. And once the Will was read and details of their transaction made known, Adam would know that however much he detested the idea, their lives were still intertwined, more closely than ever.

She ran her tongue over her dry lips. Why he should detest it so, she didn't understand, nor ever would. But her pride still remained, whatever else she had lost. Her head tilted back, and it was to Sarah that she spoke.

'If you need me for anything, you know where I am, Sarah. If you will let me know the time and place of the funeral, I shall close the shop and attend.'

'Bless you, Loveday,' Sarah hugged her. She whispered in her friend's ear. 'Forgive him, dearest. It must be the shock that's made him so callous.'

Whatever it was, Adam made no attempt to speak to her as she left the house, after Sarah had called one of the workmen to take her back to Taunton in the pony and trap. Somehow she kept her head high, stemming the flow of tears until she reached the privacy of her own home. And then they emerged like a torrent. How *could* he behave so cruelly towards her? What had she done? What in heaven's name had she *done*?

He never once came near her in the week that followed. If Loveday had expected him to ride into Taunton and sort out the differences between them that were completely inexplicable to her, she was bitterly disappointed. She could only assume he had found another, more worthy young lady on whom to shower his affections, one who didn't bear the name of Willard, with all the unsavoury associations it implied. She had never taken him for a snob, but it was the only explanation she could find.

She was hesitant of approaching the Goss family at the burial. There they all were, dressed in black, and it was a world removed from the undignified happenings at her mother's funeral, when she had leapt like a wild cat at her cousin Matt, and started up more family wranglings. This one was conducted in genteel sobriety, with gentle snufflings into lace-edged handkerchiefs, and once when she looked across at Adam and caught his hard glance, her heart skipped a beat, that he could look at her so coldly.

Sarah stepped over to her when the burial was at an end, speaking awkwardly.

'I'd ask you back to the house, Loveday, but Adam has insisted that it should be a private affair, with just the immediate family. I hope you don't feel slighted, because both Father and I regarded you most warmly, you know that.'

'I do know it,' Loveday's voice was tight. She looked into Sarah's face with brimming eyes, aware that the ever attentive Doctor Geoffrey Chard, presumably included now in the 'immediate family', hovered near.

'Do you know why Adam hates me so, Sarah?' she whispered.

Sarah shook her head helplessly. 'I'm sure he doesn't hate you. How could anybody?' She leaned forward and kissed Loveday's cheek. 'I'll come and see you soon, I promise. I'll have to go now, Loveday. The solicitor will be at the house, and Grace and Aunt Lucy want to get back to London very soon.'

She picked her way back to where Doctor Chard waited for her, to have her hand tucked in his arm. Loveday turned away abruptly, unable to watch the caring way he helped her back to the carriages, emphasizing the loneliness in her own heart.

'Loveday.'

All her nerves jumped as she heard the sound of her own name spoken on Adam's lips. She whirled round, but there was still no vestige of warmth in his face. His dear, dear face, that even now she loved so much . . . she swallowed back the rush of emotion that made her want to fling herself into his arms.

'My father's solicitor has had a private word with me concerning the property in which you live,' Adam said carefully. 'I merely wanted to reassure you that I've no wish to turn you out or make any different arrangements. You may continue to be my tenant as long as you wish, and though I will be residing at Goss House from now on, there will be little need for us to meet. The stock will be delivered as before, and I trust you will continue with the accounting as usual. I wish you good-day, Miss Willard.'

He moved away from her, and she watched him go as if it was all part of a horrible dream. He spoke to her as if she was nothing less than one of his minions. How *dare* he treat her so! His tenant indeed. And he the Lord and Master of all he surveyed. She was right. He *was* a snob, and she was well rid of him. She told herself so all the way home, and then once inside she had to get out, because the occasion had aroused all her jittery memories of Finch and finding him in a pool of his own blood; in the end she went and visited her father and cooked him supper, which amazed and delighted him, because now at last he could regale his wayward daughter with tales of his comeuppance into the world of the Alltrades Club. It was about time she bent her ear and heard him out, and realised that not all comeuppances were bad. This one had been deliriously profitable, since he had had a wooden plaque made to go in his window, not being elegible for a brass one for a year, but all recognised it, and patronised his store because of it. The best thing Polly Reeves had ever done for Ralph Willard was to skip off with all his savings, he often thought gleefully.

And Loveday wasn't the loser for it, anyway. She still had Viney's shop, even if it didn't seem to do her a power of good by the looks of her, with the dark shadows under her eyes as if she never got enough sleep. But mebbe that was because of today, since he'd heard of Norman Goss's passing.

'A good funeral, was it?' he said conversationally, when he'd lit his pipe and was clouded in a gauze of smoke.

'Oh, one of the best,' Loveday's sarcasm was lost on him.

Ralph let out a discreet high-pitched fart that would have had Polly wild with mirth at the backside pinching that had produced it.

'Oh well, he's just as dead as the next 'un, for all the trimmin's,' Ralph remarked, and told himself he'd never understand women if he lived to be a hundred, as his daughter burst into noisy, releasing tears.

Adam lay sleepless in his bedroom at Goss House, gazing unseeingly at the changing patterns thrown by moonlight across the room. The day was done with, and his father would have been the last person in the world to want him to waste time on futile tears. Life was to be lived, Norman would say, so go on and live it; if he hadn't felt that way, he'd have put his foot down long ago at his son's decision to work as a common labourer in the Box tunnel, instead of continuing the life of a gentleman, and all because of a dream inspired by one Isambard Kingdom Brunel.

Adam moved restlessly. He belonged here now, and any lingering regrets were futile. Tomorrow his sister Grace would go back to London with their Aunt Lucy to continue her socialite life; Uncle Miles would leave for Bristol; Sarah's future was assured in the marriage to the doctor arranged for the end of the year. Suddenly he realised how alone he was.

All this, the property, the apple orchards, the business, even the shop in Taunton that had once been Viney's butcher's shop now belonged to him. The girls had been amply provided for, but as the son of the family, Adam could now count himself a rich man. Yet still he felt himself poor, for in his loss, there was no-one to comfort him the way Geoffrey Chard had held his sister Sarah, nor the way Grace had been supported by the older relatives. He had never felt so alone.

Inevitably, his thoughts turned to *her*. To Loveday, whose image was never far from his imagination, no matter how much he sought to cast her out. His heart had yearned towards her when he'd seen her, taut and pale, standing alone in the churchyard, a sprinkling of curious townsfolk nearby. And what had he done? Been curt to the point of insulting, demeaning everything they had once meant to each other. His hands clenched in the darkness.

And the thought that had been nagging him all day returned sharply. By now, if Adam read a woman's physiology correctly, Loveday should be showing large with child, and she was not. There was no way she could be hiding it now.

Had he been too gullible in believing all that Matt Willard told him that night? The oaf had been swilling drink even before he arrived at Goss House . . . had the whole tale been a lustful wishing and nothing more? Coloured only too well by Matt's evil mind? Adam wanted desperately to think so, and yet for all Matt Willard's coarseness, he wouldn't have taken him for a cunning person. He'd appeared in the night as someone with a tale he was bursting to tell, and who better to tell it to than his one-time friend, Adam Goss, to whom he'd made the boast that he'd be the one to deflower his pretty cousin?

It always came back to the same thing. It *could* be true, and what was even more ugly, Loveday could have rid herself of the child by taking potions. Adam was tormented anew. And strangely, or maybe not so strangely, since this was a house so newly deprived of one whose presence still remained, he seemed to hear his father's voice, admonishing him gently, as he'd done when Adam was a child.

'If you want to know something, Adam, then *ask*. All the knowledge in the world would remain silent for ever if those with enquiring minds didn't seek it out. Never be afraid to ask, my son.'

It was to Sarah that he put the first tentative questions, a few days later, when the house was gradually getting used to the new order of things with Adam as its head.

'Did you see much of Loveday after her visit with you, Sarah?' He helped himself to some choice pieces of boiling fowl at dinner, not looking directly at her.

'Not too much. She seemed to become a bit of a recluse once she went back to Taunton. And since you've mentioned it at last, I hardly blame her for feeling hurt,' she couldn't help the reproach in her voice. 'I don't know how deep your feelings were for Loveday, Adam, but I know how she felt about you. I didn't need to be told. It was written all over her – and anyone could see you were besotted with her. How do you think she felt when you disappeared the way you did, without even saying goodbye? I know what I'd have thought!'

'What would you have thought, Sarah? Tell me, since I'm obviously not too well in tune with a woman's mind?' his voice was brittle, and he wished he'd never started this. He didn't want to hear it, yet he couldn't stop himself listening.

'I'd have thought you were merely toying with me, and once you realised how involved you were getting, you took fright and escaped. I'd have thought there was probably someone else – '

'Then you'd have been wrong!' Adam burst out, piqued at her bluntness. 'There's never been anyone but Loveday for me, nor ever will be.'

'Then why don't you tell *her* that, instead of me? It may not be too late to put things right, though it depends on how forgiving a nature she has, and how deeply you've wounded her pride.' She put her hand on his arm. 'Don't let pride drive you apart for ever, Adam. Whatever it is, forget it and go to her. She loves you, Adam, and in the end that's the only thing that counts, believe me.'

It was so simple for her, sitting there so earnestly, with the love of a good man assured, and her life as serenely mapped out as the merging of the seasons. Love had put a bloom on her that was almost embarrassing to his eyes, and he threw down his cutlery, his appetite suddenly gone.

'I'll think about it,' he said curtly. 'Let's talk about something else, shall we?'

Sarah acquiesced at once, but Adam knew the moment had to come when he faced Loveday and demanded to know the truth. The fact of not knowing gnawed away at him, and during the next week Sarah noted how often her brother strode off alone through the orchards, as if to seek solace among the blossoming trees.

He was inextricably bound up with her now, Adam told himself over and over. It was just as if his father, even from the grave, had decreed that Loveday should be part of his son's life. Buying her premises in Taunton so privately, so that not even Sarah had been aware of it until the Will reading and the extra legalities concerning Loveday's shop had been disclosed, bound the two of them together. There was no way Adam could avoid an eventual meeting, and it was only putting off the day.

He rode into Taunton at last, armed with some legitimate

queries concerning the cider business in which they now were both concerned. It was evening, and Loveday had closed the shop for the day, but she responded as usual when the bell rang out. She had been Ralph's daughter for too long to refuse a customer.

Her face flooded with painful colour when she saw Adam standing there. Her heart leapt in her chest and involuntarily she pressed a slim hand to her breast. Adam refused to stare at the rounded softness he remembered so well, and gazed sternly at her face instead. Even there, those large luminous eyes of that deep midnight blue stirred him frighteningly fast, and if he didn't keep a firm control on himself he knew he'd be sweeping her into his arms and forgetting all about recriminations.

'Well? Are you going to ask me in, or do we have to conduct our business on the doorstep for all of Taunton to hear?' he spoke roughly, and if Loveday had thought this was to be a lovers' reunion, the hope died in her at the remoteness of Adam's face. She held back the door and bade him come in.

'Will you take some refreshment with me, Sir?' she spoke in an exaggeratedly servile way. She was incensed and bitterly hurt at his manner. 'I can offer you hot milk or porter, or cider, of course.'

'Maybe later. I'd like to see the place first, since it now belongs to me.'

She had forgotten that he'd never been inside it before. She showed him the shop premises where the rows of cider jugs stood on shelves, and the back room where she took charge of the accounting, opening the books silently, resentful of the way he was treating her. Never guessing at how hard it was for him to ignore the womanly scent of her, nor the way his hands occasionally brushed hers, or the swing of her golden hair on his face, let down out of its confining pins for the night as it was.

'And the rest of the premises?' he said at last. 'I should like to see all that belongs to me, if you please.'

She stared at his unflinching gaze, hot with colour as she

wondered if he included her in that statement.

'There's an attic in the roof, and a bedroom and parlour.'

Adam nodded. 'Lead the way, please.'

He didn't really know why he was doing this, humiliating her in this way. He scarcely glanced into the attic, but in the bedroom he lingered, his eyes taking in the bed on which she slept, and the patchwork coverlet she'd no doubt worked herself. Beneath the covers was a bulge that was probably her nightgown.

Was he going to demand the use of her body as well, Loveday thought feverishly? He was so overbearing, so different from the Adam she'd loved for so long. Why did he look at the bed so intently? Her nerves were razor-sharp. What did he want of her?

'This is the marriage-bed, I presume?' Adam said.

'Yes – of course – Adam.'

He looked at her, his eyes dark. 'Where the poor impotent butcher found he was unable to perform satisfactorily.'

Loveday felt herself begin to shake.

'I told you that,' she whispered. 'No-one else but you knew the truth of it, Adam. My marriage was never a true one.'

'Then it couldn't have produced a child?'

The question was so unexpected, so bullet-quick, that Loveday gasped with the shock of it. *He knew* . . . all this time, this was what it had all been about. Somehow, God knew how, Adam had known about the child she'd been expecting. *Matt Willard* had done this . . . her thoughts tumbled over themselves in her head. That night at Goss House, when Adam had been near drowned in the cider keg, fighting with a ruffian . . . it had been *Matthew* . . . she knew it as surely as she breathed.

Adam had intended shaking the truth out of her, but he was almost overcome with nausea as he watched the changing expressions on her face. She had burned with colour at first, then whitened, and now she was a sickly grey colour. She was incoherent as she tried to stammer out some kind of explanation. But he didn't want to hear it. He had found out

247

what he'd come to find out, and he couldn't listen to any more.

What had happened to the child didn't matter any more either. Nothing mattered, except that he had to get out of here fast, for the place had become more cloying than a whore's bed. He turned and ran down the stairs and out into the clean night air. He knew the truth of it now, and he'd give the earth to un-know it.

CHAPTER EIGHTEEN

The day of the Summer Fair dawned bright and sunny. Loveday awoke to it with mixed feelings. An eternity ago, it seemed, Adam Goss had said he'd dance with her at the Summer Fair on Castle Green. She wondered now if he'd even be there.

It was always a brash, noisy affair, and one to which everyone flocked for miles around. Some shops closed; others stayed open hoping to catch extra trade. Folk came in from the Quantock farms, and gawped at the fine parading townsfolk who never tried to hide their superiority. Loveday's cousins always came to town for the Summer Fair.

'It'll be a nice day out, Adam,' Sarah persuaded him. 'It's a month since Father died, and what good does it do to sit around with long faces? Please say we can go. Geoffrey says he will come in the evening and bring me home, but he can't spare the time during the day because of his duty to his patients. But I don't want to waste a whole day's entertainment!'

He looked at her with a mixture of amusement and exasperation. Couldn't she guess why he was so reluctant, and that it had nothing to do with the mourning for their father?

Wasn't it written in his face for all to see that the less he saw of Loveday Willard the better it was for his peace of mind?

He supposed she didn't guess. Why should she, when she lived in a world of her own that began and ended with Geoffrey Chard, which was just as it should be? And of course Loveday would be there. He'd heard her speak of it on one of their morning walks, when everything on their horizon had been rosy, and he'd listened with enchantment to the soft timbre of her voice as it grew ever more animated.

'This year will be special, Adam, because we'll be there together. You'll love it, I know. I can't think why you didn't go last year, but maybe you were too much the foreigner then,' she teased him. 'You're a part of it now, though. A part of *me*.'

She'd stopped, suddenly modest at sounding so bold, and he'd swung her into his arms and kissed her mouth, murmuring against it.

'So much a part of you, my dearest, that I'd be only half alive if I ever lost you. No – even less than that. I would cease to exist at all.'

'You've got that shut-in look on your face again, Adam,' Sarah's voice was tight with disappointment, not understanding. 'You won't take me, will you? And I'll have to be content with just the evening as soon as Geoffrey can get away.'

Her face came into focus again. He was being grossly unfair to her, Adam thought, spoiling her pleasure because of his own misery. That he was prolonging it by his own wish was something he couldn't explain, except that in punishing himself he was also punishing Loveday ... if she cared at all.

'Of course we'll go,' he forced himself to say heartily. 'It's time some of these Somerset folk met the new owner of Goss Cider anyway. I'll give some of the tradesmen's pretty daughters a jig around the trees! I daresay there'll be more than one to catch my eye.'

And one with whom he *wouldn't* dance, Adam vowed. He'd make it so pointed by dancing with every other girl in sight, she'd be bound to notice. His steady gaze dared Sarah to make any comment on his remark, and she merely shrugged and thought what a mess those two were making of their lives.

Matthew Willard was preparing his game-cock for the great day, making sure to starve it the day before the Fair, so that Prince would be bursting to get at any rival cock's throat for the taste of blood, and the titbits that always followed a cockfight. Matt always expected to make a bit of money at the Summer Fair, and was sure to have his name entered on the list of participants in the cockfighting arena.

'We'll beat all the buggers, Prince, me beauty,' he stroked the gleaming purplish-black feathers, and then swore profusely as the bird turned and nipped his hand. Prince was no respecter of humans. Matt flung the bird away from him and picked up the little steel spurs Prince wore at the fights, checking that they still ran freely.

Zeb ambled into the barn to tell him sullenly that their Ma was callin' 'em for their victuals. Matt looked at his brother irritably. Zeb had been as touchy as a virgin with him for weeks now, and he didn't care for it. The loon was clearly put out about summat, but whatever it was he was bein' as close as a clergyman's purse about it.

'I s'pose youm comin' to the Fair on Sat'day, Zeb? Hopin' to catch some girl's eye, eh?' he grinned, thinking it was a fat chance any girl would look at *him*.

Zeb glared at him. 'Don't want no girls,' he muttered, and then he brightened. 'Me an' Silas an' Tom'll be lookin' out for the jugglers. I might take me chances in a boxin' match.'

Matt guffawed. 'They'd think it were one o' the dancin' bears if they seen you lumberin' about! Time you've thought out your rival's next move, 'e'll have kicked your head in. You'd best leave the boxin' to folk wi' a bit o' brains!'

'Like '*ee*, I s'pose?' Zeb growled. 'Thy brains are all in thee breeches, far's I can see, brother.'

Such a retort from his normally placid brother was

enough to make Matt slap his sides with laughter. Why, the dunderhead was becoming almost human at last, and he didn't bother to argue with Zeb's comment. There was no disgrace in knowin' himself for a randy bugger. He followed Zeb out of the barn, cat-calling after him.

'Mebbe your turn'll come if you spruce yourself up a bit for the Fair! There'll be plenty o' flash-eyed wenches about for the takin'.'

And Matt intended havin' his fill on 'em. His sweet little cousin 'ould be there, but he'd be wary o' givin' her the eye, since her last wildcat attack on 'un. She didn't matter. There was fish and plenty in the sea, and plenty willin' to take on Matt Willard . . . he went into the farmhouse whistling.

Loveday wore a new muslin dress of palest blue, with trailing ribbons and lovers' knots sewn around the hem, and on her head was a matching bonnet. It was the lightest colour dress she'd worn since Finch's death, but it was six months now, and she felt free of all semblance of mourning at last. She looked as fresh as a summer butterfly, and in some ways it was how she felt. As if she was emerging from her frozen chrysalis state and looking eagerly towards a new life. The feeling had grown inside her ever since she had begun to get ready for the walk to Castle Green. Gathering strength and excitement as she saw and heard the chattering folks passing her window on the noisy street. She saw the girls' bonnets bobbing along like a sea of colour atop shining hair and flushed pretty faces, and dresses chosen 'specially to catch a young man's eye. Many a courtship had begun at the Summer Fair . . .

When she was ready, Loveday left instructions for the Mundys that they were to avail themselves of cold meats and pickles and a jug of cider for their middlings, since they were to be at the shop all day. Business should be brisk, with so many folk in town – and if there was any trouble, they were to call on the wheelwright along the street, who would soon sort out any brawling. They assured her they would be capable of handling anything, and Loveday went off with only the slightest misgiving that old Chipper would be unlikely to hold off the feeblest attacker, though Pru Mundy wouldn't be above throwing a jug or two if danger threatened.

But within minutes Loveday was part of the throngs heading towards the Green, and promptly forgot the Mundys. Excitement took hold of her. It was Fair Day; the sky was a cloudless blue and the sun caressed her; she was young and pretty, and if God was feeling generous, Adam Goss might relent towards her.

The Green was a large area, dotted with fruit trees where on normal days folk could wander and sit beneath the shade, but on this day it looked anything but its normal self. There was hardly walking room between the canvas stalls and various arenas, put up almost miraculously overnight it seemed. Arenas for bear-baiting and cockfighting and arm-wrestling; penny stalls containing a hotchpotch of goods; sideshows and barrel organs with brightly-dressed monkeys holding out their paws for money; the smell of hot potatoes and onions.

Trees were decorated with posters, and flags hung from every available branch. Somewhere a band was playing, and drums banged unmercifully as a cryer announced where the boxing area was to be, and for all interested to make their wagers on the contestants. Loveday saw Adam Goss and heard Matt Willard, almost at the same moment.

'There ain't a man here who can compete wi' me at the boxin',' Matt was boasting to a crowd of giggling shop-girls. 'But first off, I'm puttin' my Prince to the test. Did any of 'ee ever see such a wondrous cock?'

The giggles changed to screams of laughter at the daring talk of the bawdy good-looking farm-boy, the girls in no doubt as to its double meaning. Matt was enjoying himself. With all the wenching available here today, even he'd be put to it to last out the course; but he meant to have a bloody good try, he told himself gleefully.

'Loveday!' Sarah still held Adam's arm as she caught sight of her friend, so he had no option but to walk across the patch of Green dividing them with her. Sarah's eyes sparkled. 'Isn't it all exciting? Oh, and you look so pretty. Doesn't she, Adam?'

'Very pretty.' His voice said the words but his expression stayed as remote as ever. The hope in Loveday died a little, but he wasn't going to spoil her day. Her chin lifted as Sarah asked her eagerly if she'd seen the stiltmen yet.

'I've only just arrived – '

'Well then, if you two young ladies want to stay together, I'll take a look elsewhere,' Adam said at once, just as if he couldn't get away from her fast enough. 'You won't want to watch the rougher sports, will you?'

Before either of them could answer, he'd twisted away from them and was swallowed up in the crowd. Sarah tucked her hand in Loveday's arm and gave it a sympathetic squeeze.

'Come on, there's such a lot to see, and I want to do everything at once! Forget about Adam.'

She could as easily forget to breathe . . . but Sarah was right. There was an endless variety of attractions at the Fair, and by the middle of the day when the sun was at its highest, they had barely seen half of them. They paused near the Castle walls, leaning their backs against the old weathered stone as they fanned their mouths from the hot potatoes they'd purchased, and watching the rest of the world enjoying themselves.

There would be a procession very soon. Loveday wondered idly if her father would participate, since some of the local clubs were usually involved. She hadn't bothered to ask him if it included the Alltrades Club, but later on she saw his proudly smiling face, bulbous nose a'shine with sweat, as he held his flower-strewn banner aloft. Ralph was happy, Loveday concluded, and that made her happy too, because he'd be unlikely to bother her. He only came near her to grumble or when he was in trouble.

A large shape she recognised came shambling across to the two girls, and Loveday smiled at her cousin Zeb.

'Enjoying it all, are you. Zeb? Are the younger boys here as well?'

253

'Oh ah,' his rough face beamed at the sight of his pretty cousin. The prettiest maid there, he thought stoutly, though the one wi' her weren't a bad second. 'Matt's over yonder wi' the cocks, and the young lady's brother's been winnin' a fair bit off 'un. Matt ain't so cocky 'imself now!'

He honked at his own joke, but he didn't miss the way Loveday's mouth froze a little at the mention of Matt's name. The maid was still smartin' at the ill his brother had done 'er, and it was something Zeb brooded on. For all his slowness, when he took to ponderin' long about summat, it hacked away at his mind and wouldn't let go.

'I don't know how Adam can be so interested in cock-fighting,' Sarah said crossly.

'Ah well, he ain't no more. He's over prancing wi' the girls now, missy. Over yonder, where the band's a "playin".'

Loveday's heart jolted. She craned her neck, and could see the young men picking out their favoured girls and leading them out to dance. Without waiting to see if Sarah would follow, she pressed through the mass of people and joined the edge of the dancers. Adam was spinning round with a pink-faced girl in a white dress. He saw her. She knew very well that he saw her.

Half on hour later she gave up any hope that he'd ask her to dance. Eyes stinging with the effort of holding back the tears, she watched him dance with every girl in the circle, save her. Other young men were only too glad to take pretty Loveday Willard by the hand and lead her in a merry jig, but none of them mattered a fig to her. Adam was publicly humiliating her. Maybe none but the two of them knew it, but that didn't make it hurt any less.

When she'd had enough of it, Loveday slipped away from the dancing to look for Sarah again. She seemed to have disappeared for the moment, and then she heard Matt's raucous voice baiting her friend. Loveday felt her nerves prickle. How dare he! Showing himself and the whole Willard family up by being so uncouth and loud-mouthed. She pushed through the onlookers, not counting her own behaviour as anything like her cousin's.

254

'Sarah, I've been looking for you,' she said loudly. 'There's something on the other side of the Green I want to show you – '

'What's your hurry, little Lovey-dovey?' Matt drawled. To Sarah's fury, he put his arm round her waist. She shrugged him off, but he wasn't got rid of that easily.

'Let go of me, you lout,' Sarah hissed. 'Don't you know I'm engaged to be married? What will people think?'

'I could tell 'em a thing or two, my pretty maid,' Matt whispered coarsely in her ear, but loudly enough for those nearest to hear. They leaned forward, but like a tornado they were suddenly scattered by Loveday Willard's threshing arms as she marched up to that oafish cousin of hers and hauled his arm away from the other young lady.

'Get back to your pigsty, Matt Willard,' Loveday's eyes blazed at him. Her presence seemed to set the company alight with interest, and Matt's eyes sparkled. Hardly realising how he'd done it, Matt had his arms round two lovely female bundles, huggin' 'em tight amid the laughter of the approving crowd. At that precise moment they seemed to be surrounded by urchins, who saw nothing wrong in a bit o' sport at the Fair, partic'larly when the two maids weren't bein' hurt, and added to the sport by the way their eyes were flashin' fire.

Suddenly Loveday caught sight of her older cousin shambling nearby, his eyes agog at the sight of the young men shinning up the greased poles for a leg o' mutton as prize for the winner.

'Zeb, help me!' She screamed out, her fists beating at Matt's chest. He turned so slowly she could have wept, and even his lurch in their direction seemed to be happening in slow motion . . . before Zeb reached them, Matt was suddenly hauled off Sarah and herself, and it was Adam who stood blazingly in front of him, his hand at Matt's throat as the crowd pressed closer.

'Someone's going to swing for you one of these days,' Adam grated. 'You randy bastard.'

'T'won't be you, fancy-boy,' Matt managed to croak, his bravado never leaving him for a second despite the pressure

255

on his throat. He dug a vicious punch at Adam's groin, but he dodged it neatly. There was a sudden roar from the crowd.

'Put 'un to the test, young Sir. Into the boxing match with 'un! play fair by the rest on us and let's 'ave proper wagers on 'ee!'

Whether they wanted to or not, they were swept along by the excited onlookers. There was a corner of the Green set aside for boxing contests, a crudely roped-off affair that was hopelessly inadequate for holding back the crowds, and more often than not they ended up joining in with their favourite, so that it ended up as a free-for-all. Word spread like wildfire that a Willard was involved in the fight, and Loveday gasped at the interest the fact caused. Her father would be incensed, the thought rippled through her mind, but that was the least of her worries. She was more concerned with what Matt might do to Adam.

She heard the jingle of coins passing hands as wagers were made, and she and Sarah clung to each other's hands as the match was set up. Right and proper, the stout organiser boomed out, and if the wagers were all done, then let the contest begin. Adam had handed Sarah his coat, but somehow Loveday found herself clutching it as if it were a lifeline.

Afterwards, she couldn't have related the course of the match. She was too pressed in from all sides, too sickened by the jeering, foul-mouthed crowds, drunk on scrumpy and lusting for blood, jostling and bellowing and blaspheming. Matt was in an angry mood anyway, since Prince had lost his fight in the cockfighting, and he didn't aim to lose this one against the high-an'-mighty Goss bugger.

After a bloody fifteen minutes, which was all the crude rules allowed, the organiser raised Adam's hand high in the air and declared him the winner, to the roars of disgust from Matt's supporters. It was only by virtue of Matt lying on the ground at the minute the handbell was furiously rung, they hollered, and from the beatin' both men had taken, it could have been either on 'em. The organiser was adamant, and the winnings paid out in Adam's favour.

Matt struggled to his feet, grabbing Adam by the ankle as

his did so and hauling himself up by his opponent. His eyes were streaming as blood gushed down his face from a cut brow.

'This ain't the end, you bugger,' he made no secret of it. 'We'll battle this out again, never fear.'

'Adam, let's get away from here, please.' Sarah pulled at her brother's arm, wincing at the way his cheek was swelling from the rain of blows from Matt's fists. Thankfully, she saw Geoffrey striding towards her, though her relief was mixed with embarrassment. What would he think of them all – her brother engaging in a common brawl under the guise of a boxing match! It didn't take much imagination to realise that the two contestants were bitter enemies.

The rules stated that the participants of any boxing match must be removed as far from each other as possible once the fight was over, to make room for the next contest and to stop the crowd being deflected away from the proper arena. Zeb dragged Matt away, with his vicious words still ringing on the afternoon air. While Adam was helped by the two young ladies and the doctor's supporting arm to the comfort of Geoffrey's trap, where he could take a professional look at him.

Adam shook off the helpers and walked unaided.

'Do you want to make me look a milk-sop?' he growled. 'I'm able to walk upright, and there's nothing wrong with me a few jars of cider wouldn't put right.'

'You must let me take a look at you,' Geoffrey insisted. 'Take a look, and that's all. I doubt there's much medical treatment needed. You're obviously superior in the art of boxing.'

'A legacy from the fine education my father gave me,' Adam was heavily sarcastic. 'I hope he's not squirming in his grave to see the use I've put it to today.'

He never looked at Loveday, but she felt the smart from his words all the same. He'd be cursing the minute he set eyes on her and became involved with the Willards. She watched as Adam climbed adequately enough into Geoffrey's trap and succumbed to the brief checking over by

257

the doctor. Sarah stood silently, and they were suddenly estranged. Loveday swallowed, and thrust Adam's coat into his sister's hands.

'I want to find my father, Sarah. I'm glad Geoffrey got here earlier than you expected. I – good-bye.'

There was suddenly nothing she could say to her friend. Sarah wouldn't want her around now that Geoffrey was here, and Adam certainly wouldn't. He was probably choked to his soul with anyone by the name of Willard. She twisted away from them all and merged into the Fair crowds before Sarah could make any protest. And of course she didn't want to seek out her father, but he saw her first and made his way across to her, his face peevish.

'A fine display by young Matt,' he grunted at once, just as if he'd never got into a fight himself. Loveday was nauseated by his pious tone. Ever since Polly had run out on him, never to be heard of again, Ralph had become the epitome of virtue – on the surface at least. Loveday thought she knew him too well to believe in it entirely.

'He got the worst of it for once anyway,' she stated without any inflexion in her voice. Ralph glanced at her keenly. Proper wound up, she looked. He made a generous gesture.

'How 'bout you coming back to the store an' having a bite to eat wi' me tonight, Loveday? It's a while since you've been inside your old home, and your mother wouldn't like to think you was staying away.'

The same old emotional blackmail, she thought wearily, but why not? What else did she have to do? Who else cared whether she ate or starved? She probably wouldn't even get a dance now, for fear that any young man showing an interest in her would get his head broken by that ruffian cousin of hers. The Fair had begun to pall for her, and she nodded quickly, not wanting to show by her bright eyes that she felt suddenly adrift, with nothing and no-one. Only her father, and the ties of blood that bound her to him, she owned. When all was said and done, her mother had been right. When all else deserted you, there was only the family to rely on, and this little part of it was offering her a rough

258

comfort when she most needed it. Slowly, she took his proffered arm.

'All right, Pa,' she said huskily. 'I'll even prepare a meal for you, if you like.'

Ralph chuckled. 'I was countin' on it, girl!'

It was late when she left Willard's General Store. All evening, they could hear the distant music and hullaballoo coming from the Fair on Castle Green, but by the time Loveday made her way home along the resounding stone streets, all was quiet from that direction. A few late-night revellers made ribald remarks as she passed, but something about the freezing looks Loveday Willard threw in their direction quenched their zeal.

' 'Twould take a brave man to take on that hellcat of a wench,' they fervently agreed and thought no more of her.

Loveday let herself into her shop. The Mundys had long since gone on home and locked up, as she had expected. The house was silent, and she felt desperately alone. The day that had begun so cheerfully, with, she admitted, hope in her heart that she and Adam might end up on friendlier terms, was dashed to a painful memory of the degrading fight between Adam and her cousin. She hated Matt Willard, she thought passionately. Hated, hated, *hated* . . .

There was a small noise in the midst of the silence that stopped her heartbeat for a second. Bloody rats, Loveday raged the next minute. That was all she needed tonight. They had never left the premises, even though all trace of Finch's butchery business had gone. They still sought the blood and carcasses of the meat. Unafraid, Loveday stormed through the rooms, and then realised the noise came from upstairs. If one of the disgusting creatures was in her bed, she'd beat it to a pulp, she thought hysterically.

As soon as she entered her bedroom, Loveday knew it had been a human sound she'd heard. She heard it now, the small movements and the breathing of another human being. Her heart began to thud. Oh no, not Matt . . . please God, not Matt . . . she could only make out the masculine shape in

259

the pale light from the moonlit window, until suddenly the shape moved, and her face flooded with burning colour.

'You've taken your time,' Adam said.

Loveday ran her tongue round her dry lips. She could hear herself stammering, feeling gauche and unnerved.

'What – what do you want here?'

He gave a harsh laugh. 'I've come for what's mine,' he made his meaning insultingly clear. 'My father bought this place and all that's in it, and now it belongs to me. And tonight I mean to have it.'

He was off the bed in one swift movement. Evidently his fight earlier on had done nothing to lessen his reflexes, and she could smell the cider on his breath as he pulled her roughly into his arms. She felt the push of one hand against her breast, as crudely as Matt would have done. She felt the sudden bruising of his mouth against hers, and the forceful thrusting of one knee between her legs. And stunned though she was by his appearance and the violence of his intent, Loveday felt herself melt against him, her arms winding around his neck, combing through the crisp dark hair in a sudden erotic need for him.

Wantonly, she didn't care if Adam had come here intent on shaming her. The reasons didn't matter. He could insult her and degrade her and make a savage attack on her body, if he needed to prove to himself that he was master of her . . . she had craved for his touch and yearned for his love for too long for this to seem anything less than miraculous. As yet, he seemed unaware of her mood, and took her reactions to be fear, as he pulled her hands from his hair.

'Don't bother to scream,' he said coldly. 'Those who aren't still at the Fair on similar business will be too drunk to heed any noises in the night.' He pointed to the bed.

'Undress,' he ordered, pushing her toward it.

He was treating her like a whore and she didn't care, the thought radiated through her. Unknown to him, she gloried in his arrogance, and his hard masculinity. Quickly, she took off her clothes, realising he was doing the same. Her eyes were more used to the half-light now, and she drew in her breath at her first sight of his body, the wide, muscular shoulders and tapering waist, the hard flat stomach and the hard bone of his manhood that was ready for her, circled by a tangle of dark hair that also matted his chest. Adam was no milk-sop, the dizzy thought entered her head.

He saw her naked beauty for the first time, and a shudder of raw delight ran through him, despite his savage errand here. The breasts were full and rosy-peaked, her shape more womanly than he had guessed from its usual covering of clothes. The flare of her hips invited his gaze to the golden downy triangle in which he longed to sink himself, and desire pulsated through him like a flame. As if her legs grew suddenly weak at his gaze, Loveday sat abruptly on the bed, and Adam crossed the room in two strides, to push her gently downwards until the golden spread of her hair fanned out like a rippling sea of sunlight on the pillow.

He wouldn't let himself be swayed by her beauty, he told himself savagely. She had driven him mad for too long to be gentle with her now. He'd come here with one purpose in mind.

There were no preliminaries. He thrust her legs apart with his body, not noting the lack of resistance. With one lunging movement he was inside her, pinning her flat against the bed, and driving himself into her with violent exertions, while his lips fastened over the tips of those tantalising breasts.

He waited for her struggles, her screams of pain, her blaspheming, but none of it came. And the sweet torture of Adam's intention suddenly changed as he realised the movements were becoming more fluid, more mutually shared, that Loveday's body was arching towards him, as if this was not an act of rape, but one of love ... the magic of their union tempered his rage, and became more sensually charged. The thrusting movements slowed to long deep forgings that were acutely pleasurable. He was sharply aware of the musky womanly scent of her filling his senses, and the abandoned way she rose to meet his passion. Her arms were around him, pulling him closer, her sensitve fingers stroking his back, from his shoulders down the lean length of his spine, adding to the sensuality between them.

'Adam, oh Adam,' she breathed his name on a sigh of pure happiness. How this night had all come about, she neither knew nor cared. All that mattered was that he was here, and so was she, as close as one person. Rapture was transporting her to heights of which she had never dreamed. Her skin was damp and flushed, fusing them together, her eyes blue-hazed with joy. She was warmed by his flesh and exalted by the knowledge that he wanted her, needed her, with a hunger that transcended all other considerations.

'Oh Adam, I love you so much,' Loveday whispered. 'If you only knew how it's hurt me to have you so cold towards me.'

He listened to her, generously forgiving him everything, and despised himself. For in his soul, he knew he still didn't forgive her. No matter how ecstatic their union had been, there was still a devil inside him that remembered she had lain this way with his enemy, Matt Willard. That she had been with child from their coupling, and had married the butcher to hide her shame.

His passion evaporated. He rolled away from her before he too could pour his seed into her and be trapped in the same sweet net. Loveday's spirits plummetted at the sudden removal of his warmth, and her soft mouth trembled. His hand suddenly pressed hard against her stomach, hurting her. She whimpered, wondering how God could be so cruel as to give her a glimpse of heaven, and then snatch it away, for there was no love in Adam's glittering eyes now, only contempt.

'Don't think you can pull the same trick to wed me, Loveday Willard,' he said, thickly. 'I'll take what I want of you and no more, any time I feel the need. You belong to me with all the goods and chattels in this place. Do you understand me?'

She couldn't speak. She could only stare up at him with tear-drowned eyes, feeling less than nothing at his words. Savagely, he grasped her chin in his hand and bent to kiss her

262

mouth, a brutal, bruising kiss that shamed her. And she still lay there, stunned, as he threw on his clothes and cannoned out into the night, appalled at himself but totally unable to make amends. The sawing ache of unfulfilment in his loins was echoed in Loveday's frustrated weeping that followed him along the darkened streets. He hated and loved her. She was like a penance from which he could never be free.

CHAPTER NINETEEN

Sarah watched Adam striding about the apple orchards with troubled eyes. Ever since that night of the Summer Fair, he had been impossible to live with. She didn't even know what time he'd returned to Goss House that night, but it must have been in the early hours, and she could only surmise where he had been all that time. She'd never ask. She preferred not to know. As she stood at the drawing-room window, Geoffrey Chard came up behind her and put his hands on her shoulders.

'There's nothing you can do about Adam's temper, my darling, so I wish you'd stop fretting about it,' he said quietly.

She twisted round in his arms. 'How can I help worrying! He's so changed, Geoffrey. He was always so gentle, so approachable! He seems more like a stranger these days!'

'You're remembering the brother you knew before he worked in the Box tunnel,' he reminded her. 'Such a hard existance, brushing with death every day, can have a strange effect on a man. And then to cope with your father's death after he'd left so abruptly may still be playing tricks with his mind, darling. You must give him time to adjust and to come to terms with himself. It's easier to come to terms with the outside world than to accept your own shortcomings, I fear, and Adam certainly seems like a man tormented at the present. '

What he didn't add was how disturbed he'd been on several occasions to see Adam in the company of the farm-boy with whom he'd had the boxing match at the Fair. Geoffrey thought Adam would have had enough of Matthew Willard and his kind, but it seemed as if the two had a fatal fascination for each other that to him was unhealthy, not in an intimate context, but alarmingly, completely the reverse. They weren't friends, yet each sought out the other, as if compelled to do so. Almost as if each had a death-wish to be perpetrated by one or the other. Geoffrey told himself a hundred times that he was being hypersensitive, and that his diagnosis of Adam's state of mind was correct. He needed time to accept the fact that he had never really made his peace with Norman Goss before his death.

Watching Adam now, Geoffrey thought it a pity that the elegant young man of old had now resorted to slopping about in clothes that would be better suited to the workers he employed. As if nothing mattered any more . . . perhaps his and Sarah's wedding later in the year would bring a lighter feeling to the house, he thought keenly. Discussing their wedding would certainly dispel the gloom from his Sarah's pretty face, anyway, and Geoffrey put the thought into action and promptly forgot her brother.

The engaged couple weren't the only ones to be anxious about Adam. Only in Zeb's case, it was his brother Matt's gleeful crowing over the Goss bugger, as he'd taken to calling him, that agitated Zeb's placid thinking. His thoughts were all topsy-turvy these days. He'd waken in the morning with a gnawing in his stomach, where before there had only been an eagerness to see the new day, that could delight him whether bright or grey, wet or dry. There was always summat of interest for Zeb to be seeing in the countryside, and each new day had allus been an uncomplicated stretching of hours until nightfall. Matt had spoiled all that.

264

Ever since that night Matt had come home rip-roaring drunk on the back of a pony and persuaded Zeb to go into the barn with him to hear all about Matt's lyin' with Loveday, he'd felt a sickening unease. Matt had assured 'un his Lovey-dovey had been spoilin' for it a long time, and had been as eager as Matt for the couplin'; but then had come that other time, when he'd seen her cringe away from Matt and scream at him about the bab he said he'd put in her belly. Loveday hadn't been eager for 'un then, Zeb's mind had rambled on. Loveday had been a'feared and upset, and Zeb cared for Loveday the way he cared for small pretty helpless creatures.

And then at the Fair, Loveday had called for his help, and he hadn't been the one to give it. He'd been too slow and lumbering, and it had been Adam Goss who'd come to her rescue, and the jeering crowd had called for the boxing match atween 'em. Matt still hadn't paid his dues for the wrong he'd done to her. It festered inside Zeb's mind to know it. It crowded his thinking, hour after hour.

He'd thought Matt would keep well away from Adam after that, but he'd seen 'em scrapping a few times, and Matt had made sure Adam knew when he'd set up his little cockfighting arena, knowing his weakness to make a bet. Adam had been to the farm on those occasions, and if he'd won, Zeb would hear Matt shouting abuse after him as he rode back to Goss House with his pockets jingling. An instinct Zeb didn't fully understand told him the hatred atween 'em all stemmed from wantin' Loveday. Matt lusted after 'er, and it was slowly dawning into his brain that Adam Goss wanted 'er too.

As Matt would say, it took a long while for it to sink into Zeb's old brain-box, but when it did, it was like a stone dropping into a well. There for all time.

He saw Matt swaggering round the corner of the barn now, whistling tunelessly as if he was well pleased with summat. He sprawled out on the grass near the barn, hands behind his head as he leaned against the wooden side, and grinned, squinting up at his brother in the sunlight.

'Well, me old loon, that's fixed up a contest I ain't going to lose with Mister fancy-buggering Goss! You be sure an' put your wagers on me next Sat'day night, Zeb, an' you'll make a pretty penny.'

'What contest, then?' Zeb grunted. He knew without the tellin' that there must be a catch in it for Matt to look so confident. He dropped down on the ground beside his brother, idly crunching a sweet young blade of grass in his teeth. Matt chuckled, tapping his finger against his nose.

'Now if I tell you, you'll be as wise as me, won't you?' he said in the infuriatingly way he often did. Zeb knew it would only be a matter of time afore Matt couldn't keep it to himself any longer. Whatever it was was burstin' to be told, by the looks on it.

'Suit yourself,' Zeb shrugged.

Matt looked at him in surprise. What was this – his dunce of a brother actually having thoughts of his own and pretending he weren't interested in Matt's doings? He prodded him in the gut, just to remind him who was boss around here.

'Well then, I'll tell 'ee,' he confided. 'On Sat'day night we're goin' up in the hills to find us a couple o' wild ponies, then we're goin' to race 'em back to the farm. There's folk who know about it already, and are puttin' wagers on it, only 'tis best not to say nothin' indoors, if you know what I mean, see? There's about a dozen folk who'll be waitin' for me to ride first through Long Field and collect, and you can be one on 'em if youm clever!'

'Adam Goss might win,' Zeb argued. 'Then I'd lose all me money, and I ain't got any to speak of.'

Matt gave a chortling laugh and dug him again.

'You won't lose, blockhead! That's what I'm a 'tellin' of 'ee!'

'How d'you know that then?' Zeb said sullenly.

Matt stared at him thoughtfully, but the plan was too good to waste on keeping it to himself. Besides, telling Zeb was the same as telling the bees. Good for the soul, but with no danger of it bein' passed on.

266

'I know it, 'cos snot-nosed Adam don't know of the short cut through Dingle Wood, see?'

'You ain't ridin' down there at night, be 'ee, Matt? There's ruts and gulleys and – '

'If you say there's ghosts and phantoms as well I'll 'ave 'ee put in the looney-bin sure's my name's Matt Willard,' Matt snorted. 'Now you just keep your mouth shut and put your wager on me, see? I'll expect a jug or two o' scrumpy out of 'ee when you collect your winnings.'

Zeb looked after him broodingly as Matt swaggered off to the farmhouse. Cocky as ever . . . but Zeb wouldn't ride down through Dingle Wood after dusk and that was for sure. It was a fine and pretty place by day, allus spangled with dew on the cobwebby plants growin' on the marshy ground, but nobody went there at night. Nobody who expected to come out with their senses still intact, that was. An' it was cheatin' too. It took a while for all the arguments to seep into Zeb's brain, but he knew how useless it would be to get Matt to change his mind an' do things right by this contest he'd sparked off with Adam Goss. He was still aimin' to win over 'un.

Zeb's thinking meandered on. Without realising what he was doing, he wandered out of the farmyard towards the slope of the hills. He was s'posed to be checkin' on the sheep, but he could allus say he'd gone after one caught in a bramble. It was an unusually devious thought for Zeb. He walked and walked until he came to the edge of Dingle Wood and plunged into its dank black silence. The leaves on the trees were polished to a high green gloss with the dew on 'em, and sunlight sparkled like diamonds through the top branches. But at ground level, their roots were twisted and half-exposed as if striving to get out of the inhospitable red earth. Nobody came here much, even though Zeb had allus liked its majesty. But then, Zeb allus liked things other folk found odd. All the same, he wouldn't do like Matt planned, and ride a wild pony down through here at breakneck speed on Saturday night. It was asking for trouble.

Their folks thought the two older Willard sons were off out

for a jug or two at an alehouse some ways off on Saturday night. But once away from the farm, Matt couldn't contain his excitement. Tonight was the night he'd beat the Goss bugger once and for all, he told Zeb gleefully. They walked to the arranged meeting-place, where a dozen lusty farm-boys like themselves eventually joined them, along with Adam Goss.

The arrangement was for them all to ride in a couple of farm carts to the top of the hills, where the wild ponies roamed. Once Matt and Adam had caught their chosen beasts, then the rest on 'em would hightail it back to the starting-place and make their bets, with just one on 'em staying behind to make sure the two contestants started together, fair and square. Once off, the route down was up to them, but there were only two good tracks, and whichever one the smartest one took, it was fair guessing the other would follow the second route. The carts started off, wheels digging into the soft earth with their heavy load of bodies.

Adam had his supporters. There were plenty who had good cause to see Matt Willard brought down a peg or two, and the two cartloads were engaged in noisy cat-calling until their wheezing animals brought them to the top of the hills. Among the sparse bracken and bushes, the wild ponies were silhouetted against the night skyline. They all slithered out of the carts, still jabbering with excitement.

'Look, shut up, you buggers, you'll frighten 'em off,' Matt snarled. 'Then the contest'll be over afore it's begun. And I aim to be the winner tonight.'

'First catch your pony,' Adam snapped at him, already sizing up the beast that looked a likely mount.

'I'll help 'ee, Matt,' Zeb said obligingly, to the guffaws from the others. Matt shook him off. Sometimes the buffoon was a useful way of gettin' a few laughs, but tonight he seemed irritatingly half-witted and mushed.

'You couldn't catch a cold wi'out help, dunderhead! This is man's work, not for soft-bellies like you. Out the way, an' let me get on wi' it.'

He gave Zeb a shove that caught him off-balance and sent

268

him staggering. He could hear the raucous laughter ringing in his ears as he picked himself up and watched them all race after the ponies. He hunched his great shoulders. If that's what Matt wanted, he'd wait patiently. He sat in the cart, stone-faced as ever, unperturbed. He could be patient. He'd had plenty of practise.

It didn't take long for the ponies to be caught, and Matt and Adam sat astride their chosen ones, digging their heels into the flanks to keep 'em still. The beasts snorted and blew, tossing their shaggy manes and stomping their sturdy little legs, but they were held fast around their necks by two tenacious riders.

'Get goin' then,' Matt yelled at the rest. 'Or I'll be back down there afore 'ee. I'll show this bugger who's best around here.'

'And I'll show you, Matt Willard,' Adam shouted back. 'You might be king of some coops, but you'll never beat me.'

'Done it once already, ain't I, poncey, in a way you an' me both know about?' Matt crowed, and Adam gritted his teeth. He had to win this contest tonight. His pride depended on it.

Finally everything was ready. Most of the onlookers had departed to wait at the finishing point, and one remained, to make his way down at a much slower pace on a calmer pony than the two fiery ones the contestants had chosen. He gave one loud yell as a starting signal, and the race had begun. Matt bellowed in his pony's ear and tore off to the right-hand track, so Adam turned naturally to the left. There was little difference in distance, and each would have a free passage downhill. He clung on for his life and prayed he'd get there in one piece as the ground thundered beneath the pony's hooves, and sky and earth seemed to be jumbled in his vision as the pony hurtled on down the steep slopes.

He could hear nothing but his own panting and the snuffling and thundering of the pony beneath him. He was dripping with sweat, and his heart hammered in his chest. He knew bloody well this was a foolhardy thing to be doing, but it seemed it was his fate to compete with Matt Willard. Ever since he'd known him, he had been his bitter rival, even if he hadn't realised it at first.

All those times when Matt had leered about his pretty little cousin, Loveday Willard, and then Adam had met her and been stunned by the golden, delicate young woman, when he'd expected a coarse, red-cheeked country wench from Matt's description. And then all that had followed . . . Adam dug his heels in the pony's sweating, slippery flank as he felt himself slide a little as the route twisted and turned down the narrow track . . . his sweet Loveday, who had been more cunning than a fox.

He tried to remain angry with her, because truth to tell, he was sorely troubled by all that had happened the night of the Summer Fair. He'd gone to her house, storming with rage, intent on ravishing her the way Matt Willard had done, though what he'd been trying to prove he couldn't have said. And it had started out that way, but he hadn't reckoned on her sweetness, or the welcoming softness of her, or the womanly excitement of her; he hadn't reckoned on love being part of that night, and now he didn't have the gall to go back to her and beg her to forgive him. He didn't know how to say the words.

The pony suddenly stumbled, and Adam's heart thumped wildly as he clutched at its neck, feeling the thick matted hair sliding out of his clammy hands. He was falling . . . falling . . . and Matt would have won; in his ears, he could hear cheering and laughing, and then there were hands pulling him off the pony's back as it was stopped in its tracks, and there were slaps on the back and promises to buy 'un a jug o' the finest ale goin', since it weren't every day Matt Willard was bested.

Adam blinked the sweat out of his eyes. He'd done it then! He looked around him, his heart still pounding. Realising there was no sign of Matt yet, and that even his supporters weren't too upset at his losing the contest. He flopped down on the ground to get his breath back, only half aware of the money changing hands as the wagers were paid out. He grinned up at Zeb, on the edge of the group.

'Didn't you have a bet then, Zeb?'

Zeb shook his head slowly. He was feelin' better with every minute that passed. He hadn't had the stomach to bet this time, but gradually the great knot of tension that had been griping his gut for so long was unravelling like a skein of yarn inside him, soothing his nerves and restoring his spirits. He'd forgotten what it was that had made him so restless for days. It was the way he was made, and he smiled at Adam Goss, who wanted Loveday.

'Weren't no need,' he muttered.

Adam suddenly became aware of the time passing. Matt should have been here long ago. He could only have been minutes behind himself. The rumblings among the rest of them told the same tale. He got to his feet, feeling his clothes cling tackily on his skin.

'Matt should've been down long afore now,' one said, suddenly anxious. ' 'Tis a straight trail, and moonlight enough for 'un to see where 'e's goin'. Mebbe summat's happened to 'un!'

'We'd best go an' find out,' another said, and there was a sudden rush of activity towards the track down which Matt should have been hurtling. If he came now, they'd be flattened by the careering pony, Adam thought cynically, but there was no stopping them. He was a little surprised to find Zeb still there.

'Why aren't you looking for Matt with the others?' he demanded. 'He could be hurt, Zeb.'

'They won't find 'un that way,' he said ponderously.

Adam felt a sudden twist of premonition, a gut-sure feeling of what was to come ∴. .

'Where will they find him, Zeb?' he said softly. 'Show me. You and I will find him, won't we?'

Zeb nodded and strode off towards the left-hand track. But when they'd only gone a little way, he turned sharply off the track, across some scrubby wasteland leading to a darkened wood, with trees reaching tall towards the sky. It was all Adam could do to keep up with him after his exertion on the pony. He didn't know this place, but evidently Zeb knew it well. He strode unerringly, and only stopped when he reached a hard-packed mound of earth and stones forming an impassible ridge across the narrow passage through the trees. In front of the ridge, sprawled out with his neck at a horrible angle to the rest of his body, was Matt Willard.

Adam drew in his breath in a gasp of shock. He knelt down to feel for a pulse, but he knew before he touched Matt, that there'd be none. He was too twisted to be still alive. He'd gone straight over the ridge and broken his neck instantly. Of the pony there was no sign. Adam stood up slowly. He was breathing heavily. He turned to look at Zeb, standing motionless nearby. A shaft of moonlight through the trees lit his pale face. There was no expression on it. No grief, no surprise. Adam looked from him to the ridge of earth and stones.

'He hurt Loveday.' Adam was startled to hear the words Zeb intoned. 'Loveday were allus sweet and good. Matt were the bad 'un. Like one o' your rotten apples, needin' to be cast out afore it did harm to the whole tree. Loveday needs 'ee to look after 'er.'

Adam's mouth was dry. It was clear as daylight to him now. Zeb had known Matt was taking this short cut and had chosen his own way of ridding himself of a brother who had ruthlessly baited him every day of his life.

'What do you know about Matt and Loveday, Zeb?' he said carefully. He saw Zeb frown.

'He hurt her. Did summat bad to her. He told me about the bab, but I don't rightly remember now.' He gave a lopsided grin. 'Matt allus said I bain't no good at remembering. Allus get it wrong, I 'ould. Matt said God wasted His time givin' me a tongue, 'cos the words allus come out stupid.'

And supposing he did go and report his suspicions, Adam asked himself? Who was going to believe this poor fool, whatever story he told? He'd only end up packed off to an asylum, and he wouldn't commit anybody there, least of all Zeb, for whom he, as well as Loveday, had a rough affection. He made up his mind.

'Can you carry Matt down through the wood?' he asked. 'The others will have realised he didn't go the way they expected him to by now. We'll just have to tell them he took a short cut, which is the truth, isn't it?'

'Ah, 'tis the truth all right. And nobody could have known

272

there'd be such a stumbling-block,' Zeb said mournfully. He swung his brother over his great shoulder, and Adam tried not to feel sick as his rival's head lolled gruesomely against his brother's back. It was clear that whatever part Zeb had had in all this, the memory of it was leaving him rapidly. He didn't even show any emotion over Matt's death. He was his usual self. Adam shuddered and followed him out of Dingle Wood, to where the rest of the searchers were gathering. They crowded round in horror as they saw the lifeless form over Zeb's shoulder.

Adam took charge, since none of them seemed to have any idea what to do.

'Matt's broken his neck,' he said deliberately. 'The pony must have reared up at something and shot him over the top. So that's it. Matt took a short cut and came a cropper, and there's no use us standing around here like spare parts at a wedding.' He spoke in a way they'd understand. 'I suggest some of you take Matt back to the farm in the cart and help Zeb with the explaining. Say it just the way I told you, since poor Zeb seems to have lost the way of speaking for the moment. He'll do his best, but it'll need a spokesman among you to break the news to his folks.'

'Ah, ah, that it will,' one and another agreed in hushed tones after a glance at the blank-faced Zeb. Poor loon looked as if he'd properly lost his wits. 'Twould be the shock, they reasoned among themselves. Looked as if it really didn't register to him what had happened, and mebbe 'twas better so, considering . . .

They helped Zeb lay his brother gently on the floor of the cart and looked to Adam Goss for further instruction. At that moment they were all as simple as Zeb. They were farm-folk, unused to coping with decisions of this kind. Death was nothin' new to 'em, but not this kind o' death. Not Matt Willard's, who seemed as indestructable as the strongest oak. His death had all but stunned them.

'His family in Taunton will need to be told,' Adam said steadily. 'I'd be glad if you'd inform Zeb's parents that I will take it on myself to ride into the town right now and acquaint

Mr Ralph Willard and his daughter of the unhappy news.'

Now he was being deliberately formal, seeking no argument and no mumblings among them. One or two touched fingers to forelocks in agreement.

'Ah, mister, 'tis the best thing to be done,' they muttered vaguely. 'Matt were allus a reckless 'un, but who'd 'ave thought he'd cock 'imself up in a contest he thought he was so certain sure o' winnin'?'

'Just goes to show,' was the general comment. 'Don't pay to be certain sure o' nothin' in this life.'

At last they were on their way, and the riotous group that had started up the slopes earlier returned Matt Willard's body to the farm subdued and bewildered. If he hadn't known better, Adam would almost say Zeb was the sanest one among them at that moment. He turned abruptly and walked away to where he'd tied up his horse when he'd arrived for the contest. Whatever the outcome of the night, he'd never expected it to be this one. Without giving himself time to think he kicked his heels into the horse's side and galloped off towards Taunton. He still had a mission to carry out, though his nerve almost balked at the thought of it.

As he neared the outskirts of the town he slowed his horse down a little. He could smell his own body sweat and he felt dirty and unkempt, and nothing like the fine-cut figure who owned Goss Cider. He didn't want to see Ralph Willard. All he wanted was to be with Loveday – and yet it unnerved him to think of facing her. It was late evening, but there were still people about here and there, particularly those who frequented the taverns. He tied up his horse and stumbled into one, to gulp at a jug of ale. He needed its support. Nobody seemed to recognise him, and why should they, from the state he was in? He looked no different from any other roughneck here. He called to the landlord to ask if there was a trustworthy man here he could pay to deliver a message. He rattled some coins to show there would be ample payment for the right man. The landlord said stoutly that he'd send his own son, and Adam nodded briefly and asked for writing paper and pencil.

He wrote a short message, since there seemed no way of glossing the facts. He re-read it and nodded slowly. It would do.

'Dear Mr Willard,' he had written. 'This is to inform you of the unfortunate accident that has befallen Matthew Willard this night, resulting in his death. Your presence is required at the Willard farm directly. Your daughter is already on her way.'

'With regrets, Adam Goss Esq.'

Ten minutes later, Adam stood outside the darkened shop with Goss Cider stamped in proud letters over the door. All the way here, there had been one desire on his mind. To fold Loveday in his arms and tell her he was wrong, so appallingly wrong, to condemn her the way he had done all these months. Being so loftily arrogant in refusing to forgive her, when all the time it was he who should be begging for her forgiveness.

It had taken Zeb to show him what he should have known all along. *Loveday were allus sweet and good. Matt were the bad 'un. Like one o' your rotten apples, needin' to be cast out afore it did harm to the whole tree.* Loveday had been little more than a child when she'd had to cope with too much emotional upheaval in too short a time. Her mother's death; the brief joy of falling in love with himself; the catastrophic intimacy with Matt; the panic-stricken marriage to the butcher ... he'd never really bothered to listen to her explantion. He'd never asked for it. He'd been judge and jury and sentenced them both to a lifetime in purgatory.

Remembering the way he'd degraded her the last time he came here, Adam felt the sickening thud of his heartbeat, and wondered painfully if it was impossibly late to put things right between them. He lifted his hand and pulled on the bell.

Loveday had just gone to bed when she heard the shop bell. For a moment she froze, and then as the ringing persisted, she picked up a candle and the heavy stick she was used to keeping near the door, and opened it a crack. For a second she didn't recognise Adam; looking as uncouth as any of her cousins,

275

and seeming to sway against the doorpost, with the smell of ale on his breath. He saw her flinch back, and it tore at his heart.

'Can I come in, Loveday?' he said hoarsely.

'I can't stop you, can I?' Her voice was bitter. 'You *own* me, remember?'

The memory of the last time he'd been here swept through him with a burning shame. He stepped inside, and followed her young taut figure, clad in shawl and nightgown, as she led him to the parlour. She dumped the candle on the table and lit the lamp, turning to face him with trembling limbs. She just couldn't bear it if tonight was to be a repeat of the last time . . . she just couldn't *bear* it.

She suddenly noticed the wild, distracted look in his eyes, and the fact that if he'd come to ravish her, then at least there was none of the brashness of his previous attitude. She saw that Adam's hands were unsteady as he clenched them, and a sixth sense told her something was badly wrong.

'What's happened?' she said quickly. He sat down heavily on one of the chairs in the tiny room, hardly knowing how to say it after all. There was only one way.

'Your cousin Matthew's had an accident,' he said harshly. 'He and I had a race with wild ponies, and he took a short cut. Somehow the pony must have tossed him, and Matthew broke his neck. He was dead when Zeb and I reached him. I'm sorry to be bringing bad news.'

Loveday felt the room spin for a second. And then Adam could hardly believe it as she broke into hysterical laughter. She couldn't stop. On and on it went, high-pitched, half-crazed hysterical laughter that frightened him . . . when he would have risen to calm her, she suddenly knelt down at his feet, looking into his face with blazing, jewel-bright eyes.

'*Sorry*? Are you so hypocritical as to pretend you're *sorry* Matt Willard's dead, Adam Goss? Well, I'm not sorry! I'm glad, glad, *glad*! It's the best news I've had in a long time. I'll wear red at his funeral and dance on his grave! Does that shock you? It shouldn't, not when you believe so ill of me already. I'm the worst thing that ever lived, aren't I? Lower than a whore, and tarred with the same evil brush as all the wild Willards. Don't you rue the day you ever set eyes on me? You must have been devil-marked on that day – '

The ring of his hand against her cheek made her gasp. Her fingernails had been digging into his arms, and Adam suddenly feared for her sanity. She looked so vehement, so tempestuously passionate, and so wantonly beautiful ... the emotions inside him were bursting to be free, and with an explosive oath he leaned forward and gathered her up in his arms, pulling her on to his lap, and smothering her eyes, her mouth, her hair, with kisses.

'Forgive me, Loveday,' the words were choked out of him. 'Forgive me for every rotten thing I've said or done to you. If I hadn't loved you so dearly all this time I might have been able to see things in their right perspective. Whatever you did, it was because of what Matt did to you. He's the evil one, not you. How could anyone ever think that – ?'

'You did!' She couldn't quite believe this contrite Adam. Even though her longing for him almost overcame her, still she held back, afraid to give credence to her own ears. 'How long will this new mood last, Adam? Just for tonight, while this is all fresh in your mind, maybe? Just long enough for me to forget the pain of the last few weeks, until it all begins again. How much longer are you going to punish me?'

She stood up with one twisting movement, proud and erect, the tumbling gold of her hair caressing her shoulders in a way Adam knew he dare not – not yet. All that she said he knew he deserved. He'd destroyed her trust, and he couldn't blame her. Why should she ever believe in him again? How could he begin to explain that something so simple as Zeb's halting words as to her innate virtue had done for him what nothing else could?

He felt crushed, beaten. He slumped in the chair, his eyes lowered. He could take her here and now, but that wasn't what he wanted. He didn't want to take what she didn't freely give. His eyes caught sight of the clumps of earth that had clung to his boots and were now scuffed on to the floor. Without stopping to think, he bent and scooped a ball of it in his

277

hand, where the dampness of it oozed between his fingers.

'I could swear on a dozen bibles, Loveday, that the love I feel for you is as deep and binding as any man felt for a woman. But I'll vow to you on something we both find as sacred as any bible. I swear by the sweet red earth of my given name, and by that which covers your mother's grave, that no woman has ever meant more to me than you, Loveday. I love you so much I could die with wanting you, and if you refuse to be my wife, I may as well join those that sleep beneath the red earth for ever.'

The ball of soil crumbled beneath the pressure of his fingers and fell to the floor. Loveday's heart thundered so loudly and so rapidly she felt the room shift beneath her. Had she really heard him say those things? When until this very moment she thought she would never again feel the sweet touch of his hands caressing her. Never again feel him holding her in that intimate way that told of his need even when the words failed him. Never again to know his body warmth, hungry for her . . .

Somehow she had covered the distance between them and was crushed in his arms. The animal sweat still clinging to him was pungent, and merely stimulated her need of him. The tears still blurred her eyes, but at long last they were happy, releasing tears, for of all the vows Adam could have made to her, this was the most poignant, more hallowed in her mind than any churchman's text. The glory of it was that Adam knew it too.

'My darling, darling one,' he breathed the endearments into her flesh, rocking her in his arms as if he would never let her go. The beat of her heart was as forceful as his own, merging into one. For these precious moments they were in a private heaven unparalleled, blotting out everything that had separated them before. 'If you knew how many nights I've lain in torment in my lonely bed, wishing I could hold you like this.'

'And I,' she whispered softly, knowing that between them there could be no false modesty. She ached for him, her desire as great as his own.

278

'We'll speak no more of the past,' Adam began roughly, but she put her finger gently against his lips.

'We must,' she said quietly, knowing that too. 'The past has made us what we are, Adam, and to leave some things unspoken will merely make them fester. We must speak of it – but not now. Please, not now.'

At that moment she was wiser than he, more sharply perceptive, and she knew she was right when he ran his hands down the length of her spine, as if he would pull her even closer to him, murmuring the words of love that were so dizzying to her ears. She was secure at last in the knowledge of his love, safe in his arms where she truly belonged.

'We must leave soon,' she whispered reluctantly. 'We must go to the farm. There are people who will be needing me.'

'But none so much as me, Loveday.' He stood up, still holding her in his arms. She could feel the hard masculine strength of him and gloried in it. Nothing could take him away from her now. 'Would it be so wrong to make them wait a little longer?' he asked huskily.

Loveday's arms tightened around his neck. Already his steps were moving towards the stairs, the soft cushion of her breasts heightening the desire in him. He saw the love in her eyes, as deep as the midnight sky, and it was all the answer he needed.